SOPHIE GRAVIA grew up in a town just outside Glasgow and has always had a love for the English language. At a young age, she found herself writing funny stories or poems to friends and family for special occasions, and after high school she undertook a performing arts diploma, flourishing in her creative writing class. Sophie now works full time as a nurse in a busy city hospital.

In 2020, Sophie started writing again as a distraction from the ongoing pandemic, cheered on by fans of her hilarious blog, 'Sex in the Glasgow City'. *A Glasgow Kiss*, her debut novel, shot straight to number one in the erotic charts and has been a word-of-mouth sensation ever since.

SOPHIE GRAVIA

Hot Girl Summer x

ORION

An Orion paperback

First published in Great Britain in 2024
by Orion Fiction
an imprint of The Orion Publishing Group Ltd,
Carmelite House, 50 Victoria Embankment
London EC4Y 0DZ

An Hachette UK company

3 5 7 9 10 8 6 4 2

A CIP catalogue record for this book
is available from the British Library.

ISBN (Paperback) 978 1 3987 1572 1
ISBN (eBook) 978 1 3987 1573 8
ISBN (Audio) 978 1 3987 1574 5

Typeset by Born Group
Printed and bound in Great Britain by Clays Ltd, Elcograf S.p.A.

www.orionbooks.co.uk

This book is dedicated to every man who has hurt me over the years. Thanks for the heartbreak that has turned my books into bestsellers. I wouldn't change any of it for the world.

Sophie x

Chapter One

Ava

'Are you sure you want to do this again?' Adam asked, breathing heavily as I tore down the zip of his washed-out hoodie and pushed him against my small wardrobe.

I ignored his ridiculous question. Of course I did, I was horny. And I needed to feel better after another petty argument with Johnny.

'Ava,' he repeated, more seriously this time, 'are you sure? It's the middle of the day.'

I took a step back. 'What the fuck, Adam?' I demanded, flustered at the interrogation. 'Do people not have sex in the middle of the afternoon now?'

He nodded and a soft smile reappeared on his face. I always enjoyed his face. He was a handsome guy, after all. Reliable, kind, a bit hipster, and he was always there when I needed him. I watched him begin to strip down. I took a few steps back, accidentally standing on one of my daughter's Barbie dolls, and stumbled onto the bed, rubbing my foot a little.

He sauntered towards me, naked. Adam's body was thin, toned and tanned. His father was Tunisian and his mum from Camden, so he had an exotic cool-guy vibe. He was vegan and teetotal, so in the long term we would never work, but his body on top of mine felt amazing for now. We began kissing slowly and passionately, and I shut my eyes as I sank into it. I felt his hands lift the floaty shirt I was wearing and caress my tits. *Jesus*, it felt good to be touched.

'You are so beautiful, Ava,' he whispered.

I wanted to tell him to be quiet, to get inside me and start drilling me like a jackhammer, but I smiled politely instead. Then I lowered my underwear to my ankles, fumbling to kick them off entirely. I could feel his dick hard against my stomach, and I waited eagerly for it to slip inside me so I could finally forget trading insults and ridiculous accusations with Johnny, even if it was only for a few sweaty minutes.

His fingers ran down my stomach, slowly teasing their way past my belly button until they were circling my clit.

'Yesss,' I moaned. *Finally*.

'More?' he asked, his cockney accent almost drying up my fanny instantly.

Please God, stop this man from talking. 'Mmmm . . .' I mumbled, not wanting to have any more conversation.

He began pushing his fingers in and out of me, hard then slow, bringing them back up, then rubbing my clit some more.

'Oh, God, yes! Keep going!' I begged. *Why do they always move their hand when they get to the good bit?* I wondered.

2

He was hovering above my body, smiling as my face jerked while he finger blasted my hole.

The thing about Adam was he was a great neighbour. He was always there when I needed a chat or a decent Wi-Fi connection, and he was great with my daughter, Georgie. We'd only started having sex the past few months, after I drank a bottle of wine and knocked at his door one night. Afterwards, I'd ignored him in the hallway for a few weeks until my hungry hole demanded more attention. He was *nice*, but I wasn't ready to commit to anyone. Not since my marriage broke down, not since my husband and I *took a break* and I suddenly, out of no where, became a single mother. Deep down, I think he knew that too.

I could feel his fingers smashing into me, hard and fast.

'Keep going, don't stop!' I whispered, feeling my body warm with desire.

'I am, baby. How does that feel . . .'

His voice trailed off. I was suddenly aware of an uncomfortable odour taking centre stage in the bedroom.

What the fuck is that?

I sniffed.

Had he just farted? Was this cheeky bastard letting rip while fingering me in my own home?

I watched his warm smile suddenly fade. I knew he smelt it too.

Act natural, Ava. It will disperse and you can get back to business, I thought. *I mean, the cunt does eat a lot of veg.*

His hand motions became slower and I noticed his neck twitch with agitation.

3

Jesus, it was getting stronger, more potent, more extreme. Then I was aware of his hand, inside of me, coming to an abrupt halt.

Fucking hell. My room smelt like the fucking sewers. I sniffed the air discreetly and felt my stomach lurch.

'Adam?' I asked cautiously. He looked down at me, as if snapping out of his thoughts. 'Did you just let rip or something?'

He sat up, pulling his hand from my vagina. 'No!' He paused. 'It was you!'

'It was *not* fucking me!' I screeched, completely offended. I tugged down my shirt with one hand and held the other up to my nose, masking the odour.

Adam scanned the room, looking concerned, and then suddenly jumped back when he clocked his fingers.

'Ava!' He threw his hand in the air, as far away from his face as possible.

'What?' I yelled back in a panic. He was making so much fuss but I couldn't see anything on him.

Slowly and hesitantly, he brought his fingers closer to his nose and sniffed.

'*Ohhhh,* Ava! It is coming from you!' He sounded horrified, and I could see his small stomach clench as he tried not to retch all over my bedroom. I watched his brick-hard dick shrivel to the size of a raisin in a moment.

'Stop! Stop! It's not fucking me!' But I was suddenly aware of a dampness between my legs. A brown liquid began running down my thighs.

I turned my back on him straight away, feeling my heart pound. *It can't be me.* But he had been down

4

there for a good few minutes before this happened – surely I would have had some warning? Reluctantly, I skimmed my hand down.

With one small whiff, my insides curdled.

WHAT THE FUCK WAS THAT?

Trying not to visibly gag, I turned to Adam, who now had tears streaming from his sad eyes.

'Leave, please!' I said.

'Ava, wait. Are you OK?' he asked as I shooed him out of the room.

Am I OK? I thought. *What a fucking question, Adam. My insides are rotting, and you're asking if I'm OK. Of course I'm fucking not.*

'Adam,' I breathed heavily, needing to get to the bottom of this by myself. 'Please leave my flat now!'

He nodded, looking relieved at the thought of fresh clean air, and began gathering his things.

I could feel myself shaking. What the fuck was happening to my body? I felt sick. Did I have an STI or some kind of severe vaginal infection? Or – I shuddered – cancer?

'Ava?' he asked, interrupting my overdriven mind.

'What?' I shouted, now panicking.

'I've heard that certain times of the month can interfere with the pH balance downstairs . . .' His eyes lowered to my groin. 'It can even get messed up, like after birth and stuff, but there's herbs and vitamins women can take that—'

'My vagina is fine, Adam,' I cut him off. 'You and your wee vegan-herbed hands have obviously caused

5

a reaction, and *she* doesn't like it. It has nothing to do with being a bloody mother! Georgie is almost five. Now fuck off!' There was thunder in my voice and he scampered away.

As soon as the flat door closed, I raced for the shower. I began scrubbing my vagina, investigating every crease thoroughly. In pure desperation, I dumped a big dod of Head & Shoulders on my loofah and went to town.

I could smell the strong odour mixing with the perfumed shampoo.

Nooooo, why won't it go away?

Eventually, I placed a soapy finger inside. That was when I felt something weird. *Oh no.* It felt spongey, but hard. I pressed on it a little and felt more stench water leak down my leg.

Oh Christ. What is that?

It must be a tumour.

I squealed loudly as brown discharge ran freely down my leg.

This is it. The end. No more Ava Little. Georgie will be motherless. Johnny would no doubt move on and I'd be forgotten about once and for all.

I hopped out of the shower and sat on the toilet seat. *What should I do?* My wet foot tapped nervously on the floor. *I'll have to call an ambulance. Or is that too dramatic? Apart from the smell, I don't have any other symptoms. Maybe I should call Johnny?* But I didn't want him to look down on me even more than he already did. I could just imagine his condescending voice on the phone: *Another drama Ava has concocted in her head.*

6

He would think I was lying, because of the argument. He'd think I was making it all up because I asked to go on the trip to the Lake District that he'd planned for himself and Georgie. He wouldn't believe me. I'd need concrete medical proof that I was ill. Seriously ill.

OK, what about a taxi? Yes, that's it. I lifted my phone from the windowsill and Ubered myself a car to St Thomas's Hospital. I fired on jogging bottoms and a jumper, scraped my long dark hair into a messy bun and raced down the close to await the car's arrival.

Standing out in the fresh air in the centre of London on a busy afternoon made me contemplate everything. My life. My shit existence. I was only thirty. How could this be the end? How could I be ready to die with no legacy? I felt my heart pounding. What the fuck was happening to me? Who could I call? Who would care? How would I even admit this to anyone?

The Uber pulled up, and I got inside.

'To St Thomas's then, love?' the driver asked as I shut the door.

'Yeah, please,' I replied, leaning against the window, grateful to the cold glass for cooling me down.

As the Uber through the London traffic, every set of lights seemed to turn red on my arrival, and every biker on the road seemed to overtake us. *Hurry the fuck up!* I glanced at the meter, praying I had enough in my bank to cover the cost. I felt my foot tap nervously as we sat stationary, then toddled through the centre of London. Was I being dramatic? I wondered. I really couldn't afford a taxi fare, and I knew how much this

7

journey would set me back, but if it was a matter of life and death . . .

Then, I felt my jogging bottoms dampen with whatever was leaking from inside me. *Shit, am I haemorrhaging?*

'Do you want the main entrance for visiting, darling?' he asked as the old dusky building came into sight.

'Erm . . . no. The A&E entrance, please.' I could hear my voice shake.

'Call it forty, love,' he smiled towards me, and I nodded as I pointed to the app and gave a thumbs up.

'Thanks again,' I said when the cab halted, immediately lunging for the car door, hoping to air it out for a few seconds for the unlucky cunt who was in here next.

I felt overwhelmed, dizzy, and nauseous.

How can you be fit and well, in your early thirties, about to get your Nat King, then the next minute you're fighting for your life?

Chapter Two

Ava

As I entered A&E, I scanned the busy waiting room. Luckily, there were no familiar faces – just rows of people with cuts and bruises, some holding sick bowls to their chins. I gulped down hard and stood in line, waiting to be triaged.

'Next here, please!' one of the younger receptionists eventually called.

I approached her station, aware of my jogging bottoms feeling damper with each step.

'Name?'

'Ava. Ava Little.' I looked over my shoulder, triple-checking I didn't recognise anyone.

'Date of birth, Ava?' She was staring at the computer screen, typing as I spoke.

'The thirty-first of July, nineteen ninety-three.'

'And that makes you . . .?' She lowered her glasses, looking at me for the first time.

'A Leo.' I managed a polite smile back.

She didn't seem impressed. 'What age, Ava?'

'Sorry.' I cleared my throat, too distracted to take a rid neck from any of this. 'Thirty.'

'Ah, here we are. And you still live in Kensington?' she asked.

I felt a wrench in my gut. I hadn't lived there since Johnny and I split a year earlier, but I nodded back, not ready to update any records with the shit-tip living arrangement I had now.

'So, what's the problem, Ava?' she asked.

I paused. How would I explain this?

'Ava?'

'I think . . . I think I might be haemorrhaging.'

Her face fell, and she began typing quickly. *Shit, even she looks worried*. 'OK. So, what makes you think that?'

'I think my friend has ruptured a tumour inside of me, and now I have a lot of stuff leaking from, you know . . .' I cleared my throat again. 'Down below,' I pointed to my groin, feeling my cheeks flush, aware of the busy waiting room.

She nodded, then stood up. 'A lot of blood?' she asked.

I shrugged my shoulders.

'Ava?'

'It could be, I'm not sure. I'm sorry!' I felt my bottom lip tremble.

'Wait there, pet, I'll get a nurse to take you through!' She walked through the back as I stood waiting, cheeks and fanny clenched, hoping not to spill my vile vaginal juice on the floor.

A few minutes later, I was escorted to a cubical and asked to lie on a trolley. My hands were cold and my body was trembling. I looked up at the ceiling and stared into the bright lights. *Maybe I should call Mum and Dad?* But they'd moved back to Glasgow a few years ago and I knew they would panic, not being close by. *Maybe I could call Grace?* But my sister's husband was still best friends with Johnny, and I knew he'd contact him immediately.

A young, handsome doctor entered my bay and smiled. 'Hello, Ava! I'm Dave, one of the junior doctors covering tonight. So, do you want to tell me what's brought you here today, love?'

He was poised and ready to take notes. I sighed, doubting that this poor man was ready for the smell that would put him off vaginas for life.

'I was ready to . . .' I paused, feeling myself blush, 'with my friend, and . . .'

He paused his note-taking. 'Sorry, you were ready to . . .?'

'We were about to be . . . you know . . . intimate.'

Dave's shoulders tensed as he began writing again.

'And he put his fingers inside me – with a lot of force, to be quite honest – and he's ruptured something. There is now a piece of me come loose internally, like, inside my vagina, and I don't know if it's septic or something. I'm unsure if it's a tumour, Dave, but whatever it is, he's done a lot of damage, and the smell is just vulgar!'

The doctor tilted his head, looking utterly confused. 'OK, let's start again – slowly. I'm not sure if it's your accent, but take a breath, calm down and tell me: before your intimate moment, did you have any other symptoms of being unwell?'

I thought hard about the past few weeks. Truthfully, I hadn't felt well for months. Maybe even years. Probably since Georgie was born. My life changed overnight and I have never been the same since.

'Any sickness, for instance?' Dave prompted.

I nodded, not wanting to divulge that it was probably the bottle of Barefoot I was consuming most nights to fall asleep.

'Temperature?'

'I'm not sure.'

'And just to formally check – your friend, he didn't put any objects up there that could be trapped?'

'Eh, no! He bloody well wouldn't dare!' I gasped.

'Just have to check, Ava, I'm sorry. OK, I'll get a nurse in here to carry out some routine observations and blood work, and I'll ask the gynaecologist on call to pop down and give you an internal examination. How does that sound?'

I nodded back. 'Yeah, OK. That's fine, thanks.'

Half an hour later, after having blood tests and being hooked up to a cardiac monitor, a young female gynaecologist was ready to examine me.

'Ava, just relax now. Open up your legs when you are ready and pop them onto the stirrups, please.'

Immediately, the smell began filling the room again.

'You'll feel some cold gel, and I'll insert the speculum. It will feel similar to a smear test, OK?'

Every muscle in my body tensed as I felt the cold equipment squeeze inside me.

'Relax, Ava. Keep your knees flopped to the side,' she advised in her posh English accent, but my stomach was churning. She angled the speculum and turned on a pen torch.

I couldn't relax, the smell was getting stronger.

'Oh my God, I'm so sorry! That's the smell,' I explained, wholly mortified.

'Hmm . . .' She cleared her throat. 'Pretty pungent, eh?'

I was horrified and terrified all at once.

'Do you see something, Doctor?' I asked, lifting my head. My dignity had been well and truly shredded to pieces.

'Hmm, I have,' she replied. 'Just relax, please; lie back down, I'm trying to manoeuvre it.'

'Manoeuvre *what*?' I called out.

The next few seconds seemed like hours as my question went unanswered and my anxiety sky-rocketed while the doctor became completely engrossed in my vagina. She pushed and prodded inside of me. The bottom of my stomach cramped, and I felt completely violated.

Eventually, she pushed herself away from me on her tiny rolling stool, muttering, 'Nope! I'm sorry. It's just too large!' As she removed her gloves, I could see her gasp for breath, having been holding it while she was nose-deep in the stench. 'Ava, I'm afraid you have a tampon stuck inside of you. It's caused an infection in your cervix. It looks like it's been there for at least a few months.'

'*What*?' I exclaimed, feeling relief flood through me. 'It's just a tampon?' I laughed a little as I felt blood rush back to my face. I thought I was dying. I thought I was writing my last will and testament – not that I'd have anything of value to leave anyone, besides my wedding rings and Doc Martens.

The doctor gave me a sharp look. 'This can be very serious, Mrs Little. It can cause toxic shock syndrome and, from the size of it, you're lucky it hasn't.'

'Toxic? Wait, what do you mean *size*?' I sat up, trying to remove my legs from the stirrups so my vagina wouldn't be such a prominent fixture of the room.

'It looks to me that it's about the size of a small plate and has wedged itself right into your cervix.'

'A dinner plate! *Jesus Christ*,' I laughed a little at the thought. How did I not feel it?

'We are going to have to take you to theatre, tonight.'

'WHAT? Wait, theatre! An operation? For a tampon?' I felt myself begin to panic once more.

'Don't worry, we can fix this. OK?' She came closer, braving the stench once more to give me a reassuring look. 'I'll take you to surgery, remove the tampon and give you a washout. You'll be home with some antibiotics in no time. But your observations and blood tests show your inflammatory markers are up, so this is causing an extreme effect on your body. It needs to be removed as soon as possible.'

I was speechless. I had never undergone surgery before.

'I'll get you prepped, and one of the nurses will notify your next of kin. I think . . .' She reached over and grabbed my notes. 'It's your husband, isn't it?'

'No! *No!* Please, don't call him!' I begged. 'We're not together anymore.'

'OK, well I have to notify someone.'

'Call . . .' I raced through everyone in my head, but since Johnny and I split, I had no one. My friends were his friends, and even my best friends I'd gradually distanced myself from.

'We need to inform someone, Ava. You'll require a general anaesthetic for this procedure and will need someone to stay with you afterwards to ensure you're OK.'

I didn't know how to tell the doctor I genuinely had no one.

'Perhaps your parents?' she asked.

I shook my head, still trying to take everything in. 'They live in Glasgow, I don't want to worry them.'

'Well, who else?' she rushed me.

'OK, right, erm . . . Can you call . . . maybe my friend Rebeka? She should come.'

I scrolled through my phone, reading Beka's number aloud to the doctor. I hadn't seen or spoken to her in almost two years, but she was my only true friend. Don't get me wrong, when I had good days or was numb from my third bottle of Pinot, I occasionally interacted on Facebook, liking the odd picture of her living her best life, socialising in the best bars and clubs of London. Beka had recently sent me an invite on Messenger to our high school reunion, which I gave a courteous thumbs-up reply to, knowing there was absolutely no chance I'd turn up. Apart from that, there was nothing. No communication. Well, not like we used to have.

'I'll give her a call for you,' the doctor smiled kindly towards me.

Fuck, what will Beka think? I covered my face as I felt cold tears trickle down my cheeks.

The doctor patted my shoulder and left the room.

How could you be so stupid, Ava? I wondered. *You could have died! Fuck, I might still die. I'm going into surgery!* My mind was racing, thinking of Georgie. Her little smiling face, her sweet dimples, her smell, everything that I could have done in the past year to be a better mother, to give her healthier memories of me. She didn't deserve a mum who was so depressed that she couldn't even deal with a fucking menstrual cycle. I felt sick. I wanted to hold my daughter, tell her I was sorry and try again at being there. Try again at being a mother. Try again at being a wife.

The doctor re-entered the cubical a few minutes later.

'Your friend is on her way. Let's take you down now, and you can see her when you're out.'

I gulped nervously. 'Doctor, wait, will I be OK?' I asked.

She held my hand and smiled. 'Everything has risks, but we've got this in time. You will be OK, Ava.'

I nodded, grasping her hand and feeling utterly terrified.

'Thank you.'

Chapter Three

Ava

'Ava, Ava, can you hear me?'

Even through the thick drowsiness, her voice was instantly familiar. I tried to open my eyes, which was a struggle, because they felt like they had dumbbells taped to them.

'Fucking hell, babe,' she giggled, with slight relief. 'You gave me a proper fright!'

Beka's friendly Essex accent brought a fleeting smile to my face, but my eyes squinted at the bright strip lighting above, and I scrunched them closed immediately.

'Ava, babe, can you hear me?' she repeated.

I noticed the worry in her voice and made an effort to nod back, still groggy from surgery. My head felt like a giant block of cement. 'Am I OK?' I croaked out. My body felt tender.

'Yeah, yeah, hun. The doctor said everything was removed and cleaned out. You no longer have—'

'A smelly fanny,' I blurted, still struggling to open my eyes.

17

Beka laughed loudly. 'Exactly! Hey, do you want to sit up and drink water or something?'

I nodded out of politeness, but all I wanted to do was sleep. Pressing my hands into the stiff hospital mattress, I pushed myself up until I was in a slumped sitting position. I could finally see my oldest friend properly. Her shiny blonde hair bounced as she spoke, floating down her back like silk. Her grin was as bright as ever and she hadn't aged a day.

'There we go! You're back with us, babe.' She rolled her heavily painted eyes in relief.

'I'm sorry they called you, Beka,' I whispered, shrugging my shoulders.

'Why?! I'm not!' She grabbed hold of my hand. 'I was assisting my boss with a shoot and the models were sassy little fuckers.'

Rebeka had been a photographer at *Inner Me!* magazine for years, shooting top-class models posing in designer clothes. Being so close to glamour rubbed off on her; I remembered how she was always name-dropping celebrities and attending star-studded events.

'But I did wonder . . .' She paused.

'Wonder what?' I asked, sipping the stale water.

'Why didn't you call your sister? Grace would want to be here, hun.' Her bright eyes searched me, and I glanced back down. 'I mean . . . I would call her, or at least let her know you're here. But I haven't spoken to you in so long, I wasn't sure if you guys had fallen out or something.'

'No, no. Of course we haven't fallen out. She's my

18

twin.' I laughed lightly. 'But Steve is also best friends with Johnny, and I didn't want him to know I'm here. It would just be something else he'd bring up to me in an argument.'

'What? The fact that you're unwell? Everyone gets sick, babe.'

I nodded. Ever since Johnny and I had separated, he'd griped with everything I did and how it would affect Georgie, from talking too much slang, to drinking too much wine, to not looking for work, to looking for work when I should be spending time with our daughter.

'Does Johnny know you're here? Are you two still . . .' She paused, not knowing how to word our break-up.

'Still over? Yep. The longest *break* in history,' I shrugged, feeling my eyes tear up.

'That's just the anaesthetic, babe. It gets you emosh! Saw it on TikTok.' She winked at me and I agreed, smiling back a little.

'We had another bust-up today. He's visiting his mum in a couple of weeks in the Lake District soon and I thought he'd ask me to go. It's part of our summer tradition.'

'What a cunt. Is she still a snotty cow?' Beka smirked, always having a comeback to make me laugh.

'She's not changed!' I rolled my heavy eyes, thinking of my posh in-laws.

The nurse walked into the cubical and grinned when she saw me sitting up. 'Ah, Ava! You're awake! How are you feeling?' she asked, popping a blood pressure cuff on my arm.

'OK, just tired,' I replied.

'Well, the anaesthetic will do that to you, pet. Everything went to plan and the doctor has left you a prescription for some antibiotics. You need to take them for the next few days, OK?'

I nodded, feeling the cuff expand and deflate on my arm.

'Your vitals are fine. You can get packed up as long as you're with your friend for the next twenty-four hours.'

I smiled apologetically at Beka, who was listening to the instructions. I felt my head spin with embarrassment. I knew I'd had to call someone, but I hadn't spoken to Beka for years and suddenly she was landed with me for the night. A pang of guilt washed through me.

'And what do I need to do if she becomes unwell?' She looked anxious at the thought of nursing me.

'Just call up for advice. I'll leave you the direct number of the ward, in with Ava's prescription. It's all precautionary.' The nurse smiled towards me. 'I'm sure you'll be fine now, pet. You were very lucky you came in when you did, though. Women die from toxic shock syndrome because of sanitary products every day! I always tell girls that if they're forgetful or have a few tipples one night, opt for a pad instead. It's a lot safer that way.'

I kept my eyes on the floor, nodding slightly at the polite advice. The nurse bustled around the room for a few more minutes before leaving.

'Jesus, she was a bit intense!' I muttered.

'No, she's right, Ava,' Beka said. 'I googled it when you were in surgery; six people died in the UK last year because of it!'

I sighed, feeling my eyes tear up. How could I have been stupid enough to leave a fucking tampon in?

'Don't stress, babe. You're fine now. I'll watch you tonight; no one needs to know.'

'No, no. You don't have to stay with me, you know,' I whispered. 'I just needed a name for a next of kin. I'll be fine to go home by myself and sleep this off.'

Rebeka gasped. 'Indeed you will not! Fucking hell, Ava. I got you. Chill.'

I looked up and smiled at her warmly.

'But we'll head to my place, if that's OK. I have some work on my laptop to email over by midnight.'

'Sure,' I nodded, feeling entirely out of sorts.

It was years since I had seen or spoken to Rebeka properly and, suddenly, the NHS had arranged a sleepover for us. Since Johnny and I split, I'd become a recluse. I couldn't face the sympathy, the questions, the absolute embarrassing reality of my entire world falling apart and people talking or gossiping about it. All because of me. All because of my insecurities. My warped mind and over-imaginative imagination. I still wasn't ready to mentally process the fact that I'd accused the man of absolutely anything and everything with no hard facts or evidence of him ever putting a foot out of line throughout our marriage. The fact is, I'd made his life a living hell – *his words, not mine.*

After Johnny's career took off and he started teaching more classes at the uni he works at, and we spent less time together, I'd instantly jump to conclusions of where he was or what he was doing. I would sit at home, bawling my eyes out, dreaming up scenarios of all the beautiful women he'd be shagging or falling in love with, and all the while he was innocently at the gym or running into the supermarket. All because *I* was struggling. Because *I* couldn't adapt to being thrust into motherhood, running a house and waiting in all day on my husband. The worst part was that I knew I was doing it.

I knew I was pushing him away, but I did try. I'd spruce up my hair, distract myself by filling my days with other mums at the park. I also started journalling my crazy thoughts but, even then, even when I knew things were getting rocky between us, I'd burst into tears or *flames* when he'd walk through the door at night. I'd demand to know his exact whereabouts throughout his day or I'd wait till he slept and plough through his phone like I was decoding WikiLeaks. Fuck, we even went to couples therapy and the experts put it down to post-natal depression, which made me feel even worse.

Having Georgie was the best thing to ever happen to me, to us. She was a constant source of joy in my life, my proudest achievement, but I'd struggled being a new mum. It changed everything about me. My body, my sex life, my confidence, my career prospects. After she was born, I struggled to find my path in life, or even recognise who I was anymore. Having full responsibility over a tiny beautiful baby filled me with so much fear that I might do something wrong. I worried that I would accidentally hurt her, or forget a vital step in motherhood that would scar her for life. I lived on my nerves, from morning to night, shutting everyone out as I focused on my family. I couldn't lose her. I couldn't lose Johnny. But that constant fear and panic was my downfall, and I drove him away. And now, that old life of fear feels like a distant memory. A distant *perfect* memory, compared to the utter hell that I'm living in now.

Johnny and I met at high school, but we only started getting serious in the final couple of years. By the time we graduated from university, we were already engaged. We got married pretty quickly and honestly, things were great. A few months into married life I fell pregnant, and when Georgie came along, I dedicated myself to being a stay-at-home mum – something Johnny felt strongly about. I'd never needed to fend for myself and, aside from a uni job, I've never worked a day in my life! I didn't have to, with him supporting us . . . well, until now. I suppose the final straw for Johnny was when I accused him of banging the dog walker and sacked the poor girl for wearing Lycra shorts to walk our pooch. I came downstairs one day to them chatting in the kitchen and I flipped. Realistically, I was jealous. So unbelievably jealous and insecure that I packed my things and moved out of my posh home in Kensington to a one-bedroom apartment in Croydon, with no income, no husband and with even less purpose in life.

23

I mean, I tried to go back. Begged, in fact, but Johnny insisted he needed the space. He offered me the house, but I could hardly make ends meet in Croydon, never mind Kensington. My life now has become more of a hazy existence and I have never felt so alone. Don't get me wrong, my friends tried to phone and text initially, but as time passed, it became less often, and I didn't blame them. I was rude. I was unsociable. I was embarrassed. They had it all. And truthfully, so had I until I threw it away. I got so wrapped up in guilt and shame that I didn't give a single fuck about what was happening in anyone else's life because mine was so goddamn miserable.

'You with me, babe?' Beka's voice made me jump from my thoughts.

I glanced around the room until I spotted a clock. *11 p.m.* Fucking hell, I'd been here for hours. I nodded back to her.

'Come and I'll help you get dressed.' Beka assisted me to the side of the bed and untied my hospital gown carefully. She handed me my top, which had been folded neatly on a chair beside us. 'You set, hun?'

'I guess,' I said.

Chapter Four

Ava

Beka lived in a rented apartment in Clapham. She had been there since landing her job at *Inner Me!* six years ago, slowly going from a shared house to a tiny flat of her own. We travelled back together in a cab, making small talk while she scrolled through her emails. I still felt woozy, watching the bright lights of London whizz by like strikes of lightning in the darkness. My stomach felt crampy, my vagina felt tender, and the hospital had given me a giant nappy-sized fanny pad to help soak up any bleeding that might occur after my procedure. I was sick, unbelievably exhausted, hungry and hurt. I wanted to go home and cry myself to sleep, but here I was, heading in the opposite direction, trying to put on a brave face.

I rested my head against the cool window and shut my eyes as the cab sped through the night, until I felt a tap on my shoulder.

'We're here, babe. Come on,' Beka said, her shiny white teeth glinting in the darkness. She passed the driver some cash and we got out. I followed her up the tenement staircase to her flat above a small bakery.

Her place was chic, sophisticated and modern. Her living room overlooked narrow streets of shops and bars. I smiled as I glanced out the window, watching the partygoers stumble down the street, full of laughter.

'Did you spot our pic?' she asked. She pointed to an old photograph of me, my sister and Beka, on our first girls' holiday to France, resting on a bookshelf.

'I fucking loved this holiday!' I laughed.

'I did too. And I especially loved Henre's big baguette!' she said, attempting a French accent, and we giggled, remembering her Parisian actor boyfriend for the week.

I turned on the spot, taking in Beka's sleek apartment. 'Your place is so stunning.'

She frowned a little. 'You've been here before.'

'I know, but it was a long time ago now. Plus, I live in a shit tip, so I can appreciate how nice this is. Trust me.'

'C'mon babe, your place can't be that bad! Surely Johnny wouldn't let Georgie live in a dump.'

I shook my head. I didn't have the energy to explain our turbulent marriage and how cold and distant he'd been since the split. I mean, I was trying. I'd pretty much promised to sit back, not speak and become invisible if it meant we could return to Kensington. 'It's complicated' was all I could muster.

'Here, come get some PJs on, and I'll make us a sandwich before bed.'

Beka motioned me into her bedroom. Her king-sized velvet bed sat proudly in the centre of the room. Unlike

26

mine, her bed-sheets looked like they had never seen a midnight kebab stain. Cream with gold embroidery, and more togs than I could count. I pulled down my jogging bottoms just as Beka handed me a pair of pyjama bottoms.

She burst out laughing. 'Why does your fanny look like a boxing glove?'

I peered down at my groin. 'It's the pad,' I giggled back. 'Shut it! I'll have to keep it on, or your fancy bedding will get ruined tonight.'

'Fucking right, you're keeping it on then, babe! The bedding is *Kylie!*' she tittered, pulling up her top and slipping on a silky night dress. 'OK, get comfortable. I'll bring us some food and we can catch up properly.'

I smiled back gratefully. 'Thanks for this,' I whispered.

She was halfway through the door when I said it but she paused, looked at me, and smiled. 'That's what friends are for, eh?' She winked and walked back through to the living area.

I hopped onto her cosy bed. *What a day*, I thought. *How could I have been so stupid?* I lay there feeling embarrassed, mortified and terrified all at once. The thought of something happening to me and leaving behind Georgie made my stomach flip. I snuggled my head on Beka's pillow and thought of my daughter. I wondered what she was up to. If she missed me, if Johnny missed me. We'd go visit his mum in the Lake District a few times a year and this was the first time he'd thought about taking her alone. I felt my eyes get heavy, wishing I was going with them. I turned to my phone, resting on the bedside table; *three missed calls from Grace*. I cleared the notifications and gazed at my daughter's smiling face on my background home-screen instead, and then drifted off to sleep.

I woke to the sound of Rebeka's alarm clock going off from the side of the bed. For a second I lay still, feeling slightly awkward at being there.

'Morning babe,' she muttered through a yawn.

'Morning,' I replied, and tossed around the bed a little.

'You were out cold in about three minutes last night,' she laughed.

'It must have been the anaesthetic. I still feel a bit fucked, honestly.' I sat up in bed, feeling uneasy at what an inconvenience I'd been to my friend overnight. The light was peeking through the blinds and I squinted my eyes, trying to wake up quickly.

Rebeka propped herself up onto her arms and turned to me. 'So, what the hell has been going on with you, Ava Little? We haven't caught up in forever! You just bloody disappeared. I've had no one to talk to, or gossip with. I've missed you!'

God, I wasn't ready for an early morning interrogation.

'I know.' I felt my mouth dry and coughed a little, distracting myself from the questioning.

'What happened? I wasn't sure if it was me? Or Johnny? Or . . .'

'It wasn't you! No way! I guess I just ran away from everything and everybody,' I said, shrugging.

'But that included me?' she said softly.

A wave of guilt washed through me. 'I'm sorry,' I said. 'I'm so sorry.'

It wasn't until now that I realised how much I had missed in Beka's life. I was so fucking selfish, hiding away; it hadn't occurred to me that she needed me. God, we were like sisters growing up. Three best friends inseparable throughout high school, university and most of our adult life. Well, until I ruined it. I felt my heart sink with regret.

'Don't be sorry, babe. I just really missed you, you know?' She paused, and for a second the silence felt heavy. 'And I missed Georgie! How is she? Still obsessed with Disneyland?'

My face broke into a smile, thinking of my perfect daughter. 'Yes, she's great. Still crazy obsessed with Disney. We have a jar in the house and any spare coin on the street or anything goes in the Disney World jar for Florida one day.'

'I love that!' Beks smiled. 'I miss telling you all about my life every day, and hearing all about yours . . .'

'But that's it, Beks,' I said quietly. 'I honestly have no life now. Since we split, I live in a one-bedroom flat with no money to do anything. When Georgie is at Johnny's, I sleep or drink myself into bed. I haven't spoken to Grace in God knows how long. I've nothing for you to catch up on. I am existing here, not living. It's fucking embarrassing.'

There was a moment of silence in the room. I felt my eyes fill and shut them briefly to hide any emotion.

'Wow. Fuckin' hell, babe,' Beks said after a few moments. She sounded shocked. 'I suppose I'm the one who should be sorry then, Ava. I should have tried harder to make sure you were OK.'

I squeezed her manicured hand. 'You did try. I know you did. This is on me. All of it.'

'Have you been going out or seeing anyone?' she asked, lightening the conversation a little.

'Out? No.' I laughed, not wanting to delve into the finances of an unemployed single mother living in the capital to my friend, who seemed to have it all. 'I've been sort of shagging my neighbour, though.' I blushed. 'Obviously Johnny has no idea.'

Beks erupted into laughter. 'I meant seeing a therapist, babe. But, *yes* to this conversation! Is he hot? It's nothing to do with Johnny now, Ava! It's been over a year.'

I felt my gut twist. A year. She was right, but how long does a break from marriage normally take? I'd started to wonder when a break became an end to marriage entirely.

'Eh, Adam? He's a . . .' I paused, thinking of Adam, knowing what Beka's reaction would be if she knew how eccentric he was, '*nice* guy, but he's not for anything more than shagging . . . and giving me sugar or teabags if I run out.' I giggled. 'What about you?' I asked, remembering how Rebeka always had a string of handsome men at her disposal. She had never been one for settling down, and even when she presumed she'd found the one, the following week she'd move on to someone else.

'Well, I've been shagging my boss. Well, technically, my boss's boss's boss. The magazine's founder.'

I gasped. 'Not Mitchell Travers?'

'*Ohh*, yes!' She reddened, shaking her head. Mitchell Travers was a well-known millionaire, originally from New Zealand, who came to London in his early twenties and was now one of the most eligible bachelors in the city. He'd inherited a portion of his grandfather's fortune and media outlets. He was always appearing on panel shows and news segments, discussing current affairs. Not that his brain was important – the man could turn Ellen DeGeneres straight.

'And are you two together? Like in a relationship?' I asked, truly gobsmacked that she had landed the hottest man in the whole of London.

'Well, it's complicated. He's technically single, and so am I, and we only see each other. He's the kindest person I've ever met. When we're together I honestly melt, it's weird. He brings out this nice, sweet side to me. Awww, Ava!' she sighed and flopped onto the mattress, 'I just want to be around him all of the time, and he's obviously the same with me. But part of my employee contract states you can't date in the workplace, which means it's a secret. We've been together for over a year now.'

I began slapping the mattress happily for my friend, shocked at her ever being exclusive with anyone. 'Oh my God, Beks!'

'What?!' she said.

'This just isn't like you! I've never seen you exclusive

with one guy like this!' I smiled at her as she covered her face in frustration.

'I hate it. I hate feeling like a teenager, but he's a fucking sort, babe. Six foot three, abs of steel, *and* he rides me like Lewis Hamilton rides that Mercedes!' She laughed loudly, and I joined in. 'And that accent, my God, his voice!'

I nodded, agreeing fully with her, having heard him on *Loose Women* recently talking about God knows what, but Jesus Christ he was carved from God himself.

'But you can't tell anyone?' I asked, still trying to wrap my head around it all.

'Nope, or go on dates or anything. Everyone knows him! I mean he's six foot three, Ava, try hiding that cunt.'

Silence filled the room once more as I thought about my friend's predicament.

'Could you not give him an ultimatum? Or make him jealous or something. He's the fucking boss, Beka. Surely he can bend his own rules?'

She smirked at the comment, and I saw her thinking hard at my suggestions. '*Hmmm,* maybe,' she said. 'Not like I haven't thought of it. But I don't want to lose him. He knows I want to tell the world, and I suppose we will one day. But, anyway, enough of that. Tell me about the neighbour! Tell me everything!'

I huffed. 'Well, he doesn't have an empire. He doesn't actually work at all . . .'

'OK, EW!'

I turned to her, raising an eyebrow, feeling suddenly self-conscious that I was also unemployed.

'You are a mum, Ava! You have a job, babe,' she said quickly, rolling her eyes and covering her tracks.

'Well, he was in a car accident when he was twenty and got a big payout, so he lives off his cheque.'

'OK, how big a claim are we talking? And any long-term effects of the accident?' She screwed her face up nervously.

'Not big enough to stop working, put it that way. He's vegan, into herbs and nature, and honestly, nothing like me . . .'

'So, quite notable side effects from the accident then,' she teased.

'Stop!' I burst out laughing. 'We basically have sex out of convenience. There's nothing in it.'

'You won't be bringing him to the high school reunion?' She smirked.

'Ha, I won't be bringing anyone! I'm not going! I thought that had passed, anyway.'

'Eh, no, babe, it's the twentieth, two weeks' time, and you *are* going!'

I shook my head.

'Why not? Get out there, Ava! Get away from fucking Professor Sprout and stop just existing! Live a little.'

I hummed. 'I just don't fancy telling everyone I'm jobless with my marriage in tatters. Plus, Grace will be there, and no doubt she'll bring Steve – and he'll tell Johnny I'm out and it'll just cause an argument.'

'Do you have Georgie on Fridays?' she asked.

'Sometimes. But that's actually the week Johnny's in the Lake District. So I'll get her back Saturday.'

'No doubt sucking his mummy's titties when he's up there!' she spat. 'Little mummy's boy, that one. Well, fuck Johnny!' I could hear the anger behind her voice. 'What you do in your spare time has fuck-all to do with him. Please come. *Pleeease*?'

I smiled gratefully. 'I'm not sure, honestly.'

'Well, I'm taking that as a *yes* then! Ahhhhhh, I'm so excited now!' she screeched, reaching over and hugging me tightly.

'Beka . . .'

'Nope, it's settled. We are going! OK, I have to pop into work for a bit. You're welcome to stay. I could bring us lunch back in? They do the most delicious cakes in the bakery downstairs. That would cheer you and your smelly fanny right up!'

I gaped, and slapped her jokingly. 'I'd love to lie around here all day, but *no*. I'd better take my minging fanny home and tidy up a little,' I laughed, discreetly sniffing the air, hoping she wasn't serious about the smell.

'Yeah, well, dust off your old dancing shoes!' She patted my thigh and swung her legs out of the bed.

'Woo, yep. Buzzing. Can't wait,' I said sarcastically, flopping back down on her cosy pillows.

Rebeka popped on her Spotify playlist of 'Summer Tunes' and began getting ready. Eventually, I dared to stand up and head to the bathroom to get organised for the day. I threw some cold water over my dry, tired face and glanced at myself in the mirror. *It's time to get back to reality, Ava.* I popped my jogging bottoms back on, brushed my long dark hair into some form of bun, and slipped back into my Converse at the door. Rebeka handed me a glass of water and my prescription, and I swallowed my first antibiotic of the day. When we hugged goodbye, I felt a warmth inside me that I realised I'd been missing for a long time.

'I'll text and see how you are later on. You're not getting rid of me this time, Ava Little!' Beks called out as I left her apartment.

'Not this time, Beks! Speak soon!'

I walked down the stairwell smiling to myself. She hadn't changed one bit from the bubbly, crazy girl I'd known at school.

I took out my phone and attempted to call Johnny to have a chat with my daughter. Almost immediately he cut me off. A text came through a few seconds later.

Johnny: *What's up?*

Me: *Hi, just wanted to chat with Georgie. How is she?*

Johnny: *She's fine. Will drop her off at usual time.*

I glanced at his reply and felt my shoulders droop a little more in defeat.

Chapter Five

Rebeka

Beka finished curling her long blonde hair, locked up her apartment, and headed towards the Travers Media headquarters at Leicester Square Gardens. As she walked into the glass tower block, she waved to the security guard, who gave her a little wink. The lift was crammed; she just managed to slip in and press for the third floor where *Inner Me!* was published. She felt her phone vibrate in her pocket and took it out, holding it close to her so no one could peek. It was a text from Mitchell.

Mitchell: *Nice boots, baby! M x*

She smirked, taking a second to appreciate the cream knee-highs she'd bought from Selfridges on a whim.

Beka: *Checking the CCTV, Mr Travers? Tut tut!*

The lift door was nearly closed when a hand shot through the small opening, and Mitchell stepped in. His hair was shaved short, but you could see the shadow of his dark hair peeking through from underneath. He wore a black suit with a crisp white shirt, and his masculine cologne took over the small space.

'Ah Mr Travers, good morning, sir,' one of the accountants said.

Mitchell acknowledged him with a slight nod.

'Which floor, Mr Travers? Twelve?' a young journalist from the news channel asked, her finger hovering over the buttons.

'Three, please. I'm checking in on magazines today.' His voice was deep; just hearing it sent shockwaves between Beka's legs.

She blushed. In her six years at the company, Mitchell had only attended the midweek meeting a handful of times. Beka wondered why he hadn't mentioned the drop-in visit – or if it was only decided on a whim when he saw her in those boots.

'So, anything planned this weekend, Mr Travers?' the same accountant asked.

Beka stood directly behind her boss, her heart pounding. He leant back a little, pressing against her subtly.

'Nothing at the moment, Miles,' he answered.

The lift halted at floor three. They stepped forward at the same time.

'After you, miss,' he said, letting Beka walk in front.

'Thank you, Mr Travers.'

Beka gazed at his ocean-blue eyes briefly and a small smirk passed over her face. With a grin, he watched her stride to her station.

'Mitchell!' a loud voice called out, and he turned to see Robert, the magazine's editor-in-chief. 'This is a surprise!' Robert seemed anxious at his unexpected arrival and began waving papers around.

'Yes, I thought I'd pop into this morning's meeting,' Mitchell said, then walked into the distance towards Robert's office, as Beka got comfortable at her desk.

'Jesus! Tell me that wasn't just Mitchell Travers announcing that he's coming to our midweek meeting!'

Rebeka looked up from her laptop to find her friend Andre hyperventilating. Andre was head of social media at the magazine and was meticulously organised; surprises threw him into a tailspin.

'I think it was, babe,' she replied, trying not to giggle at his dramatics.

'Oh, Jesus! *Jesus!* That man is practically a demigod. How am I going to pitch in front of him? What is he here for? There's going to be cuts, isn't there? We're all getting fired!' His face was turning more sweaty and red by the second.

'Woah, babe. Chill. He's done this before, OK? No one lost their job the last time. Everything is fine. He probably just fancied a change of scenery. He needs to check on all his departments from time to time. We will be fine—'

'You will be fine! You are assisting world-renowned photographers! I'm pressing 'upload to Instagram'!'

'Exactly! I have been here for six years, Andre, and am supposedly one of the senior photographers, but somehow I'm still doing the fucking coffee runs! At least you've moved up the ladder, but *hey* I don't have a pair of testicles, so what do I expect?' Beka shrugged, feeling a knot in her stomach. She had worked at *Inner*

Me! since graduating and still only assisted her boss, still did the planning and prepping. Still hadn't had her shot. She posted the most glamorous version of her life on social media and all her friends envied her lifestyle, which deep down she knew was fake.

'You have bigger balls than me, that's for sure!' Andre panted.

'Boardroom, people!' called out Tiffany, one of Robert's most senior assistants, clapping her hands loudly.

Beks rolled her eyes at Andre. Together, they walked to the boardroom. Each department head took a seat at the table while everyone else stood behind, taking notes.

'Sit down,' Beka whispered to Andre, who was fidgeting and hovering around the table. He'd only recently been promoted to head of social media and was still finding his position with the seniors. Beka mouthed 'SIT!' once more, and he pulled out a seat and sat nervously.

The room filled with chatter between colleagues, everyone speculating what Mitchell's presence at the meeting might mean. After a few minutes, Robert entered with Mitchell at his side, and silence swept over the room.

'Good morning, everyone!' Robert said, sounding unusually chirpy. 'Today, we have a special treat. Mr Travers will observe our midweek meeting to determine what is happening on the third floor. No reason to panic!' He glanced at Andre, now downing his second glass of water. 'It's always, err . . . lovely to have you here, Mr Travers.'

'Yes, it is,' one of the junior editors whispered in Rebeka's ear and they both giggled.

Mitchell raised his hand at everyone in the room. His eyes skimmed over the people willing to make a good impression, and eventually fell on Rebeka. She smiled briefly then lifted her notebook to her face, ready to work. Mitchell took a seat, and Robert continued.

'I want to start, as always, by thanking you for a great springtime edition last week! We've had fantastic feedback, thanks to Andre, who got our 'Spring Fling' story trending. Great work!'

Beka beamed with pride at Andre, whose face had lit up at the acknowledgement.

'I'll hand you over to Tiffany,' Robert said. 'She will sort out this week's segments. Tiff?'

'Yay! Good morning, *Inner Me!* fam!' she began in her usual, incredibly high-pitched voice. 'Firstly, this month's copy is looking unbelievable.' Her hands wafted around her face, full of expression. 'Thanks for your great work, team!'

Rebeka zoned out, her gaze drifting back to Mitchell. *What was he doing here?* She looked at him, his stature, his muscular arms folded, his handsome face listening intently to Tiffany's arse-licking display of solidarity. She gazed at his broad shoulders, and her mind flashed back to holding on to them tightly as he made love to her a few nights before. He was the most flawlessly gorgeous man she'd ever seen.

'OK, as usual, we'll hear from each department and see what's happening in the print edition. Let's start with Jacob.'

Jacob, head of the writers, swivelled in his seat to face the room. 'This month, we want to run a beautiful story from Trish.' Trish stood behind her boss, alongside the other writers, sporting the gummiest grin that her piece had been chosen for print. 'She wants to interview a young woman named Lina, who saved her friend from an awful acid attack. Trish saw the post circulate on social media and wants to reach out. Basically, Lina's friend was on a first date and called her to help after the guy became full-on and aggressive. Unfortunately, when Lina turned up and the pair left, he followed them home and attempted to attack his date. But brave Lina threw herself on top of her friend and, as a result, she was saturated with the acid and suffered the most horrific burns.'

Tiffany held her face in shock. 'Wow. Brave woman! But what's the angle?'

'Online dating and the scars left behind,' Jacob replied while Trish beamed behind him, nodding in full support.

Andre turned in his chair and shook his head discreetly at Beka.

'Hmmm . . . Sounds awful. Poor girl! Yeah, so, nice story, Trish, but not for *Inner Me!* It's just . . . a little deep, you know? Maybe best to keep that one for the online readers?' Tiffany's response stamped down on Trish's grin like Nellie the fucking elephant.

'Sure, Tiffany. We'll run Ian's story, 'Lipo in Turkey – great idea or greatest fear?'' Jacob nodded at Ian, who stood tall in delight.

'Oh, yes! That sounds more like it! Good work, guys! Now, Adam, how is the health and well-being segment?'

Adam, a fitness-fanatic Australian, sat up in his seat. 'It's looking great. Allison has written a great piece on the wonders of intermittent fasting. Not only for weight loss but also for the mind.'

Tiffany gave an enthusiastic thumbs up. 'And fashion?'

Miles, head of the fashion department and Rebeka's boss, leant back slowly in his chair. He was an older gentleman, around sixty, and had been at the magazine long before Mitchell took it over. He was an icon in the fashion world, a renowned photographer back in his day and great friends with Mitchell's grandfather. Miles insisted on working closely with Rebeka and she'd assisted him in all his major covers over the years: planning his diary, booking his models and designing each backdrop or location. He always said she was his prodigy, yet never allowed her to go out on her own.

'Well, Tiff, I had our front cover locked down until twenty minutes ago. I shot an up-and-coming model in Monaco last week, and I was ecstatic with the finish.'

Tiffany's head swayed. 'Yes, the cousin of the Kardashians. I remember. Can we not use it, Miles? Some legality?'

'Exactly that! The Kardashians don't want to be affili-ated with the cousin – they claim she is so distantly related that they have a stronger blood line to the late Queen and, well, without the name, it's a pointless angle.' Miles spoke slowly, while Tiffany's stiletto tapped out her impatience.

'So what else do we have, Miles?' she urged.

'Well . . . I only received word a few minutes ago. Looks like we're back to the drawing board. Perhaps I could send some of my team out to photograph for the writers' stories until I come up with the summer cover.'

Beka felt her face lift in surprise – maybe this was her chance? Something lowkey, something to start getting her name out there.

'Sure, but we need the cover for Friday,' Tiffany warned politely. 'Jacob, let Miles know if you need any snaps for your stories.'

'I'd love to photograph some of the writers' work, Miles? Maybe the girl Lina from the acid attack story— even if it doesn't make print,' Rebeka said quickly. 'It's basic photography and I'd love a chance to do some solo work.'

The room turned painfully quiet. Assistants usually only spoke during meetings if they were spoken to. Tiffany turned to her with a look of dismay.

'Oh, OK. Well, I've just said that story is cut.'

'No, you said it would be best for our online readers, who make up a considerable bulk of our readership, Tiff.'

'I'm sorry.' Tiffany exhaled. 'Don't you work in fashion?'

Rebeka could feel her heartbeat through her chest as every set of eyes darted in her direction. She glanced towards Mitchell, hoping, praying he could do something. *Why wasn't he demanding they give her a shot at a real shoot?* Rebeka watched him glare down at the table in utter silence instead.

'Rebeka, I assign the workload. Now, enough,' Miles replied sharply.

'Yeah, sure, Miles.' She stepped back, unwilling to look in Mitchell's direction now he had just witnessed her getting shat all over.

The meeting continued, and Rebeka stood rigid and quiet behind the table of men running a women's magazine. She went over every inch of her workload: the sacrifices she'd made, from early rises to working late into the night, for planning, sketching sets, arranging backdrops, assisting the models with angles – all for Miles to use her ideas. The lack of thanks, the coffee runs for the past six years, all to be shut down by her boss in front of everyone. Twenty minutes later, the meeting concluded, and Beka stormed back to her desk, still feeling her bones rattle with resentment. She sat at her desk infuriated and mortified.

'OK, what was that?' Andre approached her station, flapping his hands over his face.

'That was my crucifixion,' she mumbled. 'I'm so sick of it, Andre. I'm a photographer! My title is Senior Photographer, but I don't get a fucking photoshoot!'

'You have worked with the biggest celebrities we've had, Beks!' he said quietly, trying to avoid the gossipers.

'Yep, I have. I have planned their shoot, ordered the set, worked on their clothes, but still . . . Miles get the credit of pressing the button on the camera. I've had enough of it!'

'I just can't believe it!' he replied, staring off into the distance.

Rebeka, grunted. 'I know. It was a bit risky speaking out, but I thought—'

'No! I meant me getting praised before Mitchell Travers for my "Spring Fling" piece!' He fanned himself, then paused, looking straight at her. 'But I don't know what *you* were thinking, Beka. That was one of the dumbest suggestions I've ever seen you make! And honey, I've seen you make a few.' He lowered his voice to a whisper. 'Remember the guy a few years ago from the mail room? YUCK!' He made a face, holding back a gag.

'He had a nice arse!' she snapped. 'Anyway, I had to say something, Andre! I want to take photos of people, of literally anyone. That's what I should be doing! And I don't mean some long-lost, twice-removed cousin of the Kardashians related by fucking dog blood! I want to take photos for real stories,' she spat back.

'Gurl, this is *Inner Me!* Not some off-brand local paper. Just apologise to Miles, tell Daddy you're sorry, and we can all move on. You'll get your chance soon. The fashion department can't run without you!'

Mitchell: *Are you ok after that? xx*

Beks smiled gratefully to Andre, as she skimmed her text from Mitchell. 'I need to get this. I'll catch up with you later?' Andre blew her a kiss and retreated to his desk.

Beka: *I'm fine.*

Mitchell: *Are you sure? Don't be mad at me, I know you're wonderful.*

Beka: *I'm going to see Miles. See if he will slap me on the wrist for speaking out.*

Mitchell: *Glad you're ok. Pop down to mine tonight? x*

Mitchell: *Could always slap you somewhere else? Somewhere I know you like x*

She slipped her phone back into her handbag, too distracted by work to start a sexting session, and began answering her emails.

Later that afternoon, when the buzz of the meeting had died down, Rebeka approached Miles's office and gave a little knock.

'Yes!' he called out. He grinned when he saw Rebeka and gestured for her to sit.

She sat opposite him and shrugged. 'I'm sorry I spoke out at the meeting, Miles.'

'Uh-huh,' he replied, tapping his pen on his desk.

'It's just that I've been at the magazine for six years now, and I'm excellent at my job,' she said.

'Hmm.'

'You say all the time that I'm your right-hand woman. And I love that, babe, but . . .'

He tilted his glasses at her casual expression.

'I plan all *your* shoots, I book *you* the best models, pick the wardrobe, the sets, the lot. I'm supposed to be a senior photographer Miles. But I feel like an overpaid assistant. I need to start shooting alone, you know?' She sighed and sank into the chair, 'I just thought that could be my chance. Shooting some of the writers' work. It doesn't have to be big campaigns, not at the start. I want to show you, prove to you how good I am, Miles.'

Miles remained quiet as his rusty old cogs absorbed the conversation.

'The twentieth.' He sighed, as Rebeka held her hands up in confusion. 'I'll let *you* shoot the back Ricardo Voe campaign.' His voice was slow and full of thought. 'I know how good you are, Rebeka, and that's why you're my right-hand woman. You are a fashion photographer, that's what I've been training you up to be. And maybe you're right. Maybe it's time you took some of my workload.'

Rebeka laughed, almost not believing him.

'I am supposed to be doing the shoot, but I'll pass it to you.'

Rebeka felt her mouth fall open, unusually lost for words.

'It has a brief – glitterball disco, if I remember correctly, so lots of diamonds and sparkle for his new jewellery collection. What do you say?'

Beks screeched. 'You're fucking for real?'

He nodded back. 'I am.'

She stood up, too excited to sit.

47

'So, I call the shots? *All* of them?'

'I won't even be in the studio,' he said, holding his hands up.

Rebeka gulped. 'Miles, seriously, you won't regret this!'

Chapter Six

Rebeka

Two weeks passed and Beks was headed to her first solo shoot, a fresh wave of motivation sweeping through her. Nerves swarmed her stomach, but she pushed them aside, repeating affirmations in her mind: *I am a strong, independent woman. I am an excellent photographer, and I fucking deserve this.*

As she walked onto the studio floor, she was welcomed by an entourage of bustling staff. Hairspray clouded her vision and made her choke, billowing up from where the makeup and hair teams were styling the models.

'She's arrived. Rebeka is here!' one of the interns announced as Beks passed her Louis Vuitton handbag over.

'How are you feeling?' the young intern asked.

Rebeka held her head high. 'Great. Why?' She immediately felt self-conscious, wondering if everyone was doubting her capabilities.

'Sure. That's great. Can I get you anything?'

'Iced latte, please, babe, and where is my camera and shit?'

'It's just over there, Rebeka.' The intern pointed to the centre of the room, where her camera rested on its tripod, and Beks headed over.

A tall, thin, captivating model approached her as she fiddled with the camera lens. She had bright green eyes and long, icy-blonde hair that hung down to her waist.

Beks smiled. 'Hey, you set?'

The model gently tugged on the tie of her dressing gown, revealing a diamond necklace that spilt down her chest and, underneath, a pair of sheer nude underwear.

'I'm set!' she replied confidently.

'Babe, I'll be the first to buy that necklace if I look like you. *Wow!*' Rebeka gasped.

The model smirked. 'Where do you want me?'

'On set, babe. Just right in the centre.' She pointed to the large swath of floor coated in sparkling confetti, directly beneath a substantial glitterball suspended from the ceiling. The backdrop was comprised of multi-coloured squares to emulate a sixties nightclub vibe.

Beks followed the model to set and positioned her camera on the tripod. 'OK, what's your name again, hun?' she asked the model while adjusting the camera lens, flickers of light radiating onto her.

The model grinned. 'It's Tia.'

'Well, Tia, if you stand where you are, I'll just start snapping till I get the correct lighting and focus. Then we can start soon, babe.'

Tia stood, relaxed in her jewel-encrusted necklace, waiting for Rebeka to begin. The camera flashed over her as Beks adjusted and then re-adjusted the lens. The room was silent.

Eventually, Beks was satisfied. 'OK, do you want me to talk you through it? Or will we start, and I'll chip in?'

'Whatever. I'm fine to get started,' Tia replied, shrugging.

'Can we bring on the boys, hun?' Beks called out to the intern who stood patiently behind her. Two six-foot ripped models stepped onto set wearing sheer skin-toned underwear that matched Tia's. Rebeka stepped back, appreciating the hunks and their bulges. 'Well, I'm sure you'll enjoy this shoot, Tia darling, and if you don't, we certainly will.' She laughed, and Tia blushed.

'Yep, I'm sure we all will!' a new voice chimed in from behind them.

Beks turned to see Andre standing behind her with his phone in hand, ready to snap his own content. 'I couldn't miss my girl's big day! Let's get a behind-the-scenes for the socials!'

Beka grabbed her friend's hand and squeezed. 'You're the best!'

With a flash of the camera, the photo shoot began. Tia posed effortlessly, flowing through her angles like she was made of silk. She ran her fingers through the hanging sparkles of the necklace, carefully not exposing herself as she stared directly into the camera, while both male models gazed at her with desire.

'Yeah, Tia. Give me more!' Rebeka yelled out, becoming more animated.

Tia was changing it up, crawling on the floor, leaning against the glitterball, tugging at her silky hair like a possessed mermaid.

'You look stunning, babe. Just don't get lost in the background, yeah? I've still not got the shot. Change it up!' Beks called back, as the team behind her glanced at one another nervously.

'Tia, think of Studio 54; that's the kind of vibe we're going for, yeah?'

Tia looked confused, 'Studio what?'

'Never mind. Just look cool, fun, daring!' She egged her on.

Suddenly, Tia took a step back and, a second later, she lunged for the glitterball. Both male models stepped back and watched in horror as her long, elegant legs circled the ball and she swung chaotically through the air. The set crew gasped, clearly hoping the ceiling fixtures would be enough to hold the extra weight.

'Wait. No. Stop! Stop! Stop!' Rebeka screeched and sprang out from behind her camera, heading for Tia.

Eventually the ball began to slow down, making it less like a bulldozer, and when it was safe, Tia hopped off.

'Fucking hell, Tia. You're not Miley Cyrus!' Rebeka tutted.

'Sorry. I thought you wanted more of a selection?' Tia replied, panting slightly after her casual circus act and looking confused at the commotion she had caused in the room.

'More angles, not broken ankles, babe. Fucking hell, love.'

'OK, will I keep going?' Tia asked.

'*Hmmm*, just let me think.' Rebeka returned to her camera, flicking through and observing the snaps closely. After going through them twice and feeling uninspired, she sighed and rubbed her forehead, trying to think. 'Shit, shit, shit,' she whispered to herself. Her hands were sweating as the pressure amplified. 'You can't fuck this up, you've got this,' she tittered to herself. 'Just think. What do you need to change?'

'Beks . . .' Andre approached her sheepishly. 'Rebeka?' He took a small breath to disguise his anxiety. 'What are you doing?'

'I am trying to sell this hip-grazing, uncomfortable-looking necklace, yeah? But I can't stop staring at the crazy fucking background. Who came up with that anyway?'

He swayed his head a little to the side.

'Miles?' Rebeka laughed. 'Look, it's too much, babe!' She turned to the staff on set. 'OK, everyone, listen up. Let's make the gorgeous Tia classy. Not trashy! We're supposed to be promoting a luxury jewellery collection, but I can't keep my eyes off the backdrop and the giant fucking wrecking ball.'

The staff looked on tensely, waiting for instructions.

'So, let's change it up then. Come on, chop-chop!'

'Change it to what exactly, love?' one of the set hands puffed, looking worried as he adjusted the collar of his shirt.

Rebeka lifted her head from her camera and smiled. 'All-black background, please. And we better make it quick. I have plans this evening.'

Hastily, a group of set runners swarmed the studio, removing the props and unscrewing the giant glitterball.

'OK, can we have makeup over here?' Rebeka called out, approaching Tia once more. 'I'm thinking of crystal tears that will make the necklace pop. Make her look sweaty, wet, *really* hot. And gel the hair. I want a nice contrast to the diamonds.' She smiled at Tia, who grinned back.

'Yes!' she agreed.

'And boys!' She turned to the two male models standing off to the side. 'Do you have your ears pierced?'

One nodded, and the other looked terrified at the proposal. Beks pointed to her intern, still hovering behind and clutching her iced latte. 'Find two pairs of stunning Ricardo Voe earrings. I want long, dangly, expensive-looking ones, preferably from his new collection – one clip-on and one normal – to give to the boys.'

'OK, sure.' She handed over the latte then hurried off to the wardrobe.

Thirty minutes passed and, with an uncomplicated, plain black background and new styling in place, Rebeka recommenced the photoshoot.

'OK, is everyone ready? What you got for me, Tia? Let's do this, yeah?' Beks called out and began snapping away.

Tia started giggling at Rebeka's energy, and in seconds she was once more chopping and changing angles like she was born to do it.

'Oh, yes, babe! Stunning!' Beks encouraged her with each click of her camera.

Tia stood centre stage, the two male models on either side drowning her with desire.

'Tia, you are so fucking sexy!' Beka yelled as Tia shifted seductively for the camera, tugging her hair, touching her face, and biting her lip while the men draped off her neck and body, caressing her legs. 'Fuck yes!' Rebeka roared, and the team looked on, impressed. 'Keep this up, Tia, and you'll be on every billboard in the capital, girl! Stunning!!'

She looked editorial – sleek and simple, but eye-catchingly beautiful. The jewellery cast glimmers onto the set, making Tia almost glow. Rebeka could feel butterflies swirl around her head knowing this was about to propel her career.

'Lick the sweat on her stomach,' Beks called out to one of the men, who happily obliged. 'Yes, yes, yes!' she screeched.

Forty minutes later, and with a camera full of content, Beks called a halt to the shoot.

'And we've got it, people. Thank you, everyone!' she hollered, then took a second to breathe, letting how well she had done sink in.

'You are one crazy bitch! That was insane!' Andre clapped, looking astonished. 'I think you may have pulled that off, don't you?'

Rebeka winked and smiled. 'I totally have, haven't I?'

Andre stepped onto the set. 'OK, everyone, amazing work today. Please give me your social media accounts, and I'll make sure we tag all of your gorgeous work today!'

The models giggled with one another, high-fiving their efforts.

Rebeka lifted her phone and scrolled through her notifications, immediately noting that she had one new message from Mitchell.

Mitchell: *How's the shoot going? The second floor is empty for renovations, room 204, if you're free. M x*

Beka giggled and bit her bottom lip.

Beka: *See you in 5 babe x*

'Andre, I have to run, but I'll come back in about half an hour. If I'm any longer, will you email Miles my prints? I can edit them on Monday.' She handed him her camera.

'Darling, yes. But I will be here until the models have exited the building! So, as long as Miles doesn't mind waiting!' He pursed his lips at the two half-naked models casually sipping on some water.

'Get their details! They're *way* too hot to be straight.' Beka winked and set off to meet Mitchell.

She exited the lift at floor two and stepped into darkness. It seemed deserted, as sheets of plastic covered empty desks, but she peered around anyway, just to make sure no one was lurking. She felt a little nervous, but also massively turned-on, about hooking up in the middle of the afternoon and on the clock. She and Mitchell had only shagged in the building once, shortly after they first got together. They met at an office party and got talking when they were both waiting on a taxi outside, while Beka munched a kebab at the end of the night. Before they knew it, one drunken night of passion with Mitchell munching on her kebab escalated into a secret love affair only they could savour. Sneaking around at work was too dangerous for him, as he wanted to prove he was worthy of his grandfather's company and, deep down, Rebeka wanted to be taken seriously for her talent rather than for sleeping with the boss. So, they resorted to sleeping over at one another's homes, out of sight.

She turned on the torch on her iPhone and wandered through the corridors of empty offices, hoping not to trip on any of the loose wires or machinery lying around, and carefully checking the door numbers. 204. She paused, then gently knocked on the door and opened it.

Mitchell had his back to her, turning as she entered.

'How's my favourite photographer?' He smirked, and she laughed at the compliment.

She drew close to him and skimmed her hands over his broad shoulders, then let them rest on his chest. He was wearing a white shirt so pristine, she almost didn't want to crease it.

'This seems a little dangerous for you, Mr Travers,' she said.

He came closer to her face, and she could feel his cool breath on her skin.

'I haven't stopped thinking of you in those knee-high boots,' he murmured. He attempted to kiss her, but she pulled back playfully, keeping her gaze on his piercingly blue eyes.

'So you're willing to risk it all for a pair of boots?'

'I'm willing to risk it all for you, baby.'

Suddenly, Mitchell grabbed Rebeka's waist, lifting her from the ground; they began kissing passionately in the quiet room. He turned around, posing her on the desk, and ran his hand up her thigh, under her dress. Rebeka's back arched as he circled his thumb over her underwear, pressing down on her clit.

She pushed back against him and stood up, giving him a seductive look as she turned around and bent over the desk.

'Do you want to take me like this, Mr Travers?' she asked.

He raised an eyebrow and grazed his hand over his chin, admiring the view of her arse. 'You are perfect, Miss Hampson.'

Rebeka's face lit up as he slowly unbuckled his belt, unzipped his trousers and pulled his underwear to his ankles. She couldn't keep her eyes off his rock-hard dick. He glanced down when he noticed his penis was stealing all of her attention and smirked.

'I love that arse, baby.'

Just as he touched her, Beka's phone beeped, and he paused, looking at her questioningly.

'Ignore it,' she mumbled.

She watched him run his hand gradually up her leg and felt goosebumps travel down her neck to her nipples. She turned away from him and looked out the large window. The London skyline was as flawless as ever, especially in the daylight. The city buildings towered around them. She felt a tug on her lacy underwear and the sudden feeling of being complete. Beks let out a quiet moan as Mitchell began slow, watching his dick move in and out of her while she pushed back.

'How is that for you?' he whispered.

'Keep going, keep going,' Beks grunted. She felt electric, fucking so openly in plain sight. It felt risky, but hot. She wondered if the office workers would spot her from the building in the distance.

He tugged her hair, gently but firmly, from behind. 'And do you like this, baby?' he asked.

Beks felt the warmth travel through her body as she orgasmed loudly.

Mitchell continued to fuck her harder and harder until he finally called out, 'Yes! Yes! I'm going to—'

'No, no, not inside me, babe.' Beks halted, pushing back and turning around to face him. His face was shiny with sweat and desire.

'What? Where?' he panted, panicking, looking confused and desperate to empty his load.

The reality was, she was wearing a dress with no tights, and walking around with a spunky fanny in the office wasn't the best idea. As seductively as possible, she lowered herself to her knees, knowing she was wholeheartedly taking one for the team.

'I . . . err . . . I want to taste you,' she lied, not wanting to admit an accidental spunk splat falling out of her vagina in the middle of the lift wasn't a fun idea.

Mitchell's eyes lit up as if he'd just won the fucking EuroMillions and he began wanking over her face. Rebeka waited patiently, mouth wide open, for his ejaculation. A few moments later, she felt the warm salty fluid hit the back of her throat, and she swallowed hard repeatedly as his dick squirted down her gullet like an angry squid. *Keep swallowing, imagine it's tequila, pretend it's tequila.*

Mitchell panted loudly and tried to push his hands through her hair, but she dodged out of the way.

'Wait, no, no touching the weave, babe. I'm going out later,' she warned.

He laughed, holding his hands to his chest in apology. 'That was amazing.' He bent over and gently kissed her forehead. 'When you didn't call me back last night, I thought . . .'

Rebeka shrugged. 'You thought?'

'I'm not sure what I thought, to be honest, but since the meeting, you have been quieter than usual.' He pulled up his trousers, watching Rebeka walk over to the window.

'I wasn't upset you were there,' she said, gazing out at the city. 'I was pissed you didn't stand up for me. But I got my shoot at the end of it . . . so . . .' She turned back to see him lost in thought.

'What could I have said, Beks? I was only there observing.' He seemed disappointed that she had even brought this up.

Another message alert came from her bag, and she was momentarily distracted.

'Well, it's fine now. It all worked out in the end.' She rolled her eyes a little sassily.

'What's your plans this evening?' he asked, propping himself against the desk.

'The high school reunion. I told you about it, remember?' She stepped back across the room towards him, and he held on to her waist.

'Ah, yes. Any old boyfriends I need to be worried about?' His jaw clenched a little as she leant forward to kiss him.

'You could always come along with me and make sure?'

Mitchell puffed out a sigh. 'You know that can't happen. Not yet, darling, but soon,' he said, standing up from the desk and wandering to the other end of the room.

'Soon? Yeah, right. How soon? You've said this for the past six months!' She tutted.

'Rebeka, it's getting close, I promise!'

'Yeah, well, so is fucking Christmas, babe!' she replied sharply.

Beks was about to say something else when her phone beeped again.

'I think you better get that,' Mitchell replied, sounding irritated by the distraction.

She shook her head, picking up her handbag to retrieve her mobile.

'It's only Andre.' She scrolled down the messages and her mood lifted in a second. Beks jumped a little in the air. 'Miles loved the shoot; he was looking for me.'

A grin of relief swept over her face as she continued to read, and then it died away.

'What?' Mitchell asked. 'Is everything all right?'

'The model . . .' Her eyes were glued to her phone as she continued to read. 'The model I was photographing today . . . Andre got a hold of her social media accounts to tag her for content, and she's fourteen!' Rebeka felt her stomach twist in disgust. 'Fourteen years old! Look, Andre screenshotted it!' She turned her phone around, showing Tia in dozens of school pictures and laughing with her friends.

Mitchell shrugged a little. 'She must be with the agency we use.'

'She's fourteen, Mitchell! So fuck if she's with the agency, I shot a child practically naked with two grown men hanging off her today.' Her heart was pounding with regret.

'Rebeka, hey, hey, calm down. I know it doesn't sit right, but young girls are just part of the industry. You know that!'

She stared at him. If this was his attempt at consoling her, he was doing a piss-poor job.

'I don't care,' she spat, only growing more infuriated. 'I don't want my work to be part of that seedy circle. Someone should have informed me! I told her to look more desirable, I told the MEN to lick her body, and she was a fucking child! Why wasn't her mum there? Or a representative?'

'Beks, seriously, calm down!' Mitchell's voice echoed through the quiet room.

She jerked her head, full of rage. 'Who the fuck are you shouting at, babe? *Me?* You're not my boss right now, Mitchell. You're my boyfriend!'

He sighed and ran his hand frustratedly through his hair. 'Well, I'm not, am I? I'm both. And as much as I see your point of view, I also see . . .'

She shook her head, laughed slightly, and interrupted him. 'You know what? You'll never get it. You won't.'

'I get it, Rebeka. It's disgusting and if she was my daughter she wouldn't be getting photographed at that age! But this is a business, and agencies provide us with models who fit the brief. Her parents have consented to this today!'

'So fuck if *they've* consented. She's a child, who has been forced to grow up and be admired globally now. She could be preyed on by disgusting old men because of this.' Her voice was getting more high-pitched as possible scenarios entered her head. Then a brief silence took over the space as she regained composure. 'You will never understand what it's like to be a woman, and hey, that's OK, but that child just participated in a photoshoot half-naked for the world to see. Do you think she's old enough to make that decision?' She paused briefly to see if he would react, but he remained still. 'She's absolutely not. But you, Mr Travers, you will make a fucking fortune profiting from the pictures, so you're quite happy to turn a blind eye because of the industry we're in!'

He stepped forward, ready to retaliate, then stopped. He picked up his phone from the desk and walked towards the door.

'That's right, leave. You got what you wanted anyway, babe.'

'That's out of order, Beks. All of this,' he said quietly, reaching for the door handle.

'You're right, it is. What the fuck am I doing?' she moaned, folding down and grasping her knees.

'Look, I'm sorry you didn't know about the age of the model. I can bring it up at the head office briefing.' Beks grunted at his shitty attempt to fix the situation. 'I need to go. Are you OK to hang here for five before leaving?'

'Seriously? Yeah, fuck off Mitchell, don't worry, I'll hide out in this empty floor while you return to your penthouse office!'

'I can't argue when you're like this,' he said, and left the room.

Beks stood in shock. All the happiness from finally accomplishing her assignment had been sucked out from her in a moment. She felt a tear fall and quickly swiped it away.

She unlocked her phone and replied to Andre.

14??? WTF! I hate this industry. I got caught up and need to head home early. Can you cover for me? Thanks for forwarding to Miles. I'll catch you Monday xx

Beks waited a few more minutes then stepped to the door, took a deep breath, and headed to the lobby, keen to forget her argument with Mitchell. As she stepped out into the fresh air, she spotted the two male models sharing a cigarette.

'Hey, you were awesome today!' one of them said, immediately walking up and attempting to kiss her cheek.

Beks lost her cool for a second, hoping her cummy breath wasn't too noticeable. 'Oh hey, thank you! Yeah, thanks. So were you guys! Hope you had fun!'

'We had a blast! Hopefully we'll work with you again sometime,' the chiselled Australian model replied.

Rebeka nodded politely and stepped past them, then stopped. She turned slowly and smiled at the pair.

'Hey, what are you two doing the rest of the day? I have a different type of job that may interest you.'

They exchanged a puzzled look.

'At a good rate?' the cockier one of the pair asked.

'Same rate. I'll bill your hours extra, on top of the shoot?'

The boys chuckled curiously and stepped towards Beks. 'We're interested. What do you need us to do?'

Chapter Seven

Ava

That night, as I brushed my furry gnashers after my fourth glass of rosé, I started to enjoy the idea of attending the school reunion and trekking back down memory lane. Despite her reaching out, it had been a few weeks since I had spoken to my sister, and I knew she'd pester me about my lack of communication and, well, avoiding her. Grace was the social twin and, once I apologised to her, she'd probably spend the night on the microphone speaking on behalf of our class. She was never shy of public speaking or a healthy debate, if it was something she believed in. I suppose that's what made her a great lawyer.

Grace and I moved to London with my parents when we were thirteen. We cried for weeks when we heard about the uprooting, but my dad had been offered a senior position at an up-and-coming tech company he couldn't turn down. I loved Glasgow – *love*, I should say – and even now, having spent most of my life in the big smoke, I'd still never consider London home. I remember how difficult it was leaving my old friends behind and, worse than that, leaving my first boyfriend, Teejay Scott. I spent the first few months of our new life in London secretly hoping he'd come swaggering down and claim me just like in one of Taylor Swift's songs. Truthfully, that unrealistic fantasy still popped into my mind from time to time – until recently when I Facebooked him and saw he had four kids to three maws and still enjoyed spending his weekends binge drinking Buckfast up the bing with the young team.

But overall, moving here was hard, especially as a teenager in high school. The torments over our accent, the jokes about Scotland being inferior to England, the gags about the colour of my sister's auburn hair, the snotty little wankers in our class that thought they were better than us. Every night, we cried to our parents that we had made the wrong decision, but that all changed when we met Beka. Almost immediately, Beka latched on to Grace and me, and we quickly became a quirky trio, completely inseparable. Her Essex humour and sass were similar to our Glaswegian banter, and she felt like a little bit of home. We'd spend nights laughing, joking, and studying together. She had just moved to the city after her parents split up, and we bonded over a shared sense of being outsiders but she always felt like home to me.

Around eight, Beka phoned to tell me she was outside. I grabbed my bag, wiped down the grey dust that had accumulated over it since the last time it was used, and skimmed over my reflection once more. My red bodycon dress sat above my knees, masking the effects pregnancy had had on my body. My once perky tits hung to the floor like spaniel lugs, so I propped them up and scrunched them together like two wrinkly old pitta breads. I added two chicken fillets down my bra for some much-needed cleavage, but it didn't seem to do much. Truthfully, I had never been skinnier – heartache had helped me lose a few pounds – but I was still unhappy with my pale skin, stretch-marked stomach, my shitty attempt at makeup and the lousy eight-year-old outfit choice. Most of my nice clothes were still at Johnny's, and with him being away, I didn't have time to grab anything decent enough for the reunion. I grunted, knowing I didn't look my best.

'This is as good as it gets, Ava,' I whispered, then headed quietly down the stairs, hoping Adam wouldn't hear my footsteps and bombard me with another fucking fruit basket.

Stepping outside, I weaved my way through the evening shoppers, looking for Beks on the main road. Suddenly I heard the loud beep of a horn and turned to see a sporty grey Porsche across the street, with Beks waving enthusiastically from behind the wheel. I burst out laughing and headed straight over. Rebeka stepped out and greeted me in a gold maxi dress. Her makeup was pristine; she looked like she was attending an awards ceremony, not a gym hall in Brent.

'Wow, Beks! You look incredible – and this car!'

She shrugged it off. 'We need to arrive in style, right?'

I laughed, nodding, then noticed another face in the back of the car.

'And I made a pitstop before you! So get in and talk to your sister, will you?'

I beamed and waved at Grace, who was squashed in the back alongside a large suitcase. Her long red hair, though, was swept effortlessly to one side. I bent down, sat in the passenger seat and turned to her.

'Hi!' I smiled.

'*Hi*?' my sister replied, unusually quiet.

'What's with the case, Beks?'

She hummed suspiciously. 'Just wait till you find out!'

I turned back to my sister, hoping to share a funny exchange at Beka's dramatics but she remained perfectly still.

'What's up with your face?' I asked.

'Seriously? What's up with *me*? Do you not know how to return a call?' she moaned. 'I've tried calling you about four hundred times in the past week alone. I hear nothing, then I find out you're planning a night out with us all without saying a word to me? I'm your sister, Ava. I was worried sick about you, *again!*'

I could feel my face twist; riddled with guilt.

'I know. I'm sorry, I've had a hard week . . .'

'We've all had a hard week, Ava. I thought you were dead. I even came to your flat, and your weird neighbour Adam said you had been drinking a lot again.'

I rolled my eyes. 'Georgie's away to visit Johnny's mum. Of course I've been drinking a lot.'

'OK, OK, enough of the bloody domestic, ladies,' Beka interrupted, adding another layer of gloss to her lips. She turned the ignition and the engine roared to

69

life. 'Grace, go into the case. I wanted to do a big reveal but I'd do anything to stop you two from giving me a migraine right now. I've borrowed some items from the fashion closet. Wear what you want! But don't spill anything on them – I have to return all of this by Monday.'

'All of this? As in the car as well?' I gulped nervously, wondering how much privilege Beka had at the magazine and if she should be borrowing any of this stuff.

'Yeah, well. The car is Mitchell's. He left a spare key at my apartment. I borrowed it once before. I'm sure he won't mind. Plus, we have to make an entrance! Show the fuckers at Knightsbury who's really made it!' She laughed evilly, then sped off through the streets of London like Cruella de Vil.

The city lights flashed past us as Grace opened the case and began to raid its contents. She flicked through a range of sparkly dresses and earrings and tried on a pair of black silk gloves.

'What about this one, Ava?' She handed me a see-through sparkly miniskirt and burst out laughing.

Manoeuvring myself in the passenger seat, I slipped it on, and we all giggled as Beks continued to drive us to our old high school.

'Pass Ava the red one,' Beks said. 'You suit red, and this is an upgrade on the one you had on.'

Grace scrambled through the case. I heard her gasp and the next second she was handing me a floor-length red dress with a significant split up the side.

'Wow! But is it too much?' I asked my sister, having never been so dressed up for anything except my wedding.

'You can never be too dressed up! Get it on!' Beks stared proudly at the garment, her eyes drifting from the road a bit too long.

'Beks, the fucking road!' I yelled, and screamed as she dashed through a red light. My heart thumped hard as her concentration returned to the wheel.

'Oh fuck off, Ava. I'm watching,' she giggled carelessly.

I unfastened my seatbelt and wriggled into the dress. I laughed, thinking of the times as teenagers when we'd sneak out the house in jeans and jumpers, and slip them off on the bus to house parties, revealing the shortest denim shorts and cropped tops that our parents would never let us out in.

Beka glanced over at me. 'Yes! Yes! Yes! That's the one,' she said proudly.

'Good job I've shaved. With this split, everyone in Knightsbury will see my kebab when I sit.'

'As if they haven't seen it before, babe.' Beks winked cheekily.

'What are you thinking of, Grace?' I asked.

She pulled out a pale pink cropped-trouser-and-top combo, and her eyes expanded with love.

'What's she got?' Beks turned around again, taking her eyes off the road; the car drifted a little to one side. '*Oh, yes!* That has your name all over it, Grace!'

'Steve will wonder where your black dress has gone!' I laughed, watching my sister trying to manoeuvre herself into the outfit.

71

'As if he'd notice,' Grace muttered under her breath.

'Is he coming tonight?' I asked.

'He's going with the boys . . . obviously *not* Johnny,' she smiled kindly, and I nodded.

I felt a pang of regret as she reassured me. I loved my sister more than anything, but I didn't think she understood why Johnny and I split. She was the most married person I knew – cooking, cleaning and living for her husband. She managed the housewife role so wonderfully compared to me. Grace took my side after we split, but Steve remained best friends with Johnny, which put a barrier between us. Part of me felt I couldn't confide in her after that. I was always wary of what I told her in case she told her husband and it went back to Johnny.

As we drove through the city's outskirts, I began to recognise the familiar streets and houses from my childhood. A feeling of comfort settled over me for the first time in years. I felt like I was seventeen again.

Rebeka's phone beeped and, as she fetched it, she smirked at the screen.

'Well, ladies . . . I've got us one last surprise for tonight.' She paused for dramatic effect. 'I know you were nervous about people thinking you were a sad, lonely spinster now, Ava . . .'

I felt my face fall at the description, knowing I hadn't actually used those words.

'So . . .?' I urged her to continue, but she had one hand on the wheel and the other on her phone, not paying attention. 'Beks?' I groaned.

Suddenly, there was a bright glare of headlights. Grace let out a huge scream, and I felt my body swerve towards Rebeka as she forced the car to the side of the road. There was an almighty thud, and then the Porsche stopped dead.

'Oh shit! Oh shit! Oh fucking shit!' Beks panicked.

'Is . . . is everyone OK?' Grace managed quietly, but her voice shook with nerves.

I nodded back, staring at the smoke streaming out from the front of the car.

I turned to Beks as she removed her forehead from the steering wheel, 'I think this seems worse than it is. It was only a tap, right?' Beka looked at me. Her bouncy hair had turned into a sweaty ball of frizz so she now bore a strong resemblance to Peggy Mitchell rather than the elegant look she'd been going for. Slowly, she opened the car door and made her way to the front of the bonnet. Her shoulders fell.

'Oh, it's fine. It's fine. It's only a flat tyre.'

Grace and I sighed with relief, exchanging glances.

'Right, Ava, change the tyre, and we can get a move on.'

'ME?' I opened the car door and stomped out to examine the damage. 'How the fuck would I know how to change a flat?'

'What do you mean? You live in Croydon! It's miles away from the City!' Beks gazed at me, and I stared back for a moment, not knowing if she was serious.

'Yeah, I live in Croydon, not the country! Fuckin' hell, I can't afford a Tinder subscription, never mind a car, Beks!'

'GRACE!' she called out, ignoring my explanation.

'I've not got a clue,' she said, clambering out of the car. 'We have insurance for that.'

'SHIT!' Beka paused, then started pacing. 'How far away are we?'

'Not far,' I spotted the old sweetie shop we used to visit, which had since been turned into an off-licence. 'I reckon a mile, maybe?' I estimated.

'Right, I'll Uber us a car.' Beks took out her phone and stared at the screen.

'You can't leave Mitchell's car here,' I said. She seemed more annoyed at missing the reunion.

'Relax, I'll call someone to fix it. He'll never know. He has like four of these.'

Grace looked towards me nervously and I shrugged.

'Shit! Shit! SHIT!' Beks stamped her high heel into the road. 'No Ubers in the area!' She threw her arms out in defeat. 'We're going to have to walk!'

Grace shrugged. 'I could ask Steve. See if he's left—'

'No way!' I interrupted.

'OK, let's walk then!' Beks huffed. 'Grab the bottle of champagne, Grace, it's in the boot.' Grace fidgeted with the car and eventually pressed the right button. The boot opened and she grabbed the bottle and headed back towards us, popping the cork along the way. We all giggled as it shot straight into the air and she wrapped her mouth around the rim. Beks pressed the car key, locking up the Porsche and leaving it on the side of the road.

Only a few steps into our hike, drizzly rain began to fall. My feet were already starting to ache, having not worn heels in years.

'Tell me it's not fucking raining?' Beka sighed. 'I'm wearing seven-hundred-pound shoes!'

I nodded. 'They are stunning!'

'Stunning!' Grace agreed.

We all laughed.

'Why the fuck is this happening? I wanted us to arrive in style!' Beks threw her hands up to God, hoping for a break, but just as she did, a car passed us and a puddle of water lunged through the air, drowning half our dresses.

We screamed and, as I turned, I saw Beka's once pristine makeup melt down her face like candle wax. She began wringing out the bottom of her dress in disgust.

'How long?' She stomped her feet as we passed the local bakery, now in darkness.

'It's only around the corner,' I said, panting for breath.

'You literally lived on this street, Rebeka. Look around.' Grace pointed to a row of houses beside the shop, and we paused momentarily.

Rebeka's phone beeped again, and she jumped, glancing at the screen. Her sombre face brightened, and she picked up the pace. 'C'mon, you two! Our dates have arrived, Ava!'

She clapped her hands excitedly and let out an evil laugh, grabbing the bottle of champagne from my sister.

75

'Dates? *What?* You mean you got Mitchell to come?' I walked quickly to keep up with her. She had a new lease of life now cock was on the horizon.

Beks screwed up her face in disgust. 'No, fuck Mitchell, babe. Just wait and see, OK?'

'You have a date!' my sister screeched. 'Who is he?'

My pits began to sweat. The thought of meeting a stranger on a blind date was horrendous. Let alone in front of a room full of people that I used to know. That Johnny used to know.

'Wait, Beka, slow down,' I pleaded, feeling my hair stick to my face with a combination of sweat and rain. 'I can't date! If Johnny found out, he'd be fizzing! And besides, what guy is going to fancy me?' I panicked. 'What if he decides mid-party that he doesn't fancy me and walks out, and everyone sees I've been ditched again? Beks? Who is he? BEKA!'

'Fucking hell, chill out, babe. He's stunning, both of them are, and when word gets back to Johnny that you've arrived with this cunt, he'll be furious! The best way to make him notice you again is jealousy, trust me! Let's just have a good night and catch up with all the arseholes we used to hate and date! OK?'

We turned the corner and saw Knightsbury Secondary School lit up in the distance. I gulped nervously.

'Well, it looks like I don't have a choice now.'

Chapter Eight

Ava

As we approached the entrance to Knightsbury, it felt like I was being transported back in time. Everything was the same. The same old-fashioned brick building, the same old people. The same smell, the same nerves.

'Rebeka! Grace!' a voice called out as we passed through the gate. 'And Ava? Oh, I'm surprised to see you here, dear!' Darcia Loveton wrapped her arms around all of us. She was one of the most popular girls of the year, who ended up marrying an old ex-footballer from the seventies, meaning she never had to work a day in her life but did, however, have to put up with his saggy bawsack scraping on the floor as he walked – well, limped.

'I was surprised Beks persuaded me,' I replied, unsettled by her comment.

'Do you know, I was *more* surprised I got her away from that hot hunk of spunk she's been dating!' Beks said. 'I mean, I wouldn't leave him either, but hey, he'll probably show up tonight. He can't seem to leave her alone, Darcia! How's your old man?'

Darcia eyes expanded with the snippet of gossip, 'Very well. He's just had a minor operation, so he's staying home tonight.'

Beks nodded sympathetically, 'Hips get fragile at his age! Send him our love!' She turned, tugging my arm, unbalancing me, and we began walking again.

I squeezed down on her arm. 'Why did you say that?' I hissed, approaching the ballooned covered front doors.

'What did you want me to say? 'Hope his prostate's holding up?' I went for the hip to be kinder, now c'mon!'

'No! I mean about my date! He doesn't even know me.' I cringed, feeling flustered, drowned and an absolute mess.

'Ava, you're beautiful!' Grace insisted, nodding her head rapidly.

Beka chuckled. 'Look, tonight you can be anyone you want, Ava!' She pressed my nose and smiled widely. 'Let's have fun!'

I tugged on her wrist. 'Well, tonight I feel ridiculous. I'm drenched through to my spanx, I now have fucking mud splashed up my legs and I've just found out I'm supposed to be on a date that, when Johnny hears about it, will be sure to cause carnage!' I spat back, wondering why I'd even come here in the first place.

'Fuck Johnny! Why do you care what he thinks?'

My heart sank.

I knew I shouldn't care, but every part of me still did. I didn't want to give Johnny the ammunition to close the door on me completely. I didn't want him to fire insults at me for dating. Or being a bad mother for going out. I was much more comfortable hiding behind the crowd and, when he was ready, when he finally realised what he'd lost, hopefully he'd come back to us.

'Sorry guys, I have to head to the car park and find my husband. He can't sort his tie. See you in there?' Grace asked, seeming flustered as she stared at her phone.

Beka smiled. 'Yip! Our boys are inside. See you in there, Grace!'

Jesus Christ! What has she done? I can't do this.

I glanced at my sister nervously, and and body roll she tried to give me an enthusiastic thumbs up before walking back towards the entrance. I followed behind Beks, who was admiring the navy and yellow balloon arch, happily smiling to the familiar faces in the foyer. I skimmed my hands over my damp dress, now a deeper red as the rain clung to it. I'd felt so confident in it only half an hour ago, and now I noticed every crease it showed.

'Get a move on,' Beka called out, making me speed up behind her.

'Beks, I honestly think this is a—'

'Ava, I'd like you to meet Damien and Olly.'

I glanced up, feeling clammy from sweaty nerves and my mile-long jog, and spotted two of the most handsome men I had ever seen. My jaw dropped open and my eyes popped. They were dressed in tuxedos, and the taller one of the two had piercing blue eyes.

'Nice to meet you, Ava. I'm Damien.' The brown-eyed man put his hand out to greet me, and I smiled, still in a daze, observing their perfect bone structure.

'I'm Olly.' The taller one came over to hug me.

'I'm Australian,' I exclaimed. Beka's face screwed up. 'No, fuck. Sorry. I mean – *you're* Australian!' I corrected myself and jerked my head, trying to release any other word vomit that was in there.

'And you are . . . speak again!' He giggled, holding his hand to his chin in concentration.

'Erm . . . I don't know what to say!' I chuckled loudly and far too much, flustered by his presence.

'She's Irish,' Damien concluded.

Olly squinted his eyes playfully. 'She's Scottish!'

'She is!' Beks confirmed. 'And she's your girlfriend for the night, Oliver.'

My stomach felt as if it had just been volleyed by Black Beauty. I blushed furiously at my friend's lack of subtlety.

'Well, aren't I a lucky man?' he replied. I felt his bright eyes scan over my body. Then he looped his arm, inviting me to join him. As I placed mine through his, I glanced around, hoping none of Johnny's friends were lurking around witnessing my PDA, but strangely, I felt butterflies flutter around my stomach for the first time in years.

As we entered the hall, I smelt the old familiar scent of the musty gym from years previous. The lights were dim and a DJ played on a makeshift stage in the centre of the bustling party. I spotted a large sign saying '*Welcome back!*' Rebeka had her arm around Damien's back, and as she spoke with him, she ran her long acrylics up and down the nape of his neck. I was always envious of her confidence around men; she never seemed clumsy or gave a fuck what anyone thought of her, and she was so thrilling to watch. Meanwhile I stood as stiff as a fucking ironing board, conscious of not allowing myself to put too much weight onto my arm hold with Olly. As we pushed further in, Beks pointed out some familiar faces in the crowd. I watched her become animated as she revisited memories with each partygoer.

'Oh my God, there's Courtney Todd. Remember, she was on MSN and accidentally sent her tits to all her contacts!' Beks bellowed. I shook my head and encouraged her to keep her voice down. 'And there . . . there's Peter Picknose.' She pointed. 'I forgot about him!'

Olly chuckled at the commentary and whispered, 'What did he do?'

I smiled back. 'Well, his real name is Peter Princeton, so you can guess what he did ninety per cent of the time in class.'

'Oh, and Daisy Deepthroat!' Beka turned to us, making a blowjob choking gesture.

'Ah, OK. I know what dirty Daisy did!' Olly smiled towards me, and I gazed back. *What a beautiful fucking man.* 'Did you have any nicknames I need to know about, Ava?' he asked. I wasn't sure if it was my damp dress or his Aussie accent but something made my nipples go hard instantly.

I rolled my eyes to the ceiling, trying hard to recall any attractive name anyone had ever called me over the years. The only ones I could think of consisted of me being Scottish or a fucking bookworm.

'I bet you were too cool for a nickname,' Olly said. 'I bet you were the most popular girl in school.'

I pushed on his arm, snorting at the compliments, knowing fine well no one even knew I existed until my final year.

'Maybe a name like *Sexy Ava*?' he continued as I blushed.

'Well, actually, I have heard that a few times, to be fair,' I lied. *I have never been referred to as sexy before in my entire life.* Not even by my husband, who would occasionally say I looked *cute*.

'I knew it,' Olly said with a smirk.

There was a tap on my shoulder and then a strong, deep voice called out, 'Well, well, well, if it isn't *Arselicker Ava!*'

I turned around to see my old classmate Richard Tierney behind us. My heart fell to my own arsehole as he recited my old, dreaded nickname for being the teacher's pet.

'Richard. Lovely to see you,' I muttered through gritted teeth.

Richard Tierney had always been an absolute arrogant prick. He was practically a giant at six foot six, with black slicked-back hair and fair skin. His father was the headteacher at Knightsbury when we attended, and he would always get preferential treatment. From being appointed head boy, to prom king, to getting the best recommendations for university, the smarmy cunt had it all. He was pretty clever, but so was I, and we'd spent most of our school days debating and competing against one another, trying to see who had the best interpretation of a piece of literature. I graduated with a better mark in English, and *'Arselicker Ava'* was formed to tease me. Richard was convinced that I must have sucked up to the teacher, as there was no way a Scottish person could ever be better at the English language than him. But honestly, I was. It was my talent. My thing, and I absolutely adored writing.

Despite all this, at one point, we were all pretty close. We ended up attending university together and had practically lived like family. Fuck, Richard was supposed to be Johnny's best man at our wedding – until he didn't show up. Yep, *he* jilted *us* at the altar. Luckily, Steve stepped in, which resulted in me getting married with a shitty borrowed ring from my great-uncle Brian. Richard returned the rings the following week without so much as an apology for his behaviour. Johnny said the last he remembers was Richard partying with hookers the night before the ceremony and them having a petty argument over calling it a night. After Richard's disappearing act, Johnny was still willing to hear him out, but Richard never apologised or tried to explain, and the pair never spoke again.

But losing his friendship with practically everyone didn't seem to have had an impact on him, since Richard now ran one of the biggest publishing companies in the UK.

'It's really lovely to see you, Ava.' He stared intently at me for a second. 'Aren't you going to make an introduction?' He gestured towards Olly, who held his hand out for him to shake.

'Olly, Ava's date. Nice to meet you, mate,' Olly said warmly.

This guy was good!

'Richard Tierney, I was once great friends with your date.'

I rolled my eyes. *Until you nearly ruined my wedding, ya prick!*

'Ah, Dick! Lovely to see you!' Rebeka said, popping her head out from the crowd.

'There she is!' Richard hugged her tightly. 'And you've brought a date too?'

'Yes, this is Olly!'

'Damien,' I hissed behind her.

'Oh, yeah, *this* is Olly.' She pointed towards my date. 'And this is Damien.'

'Great to meet you.' Damien looked Richard up and down, then deepened his voice to say, 'Ah, you're wearing the Dolce & Gabbana suit. Great choice, Dick.'

I turned to Beks to share a puzzled look, but she seemed oblivious to Damien's fashion observations.

'So, how long have you guys all been together?' Richard asked.

'Erm . . .' I puffed out as if recalling a lifetime, when I had only met this man ten minutes before this exchange. 'Fuck, err . . . Three, four months?' I shrugged at Olly, who happily agreed back. His hand touched my lower back and I felt myself tense up.

'Nice to see you've moved on, Ava.' Richard smiled and I noticed his dimples appear beneath his stubble. 'You crossed my mind this week, and I wondered if you'd be here—'

'There you guys are!' Grace stood behind us, now incredibly neat and pristine again.

'Here we are!' I smiled, bopping my head happily towards my date.

'Ahh . . . I'm Ava's twin sister. Lovely to meet you . . .'

'Olly.' My date leant in and kissed her cheek. Grace giggled shyly.

'And Richard, how are you? I saw your date as you headed in! Wow!'

'Ah, *yes*. It is early days, but she is a gem. But I'm very well, Grace, how are you?'

As Grace and Richard caught up, Beks and I stood to the side, huddling together.

'So, what do you think of the boys, eh?' Beks asked.

My eyes lit up. 'Like . . . stunning! Ten out of ten! Where the fuck did you find them, Beka?'

'Honestly, I met them today at my shoot. But they seem like good guys, right? We'll have a right laugh with them regardless. I mean, look at the attention they're drawing.'

She was right. Everywhere in the room, people were sliding sly stares towards our group, nudging elbows and whispering for jobs. I was invisible to most of the people here until I started dating Johnny, and by then, half the year had left for jobs. But tonight, I felt seen

85

already. I paused, thinking of Johnny and wondering how he'd react if he heard I'd been out with the old gang. I dreaded to think what he'd say if he knew I'd brought a date. I felt a cold sweat trickle down my spine and gulped nervously.

Just enjoy your night, Ava. He won't know a thing.

Chapter Nine

Ava

As the evening passed, I caught up with old classmates and wandered down memory lane with Beks and Grace. Steve, my brother-in-law, spent most of the evening with the other men, standing halfway across the room, allowing me space to discreetly flirt and wholly admire my date without feeling my ex would receive a running commentary from his pal.

'Are you enjoying yourself?' Olly asked, handing me another glass of champagne.

'I am. The company isn't so bad.' I smirked, taking a sip as his eyes lingered on me. 'I wonder where Damien and Beks have got to,' I said, suddenly noticing their absence.

Olly gestured to the dance floor, and I turned to see Damien throwing some wild moves to Beyonce's 'Single Ladies'. I almost spat my drink out with laughter.

'AVA!' Beks stormed over towards me. 'Have you seen my date? Like, babe, have you actually seen him dancing?'

'I think the whole room has seen him, Beks. He has some moves!' I smiled cheekily as Olly agreed behind me.

'Moves? He's mastered the entire fucking choreography!' she hissed. 'He's mortifying me!'

She waltzed onto the dance floor, tugging at his arm mid-slutdrop.

'Stop it! Stop!' she demanded, pulling him to the side to have a word in his ear.

I giggled loudly as my sister approached, popping her arm around my waist.

'I'm so glad you're here,' she said quietly.

I rested my head on her shoulder gratefully.

'Ladies and gentlemen! Good evening!' a voice bellowed from the stage, and I turned to see an older man holding a microphone. 'I am Mr Davis, the current headteacher of this fine school, and it is my honour to welcome you all back here tonight.' The crowd gave a brief applause, then he continued. 'Tonight, we are lucky enough to have someone very special to speak to you about your time here at Knightsbury. Please raise the roof for Sir Richard Tierney!'

Suddenly the room filled with hoorays and whistles as Richard strolled onto the stage like he'd just won a fucking Oscar.

'Why are they calling him Sir?' I asked Grace. 'He's not been knighted, has he?'

'I dunno, maybe he has? It wouldn't surprise me.'

'What? Why would he be *knighted*?' I turned to her. 'Other than the fact he is the biggest cunt in the whole of London?'

Grace held her hand to her face as she started to laugh.

'Well, well, well, it's a privilege to be standing here representing the class of the naughty noughties!' Richard said into the microphone, so his smarmy voice was literally unavoidable. He winked as a few chuckles dotted the room.

'Ew, if you're past the age of ten and still using the word 'naughty', you are a paedophile in my book!' I whispered to Grace, who quickly nudged me to be quiet.

'Knightsbury, eh. What a bloody good time we had here. I learnt from a young age how important education is, and thankfully, because of the foundational knowledge I obtained here, I graduated from one of the best universities in the world.'

'Lies,' I coughed, and a giggle rippled through my friends. Everyone knew he had been knocked back from Oxford.

'I then spent the next few years working my way up in the publishing world and I have been lucky enough to edit and influence some of the finest works of fiction from some of the most established authors we all read today . . .'

'Is it just me, or is Richard Tierney getting hotter? Boasting aside, he is unbelievably fuckable,' Beks said. She had wedged herself between Grace and me, and the three of us tilted our heads simultaneously.

'He is very handsome,' Grace agreed.

'But he's an absolute wanker! Can we not forget what he did? I almost had my wedding cancelled because of him,' I shrieked.

'Did any of you ever have a thing with him?' Beks asked, still in a daze as he blethered on stage.

Grace shook her head wildly, sipping on her champagne.

'I was with Johnny,' I said, utterly appalled at the suggestion. 'Didn't you?'

Beks smirked. 'I gave him a blowjob one night after a study class, and let me tell you, that man is hung like a hippopotamus! Trust me, they don't call him Big Dick because of his height, that's for sure.'

We erupted into laughter and caught some unimpressed gazes from our fellow classmates. Damien stood beside us, nodding intently, wholly engrossed in Richard's speech, while Olly sipped his champagne, smirking towards me.

'So tonight, it's really wonderful to catch up with everyone. I have been utterly amazed by the conversation and the paths many of us have taken since leaving Knightsbury. And, in celebration of *us* all, I thought I ought to do something a little different. I'm suggesting we all get to know one another again.' He winked cheekily as the hall began whispering to one another, curious as to what Big Dick was plotting. 'I will bring my lovely date up here with me and . . .' The hall filled with *ooohs* as he raised one eyebrow in suspense. 'Katya, would you join me, darling?' He turned to look at the side of the stage just as a tall, slender young woman walked on. She wore a nude-coloured dress with a splash of sparkle, her hair slicked back tightly into a ponytail. *Wow.*

'She is absolutely stunning!' Grace gasped.

I glanced around the room, noticing the whispers about the girl's beauty.

'Oh my God, that is Katya Ivanov. She's a famous Russian supermodel!' Beka almost leapt into the air. 'I was part of her winter cover story for the magazine!'

'Tonight, let's revisit our younger selves, our love stories and heartbreaks, our dreams, the trips and adventures we planned on undertaking as we transitioned to adulthood. Let's look back and revisit the worries of exams, or the real pressure of England battling through the World Cup.' The room laughed as I nudged Grace; we took some serious stick over the years for supporting the Scottish team. 'I have the yearbook from our sixth form,' Richard continued onstage. 'I'll read the boys' entries, and Katya will read the girls', and then we'll invite each of you onstage to tell us what you've accomplished with yourself since leaving Knightsbury! I'm curious to know if we had *any* idea how our lives would turn out at that young age.'

The room again filled with laughter at Richard's idea of a fun game, but my stomach was churning, the walls of the old musty gym hall seeming to close in.

Shit! What would I say? I had straight As my entire time at Knightsbury, and was one of the few students to receive a fucking scholarship for university and I wasted it. Totally fucked it. *What did they expect from me now?* A swanky author or journalist? A lecturer or teacher even? How the fuck will I admit that I'm an unemployed, single mother who drinks wine for breakfast?

I turned to my friends, who also looked apprehensive.

'Starting off, Andrew Anderson – where are you, Andy?' There was a bustle around the room as the first participant, now a lot stockier, made his way up to the stage. Richard continued, 'Ahh, Andrew Anderson, you began by saying, "*When I leave school, I will take a gap year to travel the world. I will return and study finance.*" And your motto,' Richard paused, smiling at Andy, "'*To infinity and beyond!*"' The two of them laughed loudly, then shook hands. 'Would you like to say something? Tell us what happened after that . . . err . . . wise statement.'

Andy took the microphone nervously. 'Well, I travelled the world for six months. Then I fell in love with a beautiful woman and moved back home. I studied accounting finance at Bloomsbury and now work as a senior accountant in the finance district!'

The room filled with applause, but not loud enough to drown out the sound of my heart pounding as I thought up escape routes to the bathroom.

'I don't know what I'm going to say!' I whispered to Beks and Grace.

'You have a master's degree in English literature, Ava! And the most beautiful wee girl in the world. Start with that. That's an amazing accomplishment!' Grace smiled warmly, gently squeezing my hand.

'Christina Buckley,' Katya said in her European accent. Tina made her way onto the stage, full of confidence.

'Didn't she have an affair with the creepy art teacher?' Beks mumbled.

Grace shook her head. 'That was her sister.'

"*When I leave school, I will study politics with a view of becoming prime minister. I believe this country needs changing, and I am the woman to do it!*" Katya smirked as she continued, 'Your quote – '*Don't let the muggles get you down!*"

Christina took the microphone eagerly. 'Hey everyone. Nice to see you all, everyone is looking very fancy tonight. I studied politics for a while but found my real passion in baking. I now own a bakery in Bradford and have been nominated for this year's local business awards. Please add me on Facebook and give me your vote at Tina's Cakes. Thank you!' She grinned proudly at the free publicity and then exited the stage.

Together, Richard and Katya made their way through the yearbook; I could feel the pressure looming over me as my mind ran wild with what I would say. *What would Richard add to get his tuppence in?* No doubt a smartarse comment that would make me look like an absolute dick in front of everyone. Oh, God, what will Olly think? He doesn't even know about Georgie! I listened intently, feeling my foot tap the wooden floor nervously, wondering if I could copy other people's statements, or somehow intertwine them to make my own. My arsehole was twinging with nerves.

'Grace Campbelle,' Katya called out my sister's name, and I felt nauseated. Great, I would be up next for sure.

Grace looked flustered but dutifully headed up to the stage.

Katya began, '"*When I leave school, I will study law. I want to make a difference in society and push myself to the limit! I can't wait to travel with my best friends and make memories.*"'

Grace shrugged sheepishly, glancing out at the crowd.

'Your quote was – '"*It's been a blast Knightsbury! But I got this on my own!*"'

The room filled with genuine smiles as my sister approached the microphone. I watched her hand tremble with nerves as she began.

'Hello, everyone. I did indeed study law and received a first-class honours degree. I now, however, spend most of my time at home with my lovely husband, Steve, who you all know.' Grace scanned her eyes through the crowd searching for her husband. She stopped when her gaze landed on me. I noticed her eyes shut momentarily at the anti-climax of her once promising career that she gave up because Steve insisted on a housewife, like all his colleagues had. *Shit. Tough crowd, tough crowd.*

I felt my toes curl as dissatisfaction filled the room. Scattered applause followed as Grace headed offstage with her head low. My heart began pumping, knowing I was next.

'Grace was undoubtedly one of the smartest in the year; I think we all remember that! And another brainiac was, of course, her twin sister. Get up here, Ava!' Richard called out.

Fan-fucking-tastic! I pumped the air with my fist awkwardly.

94

I walked up the stairs and watched the rows of bright eyes follow me. I crossed my arms around my waist, immediately self-conscious about my mummy tum being centre stage next to a stack-of-ribs supermodel, and tried to rack my brain back to sixth form. What did I say in that yearbook? *Please don't have mentioned Johnny, Ava, please!* I couldn't remember a thing.

Katya looked down at my entry in the yearbook with a serious expression and began to read. '"*When I leave school, I will continue to write. I love everything about the English language, and want to share my imagination with the world!*"'

I gulped as I recalled that daring, enthusiastic teenage girl I used to be. She felt like a stranger to me now. I hadn't written since university, I hadn't read since Georgie was born. I had slowly but surely changed forever.

'Your quote – 'You only live once!''

Richard laughed and gestured me to the microphone.

I looked out at the eyes staring at me, the sweat flying down my arse crack. Fuck, fuck. Speak Ava. I turned back to Richard and he encouraged me to speak.

'Well, yeah, I *eh* . . . I . . . went on to get an English literature degree at the University of Buckingham, like yourself, Richard. We had a great programme there, and I enjoyed it very much. Thank you.' I attempted to walk off until I felt a tug on my arm from Richard.

'Hold your horses, Little! Tell us what life is like for you now, Ava?' He pushed me back towards the mic, and I gazed out at the faces of my peers. Beka and Grace watched on nervously. '*Erm* . . . life now?

I suppose it's . . . pretty good.' I could feel my heart dance around my chest looking for the nearest exit route, I kept my eyes fixed on my puddle-splashed shoes. 'I live with my daughter and . . . And I . . . Well . . . Do you know something? I suppose I have realised that a fandabidozi degree like mine doesn't pay the bills! I suppose I had more of an idea of what to do with my life back then than I do now; yeah, maybe one day, I'll figure out what to do. Although, sometimes, right?' I huffed and took a breath, finally glancing up from my shoes, 'Sometimes I look at all the strange things the internet has provided us with in the past decade and I think . . . fuck all those years at uni, maybe it would be a lot easier if I hopped onto OnlyFans and got my trotters out instead! Or, I don't know, fart in a jar and sell it. People actually pay money for that these days! Can you believe it?' I felt my eyes go blurry with nerves. What the fuck was I talking about? *Word vomit! Stop, Ava, stop!* I stepped back, acknowledged the chuckles from anyone in the room with a slight sense of humour, and bolted offstage.

'Wow, nicely done,' Beks said sarcastically, as I returned.

I covered my face, trying to conceal my emotions.

Grace wrapped one arm around me. 'Yes. It was funny and honest. I thought you did great,' she whispered unconvincingly.

Richard and his model girlfriend continued calling out names while I continued sipping the cheap champagne being handed out by the current sixth-form students.

Eventually, 'Rebeka Hampson' was announced by Katya, and Beks turned to us, seemingly raring to go. I watched her take it all in her stride, just like she always did. Not an inch of nerves. I couldn't help but feel envious of Beka and how far she'd come. The magazine, her lifestyle and, most importantly, how she could fend for herself.

'Well, I'm up!' She smirked. 'Hold this!' She passed Damien her glass and strutted boldly onto the stage.

'*Rebeka Hampson* – '"*I will work in fashion when I leave school. I live every day like it's a catwalk!*"'

Beks held her hands up, embracing her yearbook entry proudly.

'And your quote – once again, '"*Bring on the hot girl summer!*"'

I smiled at Grace, who shared my grin. That summer, we'd planned to move to the city together and take on the world. I remembered the three of us choosing our tiny apartment and treating it like it was a palace. We planned to spend the entire summer before uni together, careless and fearless. But it didn't play out that way – within a week we realised we had to get part-time jobs to pay the bills. Beka landed herself a great internship at a designer, and practically worked around the clock, sketching and creating dress designs. I worked as a barista in Starbucks and in my spare time I prepped for uni, reading books, or spent it with Johnny. Grace also worked part-time as a secretary in a local lawyer's office. She would read textbooks and legislations until she fell asleep at night, hoping to impress her new boss. And on weekends, if she had a spare minute, she'd spend it with Steve.

'I am indeed working in fashion. I am now a senior photographer at *Inner Me!* and . . .'

'Oh, *Inner Me!*?' Katya interrupted.

Beks turned to her. 'Yes, yes, I know. I helped shoot you for the winter edit. Great cover!' She winked.

'Miles photographed me,' Katya replied sternly.

What the fuck was this girl's problem? I turned to Grace and shrugged my shoulders at their interaction.

'Yeah, babe, but I was with him.' Beks rolled her eyes sassily to the crowd, then continued. 'Working at *Inner Me!* is a pleasure, and I am grateful to the art department here at Knightsbury for always allowing me to get creative and push myself. Thank you.' She stepped back as the room filled with admiration for her. I clapped and cheered wildly as she pointed towards me happily.

'Oh, I'm sorry! I remember you now,' Katya added, holding the microphone to her face, ensuring the entire hall could hear her. 'You were the coffee girl.' She stared at Beka, emotionless, as everyone in the room fell silent.

I gasped and felt Grace grab my arm tightly.

'What?' said Grace, baffled. 'Why would she say that?'

'I have no idea.' I held my hand up to my face, waiting, hoping for a comeback.

Beks stood for a few more dwindling seconds, and I wondered if she was about to offer Katya a square go or burst out crying. Instead, she lifted her sparkling gold dress, strode offstage, straight past us, and left through the exit.

Grace and I trekked quickly behind her, pushing through the crowd and calling her name.

'Beks, wait, wait!' I bellowed.

She continued through the empty corridors of the school, making her way up the staircase.

'Rebeka, calm down!' Grace called out as we raced up the stairs behind her.

'Beks, please!'

'Where is she headed?' Grace asked, slightly out of breath, reaching the second level of stairs.

'She must be going to the rooftop? It's all that's up there'

'What? To *jump*?' Grace shrieked. A look of fear washed over my sister's face, and we belted up the stairs even quicker. By the time we reached the top, Beks had disappeared through the exit onto the roof.

Shit, shit, shit.

A few seconds after her, we pushed open the fire-exit door with a bang and burst onto the cold, wet roof. Beka sat at the edge of the old brick balcony, dangling her legs off the side.

'DON'T JUMP!' Grace cried in horror, pulling her phone from her bag to call for backup.

Rebeka turned. 'Jump? What the fuck are you talking about? I just had to get out of there.'

I stared at my sister in relief.

We paused, catching our breath.

'Remember when we used to come up here?' Beks asked, a fleeting smile washing over her face.

I strolled towards her and leant over the railing.

'We used to look out at the city and dream about making our mark,' Grace said, hopping up onto the balcony and swinging her legs around to join Beka.

Beks turned to me and patted the wall beside her.

I slipped off my high heels and joined them, looking out to the sparkling skyline of London.

'She was right, you know,' Beka said softly. 'I'm the glorified coffee girl at work.'

I turned to my sister, who looked as shocked as I felt.

'What? I thought you were a senior photographer, Beks?'

She huffed under her breath, 'On paper, *yes*. But, in reality I assist my boss, Miles. He lets me plan everything. I do literally everything there, but in the end, he takes the shot.'

'And the credit for all that work by the sounds of it.' Grace sounded enraged.

'Until today. I actually shot my first solo shoot today.'

I gasped and rubbed her arm. 'What? That's amazing, Beks!'

'I wanted to tell you guys, but you already thought I was this big deal photographer.'

'But you are now! How was the shoot?' I asked excitedly.

'It didn't feel amazing. Not like I'd hoped.'

There was a silence. Grace and I shared a puzzled look.

'What do you mean?' I nudged.

Beks sighed. 'I did this sexy photoshoot, high-end, for some jewellery collection, and the images were great, but then I found out the model was only fourteen.'

Grace gasped. 'That can't be right! Did she lie about her age?'

Beks smiled back, still staring into the distance. 'It's the industry, though, babe. And I . . . I don't know if I want to be a part of that. I want to make women feel sexy, not have them compare themselves to children. Not to mention what that kind of sexualisation will do to a young girl.' She leant her head on Grace's shoulder, and I held her hand tightly. 'Then Mitch and I had a huge argument about it all. He doesn't understand it. He doesn't understand me. Or us, or where we're going. I'm so fed up of putting a man's opinion before mine, especially when I know I'm right.'

'You are right,' Grace added.

'Well, if it's any consolation, at least you have a job. I looked like a right fud up there tonight.' I laughed a little at the commotion.

'Ditto!' Grace replied, smiling at me. 'I don't have a job either, Ava.'

'But you have a life, a purpose . . .'

'What, making scones and waiting for my husband to get home from work?' She shook her head, seeming disappointed with herself. 'I gave up my entire career because Steve insisted his colleagues' wives didn't *need* to work. He painted this luxury lifestyle I'd have, if I stopped. How dropping my caseload would give us more time together, to maybe start a family. But it hasn't; he works around the clock, barely makes it home for dinner, and when I mention it he acts superior because '*his job is so important*',' she screeched. 'I loved my job, my career, and now every single day is the same.'

I sat up, taking in my sister's words. I'd always assumed she was happy to live as a housewife. I know I was for a long time. The life she seemed to hate so much was the one I still dreamt of.

'What happened to us?' Rebeka asked. 'We were so clever, so determined, so fucking ready to make our mark on the world.'

'Men?' I huffed.

'Men,' Grace repeated.

'Fucking men!' Rebeka tutted. 'Every single chairperson or head of department at *Inner Me!* is a man! Can you believe that? For a women's magazine?'

I laughed a little at the irony. 'I can believe it, actually. That's the sad thing.'

'We have to work twice as hard in our industries, do the chores around the house, and still—'

'We get shafted!' I interrupted.

'Right up the fucking arse, babe!'

Grace gave me a sympathetic look. 'We can't keep living like this, girls!' she said sternly. 'I don't want being someone's wife to be my only legacy! I want to make a difference, do some charity work, or help people with legal problems.'

'I don't want to be an alcoholic mother.' I shrugged.

'And I don't want to be the fucking coffee girl!' Beks screamed into the distance.

We all giggled, cuddling into one another.

'We almost died tonight,' Beks said, her voice more subdued now. 'I could have killed us in that car, and what would we have left behind to show for ourselves?'

Silence fell between us again. It was hard to think about.

'You know, it isn't too late to plan a summer of glowing up,' Beks continued, sniffling slightly as the wind blew on our faces.

'What do you mean?' I asked, giggling a little at the proposition.

'We never did get that summer of fun, planning and changing the world!' Her voice became animated and she lifted her head, looking at us brightly. 'It's clear when we're together, we work better, right? I mean, we were fucking unstoppable back then, a force to be reckoned with. And why? Because we support one another. We get it. We know how hard it is as women to work, to be a parent, a wife. I mean look at the state of us now.'

Grace sat up, gently nodding at the suggestion. 'I'm up for a hot girl summer of change,' she laughed nervously, matching Beka's infectious energy.

'Are you in, Ava? We could start again, learn from our mistakes, fucking do it right this time. We can meet up and plan it out and stuff. Get where we finally want to be in our lives, together, as a team. We can keep each other on track. No men bringing us down or feeding us shitty fucking false promises.'

I turned to my best friend and my sister. I watched their eyes shine, alive with a passion we had wholly lost over years of letdowns and isolation.

I gulped, observing the skyline of possibilities before me.

'A hot girl summer?' I shrugged, then smiled as I turned back round to my friends, 'Fucking right, I'm in!'

Chapter Ten

Ava

As we headed back down the winding staircase towards the party, Grace and Beks seemed alive, energetic and passionate about starting over, yet there was something inside me full of doubt. I loved the possibility of getting a do-over at life, but how much could I change in one summer? What if I was too far gone?

'How are you finding your dates, girls?' Grace asked.

Beks hummed. 'Is it just me, or does Damien want to fuck Richard?' she asked as we sauntered down the last few steps.

'Oh, one million per cent he does!' I agreed, giggling.

'Yes, he does,' Grace admitted. 'Why did you choose a gay man as your date, Beks?'

Beka laughed, pushing both of us a little. 'I didn't know he was gay! I only met them today.' She folded her arms sulkily. 'But yours seems to be all over you, babe!'

I raised a brow, thinking of Olly. 'Yeah, you chose well for me, he's stunning. Far too good-looking to be here with me.'

'He is not!' my sister spat.

Beka slapped my arse jokingly as we re-entered the party. 'Go and find your hot Aussie! Fuck him hard for the both of us. Enjoy your night, guys!'

I turned to her. 'Are you not coming in?'

Beka swayed her head a little. 'Nah, I think I better try and get a mechanic for this car sorted. I'll have to return it tomorrow.' She rolled her eyes and wrapped her arms around me and my sister. 'But hey, our hot girl summer is happening now. We're going to have the best fucking time of our lives, do you hear me?' Beka's bright smile took over her face, and it was so infectious I felt myself smiling too.

'Yes, we fucking are!' I waved my hands in the air, laughing loudly.

'See you, Beks!' Grace blew her a kiss as she headed for the exit, and I strolled back into the gym hall, linking my sister's arm.

'I'm going to find Steve. I haven't spoken to him all night,' Grace said.

I nodded. 'OK, well, if I don't see you, I'll call you tomorrow.'

'You bloody better!' she warned, pointing a finger in my face.

I wandered through the crowd of partygoers, smiling at the familiar faces. By now, Richard and Katya had got through the entire yearbook, and I giggled as I saw him cornered by Damien while he tried to politely edge away. The music was loud, and I could feel the floor vibrate through my legs as I walked.

'And there she is!' a deep voice whispered. I turned to see Olly standing behind me. 'I thought you had run off.'

I shook my head. 'No, but Beka did. We were upstairs chatting,' I explained, blushing from just making small talk with the handsome model.

'It's just the two of us then?' he asked, pursing his lips a little.

I felt the blood drain from my face and hit my clit in a matter of seconds. Was this hot fucking model really – like, *really* – flirting with me?

I glanced up as he stared back at me intensely. 'Yeah, I guess it is.'

Olly casually placed one hand in his trouser pocket and leant closer. 'And what would you like to do with our time?'

I could feel his breath against my skin and hoped the old janitor wouldn't jam a 'wet floor' sign between my legs, as I felt soaking already. Fuck, maybe my luck was about to change.

I pushed back against him and giggled, lowering my voice in an attempt to be as sultry as possible.

'What do you like to do, Oliver?'

Olly cleared his throat, looking a little surprised. 'Oliver?' He grinned. 'Only my mum gets to call me that!'

I laughed, but my face felt hot with embarrassment at my pitiful flirting attempt. The past few months, the only person I'd flirted with was Adam, and that took as much effort as opening my flat door and knocking on his with my onesie on and maw bun in.

He leant closer. 'Personally, Ava, I'd like to fuck you with that dress on and show you how well I've earned my paycheck from today.' He winked.

I felt my head tilt. *Paycheck?* I wondered briefly what he was on about, before my mind zoned in on the fact that he wanted to fuck my brains out. No airs or graces, no shit patter for the rest of the evening, wondering, praying about what would happen next. I liked this, and if this was how the Australians got down to business, I was applying for a fucking visa.

'Where?' I asked, my heart beginning to pound. I had only had sex with Adam since splitting with Johnny. I was out of practice. *Please, God, don't let my fanny stench come back*, I thought.

'My car's in the car park?' he suggested.

A wave of excitement rippled through me. I glanced around, ensuring no one was overhearing our conversation, and then nodded back.

'Are you ready to go back down under?' I smirked, toes curling from my cringe reply.

Suddenly, Olly grabbed hold of my arm and began marching me through the crowd. 'Too right, I fucking am!'

I laughed loudly, holding my hand over my mouth, trying my best to disguise my giggles as we weaved through the groups of classmates enjoying their night, apologising for bumping into them as Olly hauled me out to the car park. It was still drizzling slightly, and I held my hands to the sky, welcoming the cool rain on my flustered skin.

'What about Damien?' I called out to him, realising we'd left his friend behind.

Olly shrugged. 'What about him?'

I followed him, stumbling through the bumpy car park with my heels on. Lots of parked cars spread over the large space, and eventually we reached a small Volkswagen Beetle.

'This is your car?' I asked, pointing to the mint-green vehicle.

'What do you drive?' he asked, laughing as he opened the back door and ushered me inside.

'I live in London. I don't have to drive.'

I squeezed into the car, and Olly joined me in the back, closing the door behind him. All of a sudden, it felt quiet.

'This is cosy,' he said, imitating my Scottish accent.

My breathing seemed loud in the small space.

'Did you ever get frisky with a lad when you were here?' Olly began peeling his damp suit jacket off and tossed it to the passenger seat.

I shook my head and laughed. 'It was against school rules!' I thought back to my time at school, knowing I never really had the opportunity. Johnny and I didn't get serious until our final year and even then, he would never so much as touch me in public, never mind shag me on school grounds. He was never an affectionate person, and I suppose I missed out on that crazy wild love that teenagers have in the movies.

'*Well* . . . Ava.' He paused, then gave a little tut. 'I think you may be about to break a few rules tonight.'

Finally, he leant closer to kiss me, his hand slowly gliding through my damp hair.

I felt his lips touch mine, and moved my body closer. Then his hand ran all the way up between my thighs.

Oh, fuck yes.

Grace

Inside the school, Grace had finally tracked down Steve, and together they were saying goodbye to their old classmates. They began walking towards the front entrance, and without a second thought, Steve took off his jacket and placed it over his wife's shoulders. She smiled gratefully towards him.

'Nice night?' he asked, opening the door for her.

Grace's face lit up; she was still buzzed with adrenaline from reuniting with her friends. 'I had a great night. It felt like old times with me, Beka and Ava. I feel like I didn't see you all night though!'

'I stayed out of the way, you know I hate these things.'

Steve let out a small yawn. He was a quiet man who said little in any situation. He was about five-eight with dark curly hair that was greying around the sides. He and Grace had been together since they joined a study group at Knightsbury to learn about the law. Now he worked as a barrister in London.

'Ava seemed well. It was such a surprise that she came tonight,' Grace said.

'I wouldn't know. Your sister didn't even mutter hello,' Steve replied, with a slight eye-roll.

'She probably didn't see you. I know I didn't, it was crammed in there! But you could have said hello first.'

Steve let out a small grunt, agreeing with his wife.

'We're over here.' He pressed the keys to his Jaguar, and it gave out two pulses of light.

'I'm sorry I missed your speech with Richard,' Grace said. 'I was on the roof with the girls.'

He shrugged. 'I didn't even notice. It was fine.'

From somewhere in the quiet car park, Grace heard moaning. She turned her head, spotting a green car parked opposite them.

'Oh my God! Steve!' she whispered as her jaw spread wide.

'Huh?' He seemed tired and disinterested.

Grace pointed to the car, which was steamed up and rocking back and forth.

'Steve!' she screeched.

He shook his head in disapproval.

'I wonder who it is?' Grace asked, taking a small step closer to the rocking car. 'Ohhhh, maybe two old lovers reunited?' She clasped her hands together excitedly.

'I should phone the police. This is school grounds and unacceptable on any level,' Steve tutted. He brought out his phone as Grace tiptoed towards the squeaking car.

The closer she got, the louder the moaning and panting became. Squinting, she tried to peer through the back windscreen, but all the windows were thick with steam. All she could see were vague shapes moving in the darkness. She stifled a laugh.

'Grace, c'mon darling. I'll call it in,' Steve said, checking over his shoulder as a few other classmates drew closer to the car.

Grace giggled a little and walked to the back window. She used her hand to peer into the car, which was full of condensation. Suddenly, a large hand slammed the window during the throws of passion from inside, and Grace jumped back screaming 'Jesus!' But then she realised the handprint had now given her a perfectly clear view. She bent down slowly, scrunching her eyes, expecting to see a romantic Rose-and-Jack-from-*Titanic* moment. Instead, her face screwed up in horror as she watched her sister's hairy balloon-knot arsehole pounding into Olly, riding him like Seabiscuit.

Grace gasped.

Inside the car, Ava turned around, saw her sister's face and screamed.

Olly jolted, manoeuvring his naked body to cover up the window.

Grace turned her back instantly, hoping the condensation would steam up the window again and preserve her sister's dignity.

'Oh God,' she whimpered, shaking off the sight. It was then that she saw the crowd gathered behind her.

'Who is it, Grace?' a woman called out.

'Erm . . . No one we know!' she said sternly. 'It's . . .

it's OK – just a couple of kids. Go home, everyone.'
She waved the curious spectators away, her red cheeks
now matching her hair.

'Grace!' Steve called her over.

When the group began dispersing, she rejoined her
husband in the car.

She slumped down in the seat, trying to delete the
image she'd just witnessed from her mind.

'Well?' he asked, pointing to the Beetle.

'Couple of kids. Don't phone the police, sweetheart.
You know what we were like at that age.' She smiled,
placing her hand on his thigh.

He shook his head. 'I won't, but only because I have
a busy day tomorrow. Providing a statement is something I don't have time for. Bloody disgrace.'

With that, Steve started the engine and began to
head home.

As Grace sat in the passenger seat, eventually a brief smile
swept over her face, thinking of her night with friends.

They entered their plush townhouse in Kensington,
and Grace slipped off her shoes. She leant forward
to kiss her husband, and he pecked her back before
retreating upstairs. The house was large, all white, with
scattered works of art on the walls. It sat pristine and
unblemished, just like Grace.

She headed to the kitchen, poured herself a glass of
bottled water from the fridge, and sipped. She thought
about her sister's rendezvous with Olly and giggled to
herself. She couldn't wait to bring it up over lunch
or a morning breakfast call with Ava. But deep down

she felt happy that her sister was having fun, forgetting about Johnny, even if it was only for the night.

Grace was still wearing Steve's jacket around her shoulders; she slipped it off and unzipped her trousers, gently stepping out of them and leaving them on the polished kitchen floor. She pulled off her top and bra and stood naked in the kitchen. She gazed at her reflection, her petite, toned figure in the shiny fridge door, and turned as she admired herself. She'd always felt confident in her body – after all, she looked after it. But she seemed to be the only one who noticed it recently. She couldn't remember the last time her husband had paid her a compliment or initiated sex. *Maybe that's just what happens after being married for so long*, she thought.

Then, brushing back her long red hair, she walked confidently upstairs to greet her husband. She wanted a hot girl summer, like they'd planned, and felt determined to get some affection.

Steve had turned the tap off after brushing his teeth and was wiping toothpaste from his mouth when he saw her in the bathroom mirror. His eyes popped a little, and he turned.

Grace edged out a smile at his reaction, feeling desirable and risqué.

As he emerged from the bathroom, he held out his fluffy floor-length dressing gown and popped it over her shoulders.

'You'll catch a cold,' he said, then leant forward to peck her forehead before walking towards his study.

She felt every bit of sexiness smothered by his heavy towelled robe.

'Steve!' she called out.

'Yes?' he replied, completely oblivious.

'I thought we could . . .' Grace stepped towards him and put out her hand to feel his crotch, but he lurched back, grabbing her wrist before she could even touch him.

'Not tonight, darling. I have a big case to work on. Get some rest.' He turned on his heel and retreated to the study.

She remained in the hallway for a few more minutes, static, still. Then she wrapped the oversized robe around her and lay down on top of her bed.

Chapter Eleven

Ava

The following morning, I woke to the sound of the buzzer echoing around the apartment. I turned to my phone to check the time: 11 a.m. *Georgie!*

I sprang to my feet, ran into the hallway and pressed the intercom. 'C'mon up!'

I raced around the apartment, bundling last night's dress into the bedroom, and fired a hoodie over my pyjamas. I felt a sudden twinge of nerves hoping Grace hadn't told Steve about Olly, and that Johnny wouldn't storm my house with social services after my late-night dogging session. There was a small knock at the door and I smiled, opening it.

'Mummy!' My daughter's little arms wrapped around me, and I bent down and lifted her. Her mousey brown hair was in pigtails and she was wearing her favourite Rapunzel dress.

'I have missed you so much!' I said as I squeezed her tightly, inhaling her familiar scent of lollipops and toothpaste.

'Missed you more,' she giggled, as she wriggled out of my arms and ran past me to the living room.

'Hey, here's her bag,' Johnny said.

I glanced up at my tall, handsome husband. His strawberry-blonde hair seemed lighter as it was swept back to the side, and he had slightly more stubble than usual. His pale skin was tanned from a week in the Lake District and his body seemed trimmer, more athletic than usual. *Why do men always age better?* I wondered.

'Thanks. Do you want to come in?' I asked.

Johnny seemed hesitant. He glanced over his shoulder. I wondered if he was thinking up an excuse to say no. But then he agreed. 'Sure, just for a minute.'

I led him to the kitchen, feeling my heart begin to simmer. He doesn't know about Olly! Thank fuck. 'Do you fancy a cuppa? You must be tired after the drive,' I said, switching the kettle on.

'I'm good,' he said, peering around at my cluttered kitchen.

I immediately felt self-conscious and began pushing the crusty curry-stained dishes stacked on the worktop into the sink. Our kitchen in Kensington – well, *his kitchen* – was the same size as my entire flat. The bifold doors opened to a small lawn where Georgie would play with the dog and have tea parties with her dolls. I loved every part of our house together – every aspect of our old life. Johnny's parents bought it for us when we got married, and I spent months redecorating it until it was perfect. I knew he hadn't done anything wrong. Now, I was the dafty having to trade granite worktops for plastic.

'Suit yourself. How was your weekend? How was Georgie? And your mum?' I asked, craving a chat with him before he made an excuse to leave.

'Yeah, it was nice.' He sat at the table. 'Georgie went rowing with my dad on the lake.' He chuckled at the memory, and my chest felt heavy as I'd missed it. 'I'll send you the pictures.'

'I'd love that.' I smiled back, admiring him and dazing off thinking about our daughter.

'Did you have a quiet one?' he asked.

I sat down opposite him, waiting for the kettle to boil. 'No, I actually didn't. I ended up going to Knightsbury for the reunion with the old gang!'

'With Beka and Grace?' He seemed surprised, crossing his arms over his chest.

'Yeah, I had a great night. Well, Richard was there, but—'

'Prick!' He rolled his eyes. 'I hope you didn't talk to him much!' he warned.

'No, well, you know what he's like, but we swerved him most of the night. I enjoyed myself, you know. Getting back there and seeing everyone, the memories and things.'

There was a brief silence between us. I wondered what he was thinking. Maybe about our days at the school? Or how he missed me? But probably what he'd be making for fucking tea that night.

'Hey, can you remember when we both got detention for sending notes in the classroom?' I asked, trying to bring back memories of our happier days.

'Yeah.' Johnny laughed a little. 'I was trying to persuade you to study with me.'

'Study? Is that what we're calling it now?' I raised an eyebrow, and he gave a small smirk.

I glanced over his toned body again. I couldn't remember the last time I'd felt it, or smelt him. The last time it was mine.

'I better head out. I have things to catch up on. You know what it's like being away from work all week.' he said.

Nope, definitely don't know what that's like, I thought.

'OK, well . . . eh . . . I suppose I'll see you on Monday then? For Georgie's welcome day at primary?' I squeezed my hands into two fists, excited that she would be starting just after the summer.

'Right, yes. Was it ten?' he asked, glancing at his phone.

'Ten o'clock. I could even pop to the house and we could go together, if you like? I think Georgie would like us walking in as a family.'

'I'll meet you there. Remember, some of us work, Ava.' He seemed pissed off at even the suggestion. Johnny got up and began walking through the hallway. I noticed his eyes fall on my pile of dirty laundry. 'You should get this place tidied up. You don't want Georgie living like this.'

'Yep. I intend to,' I said brightly, but I felt my stomach plunge. Every time I thought we were getting some-where, he'd make a dig, and my confidence would come tumbling right back down again. 'I don't have

the wardrobe space I used to anymore, since, you know
. . .' I gazed at him, feeling a simmer of anger ripple
through me. He seemed back to being dead behind the
eyes, no reaction, no feelings, nothing.

'I know it's difficult but . . .' He stopped himself
saying any more, turned his head to the side, shrugging
off his thought, and called out, 'See you later, princess!'

'Bye, Daddy,' Georgie called back, and Johnny left
the apartment.

I locked the door behind him and sighed.

That afternoon, I caught up with my daughter and
watched the *Tinker Bell* movie for what felt like the
fortieth time that month. Around one, my phone pinged.

> *You have been added to the* **Hot Girl Summer**
> *group chat.*

I smiled at my screen and noticed Beka typing.

> **Beka:** *Hola bitches, does anyone fancy a cocktail? Xx*

> **Me**: *Hey, sorry I have Georgie back. Baw deep in fairy
> dust xx*

> **Beka**: *Sounds awful! What about dinner? Xx*

> **Grace**: *I'm up for dinner! Bring Georgie! And explain
> to us what the hell happened with Olly? Haha Ava I
> am traumatised!!!!! Xxxxx*

I suddenly felt the fear of my hangover crash down on
me. *Shagging a complete stranger in a car park at a school?*

Seriously, Ava? I still hadn't washed and could smell Olly's spunk turning sour through my leggings. I was a disgrace!

Beka: WTF happened with Olly!!!!!

   Grace: *Ava you need to explain! Lets just say I REALLY know my twin inside out now!*

I giggled at my phone, not knowing whether to cover my face or embrace the first act of my hot girl summer, knowing my friends wouldn't judge my antics but would slag the shit out of me for a while instead. I knew seeing them would cheer me up, especially after Johnny's snidey comments. I checked my online banking app: forty-two pounds and twenty-seven pence to my name. I pushed my hands through my hair and sighed, then picked up my phone again.

   Me: *Sorry, Brew doesn't cash out till Monday* ☹ *xx*

   Beka: *I got it. Move your ass! Meet at Tony's in an hour? Xx*

   Grace: *See you then xx*

I sat my phone down briefly in thought. I didn't want to be a charity case, but I did want to see my friends. I had noticed a change in my mood since reuniting with them. Even after seeing Grace for one night, I suddenly felt like I wasn't so alone.

   Me: *OK xx*

'Georgie?' I said, pausing the television. 'How do you fancy going out for dinner tonight with Aunty Grace and Beks?'

Her tiny face lit up and she cheered loudly.

'Come on then, let's get ready!'

Chapter Twelve

Ava

As I entered Tony's – a small English diner – I was greeted by a bubbly young waitress. I pointed to the booth behind her as I noticed my sister's bright red hair, and wandered over to Grace, who stood up when she saw us.

'Hello, my girl, I've missed you,' she said as she hugged Georgie, who hugged her tightly back. 'How was your holiday to see granny?'

'It was fun!' Georgie giggled, taking a seat at the table.

'Hey.' I wrapped my arms around Grace sheepishly, waiting for her to bring up my shagging antics from the previous night.

'I'm so glad you guys could come!' she said. She seemed hyper, a little ecstatic. 'Doesn't this place bring back memories?' She smiled as I took a seat.

When we moved to the city for university, we would meet here for lunch a few times a week. I glanced around the place; the same décor, tables and chairs, the same smell of built-up grease from all those years ago. We would arrange to meet, lay our books out and study for hours for exams, or come to discuss heartbreaks or crushes. It was a nostalgic, greasy part of us.

I laughed. 'It does!'

'Hola!' Beka was standing behind us with her arms out. I nudged Georgie to go and hug her, and she happily obliged. 'God, you're getting big, girl!' Beka squeezed her, then sat down in the empty chair. She grinned at us. 'I fucking love this place.'

'I do too. I almost forgot it existed,' I replied.

'Hun, you almost forgot that we all existed!' Beka tutted, giving me a slight side-eye.

'That's true,' Grace agreed.

'Until we gave her a boot up the—'

'*Hey!*' I warned, tilting my head towards my daughter, who was fidgeting with the salt and pepper.

'So, how was the rest of the night? Any dramas?' Beks asked, with a slight smirk at my sister, who was pretending to skim over the menu.

I was ready to speak when Grace interrupted, 'Well, besides my sister getting . . .' she lowered her voice, '*you know* . . . in the school car park?!'

Beka turned to me, and then Grace, with a surprised look. ''You know'?' she repeated.

'I wondered how long this would take you to cast up!' I said, feeling my cheeks grow hot.

'His beat-up green Beetle was rocking all around the car park, I'm surprised he didn't move spaces!' Grace continued.

Beka laughed hysterically. 'Stop! Beetle? Classy!'

'Yep, and Steve almost called the police! Until I glanced in and saw . . . *well,* let's say I saw parts of you I never wanted to see.' Grace shuddered at the thought, screwing up her face.

I put my hands over my daughter's ears. 'You were watching me! That's worse! It's . . . It's perverted!' I spat back.

'Now, now, girls. Enough. But tell me, how was it?' Beks asked, leaning forward at the goss.

'It was fun, yeah, a lot of fun!' I stretched my hands a good eight inches, and we all laughed. 'He also ran me home, which saved on the cab fare.'

'Such a gentleman!' my sister gasped sarcastically.

Beks laughed loudly. 'And any plans to meet up again for round two? Maybe you could park up next to a swing park or something this time?'

I rolled my eyes. 'No. It was a nice distraction but I'm only on a break, remember! That was a moment of madness.'

'Hey guys, are you ready to order?' the waitress asked, approaching the table.

'Can I have a tonic water, please, and the maca-roni with garlic bread?' Beks replied, handing her the menu.

'I'll have a Diet Coke and chicken curry, please, and can I have kids' nuggets and chips with a glass of water as well?' I smiled at the young girl as she took note.

'And a Caesar salad with Diet Coke for me, please,' Grace added.

'Perfect, I'll bring some crayons over for Rapunzel too.' She winked towards Georgie, who clapped her hands in delight.

'So, I wanted us all to meet up because I wasn't joking about what I said last night. We need to change. Our lives have to change, and I mean fucking drastically,' Beks said, sounding serious all of a sudden.

The waitress came back with a small tub of crayons and a piece of paper for Georgie. Beks swiped a red crayon from the box and grabbed the colouring paper instantly, turning it over to the blank side.

'Mummy!' Georgie looked at me for support.

'Aunty Beks will return it in one second, baby,' I whispered.

'Think of where we were before. We'd just left school, we were planning our futures, we knew exactly what we wanted to happen in our lives, yeah?'

Grace and I nodded back in agreement.

'But none of us have made it, not one!' She shook her head.

'Because . . .?' She looked at us to participate.

'Because we fell in love? Or changed our minds,' Grace suggested.

'Ava?' Beks asked.

'Because . . . I decided to ruin my marriage by having far too much time to myself?' I shrugged.

'Because we didn't have each other!' Beks said in exasperation. 'Every time we drift apart or one of us goes AWOL, our lives go to shit!' She paused and took a breath. 'Look . . .'

She began scribbling on the piece of paper, dividing it into four. At the top right she wrote the heading EMPLOYMENT, and then on the left she wrote RELATIONSHIPS. On the bottom right she wrote FUN, and on the bottom left she scribbled MONEY. She made her best attempt at drawing four straight lines to meet in the middle, and in the centre, she wrote FRIENDSHIP.

'Our friendship is key! We are shit without it! It's the thing we haven't been nurturing and the first thing we let slip. We've been so busy concentrating on shitty marriages and jobs that everything else has toppled. I don't know about you guys, but when I put all my energy into a guy, everything else tumbles, and I'm not prepared to do it anymore. If we put all our focus on our friendship, and looking after ourselves, then honestly, everything else will fall into place.'

I sat back quietly at the realisation. I had worked so hard to keep my marriage and my relationship with Johnny that I'd lost everything else in between.

'When I heard our yearbook entries, I could barely remember that strong, determined, sassy little person I used to be. I'd been full of courage and winning at everything in life. We were all badasses! And I sat up last night wondering how to get her back and I realised all I need is you two.'

Grace sat up. 'So, our friendship is the key?'

'We're the fucking key!' Beks repeated loudly.

Georgie giggled.

I adjusted myself, trying to absorb her plan. 'But we were kids, Beks. You really think if we stick together now we'll change things around?'

Beks nodded, 'Why not? We've done it before. Every time we lost touch over the years, it's all gone Pete Tong, babe. But, when I'm with you guys, I'm fucking untouchable. I can bounce things off you two. You stop me from jumping in, or tell me when I should. I need that. I need that right now!'

'But, what do we actually do for each other though?' Grace asked.

'It's simple. We be there. The way no man is there. A relationship with you guys is much healthier than any I've been in before. I mean, I love Mitchell, but he doesn't make me feel unstoppable. He doesn't see me the way you guys do.' She huffed slightly, trying to get her point across. 'Look, three heads are better than one. We just need to give one another ideas, encouragement, and help out, just like we always fucking did.' She sighed. 'We are the secret to our own success; we fight for each other to succeed, and we fucki— Sorry, Georgie.' She cleared her throat. 'We will be those young, determined, stunning girls, ready to take on the city again. I know we will.' She banged her fist down on the table passionately.

'I love the idea, Beks, I do. But I wouldn't know where to start. I need help with every part of my sad life. I mean, I want to succeed, of course I do, but who's going to hire a thirty-odd-year-old single maw who's never worked before? I think I've come to terms with the fact that my best shot at anything right now is getting my old life back, with Johnny,' I said, as the waitress came over with our drinks.

Grace reached over and clasped my hand, 'There's no harm in finding yourself in the meantime, Ava,' she said quietly.

'Ava! I'm sorry, but that seventeen-year-old from the yearbook would never have left her *best bet* up to someone else, let alone a man! Come on, girl, I know you're just getting over Johnny but for fuck's sake, do this for you!'

I felt my heart crush, knowing inside that I had no intention of getting over him. I lowered my head, feeling embarrassed. *I am pathetic.*

'Well, I will start with my relationship,' Grace said. 'My *you-know-what* life needs a little oomph.'

'Ew, gross, Grace,' I almost choked at the thought of my sister pumping Steve, the monotone boring bastard.

'And I'm going to need help with employment and a little bit with relationship, for Mitchell,' Beks declared. 'I just need the magazine to take me seriously. Today, I got an email assigning me to snap pictures of a dog that won Crufts! Like seriously, *Crufts*! I'm supposed to be a fashion photographer!'

'Maybe it'll wear a Gucci bow-tie?' I laughed.

'It could have a Gucci dildo up its arse, and I still wouldn't be impressed!'

'Could you not build up a personal portfolio? Show them how good you are, Beks?' Grace suggested, sipping her drink.

Beks shrugged. 'They know I'm good, but a lot of the time, the client asks for a certain photographer. A big name in the industry, and we have loads on the books.' She rolled her eyes and took a swig of her drink. 'I've been so focused on impressing Miles and Mitchell, working hard for them, that I've not had a chance to build my reputation with clients.'

'What about online? That's where everything is these days,' I said.

'What do you mean? Like a website?' Beks asked, shaking her head instantly.

'Or an Instagram account? Take some pictures and sort of advertise your work?' I suggested.

'We're not allowed to post any photographs from the magazine on our accounts. It's in the contract,' she replied, disheartened. 'The motherfuckers own us!'

'Do it anonymously.' Grace sat up. 'Start posting your work. Not shots you take for the magazine – you could take photos anywhere. Build an online audience and, when it's time, show your boss how people are engaging with your work. You don't have to mention the magazine at all.'

Beks smiled. 'Like a fashion guide page showcasing real women!' There was a sudden buzz around the table.

'Yes!' I nodded.

'Exactly,' Grace said.

'I could do that.' Beks smiled to herself as the idea took hold. 'I could snap around London and take everyday fashion tips from normal people. This is one of the fashion capitals of the world, after all.' Her mind was alive, and I sat back and smiled.

'Your food, ladies.' The waitress began handing out the dishes and soon we were tucking in.

'You'll need a name for the account, Beks,' Grace said.

'Hot girl summer?' I replied quickly, tucking into my curry.

'No, too seasonal! What about . . . *Girl gang*?'

Grace's head tilted. 'It sounds very . . . *young*. You're a woman now! Embrace it!'

'Well, what then?' Beks huffed. 'Georgie, what should I call my page?'

'Hmmm . . . I don't know,' she replied, shrugging her shoulders, too distracted by squeezing ketchup onto her plate.

Beka sighed dramatically. 'She obviously gets her brains from her father's side.'

I laughed, semi-insulted. '*Hey*, she's only turning five!'

'I want something that screams *Vogue* but is more accessible. Something that the everyday girl looks at on her way to work and feels inspired by, with all these different styles. I could tag the designers based on my recommendations, and maybe work with them one day.'

'What about *Rogue*?' I had a mouth full of chips in my gob as I said it. 'I mean, you are going rogue by creating it in the first place!'

Beka glanced at Grace, then back to me. '*Rogue!* I . . . love it! Ava, I love it!' She raised her glass in the air, and we all joined in for a toast. 'To *Rogue!*'

We continued chatting for another hour, catching up about Steve's work and Beka's life at the office. We heard all about Grace's workout, while I chatted about Georgie starting school. We laughed and slagged the situations we'd encountered over the years. I couldn't remember the last time I had as much fun.

'So, babe, tell us how you'll tackle your life?' Beks asked, smirking across the table.

'Please don't say you're repeating last night, Ava. That's enough fun for a while, surely?' Grace whimpered.

'Oh, piss off, she can have as much fun as she likes – she's single!' Beks replied.

I glanced at my daughter, who seemed completely unaware another swear word had been outed at the table.

'Well, yeah, last night was great. I mean *a lot* of fun. But honestly, I'm enjoying this. Just getting out of the house and seeing you guys is the most fun I've had since . . .' I trailed off, and the table grew quiet as the thought of Johnny filled my head.

'Well, you can have both types, babe. Us *and* Olly fun! Did you get a number?' Beks asked.

I made a face. 'No, but it wasn't like that. It was just spontaneous and fun!' We all laughed.

'More fun than your sister's having, by the sound of it.' Beka nudged Grace, who agreed, sipping her drink. She seemed more quiet than usual.

'C'mon then, let's hear your plan to tackle this relationship!'

Grace's face reddened a little. 'Steve's working a lot just now, so things have been a bit lonely.'

I nodded sympathetically, knowing how shy she was about any marital issues. 'When was the last time you two had . . .' I glanced at Georgie, who was now colouring in the drawing, having stolen it back from Beks earlier.

'God, *erm* . . . about four, five . . . probably about ten months ago?' Her voice sounded higher at her disclosure.

'Fuckin' hell, babe! *Jeez!*' Beks exclaimed, then lowered her voice, adding 'Sorry!'

'I know he's been busy, but I have needs, too,' Grace said softly. 'And I tried last night . . .'

'Did your sister's antics turn you on, hun?' Beks and I laughed wickedly as Grace continued.

'No! God, no! Beka! Absolutely not. But I tried, and he wouldn't even let me touch him! I was *naked*, and he wrapped a housecoat around me in case I caught a cold!' She rested her head in her hands frustratedly, then sighed.

'Maybe you should speak to him about how you feel?' I offered. 'Tell him!'

'It's not even the sex part. He's just distant, you know. It's like he has this big important life, and I'm just there at home. I'm like . . . a bloody ornament or something.'

'Well, if you're an ornament, you're a Harrods ornament, girl.' Beks squeezed her hand, and continued, 'But, you shouldn't feel like that, babe. You deserve to be seen. You deserve to feel *desired*. The silly cun—' Beks rolled her eyes at Georgie's presence, just managing to stop herself. 'The silly man probably doesn't even realise.'

'It's just . . . sometimes, I wonder . . . what if there's someone else?' Grace said.

Beka and I shared a worried glance.

'Grace, there won't be. It's Steve!' I reassured her. 'He is a prick at times, yes, an antisocial, workaholic prick, but he isn't a cheat.'

'I agree with Ava. I don't think he has it in him, to be honest with you, babe.'

'But look at you and Johnny. I'm scared to even say anything in case he shuts me out like Johnny did with you!' Her eyes were wide as she finally voiced all her worries.

I put my head down. A year later, it still made my gut wrench thinking of how much I had pushed him away.

'Well, if you really think that could be a possibility, ask him. Or better yet, look for evidence. The poor guy might just be knackered from work, babe. And not every man is like Johnny. He should have reassured his wife, not shipped her off when things got tough.'

Grace nodded.

I put my hand across the table and squeezed my sister's. 'It will be fine, Grace.'

She smiled back, but I could see how scared she was behind her eyes.

'And Ava, you're going to have to sort the employ- ment section of the list. I'm just saying,' Beks said. 'I mean, it's all right for Grace, but you need some money behind you. I'm not eating in Tony's every night. I'm more of a Shard kind of gal these days!'

'I know,' I said, with a heavy sigh. 'I just have no idea what I'd be good at. But I'm going to start looking, now Georgie's going to school.'

'Yeah, look, and we can help narrow down the options together. Right girls, I'm going to head home, I need to clean up the outfits from last night. I can't be caught stealing from work or I'll be joining the queue at the job centre with you, babe!' Beks stated, sitting back on her chair.

I laughed. 'Did you get Mitchell's car fixed OK?'

She nodded, 'Yeah, it's fixed up and I even paid for a valet. He'll have no idea,' she smiled. 'He's in the bad books anyway. He's tried to call me half a dozen times, texted like a million, but I'm letting him stew!' She winked sassily.

We continued chatting for another few minutes until the summer sunshine faded. Then Georgie and I headed to the underground for another night of Disney Plus.

Chapter Thirteen

Rebeka

On Monday morning, Beka headed towards the office laden with the outfits she'd *borrowed* from the wardrobe department for the reunion, all pressed and pristine. As she wandered through the red lanterns of Chinatown with an iced latte in hand, she noticed a car at the side of the road. She paused momentarily and glanced behind her, ensuring no one from the office was around. The window lowered, and she saw Mitchell sitting in the back.

'Hey baby.' He smiled widely at her, his strong accent catching her off guard. 'How was your weekend?'

She narrowed her eyes at him and marched past, continuing her commute to the office.

'We're not still fighting, are we?' he called out.

Never able to resist an argument, she paused and turned back.

'Are you serious right now?' Her hand rested on her hip.

'Get in, Beka. I want to talk,' he replied softly.

She shook her head and let out a sarcastic laugh. 'Now? Oh, you want to talk now? After walking out the room on Friday? Wait and I'll drop everything then, Mitch.'

Mitchell smirked, folding the newspaper that was opened on his knee. 'Well, you didn't answer any of my calls or messages. I did try. Look, I gave you some time to cool off over the weekend, but now we need to talk.' His voice was smooth and serious.

'Talk about what, Mitch?'

'If you get in, I'll tell you, Rebeka!'

'Well, we can't travel in together, can we?' she hissed, walking away. 'And I'm not going to be late!'

Mitchell shrugged. 'Have you checked your email today?' he asked through the still-open window as the car followed her slowly up the busy road. People tooted their horns at the disturbance but Mitchell didn't seem to care.

Beka froze, curious. She lifted her phone and scrolled through her work emails.

One new email from Mitchell Travers:
Subject: Update to policy regarding relationships in the workplace.

Her eyes darted from her phone to Mitchell and back while she skimmed over the email.

'You can't be serious. Mitchell, you changed it?' Her face lit up the bustling street as people barged past her.

'Now, will you get in, please?' He smiled and pushed open the car door.

Beka lunged into the car, with her bags stuffed with clothes, bulldozing towards him. 'You changed it, right? No clause?' She closed the door, unable to sit still from excitement.

'The policy has changed. I've been on the phone to the lawyers all weekend.' He leant forward and kissed her. 'Now, may I *please* take you on a proper date this weekend, Rebeka Hampson?'

She nodded, her eyes filling with emotion. 'Of course you fucking can, you silly cunt. Come here!' She wrapped her arms around Mitchell tightly as his driver began navigating the rush-hour traffic. 'This is amazing. I can't believe you've done it,' she said. Her voice shook as she spoke and she quickly cleared her throat. She hated showing emotion.

'Well, I can't lose you,' Mitchell replied softly, leaning back in his seat and clutching her hand.

'What does this mean?' she asked. 'Are we telling the office? I can't wait to see the looks on their faces!' She laughed evilly, wondering how the dynamics would shift in her favour.

'I want to tell everyone. We can announce it today, if you're comfortable with that?'

'Of course I fucking am! Mitch, I've been waiting months for this day!'

His blue eyes shone with a glimmer of guilt. 'I know, and I'm sorry it's taken so long. I had to speak to my family and convince them you weren't a gold digger!'

She snarled, '*Gold digger!* How can you be sure?' She raised her brow jokingly towards him.

They both laughed as the car entered the car park underneath the offices. She couldn't believe she was arriving at work *with* Mitchell.

As the car stopped, she grabbed hold of the costume bags. 'Shall I head up first? See you in there?'

Mitchell smiled. 'Let's go in together. Properly. We don't have to hide anymore, Beks.'

She felt a surge of happiness buzz around her body as she gazed at the man she loved. She had dreamt of this moment for so long. She leant forward and kissed him. His juicy lips were soft and warm.

'I could stay here all day with you,' he said.

'But we have an announcement to make, sweetheart, c'mon!'

She quickly manoeuvred herself out of the car, and finally, after all the hiding, all the turmoil, all the uncertainty that it would ever become anything real, they entered the *Inner Me!* foyer together.

It wasn't the glamorous reveal she had dreamt of, exactly – as usual, there was a line of people queued up to show their ID badges to security. But that didn't bother Beks; somehow the normalcy of it took on a new significance, knowing Mitchell was right there with her.

'Good morning, Mr Travers, come on through.' One of the guards spotted Mitchell and ushered him to the front of the line.

'After you, Miss Hampson,' he said politely.

She grinned as she walked past the line of her colleagues, the bulky costume bags accidentally bumping against their legs. 'Excuse me, oh, sorry!'

As they entered the packed lift, Beka smiled at Mitchell, who stood opposite her; his dark eyes remained fixed on her face, and she giggled like a teenager.

The lift stopped on the first floor, and Karen, one of the accounts staff, entered.

'Ahh, Mr Travers, we have tried calling. Do you have a minute?' she said.

Beks smirked towards Mitch, and brought out her phone. She began scanning her new Rogue Instagram feed, having uploaded an image she took on the tube. *Two new followers and five likes. Shit!* She popped her phone back inside her bag.

'Sorry Karen, can it wait? I'm headed to floor three to speak to the team.' His voice was charming as ever, yet decisive.

'As am I, but I really think you should be in on this.'

When the doors opened, Rebeka stepped proudly out of the lift and strutted to her desk. She looked over her shoulder, watching to see if Mitchell was still engrossed in her every move. But there was a shift in his expression. Karen was talking fervently at him, waving a piece of paper.

So much for our gesture of love, Beka sighed. *This problem better not interrupt the announcement.* Her moment had finally come, and she wasn't prepared to wait any longer.

Andre popped his head over Beka's desk as he glanced at Mitchell and Karen's discussion. 'I wonder what's going on there?'

Beka gave herself a little shake and smiled back at her friend. 'I'm sure we'll find out. You know what it's like in here!'

'That's for sure. Bunch of bitches we work with.' He rolled his eyes. 'Hey, did you see the email this morning? No more policy against dating in the workplace!'

Beks feigned a look of surprise. She couldn't wait to break the news to Andre. 'Yeah. Like, oh my God, wonder if some lucky gal has got her claws into Mr Travers?'

Andre glanced around the room briefly, making sure no one was nearby. 'I put money on Tiff. I've seen the way they are together, you know. Very cosy!'

Beka stood up straight, slightly offended. 'No way! I hear he has a thing for blondes.' She winked at her friend, then turned towards the wardrobe department. 'I'll be back in five,' she said. She hurried down the hallway and began unzipping the clothes she'd borrowed for the weekend, quickly straightening out the creases and firing them back on the rails.

'Rebeka, is it?' a voice said.

Beks turned to see Karen standing behind her and managed to pull on a smile. 'Yes, Karen, isn't it? Just fixing these items for a shoot,' she pretended to wipe the sweat off her forehead, hoping she hadn't noticed that she was only just returning them.

'Could you follow me, please?'

'Yeah, yeah. Of course.' Beka followed Karen back through the corridor, and shrugged at Andre as he squinted over at her getting marched through the office. *What if Karen knew she'd been stealing?* she wondered. *No, surely not. I mean, technically it's not stealing if you bring everything back, is it? It must be about Mitchell.*

Butterflies were parading through her stomach. This was it. She was probably having to sign a non-disclosure or something because of how famous Mitchell was. Maybe he'd asked Karen to fetch her for a quickie before they told the building about their secret love affair. He had pulled it out of the bag, and had most certainly earned himself a decent blowie after this, even though she squirmed at the thought, having just brushed her teeth.

Karen led her into the lift, and the doors opened. They both stood to the side, allowing it to empty before heading in. Karen leant forward and pressed for floor one.

Jackpot, no blowjob needed. That was the management floor. There was no way Mitch would risk a grope when so many executives worked there. It must be to discuss details of the announcement.

There was the familiar swooping feeling as the lift dropped.

'Nice weekend?' Beks asked.

'Hmm, quite,' Karen replied.

Jeez, Karen's a fucking bore, she thought. *She probably fancies Mitchell, too. Fuck, the whole workplace will be jealous of me by the end of the day.* Beka wondered what this would mean for her. Would she get more shoots? Would she be in the gossip mags? *'Mitchell Travers seen with blonde bombshell.'* Fuck, maybe they would do a piece on her – her life story. And since Mitchell had told his family, next it would be family dinners with the Traverses or holidays on his yacht. Rebeka could feel herself glowing with excitement.

The lift stopped, and Karen stepped out. Rebeka followed her to the boardroom. As she entered, she noticed Mitchell sitting at the top of the table with his hands clasped under his chin, deep in thought.

'Please take a seat, Rebeka,' Karen said.

'Sure.' As she sat, she tried to catch Mitchell's eye but his gaze remained solemnly on the table. Rebeka became aware of a tense atmosphere in the room. 'Is everything OK?'

Karen's heels marched past her, and she sat down opposite Rebeka.

'I'll just get right to it then. It has come to our attention that there is an issue with your financing.' She sounded serious.

Beka glanced at Mitchell, who remained emotionless, staring at the floor. 'Sorry, what? My financing? I'm a photographer, I don't—'

'We have received an invoice from a modelling firm,' Karen said, cutting across her, 'claiming an extensive overtime fee that was apparently approved by you on Friday night.'

Rebeka felt the blood drain from her body.

'This invoice states that you hired two male models for a fee over and above the working hours required for the magazine?'

Beka closed her eyes momentarily, hoping her brain would spark into action and come up with a reasonable explanation.

'I . . . I . . . did, but . . .'

'You apparently hired these models to escort you to an event, and one has also stated,' Karen reached for her glasses, looking uncomfortable as she read the email aloud, 'that the model went above and beyond to ensure the host was highly satisfied with his service', she held her chest and continued, 'and therefore would like a higher rate, as sexual favours are normally outside of his remit.'

There was a loud thud on the table as Mitchell slammed his hand on it, making them both jump.

Beka felt the room spin. 'No. No, I can explain . . .'

'Please do,' Karen said.

'I did hire the models. I hired them because I was attending a high school reunion, and I wanted my friend to have a date. I didn't know they would charge the company. I might have said a joke about overtime. God, I'm so sorry. I am more than happy to pay the fees personally. I didn't think for one minute that—'

'That you would get caught?' Mitchell's deep voice echoed through the room.

'Mitch, please,' she said.

'This is a severe contract violation, Miss Hampson,' Karen explained as she looked at Rebeka disapprovingly.

'I understand that, Karen, but please, can I explain this to Mitchell alone? Mitch, look at me, please.' Her voice was getting louder, and she felt tears running down her face.

His jaw was set, and he wouldn't look at her.

'Mitchell!' she called out, praying he'd look over.

'Do what you have to do, Karen,' Mitchell said. Finally, he looked at Beka, his gaze icy and remote. 'I'll pay for your hooker, Rebeka; I hope you enjoyed yourself. But please, have your desk emptied in the next hour.' He stood up.

'But he wasn't *my* hooker! Mitchell, fucking listen!' she said desperately, but he was walking towards the door. She followed him. 'You're seriously going to let this be it? What about the announcement?'

Mitchell held the door handle and turned to her with glazed-over eyes. 'The only announcement that will be made today is a vacancy on the photography team.' He swung open the door and walked out.

Beka began sobbing. Ugly gulping heaves.

'I can arrange for security to pack your things if you wait in the lobby, Miss Hampson,' Karen said behind her, unmoved by her tears. 'We no longer require your services here at *Inner Me!*'

Beka stared, unable to comprehend the enormity of the situation. Karen's words hung emptily in the air.

How did this happen? How have I managed to throw it all away?

Chapter Fourteen

Ava

Across town, I set off with Georgie for her visit to primary school. She squeezed my hand with excitement, adorable in her smartest navy and white dress, as we walked towards the train station. It was a beautiful day in London, and the summer clothes hung neatly on the market stalls. Our favourite food vendors were setting up, and I could smell the fresh aroma of spices lingering in the air. Georgie pointed at a stack of *Sleeping Beauty* T-shirts sitting on one of the tables at a shopfront. I nodded and *oohed* and *aahed* at how pretty they were, but continued walking, knowing Johnny would have a fit if I bought her something from here. Since we'd separated, the posh cunt regularly scrutinised her clothes. One time I saved up to buy her a sequinned Rapunzel hoodie she'd gawked at for weeks from one of the markets and he'd laughed in my face when she wore it, saying he wasn't taking her if she had it on. Instead, she returned home that night with a Burberry tracksuit, just to appease him. A brief shudder went through me when I thought of the school parties she'd have to attend in the autumn.

As we continued on, her little hand grasped in mine, I wondered what it would be like in September when she finally began school. Johnny's parents were set on her attending a private school across the city in Ealing and I knew the commute would be difficult for us. I struggled to get out of bed most mornings, never mind up, ready and on a fucking train before 8 a.m. I knew I'd need to find work, but finding a job made me more anxious than living off toast and beans for dinner. I hadn't amounted to anything my entire life. I didn't have any special talents, skills, or experience, my communication skills were piss poor and realistically I needed to find a job that allowed me to do the school drop-offs and pick-ups. If it weren't for my hairy big toe and recent fungal nail infection, selling feet pictures would have been a serious option.

A warm gush of gritty air swept past us, and Georgie snuggled into my legs as the train approached the platform. The doors opened and we stepped on.

'Are you excited?' I asked, taking a seat beside my daughter.

She shrugged. 'What will *you* do when I'm at school, Mummy?'

'Me?' I scoffed. 'I'll have plenty of things to do! I can clean up the house and visit Aunty Grace and Beks. Make din-dins for you coming home?'

She smiled back.

'It will be so much fun! You don't have to worry about me, OK?' I reassured her, feeling a pit in my stomach. *What would I do?*

147

'OK, Mummy,' she replied, resting her head on my shoulder.

We got off at Ealing Broadway station, getting pushed and prodded by the morning commuters. I lifted Georgie into my arms and hefted her onto one hip, holding tightly to the escalator with the other hand. Finally outside, we began the walk to the prep school.

'This is a long way to come for school, Mummy,' Georgie said, as I felt the sweat trickle down my arse crack.

I nodded back. 'I know. But Daddy wanted you to go to this school because it is the best in the whole of London!' I made a stunned face, making her giggle a little. 'It's also closer to your daddy, so it won't be that difficult to get here when you have nights with him.'

Georgie puffed a little, seeming quiet from the busy morning.

'Here it is, look.' I pointed to the modern-looking building. 'And it's a brand–new school! It has a swimming pool and everything inside!'

She turned to me, looking a little nervous. 'But I can't swim without armbands.'

'That's OK, neither can I,' I said and winked as we headed through the impressive gated entrance.

The Ealing Girls' Prep School had just undergone an extensive renovation funded partly by sizeable donations from the parents, and Georgie's would be the first class in the new part of the building. From the outside it looked like a hotel, as it stood tall with vast glass windows and beautiful gardens occupying most of the space. It was hard to believe we were in the centre of London. Georgie's eyes sparkled as we walked through the gate. She pointed out the science garden and wishing-well at the front of the school and I laughed. They certainly didn't have this in Glasgow; my school's entrance had been full of fag dowts and drawings of cocks on the walls.

As we headed to the front of the building, we were greeted by a stern-looking older lady.

'Hello there. I'm Ms Cross. May I have your name please?' She spoke in a posh English accent and, with her long satin dress and jacket combo, I felt like we'd just walked onto the set of *Downton Abbey*.

'Georgie Little,' I said and smiled back.

'Yes, Georgina. Come this way, and I'll take you to your teacher, young lady.'

I hesitated, turning back to look for Johnny. *Why was he always fucking late?* But I gasped at Georgie, trying my best to get her excited while she looked down at the ground nervously.

We followed the older lady through the main foyer of the school. Everything was pristine; the floors were so polished that the light reflected off them, almost disturbing my vision.

We entered a classroom on the ground floor, where a small group of parents and children were chatting together.

'Mr McGroaty, we have Miss Little here,' the lady announced.

I noticed the few mothers immediately scan me up and down, appraising my jeans and leather jacket. My cheeks felt hot.

'Lovely to meet you!' Mr McGroaty said from the centre of the group. His strong Scottish accent took me completely by surprise. 'Hello, welcome to you both.'

He stood up and stepped towards us. I hadn't expected him to be so young or so . . . handsome. He was tanned, with a strong jawline and a muscular physique beneath his smart suit. He had dark, mysterious eyes. *And* he was friendly. Everything about this man had caught me completely off guard.

He shared a puzzled glance between me and Georgie as both of us stood rigid.

'Georgina Little, yes?' he asked.

'I'm sorry. *Yes,* this is Georgie. Or Miss Little, or whatever. I'm not sure how you address the kids at schools like this, to be honest.' I was rambling. *Shut the fuck up, Ava,* I thought.

'Georgie is a great name! Do you like getting called that best?' He bent down until he was at eye level with my daughter, who was clutching my leg. She nodded back shyly. 'And finally an accent I'm familiar with, eh?' He laughed, standing once again. 'You must be Mrs Little.' He held out his hand, and I suddenly became conscious of my half-polished nails I'd meant to fix last night before binge-watching another episode of *Selling Sunset*.

I shook my head, grasping his hand quickly. 'Oh, I'm not Little now, well I am . . .' I glanced down at my scrawny body. 'But I'm originally Campbelle, *well,* for Facebook purposes mainly. Technically, I am still . . . But . . . I'm sorry, I'm Georgie's—'

'Oh, I apologise. Are you the nanny?' he asked.

I felt my face fall in disbelief. 'No, no. I'm her mother,' I responded quietly.

I heard a few titters from the parents behind him and I blushed. I was so worried about Georgie fitting in, I hadn't realised I would be the one who didn't.

'Doesn't she look incredibly young for a daughter so tall?' a deep voice said from the group.

I looked past Mr McGroaty and saw Richard Tierney step out to greet me.

'Ava.' He leant forward to kiss my cheek.

'Dick?' I replied, then heard a small giggle from Georgie. 'What . . . What are you doing here?'

'I'm enrolling my niece, Beatrice. And it looks like she'll be in your class, Georgie. Will you keep an eye on her for me?' He winked down at Georgie, who smiled back, nodding her little head.

Shit. I felt nerves grow in my stomach. Johnny hated this guy, now we were going to have to spend the next eighteen years seeing him at the school gate.

'Come, join us, Ava. Meet the parents and the children,' Mr McGroaty said. 'I'll be your teacher this term, Georgie.'

I walked a few steps further into the room and joined the circle of pretentious mothers and fathers standing together, ogling my every move. The classroom was bright and airy, with large doors leading out to a sensory garden. Chairs were laid out at the front of the room and a projector set up.

'What do you do, Ava?' one of the men asked me.

'Oh, I stopped working when Georgie came along. I see to her, mostly,' I admitted.

I felt a hand grip my shoulder, but immediately shrugged it off. 'Don't let this one fool you, Bob,' Richard said smoothly, as if he'd known the parents a lifetime. 'She's one of the most talented ladies I've met!'

I glanced up at Richard, half waiting for an insult to follow the compliment, but it never came.

'Georgie, would you like to come with me and meet your classmates?' Mr McGroaty asked. She seemed hesitant about the new environment so I nodded back, encouraging her to explore, and she toddled behind him.

As more parents entered the classroom, they were introduced to the group. No one, of course, made a cunt of the introduction the way I did, but eventually, I felt my shoulders fall and my pulse simmer down. But as the classroom filled, I couldn't help but wonder where Johnny was, so I took out my phone and texted him quickly.

Hey?? Where are you?? I'm at this prep school alone, and you're missing it all?

I slipped my phone back into my pocket and sat down, keeping Johnny a seat in the back row, waiting for the welcome presentation to begin. Georgie had settled down and was reading a book in the small library within the classroom.

'She's taking after you already.' I could smell Richards's deep, musky scent before he sat on Johnny's chair beside me.

I nodded back, still wary of his niceness towards me. *What was he after?* I wondered.

'I didn't realise she was ready to start school. How time flies, eh?'

'Why would you? You disappeared, remember?' A silence filled the space between us at my comment. 'I didn't know you had a niece.' I added, trying my best to get the gossip for Beka and Grace while also being standoffish, in case Johnny walked through the door and saw us conversing.

'Yes! She's a gem, isn't she?' Richard's dimples reappeared as he glanced over his shoulder, chuckling as he watched Beatrice play alongside the other children.

'So, Daphne's, I take it? How is she?' I replied, vaguely recalling his younger, crazier sister. I remembered she'd gotten expelled by her own father for breaking into the school one night and throwing an under-age rave in the dining hall.

'She's . . .' He paused and pulled down his shirt, looking unusually uncomfortable. 'She's OK at the moment, thank you. But B is great; she spends most of her time with me, and the school is practically on my doorstep, so I thought . . .' He shrugged. 'She deserves the best.'

'I'm not convinced by this fancy school, to be honest.' I sighed.

'And why is that?' Richard turned his body round to face me in the chair, and I immediately felt uncomfortable. I could feel him stare into my eyes, but I kept my gaze to the front of the classroom. 'Eh . . . Well, between me and you, we went to a regular school, and it didn't do us any harm.'

Richard shrugged. 'Yes, but my father was head-master. I didn't have a choice. This place has a stellar reputation.'

I sat back quietly, still unsure how anyone in their right mind could be willing to pay fifty thousand per term.

'Let's face it, Georgina would probably do well with your intellect behind her, but Beatrice needs . . .' He paused again. 'A little head start.'

He turned back to face the front and I felt relief sweep through me as he opened his welcome pack and began skimming through the pages. There was something quite intriguing about watching Richard become fully absorbed in his role as an uncle. I could never remember him being anything other than the arrogant arsehole who almost ruined my wedding day. My phone vibrated in my pocket, and I glanced down at a text from Rebeka.

SOS!

She would have to wait, I thought.

I clicked back to my message to Johnny. Read, but no reply. What the hell was going on? If nothing else, this was more Johnny's world than mine, and it would have eased Georgie's nerves to see her dad show up. I popped my phone back into my pocket.

'No Johnny today?' Richard asked casually, still skim-ming the booklet.

'He's held up,' I lied. I hated the fact I always felt a need to stick up for him.

'Shame,' Richard said smugly, raising one eyebrow.

'Shall we get this presentation underway?' Mr McGroaty called out as the other parents took their seats.

I scanned my phone again. No new messages. *Arsehole!* I could feel my entire body rattle with resentment.

'Welcome, everyone!' Mr McGroaty began, and for half an hour, I listened to the exciting opportunities and social prospects that the school had to offer.

Mr McGroaty wasn't at all what I'd imagined Georgie's teacher at a posh institute would be. I assumed he'd be some older, balding, conservative-loving prick in a fancy suit. Not this down-to-earth, handsome young Scot with a face I could sit on for hours! He was gorgeous, charming, funny, gracious and seemed great with the kids. I began to feel excited at the prospect of Georgie coming here. No bams, Buckfast or neds to distract her, just learning in what seemed to be a safe and nurturing environment.

'We also are pleased to offer the summer programme,' he said. 'This year, we've set up a one-week slot, starting on the 6th of July, for all the Year Ones to come along and settle into class. We'll welcome them into the school, play games, find their strengths, and generally make them feel comfortable with what to expect when they start in September. This is all covered in your tuition fees for the term, so if you'd like your child to come along, please fill in the application form before leaving today.'

I glanced over my shoulder to Georgie, who was colouring in with Beatrice while they chatted innocently away to each other. I nudged Richard with my elbow and gestured to the girls. I could see the relief on his face as he peeked over.

He leant towards me and whispered, 'Those two remind me of . . .'

Suddenly the door burst open, and Johnny barged in with snooty Ms Cross from the entrance.

'Apologies, I was held up at work,' he said loudly, before she even had a chance to introduce him to the room. 'I'm Mr Little, Georgina's father,' he said proudly, walking over and shaking the teacher's hand mid-PowerPoint.

'Fantastic, lovely to meet you, sir. Ava is sitting just over there. We're just about finishing off for today, but I'm sure she can fill you in.'

Johnny's eyes scanned the rows of parents until they rested on me. I watched his body tense as he saw Richard sitting beside me. *Shit.* He approached and stood directly behind my seat.

'And remember,' Mr McGroaty said, 'if you are interested in the summer programme, please complete the permission slip and leave it on my desk. It's only a couple of weeks away. If you have any questions or worries, do not hesitate to contact me. Thank you.'

My heart was pounding and my body was clammy. I didn't want to deal with Johnny making a scene in front of everyone. The other parents began standing up and collecting their children. I turned in my chair and shrugged as calmly as possible at him.

'Well, you missed most of it, but I saved you a welcome pack,' I said, trying to sound upbeat. But Johnny ignored me. His eyes were pinned on Richard.

'Why are you here?' His voice was deep and severe.

Richard smirked. 'Lovely to see you, Jonathan,' he said, then stood and walked past Johnny to summon his niece.

'Why is he here?' Johnny repeated, as tension filled the small classroom. I watched his pale skin turn red with anger. That was the thing about redheads, they can never hide their emotions.

'Shut up, will you?' I whispered. 'His niece, Daphne's daughter, is in the class!'

Johnny pulled a face and tutted, then turned as Georgie ran towards him. 'His niece? Who? Daphne's daughter?'

'Daddy!' She hugged him tightly.

'Hey! Look at you in the big school, eh! Shall we leave? Daddy has work to go to,' Johnny said quickly.

I shook my head. *He just got here and hasn't even seen the grounds.*

Johnny held Georgie in his arms and marched out of the school. I smiled as I hurried behind them, waving towards the parents I'd met, praying no one noticed our animosity. When we reached the car park, he put Georgie down.

'Why were you sitting with Richard Tierney? What was he saying?' he grunted at me, rubbing his stubbly chin.

'Why were you late?' I spat back. 'If you weren't late, maybe I'd have had someone to sit beside! It's only Richard, Johnny, for fuck's sake!'

He laughed, seeming furious at my reply. '*Only* . . . Only Richard! He tried to sabotage our wedding day. He embarrassed me in front of all our friends! Our family!'

He turned to Georgie. 'You stay away from that little girl, do you hear me? Her uncle is bad news!'

I felt Georgie hug my leg and I peered down at her.

'Stop it!' I hissed at him, rubbing Georgie's head. 'You're scaring her!'

'I have to go!' He strode towards his grey Porsche and unlocked it.

'Are you not dropping us back at the house? It took me over an hour to get here, Johnny!'

He glanced at me and then Georgie.

'I'm late for a meeting. Some of us have work to go to, Ava,' he snapped, then opened his car door and slammed it shut behind him.

I watched him pull out of the car park and drive away, then turned to my daughter and forced a smile.

'Well, that was fun! Why don't we go back on the tube, and you tell me all about your new friends, eh?' I said. Rage rippled through me, but I was trying my best not to show it for her sake.

Georgie bobbed her head, clutching my hand, and together, we walked towards the tube station. We had only dawdled along a hundred yards when I heard a familiar voice call out.

'So, what did you think of big school?'

I looked around to see Richard had pulled his car over to the side of the road.

'Fun,' Georgie yelled happily. I laughed at her cheerful face, glad she wasn't too upset about seeing her dad lose control.

'Well, would you look at those two happy girls, Beatrice,' Richard said.

Georgie waved to her new classmate as I smiled, taking a step towards Richard's black Range Rover.

'You again!' I said, pulling a face at him.

'I didn't get a chance to say goodbye. Hope you had fun today, Georgie!' He ran his hands through his thick hair and smiled.

Georgie grinned back.

'Fancy a lift home? Where are you staying now?'

I shook my head. 'God no. I'm in Croydon now. It'll be quicker on the tube. Just need to get to Victoria and then it's only a short train home. Thanks, though,' I replied. 'Say goodbye, Georgie.'

'Mummy!' Georgie moaned, tugging on my arm.

I gave her a warning stare, shaking my head.

'Ahh, Georgie prefers air-con and a leather seat!' Richard teased. 'Shall we take a vote?' Richard turned to his niece in the back, who gave a thumbs up, then back to Georgie and me. 'Hands up if you think we should drive the girls home?'

The three of them raised their hands immediately into the air, and he smirked towards me.

'C'mon, get in! You're outnumbered, Campbelle!' Richard said.

He got out and escorted Georgie around the car into the back seat beside Beatrice. I huffed hesitantly, scanning the street and hoping Johnny was well on his way, before hopping into the passenger side.

'Everyone strapped in?' Richard asked, returning to the wheel.

'Yep,' Beatrice giggled.

'And Little Miss Campbelle?' He smirked towards me cheekily.

'Yes, all strapped in here,' I replied, rolling my eyes at him.

'Excellent!'

Richard drove through the bustling streets of London as the girls chatted away in the back of the car. I fidgeted with my phone, refreshing it to ensure Johnny hadn't sent me a snidey message if he spotted me fraternising with the enemy.

'So how are things?'

I shrugged. 'Yeah. Fine,' I replied, not wanting to indulge in a weird friendship with Richard Tierney after years of hating the man. 'How's the publishing world?'

Richard shrugged briefly. 'Busy. You know how it is. He had rolled up his shirtsleeves and his tanned, muscular arms rested on the steering wheel as he spoke.

'What about you? How is,' he cleared his throat, attempting a Scottish accent, 'maw life!'

I turned to face him with my jaw open and slapped his arm.

Jesus, Ava, rock-hard bicep! Damn.

'I don't speak like that!' I giggled, my fingers twinging from touching his arm. 'But being a mum is hard, and being a single mum is even harder!' I laughed it off a little. 'I am planning on working again when Georgie's back at school, you know. I need to get out there again.'

'*Great*. Where are you thinking of applying?' he asked. 'I hear the advanced creative writing course at Cambridge has a fantastic reputation.'

I almost choked on my saliva, knowing I couldn't afford the bus fare to Cambridge, never mind a course there.

'*No*, no. Like waitressing or working at a bar. I haven't written anything in a long time, Richard,' I admitted.

He turned his head and narrowed his eyes at me, as if trying to determine whether I was joking or not.

'You can't, Ava! Come on!' He patted the steering wheel passionately.

I laughed at his over-the-top reaction. 'There's nothing wrong with waitressing!'

'I agree! If that's what you love. If that's your passion. But you have a talent; if you're not writing, at least work in that field.'

His voice resonated through me. I wasn't sure if I needed to hear his honesty or wanted to tell him to fuck off. I turned and peered out of the window. Writing had been my dream for so long, but after I got married, I'd struggled to pick up the laptop again. I suppose I'd had nothing to write about, being stuck in all day with a baby. I hated talking about my future, especially when I had no idea what I was doing, or where I would end up.

Silence took over the car for a few minutes.

'What about proofreading?' Richard eventually asked.

I hummed, wanting to drop the subject. 'What about it?'

'It's not writing your story, but more the fixing of other people's?'

'Like just reading other people's work?'

'Exactly. We're always on tight deadlines at the office, and it's a bloody nightmare finding someone with experience. I could speak to one of my staff, set up an informal chat and send you over some work.'

'*What?* Wait. No way! I've never done that before.'

'You're joking, aren't you? You proofread every one of my essays at university! You practically passed the course for me, Little! You did it then, you could do it again!'

'Your work was good, Richard. But you never could figure out how to correctly use a comma, could you?' I teased, keen to remind him that I was the better student.

He gasped in mock indignation and burst out laughing. Then he turned to me, his long, dark eyelashes getting caught in the sunlight.

'Think about it. You could work from home. Just meet the deadlines and email it back to the editor.'

'I . . . I'm not sure,' I said.

The truth was, I wanted to grab the opportunity with both hands and scream *YES!* But I couldn't help but wonder if this was all a ploy to piss off Johnny. *What was the catch?* What if I wasn't good enough? I hadn't written or edited for years. What if I made a complete cunt of myself, and Richard Tierney announced at the following high school reunion how terrible my English had become?

'Think about it over summer,' Richard suggested. 'No pressure.'

I nodded back and peered out of the window again while we listened to the radio for the rest of the journey.

An hour later, I began to recognise my area and breathed a sigh of relief that we were almost home. The whole day had been weird and uncomfortable. I struggled with social situations now, never mind introducing myself to an entire room full of judgemental parents. It had felt kind of good having Richard there, even if I could never admit it to anyone. But at least it was one person who knew the old me, and made me feel welcome.

'Right, Ava, where am I going here?' Richard asked.

'The end of this street is fine,' I said, pointing to the pub across the road.

'Are you sure? I can come closer,' he offered.

'No, here is fine, I'm just down the road.'

Richard stopped his car and unbuckled his seat belt.

'Well, thank you for the lift,' I said.

'Any time.' He grinned. His eyes rested on mine for a few seconds.

I turned to the girls in the back of the car, unusually flustered by his gaze. They were both fast asleep.

'Hard day at school.' I laughed.

Richard chuckled at the pair.

I got out of the car and opened the back door.

'Allow me,' he said, coming from behind. He leant forward and passed my daughter into my arms.

'Thanks.'

'I suppose I'll see you at school!'

'Yep, I suppose you will!'

He smiled, briefly waving as I crossed the road with Georgie in my arms. When we were safely to the other side, I turned and watched him gently peck his niece's head before returning to the driver's side.

Chapter Fifteen

Ava

I spent the following week pottering around my flat and watching Disney movies with Georgie. I needed to recover from the anxiety of the school day and finally felt relaxed hiding away at home. On Sunday morning, I heard a knock on the door. My stomach twisted at the thought of Adam showing up unannounced after my toxic vagina almost caused him to need a skin graft from fingering me. *Fuck!*

'Mummy, the door!' Georgie said as she turned to me, lying in between my legs.

'*Sssh!*' I insisted, getting up and tiptoeing towards it.

I could hear huffing from outside, and I cautiously opened the door.

'Thank God, let me in.' Grace barged past me, holding onto her nose. 'The smell of urine in that hallway is appalling!' she exclaimed. 'And your intercom is broken again.'

All I could do was shrug. I didn't disagree with her, but I had become weirdly accustomed to the smell of strangers' piss surrounding my doorway.

'Aunty Grace!' Georgie ran towards her.

'Hello, big girl! Oh, I've missed you! Here, look what Uncle Steve asked me to give you.' She rummaged around in her bag, found her purse and pulled out a ten-pound note.

Georgie gasped. 'Mummy, look!'

'Wow!' I gasped, hoping she had one in there for me too.

'That's for being brave and visiting the big-girl school!' Grace crouched down beside her, and Georgie hugged her tightly.

'Can I put it in the Mickey Mouse bank, Mummy?'

Pulling the tin from the bookshelf, I nodded. 'Of course you can!' I smiled as she pressed it in.

'Still obsessing over Disney World?' Grace hummed.

'We'll get there one day,' I said, rolling my eyes at the pressure. 'Georgie, we're popping into the kitchen for some tea, would you like some?'

'No thanks, Mummy,' she replied, more engaged in the television.

Grace and I headed into the kitchen.

'I just popped around because you and Beka have been AWOL from the group chat. Have you spoken to her?' Grace asked me, taking a seat at the small plastic dining table.

I screwed my face up to my sister, ready to defend myself, then suddenly remembered Beka's SOS message from school last week.

'Especially after she sent that weird message. I tried calling, but she won't pick up,' Grace said, looking worried.

'She's probably broken a nail, you know what she's like,' I said, laughing as I took a seat beside her.

'No, I have a feeling something's not right. She's been the one on at us for starting this hot girl summer thing, drumming it into us, telling us how we all need one another, and then she just disappears. What if something happened to her, Ava?'

I sat back and flicked through Instagram. 'She's not updated her Insta or Rogue's.'

'Which is strange, right? That phone is never out of her hand.'

'She'll be fine, Grace. Probably busy with work.'

'I think we should go round,' Grace said seriously. I could tell she was on the verge of panicking.

'What? Now?' I huffed. Till Grace came round, I'd been enjoying my seventh day in the house with my pyjamas on with Georgie. And it was my last day with her.

'Yes, now! This is what we signed up to!' Grace said. The determination in her voice echoed through the flat.

I glanced at the time on my phone. 'OK, well, Johnny's collecting Georgie soon, so we could go over after that.'

'Yes, OK. Great!' See settled herself.

'Right, I'll get organised then. Can you keep an eye on Georgie?'

'Of course.'

I dragged myself to my feet and headed into my bedroom. Sniffing the clothes piled on the floor to differentiate the clean pile from the dirty pile, I opted for a mostly clean pair of leggings and a jumper. I pulled my long dark hair into a ponytail, popped on some bronzer, and brushed my teeth.

Suddenly there was a loud knock at the door, and I felt my heart pound.

'Georgie! Daddy's here!' I wiped the toothpaste from my chin and jogged to the door.

Johnny stood with his back to me, chatting to someone on the phone when I attempted to greet him.

'Hi, you're early,' I said. He raised his hand to greet me, then pointed to his phone, basically urging me to stay quiet while he continued the call. I turned back inside, hearing Georgie behind me.

'Are you ready, baby?' I asked, bending over to zip up my daughter's jacket.

'Yep!' she replied, smiling back.

'I'll see you on Saturday night then.' I pressed her nose, and she laughed.

'Georgina, are you set?' Johnny asked, finally entering my flat.

'I'm all ready,' she said, picking up her bag.

'Just leave your bag, darling. Daddy has clothes at his house for you.' He took the bag from Georgie and sat it back on the floor.

'But I want my teddy,' she sighed, pursing her bottom lip.

Johnny huffed. 'Fine, but Teddy only!' he warned. 'And Teddy will be going in the washing machine for a bath when we get home.' As if to punctuate his point, he gazed around the dark flat, shaking his head at the clutter.

I felt my heart sink.

'Go on, baby, I'll see you in a couple of days,' I said. I winked towards her, and she hugged me tightly.

Johnny went for the door, ushering Georgie out. 'Oh, and Ava, we have to sort holidays out for the summer. I'm off the middle two weeks of July, and I want to take her somewhere.'

I raised my brows, surprised.

'*Oh*, right . . . Well, we haven't discussed holidays before. Where are you taking her? Your mum's?' I replied, instantly nauseous at the idea of not seeing my daughter more than a few days.

'I'm not sure, yet. Will you be going away anywhere?' he asked.

Georgie looked up at me, her face bright with excitement.

I chuckled under my breath at him. 'You know I can't go anywhere right now, Johnny.'

He nodded. 'Well, our dates won't cross over then. Say bye to Mummy.'

'Bye, Mummy,' Georgie replied, blowing kisses towards me.

I shut the door and pressed my back against it.

Why is this still so difficult? I wondered.

'Hey, are you OK?' Grace asked, poking her tiny red head out of the kitchen.

I stood up straight. 'Yeah, I'm fine. Should we head?' I asked, walking past her in the hallway.

'Is he always like that?' Grace asked. She seemed concerned.

'Like what?' I laughed.

'So dismissive. He spoke to you like a piece of shit, Ava.'

'He's stressed at work, and the break-up has been hard on him too. I think he takes it out on me sometimes.' I smiled, trying to brush it off.

'You are Georgie's mother, Ava. The way he spoke to you seems a bit unfair.'

'Life's unfair, sis! We should buy helmets!'

I picked up my phone and followed Grace out of my flat and down to her car.

Around two, Grace and I pulled up outside Rebeka's flat. The busy streets of Clapham were alive with businesspeople and tourists taking photographs in front of the picturesque bakeries that lined the small roads. We walked up to Beka's intercom and buzzed.

Nothing.

Grace tried again, then again.

'I told you she wouldn't be in,' I hummed after a few minutes.

Grace looked slightly defeated, stepping back onto the street. 'She must be busy with work, like you said,' she replied. 'I really thought we were all connecting again.'

I smiled at my sister. 'We are! For fuck's sake, Grace, we don't have to speak every day to be best friends. People have lives!'

She glanced at me, then lowered her eyes.

'C'mon! We can head back to mine,' I offered, gripping my sister's arm. I could see she was in need of some socialising, and by this point I was itching to get back into my pyjamas. 'We can watch a movie or something, have a girlie night?'

She managed a smile. 'That would be nice.'

As we headed back to the car, something twitched in the corner of my vision. I looked up to Beka's apartment and spotted the blinds moving.

'Grace! She's in there!' I pointed. 'Look!'

Grace glanced at her window. 'Why isn't she letting us in?'

I shrugged. Grace marched towards the intercom system and pressed down on the buzzer continuously.

'Grace! Grace!' I whispered, peering over my shoulder as people watched the crazy ginger losing her shit.

'No, Ava! She promised we were in this together, and she's bailed already!' I could see the anger build in her face as she continued to press the button.

Eventually, a croaky voice answered, 'What the fuck!'

'REBEKA, let us up NOW! You can't plan our whole summer then dinghy us after a week!' Grace squawked.

'Who's dinghying you? I'm unwell, I'll call you later.' But even through the intercom static, Beks sounded flat, unusually low.

'Rebeka, I promise I will keep my hand on this buzzer until you let us into your house!' Grace persisted.

There was silence for a few seconds, then the buzzer droned, and the door popped open.

Grace tugged down her Mac, flicked back her hair and entered.

We knocked on Beka's door, and when there was no answer, I turned the handle. It was open.

'Beks,' I called out, easing the door open.

'In here,' she replied from the bedroom.

The flat was dim and looked like it hadn't been tidied for weeks. That wouldn't have been strange at my place, but it was for Beka. When we got to the bedroom, we found the floor cluttered with pizza boxes and paper bags from takeaways. Beks was sitting in bed, pale-faced, puffy-eyed and bubbling into her pyjama sleeve.

'Are you . . . Is everything OK?' I asked.

'What do you think?' she managed, shaking her head.

Grace and I sat beside her on the bed.

'Beks, what's happened?' Grace asked gently.

'I don't want to talk about it,' Beks mumbled, then let out a little heave.

'Beks, come on,' Grace coaxed. 'You send us that SOS text, and then disappear, then we find you here crying in bed. Something's obviously happened. Tell us.'

'Yeah, Beks, we want to know what's upset you,' I added.

Beks took a few breaths.

'I was sacked from *Inner Me!*' she sobbed. Her red, bloodshot eyes began streaming again.

'*What?!*' I gasped.

'What do you mean? What happened?' Grace asked, pulling off her coat. Clearly, this was serious business.

'You know Ollie? The model from the reunion?' she bubbled.

Grace threw me a dirty look, recalling me pummelling him in the back of his Beetle.

I nodded back.

'He tried to bill the company because he shagged you!'

My mouth fell open.

'WHAT?' Grace bellowed. 'Beks, what do you mean?'

'Well, I asked them to come to the party as our dates, I said I would up the fee, like overtime or whatever, and I would have. We do it all the time if the shoot runs over. But his agency sent an email demanding a bigger fee because he shagged you!' She began crying loudly.

I felt dizzy.

What the actual fuck? I had been pumping a prostitute and wasn't even aware of it. I thought we'd connected.

'And this cow Karen brought me into a meeting and Mitchell was there. He fucking fired me!'

'So, they dismissed you because of an error in the accounts?' Grace asked, trying to wrap her head around the legality of her dismissal.

'They fired me because of Aussie the fucking prozzy. Let's be honest, babe,' she huffed, jolting her head back into the pillows.

I felt sick. I was the reason she was sacked. But I had no idea Ollie was a hooker. I had no idea I was shagging a professional escort. *Fuck, I thought I had my mojo back.*

'Beka, I'm . . . I'm sorry,' I said quietly.

'No, I'm sorry. I would never have set you up with

173

a prozzy, Ava. You know that. Unless you wanted me to,' she sobbed.

'And have you spoken to Mitchell since?' Grace asked.

She shrugged dramatically. 'He won't answer. I've called him over a hundred times, but I think I'm blocked. I've even mailed him on LinkedIn.'

'*Jesus,* Beks!' I said, taking it all in.

'I can't . . . We were going to be official. We were about to finally announce our relationship!'

I looked towards Grace, who seemed to be thinking hard.

'It's unfair dismissal. You can't sack someone on the spot. You have rights, a contract. You didn't even get to defend yourself!' Her eyes blazed with anger at the situation.

'Grace is right,' I said, 'you need to fight this.'

'And look!' Beka rustled around her bed and pulled out a copy of the magazine. It was the summer issue, and posing on the cover in glossy high-def was a stunning girl draped in diamonds. 'That's my shoot. The little girl, the fourteen-year-old, look! I made the cover,' she cried. 'They haven't even credited me with the image.'

I was shaking my head in sympathy just as I noticed Ollie posing beside the girl. *Fuck, he was gorgeous,* I thought, then shook it off.

'Listen, you don't want to be associated with an image when you didn't agree with it in the first place,' I said.

'I know,' Beks sobbed. 'I hate the fact she's fourteen, but I just made the fucking cover, Ava! Some

174

photographers never get that chance in their whole career. I should be fucking celebrating!' I wrapped my arms around her tightly.

'C'mon Beks! You'll get through this!'

She pulled away from me. 'How? How, Ava? I've lost my boyfriend and my job! Everything!'

Grace stood up. 'What about Rogue?'

'What about it?' Beks huffed.

'Well, have you posted anything on it recently?'

'I made the page, posted one old picture of my Mulberry bag, twenty-five likes from randoms, hun.' She seemed raging at the lack of interaction. 'I'm fucked. I have totally fucked everything. Who is going to employ the girl who billed the company for sex? Realistically, I'm fucking unemployable now.'

Grace tutted. 'No, you aren't. Stop this! Give yourself a shake, come on. You are Rebeka Hampson, and you are tougher than some shitty-ass magazine! Yes?'

Beka attempted a smile and nodded a little.

'Come here!' Grace leant forward and hugged our friend tightly. 'I could write a letter to *Inner Me!* A lawyer's letter – they'll have to respond. Tell them that it's unfair dismissal and put it to them that Mitchell has also broken company policy for the past year by sleeping with an employee. The full thing is just wrong!'

'I couldn't go back there, Grace. Are you joking? The entire building thinks I used the company's money for my hole!'

I held my head in my hands and groaned, it was all too much. 'Oh God.'

'Well, we'll ask Ollie to testify that it wasn't you! Get him to invoice Ava instead!'

'Me!' I shouted. 'I am the victim here! Plus, I can't afford a plumber, never mind a prozzie, Grace!'

My sister widened her eyes at me to stop. 'Clear your name, Beks. I'll ask for some money for loss of earnings and you'll be free to look elsewhere for a new job. Honestly Beks, I can do this!'

Beks looked to me for confirmation, and I nodded encouragingly. 'Sounds good to me, Beks.'

'Let me draft something, and you can look over it, OK?' Grace said.

'OK. I suppose,' Beks finally agreed.

'I think Rogue is a great idea though, to help you in the meantime. You know, take your mind off it all,' I said. 'So, what if it only has a few likes? You're just starting out!'

Beks shrugged. 'It's not a magazine though. It's just another Instagram fashion account.'

'Well, make it an Insta magazine – an online one. Get some stories and I'll help you write them. Make a website and we can link it all to your Instagram page. You're so creative, you could do this, Beka!'

I noticed a shift in my friend's face as I spoke, a small glimmer of light sparkled behind her eyes.

'I think . . . I think I might actually have an idea,' she said, her voice still croaky as she wiped down her tears onto her sleeve. 'Pass me my phone, Ava, quickly! I have an idea.'

I turned to my sister and smiled.

Chapter Sixteen

Grace

The following morning, Grace sprang out of bed with sheer determination. Today, she felt like she had a purpose – getting justice for her friend. She slipped on her housecoat and headed downstairs to prep her morning smoothie, which was full of fruit and vegetables, humming happily as she blended it. Steve had already left for work that morning, so she poured out the smoothie and headed back upstairs to use his office computer.

As she entered, she smiled at the mountain of paperwork and notes her husband had taken for his latest case. She skimmed her hands along the library of books dedicated to the law she once loved, then sat at the desk. She clicked on the desktop, opened a Word document, and began typing.

Dear Sir/Madam,
I am writing on behalf of my client, Rebeka Hampson. Miss Hampson contacted me and explained her situation regarding the recent

termination of services at the Inner Me! *magazine chain. This quick decision made by your company holds a strong case for an unfair dismissal dispute. It has been brought to my attention that many inequitable and unjust actions were carried out, ultimately leading managers to terminate her contract without considering employee rights.*

I would appreciate a meeting at your earliest convenience to discuss this matter thoroughly, and I look forward to hearing from you.

Grace Campbelle

Grace read the letter over several times, adjusting the wording here and there. When she was happy with it, she opened an internet browser to search for an email address to send it to. But before she could even type anything into the search bar, the screen filled with images of gimp suits, leather and latex. She gasped in horror. *What the hell?* She closed the browser, waited a few seconds, then clicked it open again. Just like before, multiple naked men in dog collars and cock chains flooded the screen. *Was this a virus?*

She sat back, tilting her head, trying to comprehend the content as her stomach twisted.

Then, after a deep breath, she clicked on Steve's browser history.

Grace held her hand over her mouth as she scrolled through the web pages he'd been visiting. *Pornhub, OnlyFans, FetishFreaks . . .* It was an endless screed.

She sat for a few minutes in disbelief. After a while, she noticed her hands were trembling. *What the hell has my husband been up to?*

'Grace, darling, are you home?' Steve's voice called out, making her jump.

'Yip, be down in a second,' she replied, not quite knowing what to do with the information on screen.

Then, pushing back a wandering tear, she searched for the *Inner Me!* contact details. She copied the email address along with her letter into an email and sent it to the HR department.

Grace cleared her throat, flicked back her hair, and headed downstairs to greet her husband.

Ava

Across town, I woke up to the sound of Beka calling me.

'*Babe, are you there?*'

I glanced at my watch – *9:30 a.m.* – and sighed. '*I am now. What's up?*'

'*You better get up; I need your help! Get dressed and meet me at Fleet Street at twelve.*' I was drifting off again. '*AVA, I need you to get a move on, hun.*'

She sounded eager but frantic. I pulled myself into a sitting position, still waking up properly. I'd been hoping for a day in bed since Georgie was with her dad.

'*Why? What? What's going on, Beks?*'

'I have a shoot today! I'm heading out now to buy a new lens for my camera, but I need you to go to Agent Provocateur and buy a few of the sexiest underwear sets they have and bring them with you. OK?'

I giggled. 'Beks, what kind of fucking shoot are you doing?'

'Wait till you see! It will be stunning, hun!'

Knowing how upset she'd been the past few days, I grinned, relieved at her energy. 'Can't wait.'

'I'll see you at twelve then, don't be late. I've dropped you a pin for the address.'

'Beks, wait! I don't have any cash for the underwear!' I felt my face turn red, admitting to my friend, yet again, how skint I was.

'Already transferred you! Get ready. And Ava?'

'Hmm . . .?'

'Look nice, professional kind of vibe. Bring a notepad. Love you!'

As the phone cut out, I couldn't help but laugh. What the fuck did she have in store for us today? Dragging myself out of my bed, I glanced around my bedroom and saw the mounds of clothes piled up. The sun was beaming through the cheap fabric curtains, and I looked out the window at the town below. People wandered the crowded streets, and already the buskers were playing music. Commuters with headphones marched through while bars set up their outdoor seating areas for the summer rush to begin. I opened the window and let some fresh air in before rummaging around to find clothes for the photoshoot.

An hour later, I was battling through Central London, Google Mapping my way to the nearest Agent Provocateur. As I entered the Mayfair shop, I was greeted by slender women with impeccable makeup.

'Can I help you today?' one asked.

'Emm . . . I'm just having a look, thanks,' I replied, feeling a little self-conscious at being surrounded by racks and racks of unbelievably sexy underwear. *I remember being able to wear this shit, now my mummy muffin pops out. Personally, I think I would be sexier in a wetsuit.*

And *Jesus, the prices!* Seventy quid for a pair of knickers? I started to scope out the collections, lifting some for inspection.

Crotchless – *nope.* Kittycat tassels – *nope.* The Peephole Collection – *fuck no!*

I rummaged around my handbag to grab my phone and began dialling Beka.

'*Yeah, babe?*' she answered.

'*Right, I'm in this shop and have no idea what to get. It's all crotchless, or the knicks are made from fucking dental floss!*'

Beks laughed. '*It's all sexy! It was Mitch's favourite shop.*' There was a brief silence, then she cleared her throat. '*Let me look online, and I'll phone you straight back. The model is a size twelve. I'll call you back.*'

'*Beks! Beks, wait!*'

But she had already hung up. The sales assistants looked on at me while I wandered around the shop, feeling utterly uncomfortable as I pretended to admire the whips and leg-spreading bars as if I were an expert.

Suddenly, my phone began ringing, and I hurriedly answered.

'Thank fuck, you were ages! I feel like a pervert standing here!' I grunted.

'Hello . . . eh . . . Ava? Ava Little?'

My heart began beating in my chest as I pulled the phone from my ear and looked at the screen. Unknown number.

'Yes, yes, sorry about that. This is Ava . . .'

'Fantastic, it's Mr McGroaty, Georgie's teacher, we met at welcome week?'

I felt the blood drain from my body in a second.

'Yes! Hi. We did! How are you, sir?' I asked. Sir? Why the fuck am I calling him sir?

'Erm . . . yes, I'm very well. I was calling as you didn't hand in the permission slip for the summer programme. Did you have other plans, or did it slip your mind? It's a great introduction to the term for Georgie.'

'Oh, shit! Sorry! I forgot. I left in such a rush. But, yes, she would love to be involved.'

'Ideal. Could you pop into school today at some point to sign the form? Then we can move things forward.'

I glanced at my watch – it was half past ten. 'Yep, I can probably pop down in the next . . . hour. I have a meeting at midday, but I should be able *to make both*.'

'*Fantastic. See you then, Ava!*'

The line went quiet. Stress rattled through my body. What a fucking idiot I'd made of myself – *again!* When I glanced back at my phone, there was a message from Beka.

I tried calling. Get this x

Photos of three different lacy underwear sets came through, and I approached one of the assistants, feeling more hassled than I had in years.

'Hi, could I have these sets all in size twelve, please?'

She glanced at the pictures and then nodded. 'Certainly!'

A few minutes later, she handed me a bag with the lingerie carefully folded inside, and I jogged to the tube, hoping to make it to Ealing and back in time.

I hopped off the tube and marched towards the private school entrance, sweating and flustered from a mental morning I wasn't prepared for. I pressed on the intercom, tapping my foot as I glanced at my watch. Ten past eleven. I had just under an hour to get to Beka for her photoshoot. I suddenly noticed the Agent Provocateur bag swinging freely on my arm and panicked. *What the fuck am I doing?* I couldn't enter this place with that! I was frantically pulling out the garments and stuffing them into my handbag when I saw a figure approaching the door. I crumpled the empty paper bag into a ball and squeezed it into my pocket.

The door opened, and a smiley Mr McGroaty greeted me.

'Ava! That was quick! Thanks so much for coming down,' he said. He was wearing trendy jeans and a hoodie, looking much more casual than the last time I saw him.

Jesus, he was gorgeous. *What is it about a guy in a hoodie?* I wondered. Maybe because I spent most of my childhood in Glasgow fantasising about the hot neds in trackies, taking eccies round the back of the shops.

183

'Public transport, eh.' I smiled awkwardly as I looked into his dark eyes.

'Please, come in.'

He led me through the school towards the classroom. I ducked my head to avoid some cute little rainbows dangling from the ceiling.

'These are sweet,' I said, pointing.

'Ahh, each child gets their face on a rainbow,' he explained.

'It's adorable! I didn't get that at school, that's for sure,' I laughed.

He shook his head. 'Aye, me neither! Things are different now – in a good way!'

'Definitely.'

'So, where are you travelling from? Not too far, I hope?' He said, gently resting his arse on a desk.

'Well, I live in Croydon,' I shrugged. 'But I was in the city when you called.'

He smiled back. 'Have you been to the *The Front Room*? It's my favourite place in the whole of London.'

I smiled and nodded at the mention of the popular bar down the street that had live soul music every night. 'YES! The singers are insane! How are they not famous, though? I actually stay just down the street from there.'

He scoffed. 'You're so lucky!' He leant forward and tapped my hand. I glanced up and he pulled it back immediately. 'Sorry, Ava,' he chuckled.

Jesus, don't be. I thought. He could touch much more than my hand if he wanted to.

I blushed, looking around the room, at the slight awkwardness.

'So, erm . . . yes, here's the form. If you just read through it, sign at the bottom, and Georgie can come Monday to Friday next week for her induction.'

He passed me the form, making sure not to touch me, while I glanced over it.

'Looks good to me. Do you have a pen?'

'Ahh, I should do, one second. They all seem to be coloured felt tips around here.' He rustled around his desk.

'It's fine. I should have an adult one here somewhere!' I smirked, resting my bag on my knee and rummaging through the bottom. I felt the pen and pulled it out, along with a lacy black and red G-string. I watched in horror as it sprang in slow motion from the end of the pen and onto the floor.

'Oh my God, I'm sorry,' I gasped, lunging to the floor for it.

'Wow, Ava!' Mr McGroaty clapped his hands and laughed loudly as he observed my blunder. 'Wow.'

I felt my cheeks go purple. *Kill me now, God. Please, kill me.*

'Can I see?' he asked.

'What? See what?' I asked, feeling my heart pump hard through my entire body. Even my hands were vibrating.

'Can I see what you have in your hand – I mean, if you're OK with that?'

I paused, my hand still clutched in a tight fist.

'You do know this is underwear I have, though?' I said, hoping he hadn't thought it was something entirely different and that I hadn't just made another complete cunt of myself.

He leant forward on the desk a little. 'I'm a big boy,' he whispered.

The hair on the back of my neck stood up. *What the fuck was going on?* How big? *How fucking big?!* I wondered.

'It's just a set I picked up this morning,' I said, lying and pretending they were mine. In reality I knew both my flaps would be sticking out the side of the material like a hotdog bun. I closed my eyes briefly as I unclasped my hand, revealing the tiny thong.

He leant back for a second and held his hand to his mouth. I watched his bottom lip fold as he fumbled.

'Wow! *Erm* . . . you have good taste.'

'It's very inappropriate for school. I'm sorry!' I attempted to move my hand and pop it back into the bag when I felt him clutch my wrist.

He was so close I smelled his fresh minty breath hit my face before he leaned forward and kissed me.

I could feel my heart pound heavily. His lips felt soft.

He stood back after a few seconds.

'I'm sorry.'

'No, I mean, don't be sorry,' I insisted, wondering what was going to happen next.

'After I met you the other day, I have thought about you, a lot.' There was something attractive about his Scottish accent, it felt familiar and safe.

I paused, completely speechless, raising a brow. I mean, he had crossed my mind, in terms of appreciating his unbelievably good looks, but fucking hell, I didn't expect to be winching him in his classroom.

May I?' he asked.

I looked at him curiously. 'May you? What?'

Mr McGroaty laughed a little, then sighed, like he was already regretting what he was about to say. 'May I borrow your underwear for a few days? I promise I'll return them to you.'

'Really?' I blushed. *What the fuck was he wanting with the undies? The kinky bastard!* 'I don't know if they'd fit you.' I laughed, attempting to ease the tension.

'I don't intend to wear them.' He quickly covered his face in frustration. 'I'm sorry, this is so completely inappropriate from me. I shouldn't be kissing parents or asking them for this, but I can't help it with you.'

I felt myself hesitating. I mean, he was utterly gorgeous and handsome, and it wouldn't hurt to have at least one teacher on side at the school.

'Awk, take them! And it's fine. It was a really nice kiss.' I smiled, throwing them to him.

As he caught them, I noticed his eyes roll back in relief. Giggling like a schoolgirl and too embarrassed to make eye contact, I bent over the desk and signed Georgie's permission slip.

'Well . . . this has been . . . *kinda weird*. I suppose I should go, I have to meet my friend and I can't be late. But I'll see you next week, Mr McGroaty!'

'Very weird! And yes, you certainly will, Miss Little. Next week!' With a massive grin, he walked me to the door, and I exited the building.

As I sat down on the tube, I couldn't help but giggle every time I thought of Mr McGroaty. *What the fuck just happened? What the fuck did he want with the underwear?* I blushed, wondering what would happen next between us. Could anything happen? I mean, he was Georgie's teacher. *Would that be wrong? Private tuition wouldn't go amiss, I mean, there was always that.*

Fuck, what would Beka say? She'd specifically asked for that set. My imagination halted as I approached my stop. I stood up and texted her.

> *Hey, just a few minutes away. Lost the black and red lace thong on the way. It's a long story, but I have the other two xx*

I wondered who she'd be photographing in this racy underwear. She'd probably talked one of her model friends into a shoot, and I was going to have to type up a story for her first Rogue post on sexy underwear. *'The key to a great sex life?'* I shuddered at the thought. I was damp with sweat as I exited the warm tube station. It had been the busiest morning since I was at university. Fuck, I was usually still lying in bed scratching my arse at this time most days. I followed Beka's pin on WhatsApp, which directed me to a large tenement building on Fleet Street. I opened the door, and a security man greeted me.

'Can I help you?'

'I'm looking for my friend, Beka Hamp—'

'Level nine,' he interrupted, then leant forward, pressing the lift door for me.

'Thanks.'

As I stepped out onto the floor, I was immediately met by flashing lights from Beka's camera and the sound of her strong accent calling out orders. I walked through the studio set-up and found a girl sat on a stool, allowing Beka to screentest the lighting.

'Hey!' I whispered to my friend.

'You're late!' she warned me, still snapping the shots.

I smiled a little, knowing I was a few minutes late, but that cunt had no idea the morning I'd had.

I walked around the set. It was so cool. So professional. Backdrops hung from the ceiling, while rows of expensive-looking lights, cameras and laptops sat out for Beka to use.

'Right, babe. The lighting is spot on. This is my friend Ava I was telling you about.'

I turned to the girl she was snapping. She was young, in her late twenties, with dark skin. I instantly noticed scarring down one side of her face and neck, but forced myself not to stare.

'This is Lina,' Beks said. 'I want you to interview her while I set up.'

I nodded. 'Sure, OK!' I waited for further instructions but Beks was submerged in her laptop already. 'Do you mean now?' I asked.

'Yes, I mean now. I only have this place for an hour!' She rolled her eyes sassily, but I could see she was flustered. This was her first solo job, I reminded myself. She didn't have the backing of the magazine now, so she was relying on herself . . . and me.

'Perfect. *Erm* . . .' I gulped, suddenly feeling nervous, and glanced around the room. I spotted two beanbags sitting against a wall. 'Do you want to come over here?' I asked Lina.

She bobbed her head and followed me, taking a seat.

I sat down carefully, trying to find my balance on the beanbag and to act as professionally as I could. 'I have no idea about your story, Lina, I'm sorry. This piece was just handed to me to write. So why don't we start with you telling me what you'd like me to write about,' I suggested, taking out my notepad and pen from my bag.

Lina hummed a little, and I watched her shoulders relax. 'I want to tell you what happened to me,' she said. I felt chills run up my arm and I nodded back, 'I'd love to hear it,' I smiled towards her. 'Just start by introducing yourself and take it from there.'

'Well, my name is Lina Moyo.' I smiled at how confident she came across from the get-go. 'Last year, when I was twenty-six, I was living it up with my best mate and I had just landed my dream job in advertising. My life was perfect, not that I knew that at the time. But it was. I know that now.'

I glanced up at her, feeling a stab of relatability. It wasn't until everything fell apart in my world that I realised how lucky I was, too.

'Go on,' I encouraged her, pen poised over my notepad.

'Well, my best mate was going on a Tinder date. She'd had so many dates before, and this one was like any other, I suppose. Anyway, when she's out, we share our locations with one another – just to be safe, you know? So, while she's out, I get a text saying, 'Please come and get me. This guy is scary, and I've tried to say I'm going to head home a few times now, and he seems angry.'' As she spoke, I admired her confidence. I watched her hair shine as the sunlight crept in, and I couldn't help but admire how stunningly beautiful she was. Not just physically, but she had an aura which surrounded her.

'So, I went to the pub they were in and asked her to come home,' Lina continued. 'I made an excuse and said there had been an emergency. But the guy grabbed my wrist and said she couldn't leave yet, and I had to leave her alone. That's when my friend pushed him. She basically told him to go away, but he was up in my face, you know, very aggressive, so yeah, she pushed him off me, and we ran out of the pub.'

My heart beat hard in my chest. A feeling of dread crept into my stomach. I was hoping somehow this story wasn't going where I suspected it was. I nodded, scribbling the details quickly as she spoke.

'We went on the tube, back home together, thinking that was the end of him.' She sighed briefly. 'But then as we were leaving the station and walking to our flat,

I noticed a guy striding towards us. It was weird, he looked like he was holding a coffee or something. And it all happened so quickly. We didn't even notice it was him until it was over. He walked up to my friend, calling her a fucking bitch, and threw the liquid at her. But I saw he was going to do that, so I pushed her out of the way, and . . .' She held her hands up and turned to show the scars on her face and neck. 'It was acid.'

I gasped, feeling a lump in my throat. I glanced at the streaks of damage he'd caused; from her eye, the smooth texture of her skin became waves of scar tissue, spreading down to her neck. I felt my eyes fill. *How could anyone do that to someone?*

'I mean, who the fuck carries acid with them on a night out?' She chuckled a little under her breath.

'So, what happened next?' I asked, trying not to let my reaction show too much. I wanted her to trust me, not to feel like she had to comfort me.

'He went to prison for five years. He'll be out in three for good behaviour, and I'll be left looking like this for the rest of my life. I've had nine surgeries, multiple skin grafts. I lost my job because of how much time I had to take off to recover, and I hardly go out anymore.'

I shook my head, observing the strong woman in front of me. She was bright, resillient, brave, beautiful and unique. I couldn't believe how she'd managed to cope after what happened to her. I felt a glimmer of guilt wash through me thinking about how dramatic and pitiful I'd been following a break-up, when this girl had overcome this horrific attack.

'How is your friend?' I asked, hearing my voice quiver as I continued.

Her face lit up. 'She's OK. She's glued to my side and works hard to pay our bills now, you know?'

'She's lucky to have you.' I leant over and squeezed her hand, but she shook her head.

'I'm the lucky one. I would do it again tomorrow for her.'

I glanced over at Beka, who was fidgeting with the lights, perfecting her shot set-up, and felt a warm gush of love for my friend.

'So today, I take it we are bringing awareness to what happened? For girls to be safe on dating sites?' I asked.

Beka walked towards us. 'Today, we're making Lina feel like the sexiest woman alive. We are showing her scars and how incredible she is – *and* raising awareness in the process! Isn't that right, babe?' Beks smiled.

'Too right it is!' Lina clapped her hands excitedly.

Beks cheered. 'Right, let's get this started then!'

I dove into my bag and passed her the undies, and she grinned wide.

'Holy fuck, these are sexy!' She laughed out loud, and the sound echoed through the studio.

We spent the rest of the afternoon snapping Lina Moyo.

Chapter Seventeen

Ava

After the photoshoot, I left the studio with Beks, feeling more hyped up than I'd been in years. My legs were bouncing as we walked down the street, invigorated and ecstatic about what she had created.

'That was amazing, Beka!' I gushed, looping my arm through hers.

'It was, eh!' She was radiating pride and, more importantly, contentedness.

'How brave, and the story. *Oh my God,* I love her!' I replied, reflecting back on the afternoon spent with Lina.

'Well, make sure you do her justice!' Beka winked and pulled out her phone. 'I know you will, babe. Hmm, should we text Grace and grab a drink together?'

I hesitated. I wanted nothing more in that moment than to celebrate with the girls, but drinks in this part of the capital started at twenty quid a pop.

'My treat, obviously, hun. For a hard day's work!' Beka added quickly, as if she read my mind.

I nodded back. 'OK then, but just the one!' I insisted. 'I want to get started on that article.'

Beka: *Hey babe, fancy meeting up? I'm with your sis, and we're going for a cocktail. Lots of exciting things to discuss! xx*

'Should we pull a cab for Sexy Fish?' Beks asked, scanning the limited number of cocktail bars around.

I smiled. 'Let's walk. It's only up the road, and it's a lovely day!'

We set off towards Mayfair, arm in arm in the sunshine.

'I haven't even told you what happened at Georgie's school induction! Or, what happened today when I went to the fucking school!' I said.

'Oh babe, I hate when people with kids start telling single people who don't have kids about this sort of thing. Honestly, I love you, I love Georgie, but school inductions . . .' She threw her head back dramatically.

'That's fine then. I was actually going to tell you about Richard Tierney being there, but fuck you then, Beks!'

She stopped in her tracks and turned to me.

'*Dick?* I take it all back. You have my attention! Why the fuck was Big Dick there?'

I began telling Beka all about our unexpected meeting and how Johnny reacted when they saw each other. She laughed and gasped as I divulged about the job offer and how he ran me and Georgie home that afternoon.

'I didn't realise that mad bitch Daphne had a kid!'

'Beks!' I warned, 'But yep, she's lovely. A tiny, shy wee thing, Beatrice.'

Beka screwed up her face. 'Poor girl!'

I gasped and nudged her arm. 'Beks!'

'Imagine growing up in this day and age and calling your child Beatrice!' She shook her head in dismay.

'Well, you know that family, they're into literature. Maybe it's after Beatrix Potter? I'm not actually sure if she spells it that way.' I shrugged.

'And I'm into fashion, but I wouldn't call my kid Balenciaga, Ava, would I?'

'Well, Richard calls her B,' I said, feeling the need to stick up for the poor child.

'I'm not surprised. He's probably mortified with Beatrice!' She paused and then said, 'So, are you taking him up on the job? It would properly piss Johnny off.'

I huffed. 'I don't think he's reliable. I mean, after my wedding day. And he obviously hates Johnny. I just think it's a little too much to accept. It'll rock everything with Johnny.'

Beks turned to me. 'Babe, it's an offer nevertheless. Even if it's for a few months, it'll get you some cash, some routine, *and* some experience.' She shrugged. 'I think it's a no-brainer. You don't know where it could lead. And besides, does Johnny have to know?'

I tilted my head, thinking it over. It was the only offer of work I'd had in such a long time and I needed the cash. Realistically, working for Richard and being able to work around Georgie's school hours was the best offer I'd probably ever get, but I didn't want to upset Johnny. I wanted him back – I needed my old life back – and accepting a job from Big Dick Tierney would set us back massively.

At the same time, our phones beeped.

Grace: *Sure, where are you guys thinking? I will get a taxi now, need out this house! x*

Beka messaged her back, and we made our way towards Sexy Fish in Mayfair. A restaurant so fancy it had security men outside. As we walked through the entrance Beks winked at one, who smiled as he held the door open for us.

I turned to her and laughed. 'How do you know him?' I asked.

'I come here a lot.' She shrugged. 'Evannah, how are you?' Rebeka approached the hostess, kissing her on both cheeks.

The young, elegantly dressed girl smiled brightly. 'I wasn't expecting you! Is it a private lunch?' she asked in a Russian accent.

'No, no, just a few celebratory drinks with two friends.'

Evannah nodded, lifting menus and leading us through to the seated area at the bar. I glanced around as I sat down; vivid oceanic colours and designs swirled along the vast ceiling. All of the servers exuded a welcoming vibe and, in their bright suits, they looked as if they'd just stepped off a catwalk. I gazed at a stunning mermaid statue and huge crystallised blue whale hanging from the ceiling. Wow. I'd never been anywhere like this.

'Lush, eh?' Rebeka smiled, glancing over the menu.

I nodded, still admiring the restaurant. 'So nice!'

'It's Mitchell's favourite. We come here a lot,' she said quietly, still skimming the cocktail list.

My heart felt heavy for my friend. 'I thought you couldn't . . . like, go out . . . in public?' I asked.

She popped the menu down and pointed to the other end of the room. 'There are private dining rooms in there with the most stunning wall aquarium. We'd come here a few nights a week and the staff were always great at keeping it discreet.'

I reached over and squeezed her hand.

'But that was before he was a cunt. Now, pick a drink! I'm having the Bergamot and Jasmine, it's unreal!'

I smiled as my friend brushed off her ex in a heartbeat, wishing I could do that with Johnny. Even though I knew she didn't mean it; I could see she was hurting deep down.

'I'll have the same if it's that good!'

We ordered our drinks and indulged in some salted sugar snap peas while Beka flicked through her camera.

'These pictures are really fucking nice, babe. I am so good. Wow. Lina's going to love them,' she said.

I had a mouth full of peas when my sister barged in looking much more dishevelled than her normal prim and proper self. She was wearing a black jogging suit and had her hair scraped back into a ponytail.

'Oh, I love this place! I came last year with Steve. The grilled prawns and truffle fried rice is honestly stunning!' she said quickly, taking a seat.

'Finally, you're here. Ava has almost demolished the second bowl of peas!' Beks said, smirking in my direction.

I hadn't eaten anything other than a packet of Frubes in two days, still scrimping to get by. I wiped my hand on my napkin and swallowed the veg.

'How's things with you, Grace?' I asked, noticing my sister's tense behaviour.

'Good, good. I sent that email to *Inner Me!* – still waiting on a reply – and I had a workout today. And . . . and . . . and I think my husband's a pervert, so yes, good apart from that.' She reached across the small round table, grabbed my drink and downed it.

I laughed a little and glanced at Beka, who was sipping at her cocktail.

'Wait, what?' I asked.

Grace put down my empty cocktail glass and politely wiped the sides of her mouth on a napkin. 'Yes, my husband is a pervert. I saw his computer history and he's been looking at the most frightening, disgusting things.' I could see the worry behind her eyes as she sat back in the chair. 'Excuse me,' she asked a passing waitress, 'could I have another one of the cocktails they're drinking?'

'Can you make it two?' I added.

'Hun, you better make it three,' Beks piped up. When the waitress left, Beka turned to Grace. 'OK, so all men are slightly perverted babe. It's a fact. What exactly did you see?'

'Well, he's been looking at a lot of Lycra things and fetish things on Pornhub, that seems to be his favourite genre.' Her pale cheeks began to redden. 'But he has also subscribed to Kinkycock91's OnlyFans.'

'Ok. Well, Pornhub is basic, babe. It's porn.' Beks shrugged. 'Fuck, if you checked my browser I'd be the same! I don't think it's a perversion, it's more human nature. But OnlyFans . . . that's subscribing to someone.'

I sighed. 'Have you asked Steve? Maybe he was researching for a case?'

Both of them glared at my naive response.

'I don't like it. Any of it. He won't have sex with me, but he wants to watch these big-titted porn stars with peroxide hair instead?'

'Well, fucking tell him that, babe! Tell him you're not comfortable with that. Ask him what turns him on in the bedroom. Do a bit of roleplay or whatever, and that will get him going!'

Our drinks arrived and I watched my sister gulp hers down quickly once more.

'When is he due home tonight?' I asked.

Grace glanced at her watch. 'He's home now.' I watched as her eyes filled with tears. But she held them back. Grace didn't do public breakdowns.

'Babe, I don't think this is as big a problem as you think. Honestly. Mitch and me would watch porn together,' Beks admitted proudly. 'Some Fake Taxi shit always got him going!'

'Johnny was the same, he liked the fuck-the-hotel-maid genre. No wonder I was so fucking paranoid,' I shuddered.

I watched my sister's face twist at the thought. 'I just don't get it. He's never tried anything like that with me! Anytime we have sex it's plain old marital sex. Nothing spicy, and it has certainly never involved Lycra!'

'Maybe he's embarrassed,' Beks said. 'I think sex changes when you get older. Maybe he's found something that turns him on and is afraid you'll judge him for it.'

I agreed, watching my sister's brain buzz around like a beehive.

'I should go. I should tell him what I found.' Grace stood up and took a long, deep breath. She reached across the table and grabbed my cocktail. 'Another sip for courage!' she said, and gulped down half my drink.

'Grace, don't go,' I said half-heartedly, but I could tell she just wanted to be alone.

'I'll call you later,' she said quietly, and left.

'So much for celebratory drinks,' Rebeka scoffed.

'So much for drinks! All I can taste is peas!'

'That's because you ate them all, you greedy bastard!' She burst out laughing and I joined in. Then we both glanced out the window and watched my sister hail a taxi.

'I didn't think Steve would have anything like that in him,' I said, disheartened as she zoomed away.

'They all have it in them, Ava. That's the problem.'

Chapter Eighteen

Grace

As Grace walked up the steps of her townhouse, her heartbeat rang heavily in her ears at the thought of confrontation with her once perfect husband, but she knew she had to. There was an increasing part of her that didn't want to know the extent of what was happening. *What if everything was about to change?* What if she was left unemployed and homeless like her sister? For a moment, she wondered about saying nothing. Maybe everything would remain the same, and she could get on with life as normal. But deep down, she knew something in her marriage had shifted. It hadn't been right for a while now. She wondered if this could be it. Maybe Steve's obsessing with random women online had made him lose focus on her. Maybe that's why they didn't have sex anymore. Perhaps that's why she'd been feeling lonely. She paused at the door and checked her emails, stalling, hoping for a reply from *Inner Me!* – nothing. Grace hummed. *Am I overreacting?* She wondered. *Do most men watch porn?* But inside she couldn't help but feel disrespected. Steve had never tried anything kinky or fetish-like on her, and why not? *Does he think I'm so uptight I couldn't put on a gimp mask or talk dirty to him?* She shook it off, knowing she had to confront him; it was too humiliating.

Grace eventually inserted her key into the lock and watched her hands tremble as she turned the door handle. She stopped and took a breath before walking in.

'Steve,' she called out, slipping her shoes off in the hallway.

'In here, darling.'

She followed his voice into the kitchen, where he sat reading a newspaper. He didn't look up as she entered.

'Good day?' he mumbled, turning the page.

Grace resisted a smile, feeling a punch in the gut. 'I've had better. And you?'

'Pretty similar.' He closed the paper.

'I need to talk to you,' she said, walking towards him.

He rolled his eyes slightly, not looking keen to participate in a discussion. 'Isn't that what we're doing?'

Grace stood a few feet in front of him and sighed. 'Today, I wrote a letter for Rebeka to her company's HR department for unfair dismissal,' she began.

'She was fired?'

'Yes. And unfairly. So, I said I'd represent her. Try to get some compensation or apology, at least.'

'And . . . you'd like my help? Darling, I'm swamped at work. I'm far too busy to get involved in some silly—'

'I don't need your help, Steve!' Grace snapped.

He raised his brows at her reaction and crossed his arms in his chair.

Grace composed herself. 'I was in your office sending that email and saw your browsing history,' she said.

Steve remained incredibly still. Silence filled the space between them.

'Steve?' Grace pushed.

'What are you trying to say, Grace?' He seemed uneasy, fidgeting around in his chair.

'I want you to tell me what the fuck is going on? *Fetish Freaks? Pornhub? OnlyFans?* What the fuck are you doing, Steve? Do you think you can treat me like an idiot?' She hadn't meant to lose her shit, but all the anger, confusion and anxiety came out now, tears streaming down her face.

'I don't know what you're referring to, Grace.' Steve shook his head, attempting to laugh a little. 'I've never heard of those sites.'

Grace's heart plummeted as the lies flew out of his mouth. 'I saw everything! Tell me.'

The room remained painfully quiet. Steve's face was blank, refusing to give anything away.

'Jesus Christ, I'm your fucking wife!' Grace shouted, her voice echoing through the room.

Steve opened his mouth, then paused. 'I . . . OK,' he sighed, 'on occasion, I have looked at websites like this. But you should know, darling, most men do.' He laughed it off a little. 'Research it.' He paused again, and for the first time he seemed to see her face properly. 'I don't want you upset now, Grace. It doesn't mean I love you any less.' He stood up and took a step towards her.

'But you won't touch me! You won't come near me! And you have never tried or discussed anything kinky or out-of-the-ordinary with me,' Grace said.

He looked uncomfortable, shaking his head at the conversation as though he could dispel it completely.

'Are you having an affair, Steve?' she asked quietly.

His head swerved towards her, his eyes wet with sadness. 'What? Of course I'm not, Grace. How could you think that?'

She felt a brief wave of relief sweep through her.

'How the fuck do I know what to think? I feel like I don't know who you are anymore.'

'What? I look on the internet on the odd occasion. I'm sorry, but . . . look, I'm sorry.' He held his hands up apologetically. 'I had no idea it would upset you like this.'

'Well, what sort of thing do you look at?' she asked, wiping away a tear dripping down her cheek.

He paced the floor, sweat making his shirt sticky on his back. 'What sort of question is that? Generic things, OK? Sex, sexy underwear, dressing up – for crying out loud, Grace, I don't even know.'

She huffed. 'It didn't look generic to me.'

He turned to her with sadness in his eyes.

'Would you not rather tell your wife? Tell me your fantasies and act them out with me, rather than in a creepy old office alone? You're signed up to fucking OnlyFans, messaging a sex worker, paying for someone's photographs! Do you know how humiliating that feels for me?' She paused, feeling sick to her stomach at his betrayal.

Steve ran his fingers through his thick, curly hair. 'I . . . I didn't think, Grace. I honestly didn't.'

Grace walked over to the dining table, sat, and rested her head in her hands. 'Things haven't been right with us for a while,' she said.

Steve turned his head quickly towards her. 'What? What do you mean? They have. Yes they have, Grace. What do you mean?'

'I mean, since I stopped working and became your housewife.'

His face screwed up. 'That's not true. You know that. You're just angry, darling, because of all of this.' He held his hands towards her.

She folded her hands across her chest, declining the invitation. 'You have lost respect for me,' she said softly. Her eyes were now painful with tears. 'You told me to stop working. You told me, and I didn't even want to, Steve. You said you wanted to start a family, to have the *perfect* life, but I'm just here cooking meals, washing up, while you go and wank by yourself in an office, using our money to pay some stranger when you could be spending time with me. Having sex with your fucking wife! It's disrespectful and seedy.'

Steve gripped her shoulders tightly. 'I could never respect anyone as much as you, Grace. I'm so sorry if I've been distant. But I can change. I promise.' He looked pale, worried and nervous, as the life he thought they had began to crumble.

'I need to change. I want to work, whether it's charity work or joining a firm. I want to have a life again. I want to be respected by my husband. I want to be part of all your sexual desires. I want you to share these things with me, Steve. Or else . . .'

He nodded his head, immediately agreeing with her demands. 'Or else?' he repeated softly.

'Or else, I'm done. I can't live in a man's shadow. That's not who I am or who you fell in love with.'

He paused, acknowledging the severity of the situation. 'Right. I see. I'm . . . I'm sorry.' Steve wrapped his arms around her, kissing her head over and over again.

Grace closed her eyes and finally breathed.

Ava

Later that evening, after finally enjoying some fruity cocktails, I dragged myself up the stairwell towards my flat. My feet and legs ached from trekking around London all day. Usually I was lucky to get in a hundred steps the entire day. When I finally reached my floor and began digging through my bag for my keys, I heard Adam's door open across the hallway.

'Hey, Ava,' he said politely, pretending my presence had surprised him.

Obviously spying through the peephole again, Adam. Great!

I turned slowly. 'Oh, hey, Adam.' I forced a smile onto my face, feeling awkward after our last encounter.

He stood there with no top and his rugged jeans on, barefoot.

'How are you?' he asked.

'Good. Be better if I could find my keys here,' I joked, my hands frantically searching the bag to avoid the conversation. 'And you?'

'I'm good.'

There was a brief silence between us, and I glanced up at him. But as soon as our eyes met, I looked away again.

'You know, there was a guy here earlier looking for you.'

My hands stopped for a second, curious.

'Johnny?' I asked.

'No. No. A business-looking guy. He was wearing a suit.'

'Probably a debt collector,' I mumbled quietly. 'Or . . . TV license guy? They've written to me since I moved in. Ha, got it!' I beamed as my fingers closed around my keys. I pulled them out and turned the lock.

'I'm sorry about the other week, Ava,' he said.

I finally turned to him. 'No, no, I'm sorry. I completely overreacted.'

'No, I overreacted. I understand women can some-times have times of the month where—'

'*God,* no, Adam, that smell was not normal. It turns out I had a tampon stuck up there. So, you did me a favour by prodding and dislodging it. Apparently, it could have been fatal.' I laughed for the first time, thinking of my near-death experience, while he seemed completely taken aback.

'Jesus!' he gasped, then giggled a little at my reaction. 'Well, you're welcome then, I suppose. I'm a lifesaver, eh?'

'I suppose so!'

We both laughed.

'No Georgie tonight?' he continued, leaning against the doorframe.

My eyes darted across his body, his toned torso, the little landing strip of hair that ran from his belly button down underneath his jeans.

'No Georgie, she's at Johnny's.' I blushed, knowing where this conversation usually led. 'I do have work to do, though. Believe it or not, I'm writing a story for my friend's new online magazine – well, Instagram page.'

He tilted his head, seeming impressed. 'Wow. That sounds fun.' His voice was warm, familiar, and kind. 'Well, if you get bored, you know where I am.' He smirked and stepped back inside his flat.

I shut my eyes briefly.

Don't do it, Ava. Please don't do it.

'I . . . I . . . do need to get this done,' I sighed, taming my horny vagina at last. *Down, girl! Last time you touched that man you ended up in hospital.*

He nodded. 'Yeah, that's cool. Catch up soon, then?'

'Sure. Night, Adam.'

He closed his door, and I felt my shoulders relax. That was the right thing to do.

I wandered into my flat, flicked my shoes off into the pile accumulating in the hallway and finally sat at the kitchen table. I stretched my arms wide, then took out my notepad, rereading Lina's story. I felt even more enchanted by her courage now. I could see the article taking shape in my mind, but I didn't have the words in me to do it justice. I could feel the pressure building inside me. *What if Lina hated my take on it? What if my writing was rusty? What if I made Rebeka's first interview piece for Rogue a massive flop? I had no idea why I'd agreed to this. Who the fuck did I think I was? I hadn't written anything in years.*

I sighed and put my head on the table. My thoughts shifted to my daughter, and I wondered how she was doing. *Did she have fun today?* Johnny had probably taken her to the park, or Hamleys. She loved that place. I smiled, imagining her excitement at bringing home a new toy. I hated how I couldn't get her anything. Not like the toys Johnny got her. But even more than that, I hated how she knew never to ask me. She was almost five years old, and she understood so well how badly I felt about our financial situation, that she didn't add to it. My stomach twisted and I glanced towards the fridge, knowing there was still half a bottle of rosé from the night before.

As I got up to open the fridge, I knocked the notepad to the ground; with a grunt, I picked it up, and my notes on Lina stared at me. *What if this is my chance? a voice inside me said. Not only to tell Lina's story, but to write. To get my name out there again and change my life. To change Georgie's life.*

I paused for a moment, then sat back at the table. *Come on, Ava. You can do this.*

I lifted my pen and flipped to a new page. First, I rewrote the interview with Lina, feeling myself becoming more and more absorbed in her story and how to tell it. The words flowed as easily as the ink. I forgot about the wine, forgot about the time or feeling hungry. It was the first time I'd felt truly alive and passionate in years. The words flew out of my pen and onto the page like magic. I continued late into the night.

Finally, in the early hours, I sat back and smiled. Outside, the sky was turning pink and the birds were awake.

I flipped through the pages, crammed with writing. *My* writing.

I'd done it.

Chapter Nineteen

Ava

A few days later, Beks finally finished editing the shots from Lina's photoshoot. She set up a website and scheduled an Instagram post linking the article I'd written. I waited patiently for the piece to be uploaded, and together, we planned on sharing it across all our social media accounts to get Beks as much traffic to Rogue as possible.

Beka: *One last thing, Ava. Will you be Ava Little or Campbelle?*

The question made me feel nauseous. It's funny how strange it is to change your surname when you're first married. I remembered giggling when someone called me Ava Little; it felt like they were calling on somebody else, and once it finally sank in that *I* was Ava Little, it sort of felt like I'd lost my identity somehow. Now, though, I couldn't remember being anyone else, and the idea of not having the same name as my daughter made me uneasy. Let alone the idea of not being tied to Johnny.

Me: *Can I be Little? It feels weird changing back x*

Beka: *Course babe x*

It was 8 a.m., and I was up and dressed, waiting for Johnny to drop Georgie off. He had early meetings scheduled so I was left with the school run. She was about to attend her first day at summer school, and I couldn't help but feel apprehensive about seeing Mr McGroaty again. *What the hell even happened the other day?* I wondered how he'd act in front the other parents. Maybe he would drop me a secret note or cheeky wink about how good I looked today. *And what about the knickers?* I laughed to myself. *What the hell has that kinky bastard got planned with those?*

There was a knock at the door, and I could hear a playful scream from the hallway as I opened it. Johnny held Georgie in his arms, and the pair smiled at one another.

'Morning,' I said, happy to see them.

'Mummy!' She reached over into my arms.

I hugged her and popped her down to the ground. 'I missed you!' I said, ruffling my hands through her hair.

'You look . . . *nice*,' Johnny said, glancing at my red floral dress.

'Thanks.' I blushed. I couldn't remember the last time he'd paid me a compliment.

'You seem different.' He paused, his eyes skimming over me.

'Maybe just dressed?' I laughed, crossing my hands over my waist while sucking in stomach. 'Do you want to come in?'

'Working. But . . . maybe next time?'

'Sure, yeah.'

He stepped towards the stairwell, and I began closing the door.

'Ava.' His hand pushed it back open. 'I think we should talk about a few things.' His eyes stared into mine, and I felt my pits sweat instantly.

'Sure. OK. Yeah,' I smiled back nervously. *Talk about fucking what?* I wondered. *About us? About our break being over? About a divorce?* My head spun; I felt dizzy with possibilities that could make or break my mental health. His mind games made me want to dive straight into my one-inch mattress for a fortnight and hide like Anne Frank. *What the fuck did he want?*

'OK, good.'

'But wait – Johnny?' I said quickly, before he disappeared. 'Talk about what exactly? You make me nervous when you say that.'

He chuckled, holding his hands up to his chest. 'Don't be nervous. It's all positive.'

I gulped down on my dry mouth. 'Right, OK. So, when?'

'When?'

'When do you want to talk?' I asked.

He raised his shoulders slightly at my reaction. 'Next time I see you, perhaps?'

I nodded, 'Sure. Yeah, OK. Well, we need to head

soon anyway. We have big school today!' I gushed at my daughter, who was standing between us.

Johnny crouched down and kissed Georgie's forehead. 'Well, you, Miss Little, behave and have fun.' He stood up again. 'I'll pick her up Friday?'

'Yeah, from school, or . . .?'

'I'll message you. Depends if I can get away on time. Have fun today, and no tears, Mummy!' He pointed at me and grinned. It was the first genuine smile I had seen him produce since I surprised him with a freshly shaved fanny for his birthday.

I felt a cramping in my stomach almost immediately. *What did he want?* His demeanour was kind and warm, but I didn't trust it. Last week he wouldn't even have donated me the steam from his shit, and now he was on my doorstep offering me compliments? *What the hell was going on?*

Closing the door, I turned to Georgie.

'Shall we go? The tube is going to be busy and very warm! The sun is out already!'

She threw her head back in dread. 'OK, Mummy.'

We made the stuffy journey towards her school and arrived with a few minutes to spare. Georgie seemed excited about going in and meeting her new friends again, and I snapped a few pictures of her standing outside to send to Johnny.

Beka: *The post is up! Share it, girls x*

Grace: *Ahhhh. Going on now xxx*

I frantically came off my camera, clicked on my Instagram app, and immediately saw the most exquisite photo of Lina at the top of my feed. *Wow.* I scrolled down, saw the link to my written story, clicked on it, and began skimming. **Share.**

'Good morning! And how is Georgie Little feeling about her day at the big school?'

I looked away from my phone to find Richard clasping Beatrice's hand. I grinned as my daughter nodded happily and waved to her new friend.

'She's excited! Aren't you, big girl? Are you excited too, B?' I asked the shy child clutching onto her uncle.

She shrugged a little just as Mr McGroaty approached the door.

Fuck, I felt my heart race. I swooshed back my hair as elegantly as I could.

'Good morning, everyone! Wow, what a lovely day. The sun's come out to welcome you all!'

I laughed hysterically at his pish patter, trying my best to get his attention.

He blushed, locking eyes with me, 'Shall we head into class, everyone? Say goodbye to your mummies and daddies.'

I hugged Georgie tightly before she walked in behind a group of kids, then turned to see Beatrice reluctantly get pushed into line by Richard.

'She'll be fine in a few minutes,' Mr McGroaty said reassuringly, clasping her hand.

The kids walked into the building, and the door closed behind them.

Well, no secret love letter, Ava! Damn.

I suddenly felt a whisper in my ear from behind.

'No tears now, Mummy.'

I laughed. 'Why do you make even the sweetest moments sound creepy?'

Richard bowed his head in mock humility. 'It's a gift I've been blessed with.'

Some of the parents hung around to chat in small, cliquey clusters, but the only person I knew here was Richard. We turned and steered out of the gate.

'So, how have you been?' he asked.

I smiled immediately. 'Good, actually. The past few weeks have been really good for me.'

'I'm glad to hear it!' he replied, raising an eyebrow. 'Anything you'd care to share?'

I shrugged. 'Well, Beka started an Instagram account about real women and their stories, and I wrote her first piece. And, well, my first story for a *long* time. It felt great writing something again. It's probably the first time I've used my brain in months.'

'Wow.' Richard paused, folding his arms across his chest. 'Can I read it?'

I stopped, suddenly hesitant. *Shit, this man scrutinises writing for a living.*

'It's only a small piece. For an Instagram account. It would bore you.'

'Don't downplay it, Ava. I want to read it.'

I felt my face turn red and began wafting the clammy air between us. 'OK. Well, I'll forward it to you when I'm home.'

'Can't I read it now?' His charming dimples appeared as he asked.

I stepped to the side of the path as some of the other parents tried to pass by us. 'Really? Like right now?' I glanced around at where we stood.

'Yes, right now. No time like the present, Ava.'

Somehow the idea of people I didn't know and wasn't connected to was much easier to stomach than *Richard Tierney* reading the first thing I'd written in years. We'd been so competitive in school and, whether I liked it or not, he knew me. He knew what I was capable of.

'Well. Hmm. OK.'

I took out my phone, loaded the article and handed it over. His hand briefly clasped mine, and shivers trickled down my spine. I pulled my hand back and turned away as he began to read. But after five seconds of staring out at the road, I realised I wanted to see his reaction. I looked at him, his dark eyes roving over the words, his brow pulled down as he became lost in what I'd written. *What was he thinking?* How would he react? The man had no filter, so I wasn't counting on him to be diplomatic or sugarcoat anything; I just hoped his comments would be more constructive than when we got caught in a literary debate at university.

After a few minutes, he raised his brows, blew out a little breath, and looked up at me. 'You certainly haven't lost your touch, have you?'

'You think? Be honest. I know I probably could have improved the second paragraph some more. Maybe I should have added in a little more background information,' I said, gnawing nervously on a fingernail.

His face lit up. 'Ava! It's brilliant. So insightful, tragic and yet strangely empowering!'

I lowered my head a little, not used to a compliment. 'Thank you!'

Richard passed back my phone, and we took a few more steps.

'I'll share the piece, if you'd like? I have a few of my writers on my Instagram.' He squinted as the sun beamed into his face.

I felt my jaw drop in excitement for Rebeka. 'Shut up, Richard! Yes! Oh my God, Beka would love that!' I felt my fingers twitch, desperate to tell my friend the news. Richard had a huge reach thanks to all his connections.

He reached into his pocket and popped on his sunglasses. 'Consider it done!'

I paused, feeling a wave of gratitude pass through me. 'Thanks, Richard.'

He smiled. 'It's a pleasure, Ava.'

'Well . . .' I continued, glancing in the other direction, towards the tube.

'Fancy some breakfast?' Richard asked. 'We could . . . talk shop? We still have a position for proofreading with your little name on it.'

I turned to him. His white shirt was open at the collar, his hands resting casually in the pockets of his smart suit trousers. He was handsome, but he was Richard. Serial fuckboy, arch-nemesis of my husband. The cunt who almost ruined my wedding day.

'I don't know, honestly,' I sighed, weighing up the idea of a meal alone with him.

He shrugged. 'OK, but I do make great pancakes.'

Jesus, he wanted to *make* me breakfast!

I stood there on the sunlit pavement, pondering. Sure, we had history, but that was years ago, and I had to remind myself that things with Johnny hadn't exactly turned out peachy. And he had just offered to do Beks a massive solid. *Take one for the team, Ava.*

'How about we talk at your office?' I suggested, hoping to ignore any tension between us.

Richard laughed under his breath. 'I'm working from home today, Ava. I can assure you our meeting will be strictly professional.'

I felt myself blush at my assumption.

'C'mon, you know me,' he said, shaking his head a little.

'Yep, I do!'

He began walking down the sunny street.

'And that's what I'm afraid of,' I mumbled quietly.

Richard took a few more steps and turned back towards me, holding his arms out. 'Are you coming or not?'

I sighed, considering my options. I glanced back in the direction of the tube and saw the school again. This could be my chance for a real job in an industry I loved. If for no one else, I had to do it for Georgie.

'Yep, yep, I'm coming!' I quickly caught up with him.

We strolled towards his home which turned out to be just a few streets away. He turned his key and disarmed the alarm as we walked in.

'Welcome,' he said, picking some mail up off the shiny mahogany floor.

I glanced around. The house was painted pristine white, punctuated by large, impressive artwork hanging on the walls. I noticed Beatrice's little coat hooks hanging in the hallway and smiled.

'Nice place,' I said, reaching down to loosen my trainers. I could feel myself wobble.

'No, please. You don't have to,' he said, as he walked forward and held my waist, preventing me from falling.

I gulped, suddenly feeling very alone with him. With someone I had known for most of my life. But it felt like he was a stranger again.

Richard lowered his hand when I caught my balance. 'Please, come in.'

He led me through his sizeable open hallway, slipping off his shades and popping them on a side table. As we walked, I glanced through a doorway to the living area and caught sight of a white leather corner suite and a huge television covering most of the wall. We carried on to his kitchen. The worktops were grey granite, and the units had a pale grey finish. If it weren't for the small drawings on the fridge, this place could have passed for a show home. Jesus, if this man knew the state I'd been living in, he'd be disgusted. I couldn't believe he'd done this on his own. Part of me wondered what my life could have been like if I hadn't married Johnny. I had better grades, better results, better knowledge, but I gave up on everything.

'Coffee?' he asked.

'Mmm, please. Black, if that's OK,' I replied, watching Richard place a mug under his fancy cappuccino maker. 'So, how long have you lived here?'

He waited patiently for the noise from the machine to stop, then lifted the mug and handed it to me. A strong coffee aroma filled the space. 'Not long. Six, seven months. When I got full custody of Beatrice, I researched the best schools and thought I better move a bit closer to the area. No more fancy penthouses for me, I'm afraid.' A vulnerable smile appeared on his usually composed face.

I blew the steam off my drink. 'I didn't realise you had full custody.'

'Yes, well. Daphne is in a bad place, and Beatrice deserves something more stable. And quite honestly, she's the best thing to happen to me.' He smiled. 'Which I'm sure you understand.'

I agreed, feeling I shouldn't press him for more information on his sister. 'So, the job. I've been thinking about it, and I'd like to apply. Would you like to interview me formally, or . . .?'

'Jesus, Ava, I couldn't give a fuck about all that. It's yours if you want it.' He opened the fridge and took out a bottle of water for himself.

'Really? Erm . . . OK. I'm just worried that—' I stopped myself from talking him out of giving me the position.

'Go on.' Richard leant towards me on the worktop and grinned. His teeth were clean and white, his lips were plump, and his stubbly jawline was more defined than Cillian Murphy's. *Why hadn't I looked at Richard like this before?*

'Erm . . . I suppose I'm worried that I'll struggle. I've never professionally proofread someone's work before.'

He laughed and stood upright again. 'Sure you have. The university monthly review? I remember writing an article and you returned it with red ink highlighting my grammatical errors, lady!' He winked, and I felt my lungs collapse.

What the hell is happening to me?

'Yes, but c'mon, that was basic. It's not like the university paper had an impact on how books were written.'

'Oh, for fuck's sake, Ava! It's all the same! Writing is writing. I'll send you a sheet with all the proofreading marks you need to use, but the rest you already know.' He ran his hand through his thick black hair and allowed a smile to take over his face again. 'Why don't you try one piece? I'll email you one tonight. Edit it and have it back to me in . . . two weeks. And we can take it from there?'

I finally agreed, sipping my coffee. 'Like a trial period?'

'Exactly!'

'OK. I think I can do that,' I replied.

'Great.'

There was a brief silence as we got business out of the equation, and Richard strolled back into the hallway.

'Are you coming?' he called out.

I turned on my bar stool, standing up. *Jesus,* was he walking me to the door already? I reached the hallway again and looked around.

'Where are you?' I asked.

'Up here!' I heard his voice call from upstairs.

Oh, no. Was he thinking I was going to have sex with him? Was this a trade-off? *I'll give you a job if you give me a blow job, Ava Little?*

My heart began pounding as I stepped hesitantly up the stairs.

I could make an excuse, tell him I had to go. Tell him Georgie's sick. *Shit, he'd see me at the school gate when she finishes.*

'Richard . . . I . . . think you might have the wrong idea?' I called out to him as I approached the top of the steps.

'And what idea is that?'

I followed his voice and turned to see him in a large study surrounded by books. I felt my shoulders relax immediately.

'Oh. You're in here.'

'Where would you like me to be?' he asked cheekily.

I cleared my throat. 'Exactly where you are!' I warned before stepping into his office.

Bookcases were wrapped around the walls, and a desk sat proudly in the centre of the room.

'Wow!' I gasped, turning in a circle to take it all in.

'I knew you'd like it!'

I stopped spinning and he gestured to the chair behind the desk.

'Please, take a seat.'

'Are you kidding? I need to examine these books!' I laughed at his pristinely organised collections, from history to crime to classics.

Richard folded his arms, watching me.

'Oohh, remember this one!' I laughed, pulling a copy of *A Midsummer Night's Dream* from a shelf. 'We studied it in fourth year at Knightsbury.' As I thumbed through the pages, Post-it notes flashed by, scribbled with his handwriting. 'Wait, is this the same book from school? Did you steal it?'

Richard reached over my shoulder, shutting the book with a thud. His body pressed into mine, and I momentarily felt myself leaning back into him. I stood up straight and half turned around.

'It's one of my favourites.' I smiled, feeling my cheeks hot from his closeness. 'I hope Georgie's into old Shakey.'

'I'm sure she will be.' His voice was unusually soft, and I could still feel his presence against me. 'Did you know, I remember reading this book and comparing us all, our friend group back in school, to the characters.'

I laughed, turning to him. 'Oh yeah, and who was I?'

'Well, you were Hermia, of course, and Johnny, he was Lysander, desperately in love.' He scowled jokingly at the mention of his name. But I felt a weight suddenly press on my heart, thinking of how inseparable Johnny and I were back then. 'And I . . .' He sighed. 'I was Demetrius, desperate for your love and attention.'

I felt my insides twist.

225

'For my love and attention?' I questioned, smirking slightly. The cunt used to stick chewing gum in my hair and make fun of my accent.

'That's right,' he said. 'To me, we always made sense. Both fun, clever, reasonably good-looking.' He winked again. 'And, well, into the same things.'

'You didn't like me, Richard,' I stated bluntly.

'What? Of course I did. I should have tried harder to let you know,' he conceded. 'I think about it from time to time, even now.'

I paused, waiting for him to break into laughter and reveal that he was taking the piss. About this, about the job, about everything.

'You should have tried to let me know? Richard, I hated you in high school. You were evil, and you'd take the piss out of me constantly. I actually only started to stomach you at uni because Johnny liked you so much.'

His head bowed, 'Well, like I said, I'd do anything for your attention. I didn't know how to get it from you. Classic schoolboy behaviour, teasing the girl you like, I guess. I honestly had the most ridiculous crush.' His voice was low from his admission.

I felt my shoulders tense at the heavy conversation. I looked up into his brown eyes, gazing down at me.

'And is that why you're helping me with this job, Richard?'

He placed his hand on my shoulder. 'Trust me, Ava, you'll be the one helping me.'

'Or because it'll piss off Johnny?'

Richard face screwed up his in disgust. 'Johnny? *No!* Like I said, I know you'll be good at it, Ava, and I hate to see an old friend struggling because of a tosser like Johnny Little.' He paused for a moment, his eyes wandering into the distance. 'I should have spoken to you before you married him, Ava.'

My entire body went stiff with nerves. *What the fuck was happening?*

'Well, is that – is that why you bailed on our wedding day? Because you had feelings for me?' I asked, feeling the blood pump through every part of me as things started to make sense.

He was still so close to me. I could feel the warmth of his breath on my face.

'Partly. Perhaps.'

I took a step back. 'And the other part?' I asked.

'Well, that's a lot more complicated.'

Suddenly Richard broke away and went to his desk, leaning on its edge. I felt the tension in the room build. *Did Johnny know Richard had feelings for me? Did something happen between them that night before the wedding? Is that the real reason Johnny hates him so much?*

'Tell me, who did you see me as when you read it? *A Midsummer Night's Dream*?' Richard asked.

'Honestly? That's easy. You were one hundred per cent the donkey! I mean, apart from being silly, the resemblance is uncanny!' I said, and to my relief he started laughing.

'Well, I promise my teeth are not from Turkey, Ava!'

'I'm just glad to see you've grown into them as you've gotten older!'

'Ouch!' he replied.

I felt flustered just talking so closely to him, so I pulled back a little, scanning through other books on his shelf.

'Hey, how are things going with the supermodel? The Polish girl?' I asked, changing the subject.

Richard grinned, looking thankful for the change of conversation too, 'The *Russian*. That was a . . . weekend thing. We're good friends. And Oliver?'

I shook my head, hoping any PTSD flashbacks of shagging the prostitute wouldn't flood back. 'It was short-lived.'

'And what about Johnny?' He adjusted his watch casually as he waited on my answer.

Just the mention of his name made my eyes feel heavy. I wasn't ready for this. I wasn't prepared for a relationship with anyone who wasn't my husband.

'That's a lot more complicated,' I said.

He smirked at my response, then bopped his head.

'Remind me, how do you like your pancakes, Little?' He stood up and strode out of the study, his heavy footsteps carrying back downstairs.

'With as much Nutella as humanly possible!' I called back, feeling my stomach pang. I stood for a few seconds, catching my breath.

Chapter Twenty

Ava

A few nights later, Georgie and I were hanging out at the apartment. I was scrolling through my phone every half hour watching Rogue's story of Lina being shared hundreds of times, with a bubble of excitement rippling through me. I couldn't believe so many people were reading what I had written from across the globe. I was glued to Beka's Instagram, watching her followers grow as she continued to post cool snaps from across London. From iconic backdrops, to headshots of stunningly diverse women she met on the street, Beka made each of them look like they belonged on the cover of a magazine. But my favourite to watch was her reels; Beka spent an entire afternoon stopping and interviewing random women from across the city, asking them about their fashionable outfits, style advice and personal goals to success, she then posted them on Instagram, racking up views from thousands of followers. Rogue was booming full of body positivity and I felt incredibly proud at how well my friend was doing, just starting out on her own.

Beka's online project was a much-needed distraction for me too, as Georgie had attended summer school for a few days now and I'd had absolutely zero interaction with Mr McGroaty. I was so confused. Especially after the kiss and stealing my – well, *Lina's* – underwear, I was completely baffled. Surely that's not normal behaviour? *He must be into me. He did say he was thinking about me after we met.* But also mentioned how inappropriate it was. *What the fuck did he want?* I spent hours tossing in bed, overanalysing our conversation, our similarities. I mean, we were both born in the same country for fuck's sake! But he'd stolen my knicks and ran! *Maybe he gifted them to his girlfriend,* I thought, but I shook it off. That would be pretty messed up. I mean the underwear was brand new as well. I shrugged, going over it for the millionth time. It must be a *him* problem. Georgie, on the other hand, was exhausted, lounging across my lap on the sofa, rubbing her tired eyes and snacking on Lidl's dupe Pringles. I had just closed my laptop from editing some of the work Richard sent over when my phone pinged.

Beka: *Tony's Deli in forty minutes? We all need to talk bitches x*

I glanced over at Georgie, yawning as she kept her face on the television, shattered from school.

Grace: *I'll be there. I can't wait to see you guys xxx*

I began typing, then paused. I didn't want to feel like I was missing out on the buzz. Writing for Rogue and spending time with the girls was the most exciting thing to happen to us all in years, but I glanced at my tired daughter and felt my shoulders droop – I wasn't prepared to drag her down to the underground when she had school in the morning. I hesitated a little more, then lifted my phone.

Me: *Sorry girls, Georgie is exhausted* ☹ *! I'll have to miss this one out. xx*

I snuggled more into the sofa to cuddle up with my girl. She wrapped her arms around me, and I gently kissed her forehead. Not even a minute later, my phone buzzed again.

Beka: *Ava!!!! I need you! I am going to have a party to launch Rogue!*

Beka: *Get a babysitter????*

I hummed, questioning my decision, then lifted my phone.

Me: *Why don't you guys come over? I'll get some Barefoot? xx*

Beka: *Sold! I'll be over in an hour! Make sure it's chilled!*

I smirked at my phone at her sassiness.

'Georgie, I'll be back in one second,' I said, bolting up and walking through to my fridge. No wine – shit. I tapped my foot on the floor, then headed to the front door of my flat.

I wavered in the shared hallway, pacing back and forth outside Adam's door. Fuck it! Eventually, I knocked.

Footsteps approached and he opened the door wearing tartan pyjama bottoms and no top.

'Hey, Ava.' He smiled.

'Do you ever wear any clothes?' I asked, glancing over his toned physique.

He shrugged, biting into an apple. 'Georgie at her dad's?' He smirked as he asked.

Great, he does think I'm over for a ride?

'No, no. She's with me . . . I . . . was . . .'

He laughed curiously at my delay. 'What's up, Ava?'

'I don't suppose you have any wine? It's just, my—'

'Teetotal, Ava!'

I smiled as I remembered, managing to avoid an eye roll at his healthy lifestyle.

'Well . . . do you mind sitting with Georgie for five while I run to the shops?'

'Of course, I can.' He crunched. 'I love spending time with that girl.'

'Aww thanks, Adam.' Relief swept through me. He did always watch her when I first moved in, to let me run errands as we settled in. 'You're a lifesaver, Adam. I'll literally be five, ten minutes.'

'Do you want me to come over just now?' he asked, stepping out to the hallway almost immediately.

'Erm, yeah. Well, in a few minutes, is that OK? I want to let Georgie know first.'

Adam smiled, taking another crunch of his apple. 'Sure, who's coming over?'

'My friends.' I smiled, not remembering the last time I'd said those words aloud. 'Beka and Grace.'

'Ahh . . . The one who started the Instagram maga- zine kind of thing?' He folded his arms casually.

'Yeah, well, the story I wrote took off.' I blushed a little as I boasted.

'Way to go, Ava!' He nodded his head, looking impressed. 'I'll be over in five then. Let you go and celebrate your victory!'

'Thanks, Adam.' I turned to walk into my flat. 'And Adam?'

'Yep?'

'You might want to put a top on! I know it's summer, but come on.' I laughed.

Back inside, Georgie was still in the same spot on the sofa, and I knelt beside her.

'Hey baby, Mummy has to go run to the shop for five, but guess who is coming over to keep an eye on you?'

She took her eyes off the television briefly and hummed a little.

'Adam!' I gasped excitedly, and she matched my energy, clapping her little hands together.

'Is that OK with you?' I asked.

'Yes! But can I still watch *The Little Mermaid*?'

'I wouldn't be offering if you watched anything other than *The Little Mermaid*!' Adam replied from over my shoulder, having let himself in.

I looked at Georgie and we both giggled.

'Move up then, Georgie! I get scared when the sea witch comes on,' he said. He sat on the sofa, and I swung my jacket around my shoulders.

'Thank you,' I whispered, not wanting to disturb the film any more.

Adam smiled back warmly and then put his arm around Georgie.

I whisked to the local off licence and bought two bottles of Barefoot and some nibbles for my friends. I felt a buzz rush through me just at the thought of some adult company and catching up with them. When I returned home, Adam was lying across the sofa, still engrossed in the movie, while Georgie lay fast asleep cuddled into him.

'How was Georgie?' I whispered, nodding towards my daughter.

'She was as good as gold.' He laughed quietly. 'She pretty much fell asleep when you left.'

'Yip, sounds like her!' I admitted, admiring her peaceful little face as she slept.

'You know, I read your article when you were away. The one about Lina,' he added, keeping his voice low.

'Yeah, what did you think?'

'I thought she sounded amazing. She comes across unbelievably brave.'

'She is!'

'You did well with it, Ava. Really well.'

I smiled. 'Thanks, Adam.'

I stood there for a few seconds as he gazed back happily.

'Oh, erm, do you want me to lift her through to her bed?' he asked, shuffling on the sofa.

'Erm . . . yeah. That would be great. I mean, if you don't mind?'

'Of course not!' Adam stood up carefully, trying his best not to move too much as he lifted Georgie from the sofa and tiptoed towards our bedroom. He placed her down slowly and pulled the duvet across her. 'Night, Georgina,' he whispered, brushing her mousey brown hair off her face.

He came back into the hallway and slid his hands in to his jean pockets. 'Well, if you fancy having a glass of wine some time, we could celebrate your story?'

I paused, feeling guilty. 'You don't drink, Adam!'

He grinned. 'But you do!'

'Yeah sure, we'll catch up soon.'

He walked towards the door, and I followed him to the landing.

'Hey.' I reached out and grabbed his wrist. 'Thanks again for this.' I smiled at him.

'Anytime, Ava.' He bent down and kissed my forehead lightly. 'Enjoy your girls night!'

Half an hour later, I heard a knock on my door, along with screeches of laughter from the hallway.

'You made it!' I said, seeing Beka and Grace standing outside.

'We did!' Grace replied, kissing my cheek before coming in.

'Who has Georgie?' Grace asked.

'Never mind Georgie!' Beks interrupted. 'We have business to discuss!'

My face fell at her bluntness, while my sister almost choked on her saliva.

'Sshh! Beks! She's asleep!'

'I'm sorry, but c'mon! Have you seen the interactions we're getting on Lina's story!' A bright smile spread right across her face.

'YES! And it's amazing!' I said. 'Your pictures are stunning, Beks, honestly – amazing! And those reels, chatting to all those women, it's genius!'

'And so was your interview, Ava. Both of you have done a great job!' Grace insisted as we took a seat in the living room.

'I've decided to throw a launch party to get more clients and influencers posting my content. Today, I've had three companies asking me to shoot their brand and do a collaboration for my Insta!' Beks screamed, and we all joined in.

'A launch party for an Instagram account? Is that a thing?'

'It's an Instagram account that promotes amazing women and fashion. It's the future, Ava! So many more people go on Instagram than buy a magazine, you know, hun.'

'This is insane, you have people to shoot! Who are the companies?' Grace asked.

'A range. There's an underwear brand, a footwear brand and . . . wait for it . . . a handbag brand!'

We screeched again from the sofa, just as I began pouring the wine.

'And they're all going to pay?' I asked when she turned, feeling ecstatic for my friend.

'Of course they fucking are! This reminds me, Grace, that I need you to review the contract. Make sure everything is legit.' Beka explained.

Grace nodded happily. 'Of course I will.'

'And Ava, we need to find another story or person for you to interview. Everyone loved that piece on Lina,' she said.

'Yeah, yeah, of course I will. God, I'm filling up fast! Richard has sent me over a book and I'm proofreading it for him.'

My friends gasped in delight.

'You said yes then! Well done, girl!' Beka smirked.

'What? Ava, that's bloody fantastic!' Grace bellowed.

I nodded. 'Yeah, it is. But I'm really nervous. He sent over a manuscript last night, and I don't know how much I can change. Or if I'll be any good at it.'

'Of course you fucking will!' Beka said. 'You're good at everything, Ava!'

I huffed under my breath, knowing how untrue that was.

'So, I'll search for potential hard-hitting stories, like Lina's, and I suppose I'll have to work around your work with Richard,' she continued, looking fired-up and rattling from her alcohol boost. 'All I can think about is how fuming Mitchell will be. He's bound to have seen this now.' She let out an evil laugh, and Grace and I shared a worried glance.

'So, you've not heard anything from him?' Grace asked.

Beks tossed back her icy-blonde hair. 'Nope. Good riddance, that's what I say!'

The room turned silent for a few seconds.

'You know, it's OK to be upset about *Inner Me!*, Beks,' Grace said timidly.

Beka's face screwed up. 'I'm not though! I'm going to smash the fuck out of Rogue and make them realise how badly they've treated me!' She seemed like a woman on a mission.

'How's things with Steve?' Beks asked my sister, quickly changing the topic from Mitchell.

Grace's shoulders relaxed a little. 'Good. We're really great.' She shrugged. 'We spoke, and since then, things have been heating up.'

'Tell us more,' Beks asked curiously, arching an eyebrow.

'Well, after the conversation, we seem a lot closer, we're talking more, being more affectionate, and things have been . . . *well*, I have been . . .'

'Come on, spit it out, babe.' Beks rolled her eyes impatiently.

'Very experimental in the bedroom,' Grace's eyes widened, and she covered her mouth to stop herself from giggling.

'EWWW!' I gagged a bit, thinking of my sister and Steve together.

Meanwhile, Beks's eyes were bright with enthusiasm. 'Ignore her! Tell us more!'

'Well, Steve's search history seemed to be a lot of S&M. So, last night for instance, I spanked him for leaving a dirty dish in the sink.' She sat up proudly, cheeks flushed.

'Jesus!' I sighed.

'You dirty bitch, Grace Campbelle!' Beks laughed.

'I didn't realise how empowering it could be to take the lead. It's quite . . .' She sat back in thought. 'Invigorating. But we haven't, you know,' she lowered her voice, 'had sex yet. We're building it up, making tension, touching and exploring, it's really nice.'

'And you get your dishes done. Win-win if you ask me,' I added.

We all laughed.

'Anything from Johnny?' Grace asked, turning to me.

I shook my head, remembering our last conversation. My stomach clenched with nerves. 'Not really. He did say he wanted to talk soon. He's so hot and cold though, I'm not getting my hopes up. But . . .' I paused before saying, 'Richard Tierney told me he used to like me at school.'

My friends shared a puzzled glance.

'As in, he fancied me!' I said, in case they weren't getting it.

'As in, *still* fancies you?' Beka asked.

I paused, unsure of the answer. 'I don't know, honestly.'

'Wow. Richard Tierney.' Grace tutted. 'He *is* unbelievably handsome, with a very distinguished job.'

'And a massive dick,' Beka said.

I burst out laughing. 'But he was Johnny's best friend. They were like brothers.'

'And, don't forget, the cunt almost ruined your wedding day!' Beks stated.

'I asked him about that, and he said it was partly because of his feelings for me.'

'And what was the other part? His feelings for the strippers he'd been banging the night before?' Beks muttered.

I felt my stomach twist. I'd almost forgotten Johnny's explanation of why he didn't show.

'Maybe he's changed?' Grace said, smiling hopefully. 'It sounds like he adores his wee niece – what's her name again?'

Rebeka burst out laughing. 'Hermione or something!'

I slapped her arm. 'Beatrice!'

'And it is really kind of him to give you a job,' my sister continued.

Beks nodded. 'True. But he's lucky to have you working for him.' Then she paused as a light came into her eyes. 'Wait, tell him to come to the launch party! Ask him to bring that bitch who called me out at the reunion!' Beka was fired-up again, her mind falling back to Rogue.

'Why would you want her to come?' I asked. 'She was horrible!'

'A horrible bastard with nearly a million followers, babe. We need to have our business brains on here. If I can get her posting about Rogue, it will gain a lot more reach.'

'I can ask him.' I puffed my cheeks out as nervousness squirmed through me. 'I'll email him tonight. I've been working on the edits most of the day, so I should have them finished later.'

'When are you planning to have the party? I'll add it to my calendar!' Grace popped on her glasses and lifted her phone to schedule a booking.

'Thursday!'

'Thursday the what?' I asked.

'This Thursday, babe. Strike while the iron is hot! One of my reels got one hundred thousand views today! I've already popped into Sexy Fish and hired one of their function rooms.' She smiled happily. 'It's invite-only, only the best of the best. Lina's coming, of course, as well as journalists and models. I need you guys to be on top scouting behaviour.'

I shook my head at my friend, who had managed to change everything around in only a couple of weeks.

'I'll have to sort it out with Johnny; he's not supposed to pick Georgie up till Friday.'

'I'll be there,' Grace said, 'and I'll bring Steve.'

I slipped out my phone and messaged Johnny.

Me: *Hey, can you take Georgie Thursday night? Sorry it's short notice but I have a thing on with Beka and Grace? X*

Johnny: *I have the gym on Thursday?*

Me: *I wouldn't ask if it wasn't important. I never change days x*

Johnny: *I suppose, Ava. I'll pick her up at 5*

'Johnny will take Georgie!' I announced, and we continued chatting and planning the launch party for Rogue. Everything felt so exciting and uplifting when I was around my girls. We chatted and drank until the early hours, plotting the next stages of our lives.

Chapter Twenty-One
Ava

I spent the remainder of the week finishing my first proofreading task and sending it back to Richard. I had also secured him to come to Beka's party for Rogue. Before I knew it, it was Thursday. For the first time in a long time, I woke up excited to start the day. Georgie had been at summer school all week, and besides picking her up while trying to make flirty eye contact with her teacher — which failed miserably — I was glued to the laptop. Now I had a purpose and a job, and I was slowly getting my life back.

Following a brief and confusingly friendly eyebrow-raise in the playground from my underwear thief, Mr McGroaty, I headed home to make fish fingers for my daughter. While she ate away, I went to my bedroom and began getting organised for the party. I washed and styled my hair, having dusted off my old roller set. I sat for almost half an hour following a fifteen-year-old's TikTok video on contouring my face, and then slipped on a black leather knee-length dress. Finally ready, I smiled at my reflection. I hadn't felt so good in years.

Just after five, my door chapped, and I walked out to the hallway to greet Johnny. He was flicking through his phone as I answered.

'Hey,' I said.

'Hey. Is she ready?' he asked, deigning to look up at me.

'Yip.' My heart dropped slightly as he didn't acknowledge the effort I'd put into my appearance. 'Georgie, Dad's here!' I called out.

I grinned as I heard the padding of her tiny feet on the floor running towards us. She gasped, 'Mummy, you look pretty!' She seemed dazzled. At least *she* fucking noticed, I thought.

'Thank you, baby.' I attempted to bend down to her, but the leather made me hover.

'I love your hair.' She ran her sticky fingers through it, and I giggled.

'Are you ready for Daddy's?'

Georgie nodded back.

'Do you want me to take her to school in the morning?' I asked, looking over at Johnny.

Leaning against the door frame, he shook his head. He wore a navy shirt, and his blazer jacket was neatly folded over his arm. 'It's fine; I'll take her and pick her up.'

I pouted my lip out toward Georgie, who giggled loudly.

'And we'll be going away on Saturday, remember? It's my fortnight for the summer.'

I turned to him in a panic.

'What?'

'I told you I was taking a couple of weeks in July, Ava. You said you didn't have plans.' His voice was so matter-of-fact it cut through me.

'But you haven't mentioned a thing apart from that. We had that conversation weeks ago. I didn't realise it was two days away! You can't *just* mention it now. I have to see her before she goes, Johnny!' I could feel my eyes begin to fill.

'Here we go,' he huffed. 'I was going to tell you the plans when I picked her up tomorrow. It was a surprise!'

Georgie stood in between us, looking confused.

'Aye, it is a fucking surprise, all right!' My voice shook with anger.

'Not for you,' he said, motioning to our daughter. 'For Georgie!' As he crouched down to her level, her face simmered a small smile. 'Guess where Daddy's taking you on Saturday, princess?'

She jumped slightly as his tone lifted. 'Where, Daddy?'

'Disney World in Florida!'

I felt like I had been shot in the face at close range as the two of them screamed happily in my hallway. That was *my* goal. That's what *I* had been saving up for. Every spare coin I found on the street went towards my dream holiday with Georgie to Florida, and suddenly Daddy fuckin' Warbucks swoops in and decides he's taking her?

'Isn't that exciting, Mummy?' he eventually said, gazing over in my direction with a strange scowl.

Georgie glanced towards me as I wiped tears away from my face.

I nodded back, sniffling. 'WOW! Georgie! What do you say to Daddy?' I somehow managed to muster.

'Thank you, Daddy! Thank you, Daddy!' she shrieked.

'We're going to see *Cinderella, Snow White* and the castle, everything and anything you want,' he continued, and swooped her excited body off the ground.

'And Mummy, too?' she asked.

I felt my heart stop. *This should be a holiday for a family. One we all go and experience together. I wanted to take her, I wanted to watch her perfect little face taking in the magic for the first time.* He knew how much this meant to me.

'Mummy can't go, sweetheart. It's a little trip for Daddy and Georgina, just like when we visited Grandma last month.'

'Only it's across the world, as opposed to across the country!' I snapped back.

Johnny put Georgie back on the floor. 'Go get your bag for school, and we'll head. Mummy is going out, sweetie.'

She nodded, glancing back towards us as she scurried off to get her things. As soon as she was out of earshot, I narrowed my gaze at Johnny.

'I can't believe you didn't tell me this, Johnny. You didn't ask me,' I hissed.

'I don't have to run these things past you anymore, Ava,' he said. 'Anyway, you can take her on holiday when we're back.'

I laughed. 'You know I can't do that. I can't fucking afford it, can I? Fuck, I'm stressed out about paying for an *Oyster* card this month, never mind a trip to the States!' I stared at him, hoping to see the man I fell in love with peek through, but his face was rigid.

'Well, I can, and Georgie isn't missing out because you can't, OK?' He shrugged. 'You should maybe stop spending your money getting tarted up with your friends and try and get a job, Ava.'

My mouth fell open. 'What? I never go anywhere. How fucking dare you?'

His face turned red, and he shook his head, looking harassed and like he couldn't be bothered with this conversation.

'I'm sorry, but c'mon. You have to learn to stand on your own two feet, Ava.'

I felt a shudder go through me. I was on my own two fucking feet. I had dreams and a life, but having Georgie changed everything about me.

'I'm trying, Johnny. I've started to really try.'

He nodded a little, looking past me, clearly hoping Georgie would hurry up.

'Did you never think about asking me to go with you?' I asked, feeling another wave of emotion ripple through me, still trying to digest his holiday plan.

That seemed to catch him. For a moment he paused, his eyes on the floor.

Georgie walked back in with her school bag on. 'Can I see Mummy before we go, Daddy?'

'I'm sure we can sort something out, sweetie. But Mummy is busy too, you know,' he replied, holding his hand out to her.

She hesitated in the hallway between us, then reached over and hugged me tightly.

'Go have fun. I'll see you before you go, don't worry! And *hey*, be a good girl tomorrow at school, will you?'

She smiled a little. Then I pressed her nose.

Johnny sighed. 'I can drop her off in the morning then, about seven? So you can take Georgie to school. Let you see her before we leave.'

I gulped down; my throat felt dry. 'Thank you,' I said. 'Well, there you go! I'll see you in the morning, Georgie!' I managed to fake a smile as she waved to me and disappeared down the hall. I closed the door and fell against it.

How could he do this to me? I'd thought we were getting closer. I'd thought he'd want to try again if he knew how well I was doing. I sank down onto the floor, burying my face in my arms, and bawled.

I'm not sure how much time passed before I heard a quiet knock at the door. I might not have heard it at all, but with my back still against the door, I felt the vibration in my spine. I wiped my eyes, which felt swollen and irritated, and stood up, turning the handle. It was Adam, of course.

'Hey, I was just checking if you're OK. I heard you . . .'

I closed my eyes and opened the door fully.

'Wow, you look insane!' He gawked at my tight dress. 'Minus the black eyes.'

'Are they that bad?' I asked. My voice was low and hoarse.

He tilted his head to the right, then to the left. 'Yeah. I'd say so.' He laughed. 'Is everything OK?'

I shrugged. 'Johnny.'

Adam rolled his eyes. He'd seen me shed too many tears over the man. 'What's he done now?'

'He's taking Georgie to Florida on Saturday. I just found out.'

I watched his face twist. 'Ouch!' Adam knew about my big dream of taking Georgie to Disney World one day. He knew all about the Mickey Mouse jar and scraping pennies together to put in it. He knew how much this meant to me. 'I'm sorry, Ava.'

'Look at the state of me, Adam,' I said. 'I'm supposed to be going to this party for Beka, and look at me.'

He pushed open my door and let himself in. 'C'mon, get your face washed,' he said.

My head was pounding from stress and dehydration. My face felt tight. 'What? No, *no*, I don't feel like going anywhere tonight. I'll cancel.'

Adam tutted. 'And what? Cry in your bed alone?'

I mean, it wasn't a bad option. It was exactly what I was used to.

'Ava, come on! Look at you! You're changing for the better. You've started to get out the past few weeks, and it looks great. So what if Georgie's going to Disney

World? She'll have the best time there, and hey, it sucks you're not going, but while she's gone you can focus on yourself, on writing more stories and things. You deserve good things in life, too.'

I paused, still feeling numb. 'I'm going to miss her so much, Adam.' My lip trembled.

He nodded slowly. 'And she'll miss her mum just as much, trust me.'

I attempted a smile, but it fell away quickly. 'Do you think this is fixable?' I giggled slightly, pointing to my face.

He laughed. 'I think you need some soap and water unless you want to pull a *Marilyn Manson* tonight!'

I dragged myself back into the bedroom and began wiping at my blotchy face, taking off the ruined remnants of my original party look and applying some basic makeup once more. It was all I had time for, since the party would already be underway. Fuck Johnny for all of this, including messing up my painstakingly contoured glamour.

When I finished, I walked through to my living room, where Adam was lying on my sofa with his feet up.

'There she is,' he said warmly. 'You look great!'

I laughed back, shaking my head at the compliment, knowing fine well a bag of shit looked more appealing than me.

'You're too nice to me, Adam. What are you up to tonight?'

'You know, playing guitar,' he shrugged, 'The usual.'

I smiled back.

'Now go have fun. You deserve it!' he said.

I slipped on a pair of heels and turned to him. 'I don't suppose you fancy coming tonight? I could do with a bit of company. Lots of cool people are going to be there. And they will definitely have all that vegan shit on the menu.'

His brows perked up, and he stood, dusting off his denim shirt. 'Is this OK?'

I smiled back. 'You look perfect, Adam.'

Chapter Twenty-Two
Ava

When Adam and I got to Sexy Fish, we were escorted by a hostess to the private party room. As we scurried through the bougie bar, worrying about being almost two hours late, I gave Adam a reassuring smile. His hands were stuffed into his worn jeans and he seemed tense.

'Have a wonderful evening,' the hostess said with a wide smile, gesturing us into the party.

We were immediately engulfed in the atmosphere; a DJ played house music in one corner while an impressive crowd mingled and networked over cocktails and canapés. The huge aquarium Beks had talked about occupied most of one wall. The movement of the fish within cast elegant, dreamy shadows throughout the room.

'Wow,' I said, and nudged Adam. I waited for a dull rundown about how unfair it was to the fish to be locked in a glass box when they should be swimming out in the wild, but even he seemed impressed.

Stylish servers swarmed around us, offering us sushi canapés. I took one for myself and asked for a vegan option for Adam. Our fingers brushed slightly as I handed the small piece of sushi to him.

'How cool is this?' I said, feeling a little flustered at touching him.

He laughed, taking it all in. He seemed entirely out of his comfort zone, but in all honesty, this wasn't my world either.

'And free food,' I shrugged. 'Result!'

'Too right it is!' We'd both agreed to split the taxi fare because of how late I was running and now, with free food and drinks, I could maybe afford a breakfast tomorrow. 'Hey, Ava, Look.' Adam pointed to a Rogue cardboard cutout design in the corner with the cover photo of Lina.

I beamed. 'Aw, it looks so good in print!'

'Ava! Where the hell have you been? You missed my speech!' I turned to see Beks standing behind me in a skin-toned-colour catsuit, looking stressed.

'I was . . . You look . . .'

'*Ohhhh*. And who is this?' she asked, wafting her long acrylic nails in Adam's face, her eyes expanding at the possibility I had actually brought a date.

I gave her a stare, hoping she'd stop. The cunt had eyes and could gauge a reaction. 'This is . . . erm . . .'

'Adam, Ava's neighbour. Lovely to meet you,' he replied confidently.

She broke into a huge grin. '*This* is Adam! Oh, OK.' Her eyes skimmed up and down his torso, checking him out.

'Rebeka!' I tugged at her wrist. 'How is it all going? Anything I can do? I'm sorry I'm late, Johnny arrived at the house and said—'

'Mingle! Just mingle, Ava. Richard is over there with that cow of a model. But I want her to share my Instagram, Ava! Maybe even let me shoot her for content,' she hissed.

I turned to see Richard through the crowd, chatting closely with Katya. My heart quickened a little as I watched him laugh with her.

'Ava?' Beks called out, raising her hands in the air.

'Yeah, yeah, I'll see what I can do!'

She strutted off, noticing another guest heading in late.

'Do you need any help?' Adam asked.

I shook my head. 'Nah, I think I've got this. But you can . . .' I glanced around the room and spotted Lina sitting alone at the bar, sipping champagne. 'Follow me.' I pulled on his arm and barged through the crowd.

'Lina! Hey!' I said, kissing her cheek. She was wearing a long black off-the-shoulder maxi dress with her dark hair flowing down her back casually.

'Ava! Hey, great turnout!' she replied, peeking over my shoulder to Adam.

'Yes! It's so busy,' I glanced around the room, noticing the crowd of stunning women and men in smart suits beside them. 'Well, how does it feel to be famous, Lina?' I asked, giggling at the success of her story.

Lina burst out laughing, covering her mouth slightly. 'Erm . . . strange! Lorraine contacted me to go on her show last night! To tell my story. What the fuck?'

I gasped. 'Shut up! She is Scottish, we have great taste! You have to do it. I'm so happy for you.'

Lina smiled back gratefully, then her eyes darted to Adam who was hovering behind me.

'Oh, I'm so sorry. This is my neighbour, Adam. Adam, this is Lina,' I introduced them.

He immediately reached out and hugged her. 'I know who you are! I read Ava's article about you and thought you were the bravest person I'd ever read about!' he said. 'Do you mind if I join you? Ava's got some work to do.'

Lina blushed and pointed to the stool beside her. 'Please.'

'I'll try and be quick,' I said, but the pair were already into a deep conversation. I grinned, watching Adam. He always had that quality of genuineness about him. He was so open and honest that it made it impossible not to like him.

I strode through the crowd until I spotted Richard again and took a deep breath. *Why am I nervous? It's only Richard, for fuck's sake.* My number one frenemy since high school. I had been emailing him throughout the week, but seeing him made me feel strangely uneasy. *Maybe because now he was technically my boss and I wanted* to impress him. I needed the job. I needed the money. Or maybe it was because he'd disclosed he had feelings for me, even if it was when we were kids. Not that I ever felt the same; it was Richard.

As I was weaving between people, trying to get to him, I felt a tap on my shoulder. I turned to see Grace and Steve standing close together.

254

'Hi,' I hugged my sister, 'nice to see you both,' I lied. It was never nice to see a friend of Johnny's.

'How are you, Ava?' Steve asked. His arm was wrapped tightly around Grace's waist.

'Yeah, OK, you?'

He grinned back, then pecked my sister's cheek. 'We're great!'

They erupted into laughter together. This was weird.

'Excuse me, darling, I've spotted a client,' Steve said. He kissed Grace on the cheek again before darting away, leaving her chuckling like a hyena.

'You look happy,' I said suspiciously.

'I am happy. Very happy!' She seemed flustered, but in a good way, with rosier cheeks than usual.

'*Hmm* . . . have you got a job for tonight?' I asked.

She laughed loudly, turning towards Steve across the room.

'Grace?' I repeated.

'Sorry, what did you say?'

'Has Beka given you a job for tonight?'

She burst out laughing, covering her mouth again. 'I'm sorry! *Ohhh! Jesus!* I'm sorry!'

'What the fuck? Have you taken edibles or something?' I'd never seen my sister so off the ball. She was usually the perfectly composed one.

'No . . . of course not.' She pulled me in close. 'I'm wearing a knicker vibrator! Steve is controlling me from his pocket,' she tittered. As if to underline her point, her body gave a little tremble as though she'd received a small vibrational shock.

I felt my eyes bug out of my head. 'You have got to be fucking joking, Grace!'

'Nope! And he's passed me a secret key; when I'm wet enough, I unlock a secret present! I have no idea what it is, well . . . maybe a locked drawer of sexy undies or toys. Tonight is the night. We're finally going to have sex again. After weeks – no, *months* – of nothing. This buildup is everything, Ava.'

I felt my face twist in disgust. 'Tonight? You decide to explore your sexuality *tonight*? When we're supposed to be getting clients for Rogue?'

Grace rolled her eyes. 'I'm sorting the contracts. You are getting the clients!'

'Great night, isn't it!' A smiling lady approached us.

Both Grace and I jumped from our argument and went full on arse-licking mode.

'Great!' I said.

'Wonderful,' Grace added.

'You must be Ava, I just want to say your article was beautifully written, really, the awareness you have put out there for women to protect themselves is so vital in this day and age.'

I watched my sister's eyes glaze over with emotion as I received the compliment. She was always a soppy bastard.

'Thank you. Do you work for one of the brands?' I asked, trying to nudge Grace to pull it together.

'No, no. Women's Aid. We love to come out to these events and support the message.'

Grace gasped, 'Wow! That's amazing! I'm Grace, Ava's twin sister.'

She shook Grace's hand, laughing a little at her enthusiasm. 'Lovely to meet you. Are you part of Rogue too?'

Grace hummed a little, 'Well, sort of. The boring part. I'm a lawyer. I stopped practising a while back but I'm keen to help, so I handle the contracts coming in for Rebeka.'

'Well, we're always looking for lawyers at Women's Aid if you ever want to help elsewhere. You should consider it.'

'Wow. Eh . . . yes, I will. What would it involve?'

'Do you need rescuing?' Richard's familiar voice whispered into my ear. I felt his body press into me.

'I do,' I chuckled. 'Excuse me, ladies,' I said, and turned to greet him. 'Hey.' I smiled.

He stepped back, and I watched his dark eyes dart up and down my body. 'You look very dominating in that outfit.' He smirked.

I hoped he couldn't see my cheeks redden in the dim party lighting. 'Thanks. I think?'

'You're welcome.' His voice was smooth and confident. I could feel my pulse quicken as he spoke. 'How are the edits coming along?'

'Finished. Well, I'll review them again and send them over tonight.'

His hand grazed his chin. I looked around at the crowd, flustered as we spoke so closely.

'Ava?' he said.

'Yeah?'

'I'm impressed.'

I looked into his gaze, feeling myself burn inside. *What the fuck was happening to me?*

'Richard, there you are!'

Suddenly, his seven-foot model date appeared and draped her long arms over his shoulder.

'I'm bored!' she huffed.

'Ahh, Ava, this is my friend Katya. I believe you crossed paths at the reunion?'

I nodded. *Yep, the bitch that made me announce my disastrous life to my fellow pupils.* 'Lovely to meet you again,' I said.

'Is your dress Prada?' she asked, her striking blue eyes piercing through me.

'Uh-huh,' I lied. *Primark Essentials*, hen.

'*Hmm* . . . I remember it from a few seasons ago,' she muttered.

Jesus, she was more of a cow than I remembered.

'So, Katya . . . Have you had a chance to check out Rebeka's work? I'm sure she'd love to photograph you for Rogue one day! She's photographed so many amazing people with *Inner Me!* She has already got a queue of models lined up for her online account,' I said proudly, glancing over at my friend as she mixed with her guests. She was dazzling.

'I only do high fashion and cover shoots, 'Katya replied, holding her chiselled chin high.

Richard smirked. 'Ava's written a wonderful article that's gone viral for Rogue too. I'm lucky to be working with her on one of my authors' debut novels.'

She moved her face in what I could only guess was some form of a smile, but with that much Botox, I couldn't be sure. Richard passed me a look, suppressing a laugh as I rolled my eyes.

Suddenly, Katya gasped.

'Wait. Is that Mitchell Travers?'

I turned my head so quickly I almost gave myself whiplash. *Fuck*. It was Mitchell, and he was storming towards Rebeka.

'Excuse me!' I bellowed, pushing towards them as the crowd huddled around him.

'Rebeka!' Mitchell called out. Even above the music, I could hear the gasps.

As Beka turned, I watched her grin drop. There was a flash of shock in her eyes, but she quickly composed herself.

'Mitchell.' Her eyes skimmed over the room. She flicked her hair back. 'How are you?' I could tell she was trying her best to contain any tension between them and keep this civil.

'Not good. How do you think?' Mitchell replied bluntly, his deep accent turning heads in the room.

She narrowed her eyes slightly and I watched her civility get thrown out the window. 'Mmm, why, hun? You ill?'

'What is this?' He gazed around the room crammed with models and influencers.

'What do you mean? It's the launch of my new Instagram handle, babe. Do you wanna give me a follow?'

'Rebeka,' he said, looking down at the floor as though he was trying to gather his thoughts.

I edged forward. 'Hi Mitchell, I'm Beka's friend, Ava. Maybe this chat is best saved for another day?' I said politely.

'And maybe . . . *oooh* . . . maybe it's best to leave it to the court proceedings!' Grace buzzed from behind me, unable to stand still.

'Court proceedings?' Mitchell laughed under his breath. Then he turned back to Rebeka. 'And that's what *you* want?'

She paused. The entire room was staring. I watched Rebeka's strong eyes fill with pain. She looked lost, like for once she didn't know how to react. Then, without warning, she struck off towards the door.

Mitchell grabbed her wrist. 'That's what you want?' he repeated.

When Beks turned around there were tears streaking down her face. She shook her head. 'I didn't want any of this, Mitchell.'

He dropped her hand, pulled his dark trench coat around him and cleared his throat. 'Why? Why are you doing this?'

Grace edged between them. 'She has a right to make a living, mister. She was unfairly dismissed from your company, and she's entitled to some compensation and to relaunch her ideas!'

'I . . . I . . . had no choice, Mitch—' Rebeka began, but Grace held up her hand, cutting her off.

'Don't say anything else, Rebeka,' she warned, 'In case it goes to court.'

Jesus, Judge Judy didn't have shit on Grace, I thought.

Mitchell rubbed his eyes with the palm of his hand, looking tired. 'You always have a choice. I thought this was different. I thought this was never about money with you. I thought we were . . .' he paused, looking towards her. 'Never mind,' he muttered, shaking his head in disgust.

Rebeka choked out a sob and ran to the side door. I rushed after her. 'Beks, wait, wait!' I bellowed.

She stood outside, bent over, trying to catch her breath.

'What have I done?' she asked. Her voice was ragged.

'Nothing! You haven't done a single thing wrong!' I insisted, stroking her back. 'He was the one who fired you, remember?'

'I love him, Ava! I should have waited till he calmed down. I should have explained myself. But now look, I've given up everything, and for what? A silly fucking daydream? All for a fucking Instagram page! What the fuck am I doing?'

I pulled her into my arms. 'If he wasn't worried about your talent, he'd never have come. Rogue isn't silly, Beks,' I said softly, feeling every ounce of her pain. 'You said yourself, this is the future.'

The door opened, and Mitchell saw Beks leaning on me. He came slowly towards us.

'The compensation money, it's yours,' he said. He sounded heartbroken. 'I don't have it in me to fight with you anymore, Rebeka.'

'And I never wanted to fight with you. But you didn't hear me out. You cut me off when you heard

261

a ridiculous story and fired me, Mitchell. What was I supposed to do? Sit back and take it?' she said, standing to her feet.

Mitchell looked at her for a long moment, his face contorted in pain. Glancing away, he clenched his jaw. 'Congratulations on launching your new business, Beks. I hope it was worth it.' He walked straight to a sleek black car, where his driver was waiting with the door held open. Just before the door closed, he looked back at Beks.

The driver walked around the car and got in. As we watched the car glide into the late-evening traffic and drive away, my friend broke down in tears. I hugged her tightly, feeling her sobs wrack her small body. The night air was clammy and soon we were just a sweaty, snotty little heap outside the restaurant.

'I can't go back in there,' she said eventually, noticing the queue of people in line for a table staring at us.

'Yes, you can,' I said.

She let out a small laugh, pointing to her face. 'I can't go back like this.'

I grinned, noticing the streaks of mascara running down her face. 'I'll come back in with you. Me and Grace will both be there. We can get you cleaned up, no problem.'

But Beks shook her head, looking exhausted. 'No. I'd rather go home. I'd rather be alone. I just need to regroup. I'll be fine tomorrow. I have more reels to shoot in Camden.'

I patted down her bouncy hair. 'OK, if that's what you want. I get it.'

'Did you manage to get Katya?' she asked. She was back in business mode, her eyes on the prize, flicking back her hair and sniffling up the snot.

I shook my head and did my best Russian accent. 'She only does high fashion and cover shoots!'

Rebeka laughed. 'She can shove my shoot up her bony arse then, bitch!'

'Such a bitch!'

Beks stood up and panted. 'Can you send someone out with my bag? It's behind the DJ box.'

'Are you sure?'

'Yeah, hun, I'm sure.'

'OK.' I kissed her on the forehead. 'But promise we'll celebrate Rogue properly? A girls night, just us. Not with the arrogant arseholes you invited!' I turned towards the door.

'Absolutely. And, hey, it looks like I've got some compensation money coming in, so somewhere fancy, OK?' She attempted to smile, trying her best to seem happy at the payout.

'*Offt,* drinks are on you then, Beks!'

She giggled. 'As if they aren't always, arsehole!'

I smiled and slipped back into the restaurant, heading towards the party. The atmosphere had bounced back after the little dramatic glitch – or maybe because of it – and there was a buzz in the air as flutes of champagne were being passed around. I found Rebeka's bag and passed it along to the host.

'Can you give this to Beks? She's outside.'

'Of course,' she replied, moving swiftly towards the door.

I reached for the nearest glass of bubbly from a passing waitress and sighed. Realising I had left Adam for most of the night, I scanned the crowd for him. I could do with a bit of grounding right now. My eyes fell on his double denim ensemble, sticking out like a sore thumb amidst the suits and cocktail dresses. He was still talking to Lina, seeming wholly engaged and animated. He must have said something funny because she giggled and pushed her hand into his shoulder.

'Your date?' Richard's voice surprised me, and I laughed.

'My neighbour,' I replied. 'He's been a good friend the past few months.'

I felt Richard's eyes on me as I continued to watch Adam and Lina interact.

'Have I told you that you look wonderful tonight?' He kept his voice low and discreet, like he was telling me a secret.

I turned slowly to face him, surprised. 'You haven't. You said 'dominating'. But thanks.' I felt my heart trip in my chest. Either I was still coming down from all the drama, or Richard was making me flustered again.

He grinned. 'Wonderfully dominating.'

'I'm sure your date won't appreciate that,' I laughed.

Richard's face twisted. 'My date? That you requested that I bring?'

I covered my face, cringing at my earlier email inviting him and Katya. 'I know. Beka asked me. She is trying to get famous models to shoot! She wants the follows!'

'I see,' he hummed. 'And here I was, thinking you were friend-zoning me.'

I watched him take a casual swig of his drink. His shirt was slightly open at the neck, revealing hints of chest hair. There was something so manly about a man with dark chest hair that I had grown to like. Johnny always shaved his because it came in like blonde bum fluff and I had never known anything different. I was still staring, watching him gulp and his throat move as the alcohol travelled through his body. *Jesus,* I could feel my nips turn hard just admiring him. *Shit, not in a tight leather dress, Ava.* I folded my arms immediately to disguise my arousal. You could hang teacups on them bad boys!

'So, have you enjoyed editing?' he asked.

'It is tough; there's a lot I'd love to do, like really dig into it, but at the same time, I don't want to change the writer's style. But I have really enjoyed reading and fixing it all out.'

He nodded. 'That's the art form!'

'There you are!' Katya approached Richard. She was wearing her long leather coat, looking as if she was ready to perform some *Matrix*-style flying stunts.

He raised his brows at her, 'Are you ready to leave?'

'Yes. It did get a bit more exciting there for a moment.' Katya's eyes suddenly came alive remembering the drama of Mitchell gatecrashing.

I scoffed. 'It certainly did. Poor Beks. They've only just broken up, and she's finding it hard enough!'

Katya grunted. 'Rebeka, *the coffee girl*, dated Mitchell Travers?'

I felt my toes curl, ready to fly-kick her fanny, then realised I'd probably need a step ladder. 'Rebeka, the amazing photographer to the stars, and my best friend – *yes!*' I gulped down my champagne, hoping it would distract me from saying anything else I shouldn't.

'Wow. I didn't realise. What is he like? How did they meet?' Suddenly Katya was overflowing with interest.

Richard winked towards me as I was about to speak. 'Why don't you schedule a photoshoot with Rebeka? I'm sure she'll tell you all about it. That's if she's available; I hear she's swamped at the minute.'

Katya's wide eyes fell on me. 'Do you think she'd shoot me?'

I almost choked on the bubbles. '*Erm* . . . I mean . . . I could ask? Do you have a card? Or details I could pass on?'

'Richard, give her my card,' she demanded.

He rolled his eyes and reached into his back pocket for his wallet; I noticed a photograph of Beatrice smiling as he pulled out a business card from behind it.

'I'll pass this on to Rebeka,' I said, taking the card and smiling. 'I'm sure she'll sort something out.'

'I'm out of town next week, but I could fly back Thursday or Friday, perhaps?'

Wow, this cunt was suddenly desperate for work.

I glanced at Richard and smirked; he remained as cool as a cucumber.

'I'll let her know.'

'Can we go now, Richard?' she moaned in his ear.

Richard's eyes lowered to the ground. 'Sure.'

I felt my heart fall a little. I didn't know why, but I didn't want him to leave, especially not with the giant ice queen.

'See you, then,' I said and smiled. He leant over and kissed my cheek. I could smell his aftershave, deep and masculine. 'And thanks for that,' I whispered as our faces brushed.

He winked once more and headed towards the door with Katya.

I circled the party, chatting to more of the guests. Some of them asked about my story and complimented me on the writing, but it all felt strange without Beks there. This was her idea, after all. I was sad she wasn't here to enjoy it. After a while, I tried to locate Grace, but she seemed to have disappeared into whatever teenage sexual fantasy Steve had planned for her. Eventually, I retreated to the bar.

Apparently Adam and Lina hadn't moved from their spots all night, and I found them there, still chatting and laughing away, a few empty glasses surrounding them.

'Hey,' I said, standing between the pair.

'Ava, you never told me how amazing this girl is! And she is also vegan! It turns out she's been to the vegan cooking course I've been dying to try in Staines,' Adam said, full of energy and admiration.

Lina blushed.

'Wow, that's . . . interesting!' I laughed, thinking the only thing worse than a cooking course would be a vegan one. 'Hey, I'm thinking I should head home. My feet are really tired.'

Lina stood and hugged me. 'You poor thing. It's been a great night, though! Beks must be delighted!'

I laughed, wondering if they were even aware of the fuck-up from Mitchell barging in.

'Well, it was really great meeting you, Adam.' She leant over to shake his hand.

He hesitated, looking flustered. 'We could . . . *I mean,* that's if you don't mind, Ava – but maybe we could stay a bit longer? *Or* . . .' He paused, regaining control of his words. 'There's a great bar around the corner if you want to stay out a bit later. But only if you want, Lina?'

Suddenly I became aware of how they were looking at one another. Starry eyes, rosy cheeks. A pair of love-struck adults, altogether leaving me out.

Hadn't he come here with *me*?

'Well, yeah! I would love that. I mean, if you're OK getting home alone, Ava?' Lina smiled towards me. 'Or come! We'll have such a good laugh!'

I shook my head, slightly disheartened. 'No, God, no. Go have fun, you two!' I managed to say.

'Great! See you tomorrow then?' Adam stood up, squeezed me tightly, and sat back down. He was grinning like the Cheshire Cat. I had never seen him so happy, so full of excitement.

'Yeah. See you tomorrow!' I said, reluctantly waving to the pair before heading out to the taxi queue, staring at my banking app. Thirty-two pounds and twenty-seven pence, and no Adam to split the fare.

Sitting in the back of the cab, I felt a cold tear trickle down my face. What a shitty day, I thought. My mind returned to Johnny, thinking about him and Georgie in Disney World without me. How excited Georgie would be. She was old enough to remember, now, to really experience the magic. Everything she absolutely loved would be there, and I'd miss it. All because of my behaviour. My post-natal depression, my anxiety, my accusations. And now, Adam. A guy who was always there for me, always willing to stand by when I needed him. But I'd pushed him away, too. I felt myself heave in the back of the cab as the day overwhelmed me. The driver chatted, totally unaware. The reality was, I was completely invisible.

Chapter Twenty-Three

Ava

As the cab pulled up outside my flat, I tapped my mobile on the card reader and opened the door. The humid night air hit my chest and I felt a sudden relief at reaching my home. My safe place. I couldn't wait to get inside, retreat to my bedroom and hide under my duvet. Wake up in a fortnight when my daughter was finally home.

I'd crossed over the street and rummaged in my handbag for my key when I heard a car door locking behind me. *Great.* A robbery would top my night off completely. I searched quicker.

'I didn't want to leave you alone tonight,' a deep voice said.

I turned and saw a tall, broad shadow walking towards me. It was Richard.

'What's happened?' he asked as he got closer, sounding worried. 'You're upset.'

I put on a smile, wiping away my tears, feeling utterly ridiculous. 'I'm fine! I'm good!' I gulped down. 'But what are you doing here?'

His eyes fell to the ground. He looked uneasy. 'I suppose I wanted to see you,' was all he could muster.

'Oh.'

I walked towards him and plopped down on the kerb, feeling my tired body sink like it had taken a beating. Richard stood silent for a few seconds, then pulled up his suit trousers slightly and sat beside me.

We gazed at one another in the darkness. Dim, orange street lamps were the only light around.

'Why were you crying?' he asked again.

I closed my eyes. My face felt tight and irritated from all the tears it had soaked up over the past few days. 'Johnny,' I replied honestly, with no more energy to pretend I was OK.

I watched Richard's throat gulp down his initial thoughts. '*Still* Johnny?' he asked after a moment.

I shrugged a little, knowing truthfully it would always be him.

Richard sighed and leant back.

'He's taking Georgie to Disney World on Saturday. It's her dream holiday. We've spoken about it forever, and he's doing it without me. He didn't even tell me until today!' I laughed bitterly.

Richard turned and faced me. 'That's pretty shit,' he said.

'He's a good dad, but . . .'

He laughed at my comment in complete disagreement. 'He's not,' he replied bluntly.

'Well, there's nothing I can do about it. I feel like I ruined everything, Richard. My whole marriage broke down because of *me*. I am scraping by here. Waiting. Hoping. I'm praying for him to change his mind about us. All the while trying desperately not to be too loud, too opinionated or overbearing, too silly, or funny, or sexy. Too fucking mumsy.'

'Too Ava?' He raised his brow.

'Too much of anything that will piss him off,' I admitted.

Richard leant over, pulling back a stray hair that was stuck to my lip. 'For the record, there is no such thing as too much Ava for me.'

My face tingled at his touch. I closed my eyes. 'I like you, Richard, but—'

'I like you, Ava,' he interrupted, and I smiled.

'But . . . I don't think . . .'

Richard pulled me closer, and I nestled against him. He felt warm and strong. Why was I fighting this?

'Let's leave the *buts* for now. You like me?' he said softly.

I nodded, feeling my breathing getting quicker as I leant into his chest. I could hear his heart thump as I rested against it. No spiky stubble, just warm manly hair.

'Richard?' I said, looking up at his face.

He grinned down at me, and I ran my fingers down his cute dimpled cheeks. 'Yes?'

'Thanks for tonight.'

He winked. My chest tightened.

I sat up, and he did too. His hand went under my chin as he gently turned my head back towards him; he leant forward and kissed my forehead. I let my body relax. It felt good. Caring and warm.

272

Maybe it was because I felt so shit about everything else? Perhaps because I did like him? My head was running wild with questions I had been putting off answering. In an instant, I was confused and scared and didn't know what to think. I stood up, dusting myself down.

'You know, I didn't imagine I'd be sitting on the streets of Croydon when I purchased this suit!' he said.

I laughed and reached my hand out to help him up.

He grabbed hold of me, his large grip wrapping around my small hand, and I tugged him to his feet. Suddenly, in a second, I felt his nose, forehead, and chest touch mine. I closed my eyes and leant forward to kiss him. Gently, he kissed me back.

'I'm sorry. I shouldn't have . . .' His breathing was heavy.

I gazed into his dark brown eyes. His hand ran through my hair, while his glare kept straight on my eyes. Suddenly, he grabbed me, kissing more passionately this time, his tongue wrapping around mine; I was panting, leaning in for more. It felt hot, sexy and unbelievably good. He tugged on my hair and ran his lips down my neck, kissing and gently biting as he touched me.

I groaned. I'd never experienced this level of passion with anyone before. Not even with my husband. I felt his hand skim over my dress, feeling my curves, my stomach, and then he squeezed my tits. *Fucking hell!* My fanny was ready to explode. I pressed into his body and ran my hand over his crotch. His dick was hard with arousal. *Jesus Christ!* They didn't call him Big Dick for nothing, I thought, noticing the large girth and length of his third leg.

'Come upstairs?' I whispered between pants.

Richard's kissing halted. He leant his head against mine. His breathing sounded as if he'd just completed a 12k.

'I can't,' he said, closing his eyes and regaining composure.

I stepped backwards. 'What? Why?'

'Not while it's *still* Johnny,' he said in a low voice.

I felt my insides curl. Knowing it would never end with Johnny, but craving him inside me. If only for one night.

'I see, OK.' I reached down, feeling embarrassed from the knockback – I mean, the man was standing with a rock-hard cock and still didn't want to fuck me. I lifted my handbag from the ground. 'Are you sure?' I asked, hoping he'd change his mind.

He let out a groan of frustration, then nodded his head reluctantly.

I turned my back, walking towards my door.

'Ava?' he called out.

I pivoted.

'You do look beautiful tonight.' He smiled, his stare remaining on me for a few more seconds.

I smiled back. 'Thank you.'

Then, as I entered the building, I watched him return to his car.

I stumbled up the stairwell, unlocked my door and flopped down on my bed, confused, upset and with a hungry clitoris the size of a fucking basketball.

Chapter Twenty-Four

Grace

Across town, Grace was tumbling through her front door with Steve at her back. It was the most fun she'd had with him since she could remember – the most attention he'd given her in what seemed their entire relationship, especially in public. Even on their wedding day, he'd spent more time impressing his colleagues than with his bride. This newfound sexual chemistry with Steve had never been as passionate and playful as she was experiencing right now, and Grace was embracing it all. Fuck, she wished she had found him tugging the heid off his cock to random sex workers years ago. He was teaching her, suggesting new ways of intimacy through touch and devices. Grace felt like she was learning about her body with foreplay, but more than that, she was enjoying the attention from her husband. Tonight was the night they'd finally have sex again, and she couldn't wait to feel her husband inside of her.

As they entered their home, she pulled out her wet sticky clitoral device while he continued to kiss her neck.

'That was very sexy tonight,' she admitted, slipping off her shoes.

Steve smirked, pulling on her hand and leading her upstairs. 'Have you got the key?' he asked.

Grace nodded, nervous butterflies swooping in her stomach. *What's he going to show me?* she wondered. *A secret lair of a sex dungeon like Christian Grey? A locked drawer full of latex and whips?* She began to feel a little apprehensive. Grace loved the passion and devotion but was entirely new to the S&M scene and hoped he'd be gentle with her. After all, her pale skin marked so easily. *I hope he doesn't put me in a headlock and start spanking,* she thought skittishly.

They proceeded up the staircase together; there was an obvious tension as both remained silent. Grace could feel her skin turning blotchy with nerves. When they got to their bedroom, Steve put his hand out, inviting her to sit on the bed. She giggled and obeyed.

'Where is the key?' he asked.

As sexily as she could, Grace pulled a small metal key out of her bra, just like she had rehearsed in her mind earlier in the night.

Steve's face spread in a wide grin. 'Very cute,' he said sincerely.

He unfastened his belt and unbuttoned his trousers.

Grace sat before him, enjoying her front-row seat to his *Full Monty* moment. He stood with his boxer shorts on, and she couldn't help but gawk at his enormous bulge.

'I almost forgot how big you were, Steve!'

She reached out her hand to grope him, but her hand closed around something hard. Solid. Not like an erection at all. She tilted her head as she continued to examine his package. *What the hell was that?* It felt ribbed, metallic. Eventually, she knocked on it, and her knuckles hurt. She looked up at him.

'Steve, what is that?'

He cleared his throat. 'When I'm a bad boy with naughty thoughts, I lock myself up.'

'What?' she gasped, utterly confused at the entire situation. Her stomach full of excitement suddenly dropped to dread, and she wondered if she had joined the fetish scene too much on a whim.

He pulled down his boxers and revealed a metal cage surrounding his penis.

Grace covered her mouth in shock. 'What . . . what is that?'

'It's a chastity cage,' he revealed.

Grace scrutinised the instrument once more, the metal dick-shaped cage wrapped entirely around her husband's long cock, holding it in place, protecting it.

'But why?' she asked, she couldn't help but screw her face up. 'Have you had that on all night?'

'Yes. If I have bad thoughts or feel like I deserve it, I punish myself,' Steve said with a small, pleasurable sigh. 'Please punish me when you think I deserve it, Grace. You now hold the key to unlock me.'

She searched for words but couldn't find them.

'And, and you enjoy this?' she eventually stammered. 'You think this is sexy?'

He nodded. 'I do. I enjoy the release.'

'You don't expect me to put that thing, like, inside of me? Do you?'

He gasped, 'No, God no. You release me from it and then I can have sex.'

'Well, can I release you? Can I let you out?' she asked, feeling uncomfortable with the huge iron cock making eye contact with her.

'If I deserve it,' he replied, 'mistress.'

The hairs on the back of her neck stood up. She gave a fleeting smile to her husband, feeling entirely overwhelmed, and began unlocking him from his dick dungeon. When the chastity cage popped open, his penis was exposed and stood semi-erect.

'Agh,' Steve breathed a sigh of relief. 'Thank you.'

She nodded, holding the instrument in her hands, examining the weight and structure of it all. *Why does he need this?* She wondered. *Why would he want to walk about with an iron boaby?* She felt a pang of sympathy for him, wondering what had brought him to this point.

'Can I do anything else for you?' he asked politely, kneeling on the floor.

As his eyes aligned with hers, she leant forward and kissed him. Simply. No toys, no roleplay, just love.

He leant into her, and she threw her arms around him. The kissing began to intensify, and they started pushing against one another. She lay back on the bed as his body lifted from the ground and moved on top of her. Grace started tugging her underwear off and lifting her dress to her waist as his dick, now fully erect, hovered above her.

'Make love to me,' she whispered.

His passionate motion halted momentarily. Then, his tongue wrapped around hers and he started pushing his dick inside.

'Yes, yes, yes!' she moaned, feeling whole and complete after months of nothing.

'Do you like that?' Steve grunted on top.

'*Mmmm,* keep going, that's it, keep going, baby,' she replied, feeling her fanny twinge from the inside. She gazed up at him, but his eyes were shut as he continued thrusting hard in and out of her. 'I love feeling you fuck me,' she whispered, trying her best to sound sexy.

'Do you? How much?' he snarled, pounding in and out.

'So fucking much, Steve! So fucking much!'

'And I love feeling your big cock inside me!' Steve panted.

Grace's eyes shot open as he thrashed inside her, grunting loudly.

'My *what?*'

'Hmmm . . .' he continued, too distracted to converse.

'Steve, wait. *Wait.* You just said you loved my big cock inside you?'

The pumping came to an abrupt stop. The room fell silent.

'Steve?' She pushed him out of her and pulled down her dress. 'Well?'

'What I meant to say was, 'Do you love my big cock?' What?!' He laughed it off.

All Grace could do was nod wordlessly, her head spinning.

'Oh, come here.' Steve reached over and pecked her forehead, but she remained still, trapped in thought. 'Come here, Grace!' He pulled her in for a hug, but she was rigid and uncomfortable. 'It was a slip of the tongue, for goodness sake, Grace!' He chuckled again.

'OK,' she said eventually. He'd just been caught up in the moment, she told herself. They both had, the connection between his brain and his mouth disrupted.

'Water?' he asked. 'I'm parched.'

'Hmm . . . *Yes*, thank you.'

As Steve headed downstairs, Grace scrambled into the covers and lay her head on her fluffy pillows. *But try as she might, she couldn't not think about what had just happened. Why would he say that?* What the fuck was going on in her marriage? Her heart pounded heavily in the silent room. A month ago, she'd thought she knew her husband inside out. But now? Grace had no idea who he was.

Chapter Twenty-Five

Ava

My intercom rang the following morning, and I put down my hair curler, rushing to the door to greet Georgie. 'Hey, princess!' I knelt, hugging her, while her teddy bear squashed up between us. 'No, Daddy?' I asked, glancing down the stairwell.

She shook her head, 'He sent me up, all by myself,' she said proudly.

'Aw, wow! That's OK, come on in. Have you had breakfast?' I asked, directing her through to the kitchen.

'Yip,' she replied.

Thank fuck, I thought, because I was sure the milk was out of date. 'What did you have?' I asked, taking a seat and pulling her to my lap.

'Pancakes!' she replied happily.

I always loved Georgie in the mornings, even more than usual. She was so happy and pleasant with this bright spark. It was the only thing that made me leave bed with a smile.

'So Georgina Little, tell me, are you super excited about Disney World?' I asked, squeezing her.

She nodded back, still gripping her teddy bear. 'Mummy?'

'Yip!' I replied, resting my chin on her shoulder.

'I wish you could come to Disney World too!' Her voice sounded sad, like she had been feeling guilty about it. I felt my stomach flop.

'I do, too. But I have to stay here, make sure everything is ticking along back home. Plus, Daddy enjoys spending time with you. I know you will have the best time ever!' I said, feeling my throat tighten with dread.

'Daddy said I'm going on an aeroplane!' She giggled, turning her head.

I gasped and held my hand over my mouth, 'You are not!'

'I am!' She laughed happily.

'I can't believe that! Will you wave out the window to Mummy, when you're up in the sky?'

'Yep, I will!' she replied.

'Promise?' I felt my eyes glaze over with tears. I was delighted for her, but with a gutting feeling looming over me. I would be left alone, *again*.

'Pinky promise!' She held out her tiny finger, and I squeezed it with mine.

'Come on then, little chicken, last day of summer school today, before Mickey and Minnie! Let's get organised, eh?'

'Ok.' She hopped off my knee and ran to the bedroom to put on the clothes I'd laid out and I followed her in to finish getting ready. I knew I'd see Richard at the school gate, and after last night's moment, I had no idea how I'd react or what I'd say. But I did know I wanted to look good. As I finished tonging a loose wave through my long, dark hair, I wondered how he'd react. *Maybe he'd apologise for the kiss?* Or ignore me completely. Or just pretend it didn't happen. I wasn't even sure if I knew how I wanted him to react. I mean, fuck, I loved my husband; ultimately, he was my end goal, but I couldn't deny the passion behind my kiss with Richard. It was unlike any kiss I'd ever had. *Fuck, Ava, you're probably just choking for your hole, hen.* And, after all, he was Richard Tierney, the ultimate fuckboy and playboy; he had a lot more experience in the passionate fanny-tingling kissing department than me. I had to ignore the kiss, I told myself. *Thank fuck* he knocked me back for a ride, because waking up and making him perform the walk of shame before Johnny dropped Georgie off would have been terrible. Or worse, if Johnny had caught him – I felt my stomach twist with anxiety – that would have been a major setback for my marriage, probably one I could never return from. *Thank fuck it didn't go too far.* Georgie and I hopped off the piping hot tube and strolled down hand in hand towards the school gate. I sauntered slowly, wanting to make my time last with her as long as I could, listening to her chat about Florida and the private lunch Johnny had booked for them at the castle. We heard Mr McGroaty call on the kids from afar, and we hurried to cross over the road to lead her in. He held the door open as all the other children rushed in merrily, and I knelt to my daughter.

'Well, I'll see you in two weeks!' I could feel my eyes water but fought the tears away. 'You are going to have the best time ever!'

She wrapped her tiny arms around me. I paused, soaking up the moment, inhaling her perfect, slight baby smell. 'I'll miss you, Mummy!' she muttered, pulling away with her head to the ground.

'Hey, I'll miss you, but you'll call me every day, OK? And that way, you won't miss me quite as much.' I raised her chin and kissed her. 'Now, time for school. You better head in.' I winked down at her, and she grinned back.

'Love you, Mummy.' She waved to me, blowing kisses as she steered past her teacher through the door.

'I love you more, Georgie,' I said, feeling my insides curl at the thought of leaving her. The door shut, and I puffed out a large sigh, sitting on the school bench and taking my phone out. The other parents chatted around me, then slowly dispersed from the yard.

I glanced around briefly, wondering where Richard was. *Did he avoid the school run because of last night?* I felt my arsehole twitch. *Was I a terrible kisser?* Or had he just guzzled too much champagne, and woken up with the dreaded fear? *Oh God!*

I began texting the group chat.

Morning! How is everyone? I just said goodbye to Georgie for a fortnight, so are there any hot girl summer activities to fill my days? Or stories to write, you know where I am. Hope you feel better today, Beks! Last night was amazing (so sorry I missed your speech), BUT I got Katya on board xxxx

I tapped on the photo I took of her details and forwarded them on to the chat.

Pps. I also kissed Richard last night. WTF am I doing?

'There you are! I was hoping I'd see you here.' Richard was striding out of the school building with a large envelope under his arm.

'Oh, hey! Is everything OK?' I indicated to the school, and he smiled.

'Yes, fine. Better than fine. Mr McGroaty,' he made a poor attempt at a Scottish accent and I laughed a little, trying to humour him, 'said B is getting on great! And she's made fantastic progress this week already! He's given me exercises to work on over summer with her numeracy skills.' He seemed proud of his niece as he shone beside me.

'WOW, that is amazing! Well done, Beatrice!' I grinned.

'Ava,' a voice called out from the door. Mr McGroaty stood, beckoning me forward, 'Do you have a second?'

I stood up from the bench and walked inside the building; I could feel the nervous sweats descend from my pits to my arsehole. *Great, the two men I've been winching the past few weeks all together. What the fuck was I doing?*

'I was going to try to catch up with you later today, but Georgina said Dad was picking her up, so I . . .'

'Bolted outside to catch me?' I laughed, easing the awkwardness between us. I mean, fuck, the last conversation we had, I'd ended up a pair of knickers down. *I really hope he doesn't ask for these ones*, I thought; between the sushi last night and Richard's unexpected kiss, I hadn't been off the pan all night!

'Yes, exactly.' He seemed flustered. 'I just wanted to say Georgie's done great this week. Her literacy and numeracy skills are far beyond standard for her age, and I think she will do exceptionally well here.'

I beamed, grateful for the compliment, 'That's amazing. She is very clever,' I admitted, not able to take the smile off my face.

'I have a wee report card, just for the week; here you go.' He passed me an envelope and I grinned back.

'Thank you, she's loved this week.'

'I'm glad.' He stood opposite me, and an awkward tension grew between us.

'So, I better let you get on with the teaching.' I pointed one finger in the air. *What the fuck are you doing, Ava?*

'Yes!' He giggled, subtly cringing for me. 'And I wanted to return these to you.' He cleared his throat and reached down to the table. I watched him lift a small golden gift box with a matching lid and pass it to me.

'*Ohhh*, is this . . .?' I glanced up at him, and he began fidgeting with his cuffs.

'Yes, and thank you. They are very . . . *a very* admirable choice. I hope you get good use out of them,' he smirked back.

Jesus, today was one riddie after another!

'Well, I intend to.' I laughed back, and turned to the door before pausing. 'We don't have to feel awkward

286

next term after the full kiss thing, do we? Like, I'm sure you do that with all the mothers in the class?'

He burst out laughing and covered his mouth. 'No awkwardness from me, Ava. I am really sorry about that. I do find you very . . . endearing. But it shouldn't have happened. I apologise. Honestly, I think I just had to get you out of my system,'

I smiled back at the compliment and was about to leave when I added, 'Wait, can I ask you something?'

He nodded, his hands stuffed into his pockets.

'What did you do with them?'

He shrugged innocently, looking sheepish. 'I got you out of my system.'

Well, that was as clear as shit, I thought.

'Hmmm . . . ok, cool. I'm glad! Professional relationships are the best!' I scoffed awkwardly and shrugged off his unclear explanation, not wanting to press him too much. 'I'll see you, Mr McGroaty,' I walked forward a few steps and pulled open the door.

'Have a lovely summer, Ava.'

When I returned outside, I was instantly blasted with the morning sun again. Richard sat on the bench with one arm over the back, his shades on, and his suit jacket resting over his knee. His white shirt was rolled up at the sleeves, and as the door shut with a bang, he turned his head towards me.

'Well . . .'

'Well, my daughter is far beyond the standard for literacy,' I said proudly, with my head in the air.

'And what about numeracy?' he questioned.

'*And* numeracy,' I added.

'Such a little SWOT! Just like her mother!' Richard bellowed, shaking his head jokingly. 'I am going to have to find Beatrice a tutor over the summer to keep up with her. Do you realise that?'

I sat down beside him, laughing loudly at his competitiveness.

'And what's in the box? A gift for the cleverest child in the class's parent?' He tutted.

I felt my chest pound. *Oh shit.*

I held on to it tightly, 'No, a present Georgie made, I'm not sure,' I shrugged it off. 'Probably some pasta shell drawing,' I secretly wished it was, because I'd be picking it off and boiling it at this rate.

'Hmmm . . . I wonder why Beatrice didn't make me one? *Little shit!'*

'She was probably too busy struggling with her numbers, Richard,' I began giggling as his face fell, and then he burst into laughter.

We sat peacefully in and out of giggles for a moment in the warmth.

'What's on the agenda today, then?'

I shrugged, 'Well, I finished the edits last night and sent them to you. So, I suppose I have a free day. A free fortnight, actually,' I sank back into the bench at the reminder.

Richard turned his body towards me. 'I'm free this evening.'

I broke into a smile, 'Are you? Cool!'

'I mean, I could take you for dinner, if you fancy it?'

I felt myself swaying. Dinner sounded great, but I wanted to wait to date anyone, especially in public, when Johnny's spies could be floating about.

'I'm not sure it's a good idea. Like . . . dating, Richard? We will see people who might tell Johnny, and it gets all complicated and . . .'

'Who mentioned a date, Ava!' He lowered his sunglasses, '*Jesus*. I know we kissed, but that's jumping the gun.' His cheeky smirk lit up his face. 'It would be a thank you for your edits. A work dinner, *if* you have to put a label on it. I'll also need your details to pay you for your edits.'

I felt myself blush at my assumption. *Great, Ava. Making an arse of yourself again today.*

'I'm not sure it's a good idea after last night. I could text you my details?' I attempted a smile, hoping I hadn't ruined my chances of getting paid by knocking him back.

'What if I promise not to kiss you? C'mon, it was one drunken kiss, don't let it ruin our friendship. I kiss everyone.'

I burst out laughing, not knowing if he was serious or not.

'Let's talk shop; tell me about the edits, your thoughts on the book. I'm dying to know what you think. Forget the drunken kiss.'

A drunken kiss that left my fanny pounding for nearly three hours, I thought. 'It would have to be a quick dinner. And nowhere fancy. I have to be back home by eight,' I replied, knowing I hadn't had plans since 2007.

'Fantastic! I can pick you up around six?'

I nodded reluctantly, standing to my feet as Richard rose too.

'See you tonight then, boss!' I replied, giving a little salute. *Why am I full of hand gestures today?* He laughed, throwing his jacket over one shoulder as we headed out of the gate. The early morning sun was fierce on our skin, and I squinted towards the station.

'I'm this way, but I'm looking forward to—'

'Let me drop you off home,' he interrupted.

I screwed my face up. 'It's fine, look at the day it is!' I held my arms out.

'Exactly, it's too hot and stuffy to be riding on the smelly tube. Besides, I'm headed that side of the city anyway.'

I laughed 'No, you're not!'

'I am now! Come on, Little, or dinner's on you tonight!'

Well, that was only an option if they took tick, I thought, walking quickly behind him to catch up.

Richard opened the passenger door, allowing me to jump in. I popped my gift box on the floor as I felt my phone vibrate. Glancing down at the screen, I noticed a bombardment of messages.

Beka: *WAIT WHAT AND WHAT! Katya and DICK!!!!*

Grace: *OMG Richard! What the hell, Ava! How did that happen? Xxx*

Beka: *How was the kiss? And just a kiss?? Were you drunk? I thought he was with Katya last night?!*

Grace: *Is anyone free tonight for a catchup?xxx*

Beka: *Yes! We need a fucking catchup! Can you guys believe Mitchell's cheek? And how can Johnny not mention a holiday to Florida to the mother of his child?*

Grace: *Around five? No, I can't, Beks. I still can't believe he offered the compensation! Have you heard anything else? xxx*

Beka: *Yeah, babe. Tony's?? Not a fucking thing!*

Grace: *Great. Ava? Can you make it? Xxx*

Beka: *??????*

'Everything all right?' Richard asked, jumping into the driving seat.

'Yeah, all good. Just the girls,' I smiled, texting back.

Me: *I can't do it tonight! But any other day? I have a work thing with Richard! Haha 😆 xxx*

Richard and I drove into Croydon, gabbing and giggling throughout the journey. It felt effortless to converse with him. I had painted him as the worst person in my mind for so long, especially after my wedding day and listening to Johnny, but I was beginning to notice how he'd matured into a funny, kind, charming man. As he pulled up outside my home, Richard's face fell slightly, and he pointed to the vehicle in front.

'I think you have a visitor!'

I turned and noticed Johnny's private registration plates and felt vomit swirl in my throat.

'Fuck!' I panicked, 'What is he doing here?' My palms began to sweat instantly.

'Do you want me to get out with you?'

I laughed, rolling my eyes slightly. 'Absolutely not!'

Richard's face seemed stern as he glared at Johnny's car.

I unbuckled my seat belt and jumped out of the car, 'Thanks for the lift. I'll message you tonight.'

Walking along the road, I eyed Johnny as he swung his legs out of his car. His blond hair flopped to the side. He looked furious.

'Is that who I think it is?' His voice was deep with anger.

I turned to Richard's car, still parked up behind his. *Why isn't he fucking driving away?*

'Hmm . . . Oh, Richard, yeah,' I replied back casually. 'He was heading here for a meeting. Why? What are you doing here?' I proceeded to walk towards the door and pushed it open.

'Georgie's bear, she'll need it for Florida.'

I smiled, knowing how much she loved her teddy bear. My parents had sent it down from Scotland when she was one and she hadn't let it out of her sight since.

'Ah, intercom's down again,' I huffed, strolling upstairs.

I heard Johnny's footsteps marching behind me.

I could feel my anxiety soar at the quietness between us. Breathe, Ava, breathe. He doesn't know a thing.

I unlocked my flat door and headed into the kitchen.

'What's been up with you recently?' Johnny asked, striding behind me.

I looked at him, wearing his jeans and a polo-neck Ralph Lauren T-shirt that I got him one year for Christmas, just before we split.

I shrugged, defeated.

'What's up with me, Johnny? I'm sure you're dying to tell me.'

There was a look of disgust on his face as he paced my small vinyl floor. 'The way you are, it's different. The way you dress, you look . . .' He gestured his hand towards me. 'You're going out, and you seem . . .'

'Happier?' I concluded.

Until now, I hadn't even realised, but the past month with Beks and Grace was the happiest I'd been in years. From making plans to chatting on the phone, our little group chat, it had changed me.

'Yeah, well . . . maybe make Georgina your priority, Ava.' He tittered.

I grunted, feeling like Big Foot had just kicked me straight up the fanny. 'You're joking, Johnny, *right?* She is my priority. She always has been.' I lowered my voice. 'And you!'

He paused, resting his hands on my worktop, and turned to me as I continued.

'Look, I know I messed up before. I know how hard I made life for you, but I struggled adjusting to being a mother. It's more common than you think. I was insecure, terrified you'd leave me because I had stretch marks and love handles. I know I accused you of cheating and lying, but it was my mental health! Post-natal depression is an illness, Johnny, the therapist told us that. It was a horrible time, and I'll never forgive myself for it. But I honestly think it would be different now. I have more things to focus on. I've been helping Beks and spending time with Grace. With Georgie in school, I've also been doing freelance editing. All of this change you see is for us, not me.'

Johnny shook his head slightly, 'I've thought the same recently. I thought we could have maybe tried again, that's what I wanted to talk to you about, but you're out all the time. Changing times for pick ups, it's too far gone, Ava.' I could hear him talk and talk at me, but my ears rang loudly. *When would I ever be enough for this man?*

'What? Why do you think that? I changed pick up time once!'

He shrugged. 'It's what it looks like.'

I could feel my head spinning. How could he be so hot and cold? *What had changed in a week? Why hadn't he said something?*

'Where is it, Ava?'

'What?' I asked, snapping out of my thoughts.

'Her bear, she needs it for the plane.'

I nodded in a trance and walked to the living room, scanning the sofa for Georgina's teddy bear.

'Ava?'

I paused, feeling completely disarmed. Static. Numb.

'You forgot this,' Richard's voice made the hairs on my neck stand up.

Shit.

Chapter Twenty-Six

Ava

Richard's strong, deep voice leapt through my body like lightning. I turned to him at the door, then to Johnny, who seemed even more surprised.

Richard was holding the small golden box. *Shit, I must have left it in the car.*

'What the fuck is this?' Johnny's voice was direct. I could see his chest rise and fall quicker as his anger built inside.

'What is what, Jonathan?' Richard slipped off his sunglasses, tucking them carefully into the neck of his shirt.

'What is he doing here, Ava?'

I tried to speak, but no words came out.

'Ava!' he yelled at me.

'What? What? I told you he gave me a lift home. I left a gift in his car. Big deal, Johnny!'

Johnny's eyes fell on the box, and he strode towards Richard.

'What is this, eh?' He pointed to the gift. 'Why the fuck are you buying my wife presents, Richard?' he spat.

Shit, shit, shit.

Richard smirked, sighing a little, 'It's not from me, but as far as I'm led to believe, you gave up on the 'wife' title when you shipped her off, mate.'

'You think you're fucking smart, eh? How fucking dare—'

'Stop, please! Just stop this!' I screamed.

My head was pounding with the drama.

'Thanks for dropping it off, Richard.' I stretched my arm around Johnny, who stood only a few inches from his face, and took hold of the gift box. *Thank fuck.*

'Not at all. Happy to help, Ava,' he replied, with an exaggerated grin to Johnny. 'I better head off. I'll leave you two to it.' I finally breathed a sigh of relief. 'Pick you up at six, Ava.'

SHIT!

Suddenly, Johnny lunged towards Richard, pushing him against my wall. I ran towards the pair frantically, edging between the two men.

'Enough, Johnny. Stop. I've been editing books for him!' I insisted. 'I fucking told you I was working again!'

Johnny let go of his grip and strolled to the other side of the living room to calm down.

'Please, stop. Go,' I whispered to Richard, not knowing why he was making this so difficult for me.

He bobbed back, with his eyes looking heavy from the altercation.

'What the fuck is this?' Johnny's voice rippled through me.

I turned to see him bending down to the floor. The small golden gift box Mr McGroaty had handed me was lying open from the chaos, and the sexy pair of underwear was folded neatly inside.

Johnny's face turned white. I glanced at him and back to Richard, who seemed even more confused.

Johnny reached down and picked up the underwear with his finger. 'This is what you gift my wife for her editing skills?' he hissed, his face turning almost purple with rage.

My heart thumped louder and louder in my chest. *No. No. No.*

'You give her this? To what? Piss me off? Make her sleep with you? Fuck, maybe she already has,' he questioned, his eyes glancing over the expensive knickers, then suddenly Johnny launched the underwear towards the wall in revulsion.

My head was racing, but my eyes watched them stick to my council-funded paint job. Then, gradually, slide down the wall.

Oh, fuck no. Mr McGroaty had left me my own little present. He'd spunked all over my fucking knickers. *I guess that's how he got me out of his system, yuck!*

Johnny retched at the sight of my cummy pants gliding down the wall, leaving behind their very own slimy snail trail.

I diverted to Richard, who remained remarkably composed. *What must he be thinking?* No wonder my child has an excellent report because of the sexual favours to the teacher. My body was trembling, hoping this was all a nightmare that had gone too far.

'Are you trying to ruin me?' Johnny turned to Richard. 'Is this payback?'

I looked at him. *Payback?*

'From the looks of it, I don't need payback, mate. You're doing a great job of that yourself!' Richard responded, folding his arms at the commotion.

'Payback? For what?' I questioned.

Johnny's eyes flashed to me, then back to Richard. He suddenly seemed panicked.

'Ava. Stay out of it!' His eyes remained on Richard, who stayed quiet.

'Payback for what though?' I repeated.

Johnny remained silent. I turned to Richard, suddenly feeling worried. 'Richard?'

He sighed heavily, avoiding any eye contact with me. 'Johnny should tell you, Ava.'

'There's nothing to fucking tell, Dick!' His loud voice echoed.

I felt tears of panic run down my scarlet cheeks.

'Johnny?' I called out. 'What's going on? Tell me!'

He tutted, ignoring me.

'Richard, please.' I stepped towards him, worried.

'I didn't come to the wedding because—'

'STOP!' Johnny screeched, marching towards us.

'She has a right to know!' Richard shouted back.

'It's fucking lies, Ava.' Johnny held my arms tightly. I saw the fear take over his face.

'You're scaring me, Johnny.' I turned back to Richard, who lowered his head. 'The night before your wedding, I found out Daphne was pregnant.'

I gulped. 'With Beatrice?'

'Yes,' he replied.

Johnny let go of my arms and began pacing the floor.

'I also found out my best mate Johnny was the one sleeping with my sister before she got pregnant.'

My jaw dropped suddenly as the realisation came over me. My legs were weak, and I stumbled backwards. I turned to Johnny. 'You're . . . you're Beatrice's dad, and you've known about her all of this time?' My voice was weak and faint. Hoping he'd tell me it was a lie, that Richard was making the whole thing up.

'No. No. You can't be? He can't be, Richard. It's a mistake. Daphne was younger than us. A lot younger. Like six or seven years.'

The room remained silent as my head tried to process the information. I'd always had a gut feeling that something was off with Johnny. Ever since we were married, I'd thought it was me, I thought I had done something. For years, I asked him, but I never imagined a secret fucking love-child.

'You told me I was crazy. You told me I was depressed after having Georgie!' I exclaimed. 'All those months of therapy, and the experts said I was the mental case, but I was fucking right!'

'No, no, you were wrong, Ava. I swear I never cheated on you since we got married. Daphne was there, and honestly, half of the boys had a turn. I'm not even sure if that girl's—'

Thump.

I opened my eyes back up, and Johnny lay on the floor clutching his face. I was screaming.

'What the fuck are you doing?' I forced Richard back, who was clutching his fist, bending over Johnny.

'He's not speaking about my sister like that!' He pointed towards Johnny with venom in his voice. 'He is a fucking liar!'

'And so are you!' I cried. 'You have kept this from me! We were friends, we all were, and you turned up here and tried to build a relationship with me! To what? Piss off Johnny? Get some sort of twisted revenge for your sister?'

Richard's shoulders dropped in defeat. 'You know that wasn't the case. I wanted to . . . I honestly wanted to tell you. I came to the wedding that day but you looked so happy when you arrived at the church and I couldn't do it. I couldn't ruin your day, so I stepped back. But when I saw you at the reunion, and we became friends again, I spent hours wondering how I'd tell you, Ava. I knew you had to know.'

I shook my head, not knowing who to believe.

'Fuck, I even came here to your door a few times. Ask your neighbour, he told me you were out. But each time when I saw how hurt you were over the marriage, I couldn't hurt you any more.'

I dropped to the ground. 'Just leave, please, go!'

Richard stood entirely still.

'Fucking leave me alone, Richard!' I screamed.

He nodded slowly, pulled on his glasses, and left. I heard the door close a few seconds later.

Johnny sat up from the floor, massaging his face, unusually dishevelled and bruised. 'Don't believe a word that man says. Look what he's capable of!'

He lowered his hand, showing his crimson red cheek and eye.

'I don't believe any of you anymore,' I said quietly. 'Why didn't you tell me, Johnny?'

His stare was distant.

'When I found out, we were about to get married, Ava,' he said eventually, his eyes tearing up.

I raised my shoulders. 'And the sad thing is, I probably would still have married you anyway.'

Johnny lowered his head and stood to his feet, letting out a small grunt. Spotting Georgie's teddy bear behind the sofa, he bent down to pick it up.

'Will you be all right?' he asked.

I shook my head, feeling my eyes sting from the revelations, as he continued.

'Maybe we need this time. Maybe we needed this out in the open to move on. Have a think. I'll see you in a fortnight, Ava.'

I heard the door slam shut and, in a moment, I began wailing inconsolable tears.

Chapter Twenty-Seven

Ava

'Ava, can you let me in?' I could hear Adam's voice call out from the letterbox. I wasn't sure how long I'd been lying on the bathroom floor. My body felt numb and shattered, but my head questioned every part of my life with Johnny. *How could I have been so stupid not to have seen this?*

'Ava?' he repeated.

'Go away, Adam!' I wailed.

'I'm not going away until you open the door. Please.'

I couldn't move. I was lifeless. Comfortably lifeless. The knocking continued more persistently.

'Fuck off, Adam!' I cried.

'Nope!'

I could hear the small hatch on the letterbox tap up and down, up and down, and eventually, I rose to my feet and stormed towards the door, swinging it open.

Adam's cheery face dropped the moment he saw me. 'Ava, what . . . Are you OK?'

I jerked my head, too tired to explain or talk.

'Ava? Are you alone? Did something happen?'

I walked out onto the cool landing and sat on the top step, still feeling the tears trickle down my swollen face.

'Ava, you need to tell me what's going on,' he demanded, fuelled with worry.

'Why am I never enough, Adam?' I said quietly.

'What?' He sat down beside me.

'Today, I found out Johnny has a secret child, a daughter. He knew throughout our full marriage. He found out the day before our wedding he had got his best mate's sister fucking pregnant, Adam.'

He seemed lost for words, then eventually managed, 'Fuck!'

I nodded, gazing down the stairwell.

'And the guy Richard I've been working for? I thought he liked me, but he only really used me to piss off Johnny.' I paused, then turned to him. 'And you,' my voice quivered, 'I feel like I've messed you around, but now you've met Lina, and seem so much happier without me. Everyone is happier without me.'

Adam wrapped his arm around me tightly, cradling me.

'Hey, don't go comparing me to those pricks.' He laughed a little, then his voice sounded more serious. 'Ava, you don't want me,' he said quietly. 'Deep down, we both know that. You never have, not like that anyway.' Adam paused slightly, thinking of his following sentence. 'I would do anything for you, and I'll always be here, but you don't need someone to want you. Who do *you* want?'

I could feel my aching eyes sting with tears. 'I thought I wanted Johnny.'

303

'And now?' he pressed.

I found a smile washing over my face. 'Well, right now, I only want my friend Beks and my sister.' I managed a laugh.

Adam tilted his head. 'There you go then,' he said and gently kissed the side of my head.

'I just don't know what I will do, Adam. How will I tell Georgie she has a fucking sister? Do I even need to tell her? She knows this wee girl; she's in her fucking class at school!' I ran my hands through my hair in frustration. 'I don't think I'm ever going to get over this.'

He agreed. 'It feels like that now, but it's because you've taken another blow.' He paused, searching for the right words. 'You know, the past month is the best I've seen you. You're changing, Ava. You're working, and writing, and taking Georgie to school. I walk past your door and hear laughing all the time now. You have finally done it, Ava. Don't go back to the dark place you've been in.'

I wiped my arm across my running nose and sat up a little, thinking about what he'd said. 'It's because I met up with the girls again. It's not me, it's *them*. I don't know what I'd do without them.' I paused, thinking of Rebeka and Grace and how busy they'd kept me. How motivated and fun my life had been with them.

'Well, keep going with that. That's what's going to get you through this. You have a job now, income . . .'

'I don't think I have anymore.' I rolled my eyes, thinking of Richard.

'Well, you're a writer, for God's sake. Write about something, and stop editing other people's work! Write more stories for Rogue.' He chuckled a little. 'You have options, Ava.'

I gulped down, appreciative of his positivity throughout my shitstorm.

'Do you want me to come in with you for a while?'

I shook my head. 'No. Thanks, though.'

Adam placed his palm on my face, and I leant into it.

'Pain makes you stronger, kid.'

'Well, I'm gonna wake up one day like fucking Arnie!' We both managed to smile.

'I'm serious! You're just getting started. Look what you've managed in just a few weeks!'

I glanced gratefully at my friend, pulling myself back to my feet, though my entire body felt like lead, and stumbled towards my door.

'Any more words of wisdom before I go in?' I asked.

'Yeah, fuck Johnny Little!' He smirked.

'Fuck them all!' I said and closed the door.

I headed into my living room and picked my phone up from the floor.

I can't make it tonight, but can we catch up tomorrow? I really need to see you both. I'll explain then. And I know I don't say it enough, but I love you both so much xxx

I wandered through to the kitchen and slumped down on the chair. Every part of me ached. I wanted to phone Johnny and go over everything with him. Had he seen Beatrice? Did he pay child support? How long was his fling with Daphne? But I had no energy left to argue, no words could make me feel better. My laptop suddenly pinged from the table.

One new email: Dave Michael cc. Richard Tierney

Hi Ava,
It's Dave, Richard's assistant – many thanks for the quick turnaround on the edits. Great job! I will send another novel through ASAP.
    Regards,
    Dave.

I began typing, then stopped. I didn't know if I wanted to be associated with Richard or his company anymore, but I knew I needed the money and the experience.

Beka: *YES! Love you too, boo x*

    Grace: *Ahh, that›s nice. We'll miss you tonight. Beks is taking me to a club aghh! I'm up for tomorrow!! I loved you since the womb, Ava! Xxxx*

I smiled at my sister's chirpy reply and wondered how they'd react to Johnny's secret-baby love affair. *Love?* Did Johnny love Daphne? Or was it just meaningless sex? I felt pains in my chest just thinking about his lies. How could he walk down an aisle before all those people and pretend it hadn't happened? I wondered if Steve knew. Or Grace? I felt sick scorch the back of my throat at the thought. I'm sure she'd have let it slip. That girl couldn't hold her water, never mind something as big as that.

I felt dazed. My brain had too much information and questions rattling around it, but I knew the feeling of betrayal would never shift, even after getting the answers. *How many times can Johnny knock me down?* He'd taken so much from me, and just as I was slowly building myself back up, he hit me with a bastard child. But something felt different this time around; I was less alone. Even when Beks or Grace weren't with me, I knew I still had them unconditionally. And I wasn't going to let him take them away, not this time. I wouldn't allow it.

My eyes diverted back to my laptop as another email from Dave with more work popped up. I sighed at the thought. I loved writing, but fixing other writers' work wasn't my end goal. I stood up, pacing my small kitchen floor. My head was bulging with emotions and anger and thoughts. I needed a release. I needed a distraction. I sat back at the table, opened a blank Word document and began typing without a second thought.

I typed and typed, writing from my past experience of all the hurt and pain I'd been through. It sort of felt like therapy, a way of letting the world know how wrong I'd been, and that I was still here – still wanting to make something of my life. I planned out a book and broke it into chapters, focusing on happiness, money, fun, career, sex and finding your purpose. I knew from failing in every single one of those areas how shitty it felt, and I knew exactly how to overcome it. I incorporated Beka's banter and Grace's wise words, relating to my slump. Even through the numbness and pain that sat in my chest, I somehow began to feel invigorated, as I recalled every piece of advice they had given me. The time flew by as my mind buzzed with ideas. Eventually, I slumped over the dining table after 4 a.m., fast asleep.

Chapter Twenty-Eight

Ava

I woke to a loud banging from my front door.

'She's in there, I know it.'

I raised my head instantly, feeling the pain from lying face down on a table all night. *Ouch!*

'Ava?' the voice continued.

'Maybe she's shagging the vegan? We could check his place out?' another voice said.

'She isn't.' Adam's deep voice echoed in the stairwell.

Oh, shit. My stumbling walk grew into a scurry as I moved quickly through the hallway and opened the door. The bright light shone off my eyes, and I squinted at Beka and Grace.

'Oh, thank God!' Grace bellowed. 'We got her, Adam!'

I looked past them and lifted my hand, giving a half-arsed wave to him standing at his front door.

'What are you guys doing here?' I asked.

Grace barged past me. 'Johnny told Steve what happened yesterday! I can't believe you never told us!' she called out, striding past me towards my living room.

Beks shrugged with sorrow in her eyes and followed her inside.

I closed the door and continued into the room.

'What happened here, hun?' Beka's eyes skimmed over my chaotic home.

'Yeah . . . So, Richard punched Johnny for talking shit about Daphne, and this place was already a bit of a mess, but that made it worse, I suppose.' I was still waking up, feeling lifeless. *What time did I fall asleep?* I wondered.

'Wait, what?' Grace seemed more intense than usual.

'Tell me he hit him fucking hard,' Beks screeched loudly, rummaging through her bag and cracking open a cold bottle of rosé wine. She swigged it, then passed it to me.

I nodded back, taking a sip.

'Ava, are you ok? We've tried phoning all morning as soon as we found out. Then Beks panicked because of the weird emotional message you sent, and we put two and two together.' Grace wrapped her arms around me tightly.

'I'm fine, honestly. I'm OK.' I patted her back until she eventually let go, and we all sat down, squashed up on the one sofa.

'I am lost for words about Johnny, babe. I mean, Daphne, fucking hell!' Beks scoffed, recalling Richard's young, hectic, crazy sister.

'I know. That was a kick in the teeth,' I admitted, passing the bottle to Grace.

'A kick up the Jack 'n' Danny,' she stated. 'What did he have to say for himself?'

I shrugged, thinking of how composed Johnny was. 'I don't even think he said sorry. He just said it was before we were married, and he'd never cheated since.'

The girls scoffed.

'He also said everyone was shagging Daphne, so he wasn't sure if Beatrice was even his. That's when Richard decked him.'

'And quite right, too!' Grace added, gulping heavily on the wine.

Beks sat up. 'You seem calm, Ava. Weirdly hinged considering . . .'

'My husband has a secret child?'

'I was going to say you have a stepdaughter called Beatrice!'

We all burst out laughing.

'Stop, that's a sin!' I smiled. 'I think I'm in shock. I just feel numb,' I admitted.

Grace's eyes filled with tears, and I leant on her shoulder.

'He made me think I was crazy. I thought I was the reason our marriage broke down but I always had a feeling he was hiding something.'

'I can't wrap my head around any of it,' Grace blubbed.

'I'd love to wrap my head into Johnny fucking Little's right now, babe!' Beks replied, pulling the bottle of rosé from Grace's grip.

'How could you lie for so long to the woman you supposedly love? How could he make up a big fake story, turning all his friends against Richard, when he was the one in the wrong?'

'Because he is a cunt!' Beks stated.

'A massive narcissistic cunt!' Grace continued.

'But last night, after I heard, I sort of felt relieved. I wasn't crazy. I mean, I still probably had post-natal depression after Georgie, but I wasn't crazy with my accusations towards him. This wasn't my fault.' I paused, cringing for myself. 'And I began writing again. Don't laugh, but I sort of began planning a submission to write a self-help book. For people who don't have a best friend.'

My two friends shared a look.

'But you have best friends, babe?' Beks replied.

'No, I know that. That's what I mean. I thought about how much reuniting with you guys has helped me, then I thought, what do people do who don't have friends like you?'

'They lie in bed all day and forget they're wearing tampons!' Beks giggled.

'Exactly! I don't know what I'd have done without you girls this summer,' I admitted.

'It's our hot girl summer, Ava! And we're not going anywhere,' Grace smiled.

I nodded back, still feeling emotionless from the events.

'I would never have managed to book a shoot with Katya if it wasn't for you two, that's for sure!'

Grace dived into her handbag, 'Oh, I forgot, this arrived for you today, Beks. It's from *Inner Me!*'

'What is it?' she asked.

Grace handed Beks a large white envelope and she began tearing it open with her long acrylics. She skimmed over the pages, saying '*Bla, bla, bla. Bla, bla, bla, bla,*' and then shrugged, handing it back to Grace. I chuckled as Grace popped on her glasses and looked over the letter. 'It's a non-disclosure contract. They want you to sign it, stating that you can never discuss Mitchell on any public forum.'

Beka rolled her eyes and threw her body back into the sofa.

'Why the fuck would I want to?' she hissed.

Grace carried on turning the pages, 'WAIT! Beks!' Her voice suddenly got higher. 'They've given you a cheque for one hundred thousand pounds!'

I gasped. 'Fuck off!'

Beks remained still, and I wondered if she was in shock.

'Beka, that's amazing!' Grace nudged her.

She smiled. 'Yeah, whoopie!'

'Are you not pleased, Beks? That money could change your life. You could invest it back into Rogue. Or put it towards a house or office or something.'

She seemed hesitant. 'It's hush money,' she sighed. 'It's as if my relationship was wrong, and I'm getting paid off to keep quiet, to delete the past or something.'

Grace stood up. 'It's money because they mistreated you, Rebeka. They wrongly fired you. Companies like that have legislation they need to follow. You can't just sack an employee out of the blue. You had a contract.'

I agreed with Grace. 'Just think about it. This is a good thing.' I smiled, hoping she'd see sense. Part of me wondered what I'd get if I went to the papers about the affair. Maybe then I could afford to eat.

'Just wait.' She held her hand up, eager to move on from the subject. 'Tell me more about the book, Ava! When will it be finished?'

My eyes skimmed to Grace, realising Beks wasn't able to process the letter yet.

'I honestly don't know. I've made an excellent head start though, with the proposal,' I replied, waking up fully and feeling proud of last night's achievement.

'I can't wait to read it,' Grace smiled, sitting back down.

'So, how was last night?' I asked. 'What club did you go to?'

Both of them turned to one another and burst out laughing.

'*What?*'

'Beka got us VIP tickets to Fabric! It was awesome.' Grace giggled.

'And we met up with some Italian footballers. It was a great night.' Beks continued to laugh suspiciously.

'And? What did I miss?'

'Well, while you were busy writing a novel, Beka was . . .'

'Getting her tits sucked in the back of a cab!' She held her hands up proudly.

We all laughed together at the image.

'Classy!'

'How was it?' I asked.

'The tit sucking?'

I nodded back, excited to hear all the details.

'It wasn't a patch on Mitchell Travers gnawing at them. But . . . a pretty standard tit suck.'

I smiled back, knowing exactly how it felt to be broken up with someone you loved so deeply.

'So, Mitchell was an excellent breast licker? I didn't realise that was a niche,' Grace stated, overthinking the act entirely.

'And I didn't think cock cages were one, babe!'

Grace suddenly turned bright red as she slapped Rebeka's arm. 'All I'll say is Mitchell was most definitely breastfed!'

'Wait, what? Rewind. What's a cock cage?' My mind reeled with hilarity and shock as my best friends filled me in on their night in the city. Grace told about Steve and his cock cage and his unfortunate slip of the tongue. We laughed until tears ran down our cheeks together. Eventually, Beks sprang up, noticing the time.

'I need to head, ladies. I have a shoot! And Ava, I have a great story for you to write! Like in the next couple of days, please.' She rubbed her hands together excitedly.

I smiled. 'I'd love to!'

Grace stood up and joined her. 'I better go back too. I've been speaking to Women's Aid about working for them. Helping women who might be less fortunate get justice.'

Feeling proud of my sister, I gasped. 'That's amazing, Grace!'

Beka nodded. 'She's getting back out there. We all are!'

'And it's because of you, Ava. It boils my blood seeing women getting treated badly by their ex-husbands. I've had enough of them all!'

I laughed and nodded. 'Good for you, Grace! Get the bastards.'

She seemed serious, zipping up her bag. 'Oh, I intend to.'

Beks took one last gulp, and left the rest of the wine on the coffee table.

'Who are you shooting, Beks? Katya?' I asked.

The pair began walking towards the door. 'No, remember the fourteen-year-old model, Tia? I've got her in for a 'face of the future' segment. All very PC this time! I want to show her youth.'

I smiled at both of my friends.

'You can join me if you like, Ava?' Beks offered. 'Or I can pass you her number and you could interview her by phone? Write a 'getting to know her' segment?'

I shook my head. 'If you pass me the number, I'll give her a call. I'm going to work on this book idea. I need the distraction.'

'Will you be all right?' Grace asked, reaching for my hand. I nodded, getting to my feet.

'I think I will.' I managed a smile.

Grace leant over to hug me but paused, 'Ava? What the hell is that all over your wall?' she asked, pointing to Mr McGroaty's spunk trail.

'Eh . . . Georgie spilt a yoghurt,' I muttered, without energy to explain the story.

'Hmm . . .' Grace hugged me and headed through the hallway.

Beka leant forward and whispered, 'I know a cum splat when I see one. Good for you, girl!' She winked and began walking to the door. 'We'll message you, hun!'

'Bye!' I felt my cheeks hurt from their unexpected visit. No one in the world made me happier than the pair of them. Beks closed over the door, and I sat back at the laptop – *time to work*.

Rebeka & Grace

As Beka and Grace wandered through Croydon together, chatting, Beks paused momentarily, then asked, 'Babe, do you think I should sign the non-disclosure?'

Grace put her arm around her back, encouraging her to walk. 'I think it's a great offer with the money. And Mitchell's lawyers have probably advised him to hit you with both at the same time. That way, you both get what you want. Silence, no drama, and an obscene payout for you to keep his name out of your Instagram account or anything else you end up doing. People become bitter after a break-up, and if the tabloids knew you were dating, they'd offer you mega money to sell your story!'

Beks shook her head. 'That's never what I wanted.'

'I know.'

'Have you got a pen, babe?'

Grace nodded, reaching for her bag, and pulled out a customised ball-point pen. Beks bent over, leaning on her knee, and signed the non-disclosure quickly before handing it back to Grace.

She walked a few steps, replaying Mitchell accusing her of wanting his money at the launch party over in her mind, then stopped.

'Send back the cheque, too. I don't want any of his money,' she said, walking to the side of the road to pull a cab.

'Beka, as your lawyer, you need to rethink that.'

'And, as a friend, you need to send the cheque back. He's not thinking that I became successful because of *his* dosh. I'm doing it on my own. I don't want to sell stories about him; he can get his non-disclosure, but I don't want the money!'

A cab pulled up, and Beks opened the back door.

'Speak after the shoot?'

Grace shrugged, feeling emotional at her friend's reasoning. 'Love you, Beks.'

Beka winked back and then nodded.

Chapter Twenty-Nine

Grace

Grace steered home and began researching for her interview. She headed upstairs to Steve's office while he was at work and set up his computer. As she sat there waiting for the computer to load, she felt a strange feeling of déjà vu, recalling the last time she'd used his PC, but shook it off immediately. *We're doing better now*, Grace told herself. She browsed and started researching the background of each charity, while taking notes on her pad. After around forty minutes, Grace clicked back on the browser to research some more. She found her eyes steered towards the search history button. She dropped her pen on the desk, feeling distracted. *You don't have to check up on him*, she told herself. She then lifted the pen, examining the screen. A few moments later, she sighed deeply. *Why am I doing this? It's a complete invasion of privacy! I'm not the type of person who doesn't trust her husband!* She took off her glasses and began rubbing her face frustratedly. Her fingers hovered over the mouse, wanting to click but torn with integrity. *OK, maybe just one last look, just to see if his history's changed since we spoke,* she told herself. Grace clicked on the browser history. Empty. *Why has he deleted his searches?* Her foot began tapping the floor nervously. *Stop, Grace, you are overthinking.*

She stood to leave the office and lifted her handbag from the desk. She didn't want to be the insecure wife who questioned everything about her husband. She didn't want to be like her sister, driven crazy by meaningless accusations. But then again, they weren't meaningless, not now. She paused, then shook her head, beginning to storm out of the room, but her eyes caught a glimpse of the contract from *Inner Me!* that Beka had signed. She turned to the cabinet, bending down as she rummaged for an envelope to return the cheque and agreement. Finally, after a few seconds of lifting out papers and notes from Steve's work, she found a stack of envelopes. Grace lifted them out of the drawer but then gasped. Underneath the envelopes, squeezed at the bottom of her old oak cabinet, was a stack of magazines.

Nude men magazines.

She felt her heart race, lifting them out. 'What the fuck?' She suddenly felt dizzy. It was crammed full of topless bodybuilders, cowboys, buff men with bare arses, huge dicks and thongs. She slumped to the floor, wondering why the fuck her husband would have such a collection of naked men. *Was he working on a case for one of the models?* But then, surely, he would have mentioned it. *Was he reading a particular segment that caught his eye?* But, the more she flicked through the crispy, worn pages, she realised that apart from jock straps and huge dick bulges, there was not much content. Grace was beginning to hyperventilate as she finally digested: *was Steve gay?*

That evening, Grace had composed herself enough to come downstairs and make dinner, awaiting her husband's arrival. She cooked a honey roast ham with all the trimmings in a complete daze. She set out the table with the finest cutlery and piled the magazines at the side of the worktop. Everything over the past few months was adding up: *the lack of sex, his newfound love for bondage, his panic when she saw his browser history, and then deleting it.* She had a solid case for any lawyer to fight – the pornographic evidence was compelling – but part of her wanted to lose. She wanted him to have a reasonable explanation. *What would I do if he was gay?* she asked herself, while heating the plates in the oven. *Is my marriage over?* Grace felt a heaviness weighing down on her. She needed answers, but first she required the truth.

Around seven, she stood up as his key turned in the door.

'Hi, honey,' Steve called out.

'Hi, dinner's ready,' she replied, brushing back her hair and standing to greet him.

'Mmm . . . Smells delicious!' He walked to the kitchen, slipping off his coat and handing it to her. She smiled politely, hanging it up in the hallway.

'Good day?' Grace asked.

'Hmm . . . OK. Meetings and things. I have court in the morning,' he replied.

As she returned to the kitchen, she noticed Steve sitting at the table, waiting to be served. Grace brought out the two fully packed dinner plates from the oven and popped them down.

'How was your day?' Steve asked, leaning over and pouring a glass of wine. He signalled to Grace for a top up, and she nodded politely.

'My day,' she chuckled. 'I went to see Ava to make sure she was holding up OK.'

Steve nodded sympathetically. 'And? How is she?'

'Great. Amazing. She's writing again.' She began chopping up her meal as her husband tucked in. 'How's the ham?'

'Delicious, darling, thank you.'

Grace continued eating. 'So I have a question; it's silly, really. Do you prefer ham or sausage, Steve?'

He laughed a little. 'Well, that depends, Grace. I like both!'

She turned white and chugged her drink.

'Easy, darling,' he laughed. 'Everything all right?'

She could feel her emotions ripple as she sliced through the meat, 'Well, yes, I suppose, but I have another question. Steve, will you be completely honest if I ask you something?'

He huffed, throwing his head back in despair. 'Can't we enjoy a meal together?'

She levelled her stare sternly at him.

'OK. OK.' Steve wiped down his chin. 'Go on then, I'm listening.'

'Are you gay?'

His eyes grew three times the size. 'Excuse me?'

'*Or* bisexual, maybe?'

He scoffed, then shook his head at the question. 'I will not dignify that question with an answer, Grace. How dare you!' Suddenly, he seemed furious, dropping his cutlery with a bang on the table. 'Is this because of the other night? Because of what slipped out in the bedroom?'

'No,' she replied softly.

'It's ludicrous.'

Grace stood up, feeling tense about what might happen next. She lifted the pile of magazines and turned to Steve. His face turned pale and clammy.

'It's because of the secret stash of male pornographic magazines in our home,' she said, staring into his eyes.

He was gone. Entirely speechless.

'Grace, I . . .'

'Steve. I am your wife. Before you say anything, please know that I will not judge you. We have been friends since we were kids. But I demand to know the truth. I need to know the truth.' She could feel her eyes fill as she looked at him. 'I am your fucking wife!'

His face remained motionless as his mind caught up.

'Please,' she pleaded.

'I don't know why I have them, Grace,' he said at last. 'I honestly don't know.'

'Are you having an affair, Steve?'

'What? Please, no, I have *never* cheated on you, and I would never hurt you like that.'

'OK,' she breathed a sigh of relief, sitting back at the table.

He squirmed around the chair, trying to find an explanation, then finally burst into tears. 'I don't know what's fucking wrong with me!'

Grace felt her heart break, having rarely seen him this emotional throughout their entire relationship. She reached over and held his hand with great difficulty, trying her hardest to not overreact. 'There isn't anything wrong with you, Steve. That's if . . . well . . . If you are attracted to men, then . . .' She felt her heart sting with pain, trying to make him feel better but knowing how much she was hurting inside. 'If that's who you are, then I suppose I'll have to deal with it. But I thought it was me, *you* made me feel like it was *me*. I thought there was something wrong with me.'

He nodded between sobs.

'I'm sorry. I'm so sorry. We were married so young, Grace. And I love you with my whole heart. But . . . they are mine. I am so ashamed.'

She felt like someone had jabbed her in the gut.

'But when? When did you start liking men?'

He held his face in his hands and raised his shoulders, 'I . . . I first noticed being attracted to men at school, but when we met, I fell madly in love. I thought those feelings were gone. I want those feelings to be gone.'

'School?' Grace repeated, trying to digest his words.

He bobbed his head guiltily.

'We got married young, and people change, Steve.'

He rubbed his eyes and glanced at her. 'I've not changed how I feel about you.'

She managed a smile, still feeling numb.

'But as a husband and wife, we've not been great for a while, and maybe this is why.'

He nodded. 'I'll stop. I know I can stop. It's revolting, I know it is.'

Grace leant over and grabbed his shoulders, 'It's not revolting, Steve. OK? Stop!'

He rested his head against her hand as she touched him.

'Is that why you use . . .' she cleared her throat, 'the cage?' she asked. 'To stop yourself?'

He darted her a look, unable to speak.

Grace leant back on her chair, pushing her dinner plate away. *Why didn't I see this coming?* She turned to her husband, who was utterly broken with guilt. *I can't do this.*

'Maybe . . . Steve, I think . . . What if this is something you need to explore?' she said, her voice quivering. 'It's unfair for me to want to change you. As you said, we got married so young and recently, we've not been happy.'

'No. No. Grace, this isn't ending. I love you,' he pleaded, falling to his knees and kissing her hand.

'And I love you. I love you so much that I've realised I'm not what you need. This marriage is holding you back. God, it's holding me back, too. There isn't anything wrong with you if you are gay, bisexual or whatever, but you will never be happy in a marriage if you don't figure out what you are. Who you are!' She could feel the cold, salty tears stream down her face.

'I can't lose you,' he sobbed.

Grace managed a fleeting smile towards him, knowing he already had.

'Grace, I can't. I just can't.'

'I think you have to. For both of us. How could I trust you? Or live knowing you're unhappy? It's not fair to me, and it's not fair to you,' she replied.

He ran his hands through his head of thick curls.

'So, this is it? This is how it ends?' he asked, broken, staring into her eyes.

Grace sobbed and shook her head bravely in disagreement. 'Maybe this is where it starts.'

Chapter Thirty

Ava

Almost two weeks had passed, and I was walking into Tony's to catch up with the girls. The weather in London had been stunning, but rather than spend the day down Hyde Park ogling the DILFs at the outdoor gym as I'd hoped to do when Georgie was away, I used my time productively and locked myself up in my tiny apartment in a writing bubble. My body leaked creativity for the first time in years and, crammed to the brim with canned soup and the odd kebab, I completed two more interviews for Rogue, worked on edits for Richard's assistant, and completed my self-help book proposal. It allowed me to put Johnny at the back of my mind and concentrate all my focus on *The Best Friend's Diary*. I had yet to speak to Johnny, but Georgie called me every evening from his phone and told me about her Florida trip. I sometimes wondered what they were up to or if maybe he'd met a single mum over there and sparked a relationship with her, but when the anxiety took over, I lifted my laptop and kept on writing.

As I walked into Tony's, Rebeka was waiting at our usual spot, and I headed over to greet her with a hug.

'Hey, babe!' She smiled cautiously. 'You OK?'

I laughed. 'Honestly, considering everything . . . I'm . . . I'm OK. I feel strangely fine. I'm trying not to think about Jonathan Little or Richard Tierney.' I smiled, pulling out a chair and taking a seat. 'How are you?'

'Yeah, yeah. Good, babe. Well, great, actually! I didn't want to say that because I know you'll be feeling like a bag of shit, but I've had a few shoots this week. Had Katya in, and I've lined up a couple more stories I need you to write!'

I nodded. 'Of course!'

'Only when you've finished that book idea of yours, babe! How's it coming along?'

I grinned widely and reached into my handbag, bringing out a printed copy. 'It's finished!' I buzzed.

Rebeka's jaw dropped. 'No way! You smashed it, girl,' she said, reaching out and flicking through the pages. 'I don't have to read all of this, do I?'

My shoulders dropped slightly at her reply.

'I'm joking! Of course, I will!' She laughed loudly just as Grace entered.

'That's only the *proposal* for the book. Wait until you have to read the full thing!'

Beka's smile faded. 'Just make sure it's in an audio version, hun. I'm too busy for more than a few pages.'

'Hi, guys,' Grace said quietly.

'Hey,' I smiled. 'Don't worry, I'm OK,' I laughed a little as she took a seat.

'Fuckin' hell, babe, you look like shit,' Beks blurted, noticing how tired and pale my sister looked.

'Beks!' I warned. 'You do not!' I nudged her, and she burst into tears.

'Christ, I was only saying, Grace. If I had a bad day, I'd expect you two to tell me, you know?'

Grace rolled her eyes. 'It's not that. *God*, everything at home is such a mess!'

'What?' I questioned, feeling confused. The last time I saw her and Steve, he was making her artificially squirt in her knickers at a party.

'It's Steve. He's moved out,' she whimpered.

I gasped, immediately looking at Beks in disbelief.

'What? What happened?' I asked, getting more worried as Grace stayed silent. '*Hey!* Come on! Don't worry, I'm sure you will sort it out!'

Grace shook her head sternly.

'Well, what happened then, babe? Spit it out, for fuck's sake,' Beks pressured.

'I think . . . *well* . . . I don't even know. Where do I start?' She panicked, her neck and face turning blotchier by the second. '*Well,* I found . . .'

Beks groaned impatiently at the table as Grace struggled with the words, and I flashed her a look.

'Steve's gay. *Well,* yes, I think he might be gay.'

The table turned silently cold.

'SHUT THE FUCK UP!' Beks eventually said, her mouth gaping as wide as the Clyde.

Grace shook her head and whispered, 'I found magazines of nude men!' She turned behind her cautiously, making sure our conversation remained private. 'He admitted to me they were his!'

'Grace, I really don't know what to say,' I admitted, shocked. 'There must be a mistake.'

Beka's mouth was still hanging open.

I screwed my face at her to snap out of it and urged her to speak.

'And has he been banging guys behind your back?'

'Oh, Beks, for fuck's sake!' I snapped.

She shrugged innocently towards me.

'But has he? Like, did you ask him that?' I asked.

'Of course, he hasn't! He is completely ashamed of it. He didn't want to separate, nor do I, but can I live with that on my mind?'

'You fucking can't!' Beks scoffed.

'When did this happen, Grace?' I asked, still wrapping my head around it all.

'I found out last week. *I know,* I know, I should have told you guys sooner, but I didn't want to believe it. I just needed time to process this before saying it out loud. He moved to his mum's last night.'

I sank back into the chair.

'So, you're keeping the house?' Beks asked.

She nodded. 'For now, anyway. But I was offered the job at the women's charity.' She smiled briefly, but it slipped away just as quick.

'That's amazing!' I said, rubbing her back.

'Yes, girl!' Rebeka winked towards her.

She let out a sigh, and we sat in silence together.

Eventually, Rebeka stood up and said, 'Why don't I

330

order for us at the counter? The service has nosedived in here!'

'Cola and a cheese and bean tatty for me.'

'Just a glass of water, thanks, Beks,' Grace replied.

As Beks stepped away, I turned to my sister, 'You know you're going to be OK, don't you?'

She stared into the distance, her eyes heavy and glistening, holding back the tears.

'Grace, look at me. I came through it, and if you ever want a night away, sleep with me and Georgie. You don't have to be alone. I remember hating sleeping alone at the start, all the weird noises you would hear during the night, and the people outside chatting. But now, I love my own space. I love it because I know I'm not alone. Not really. I have you, Georgie, Beka and Adam, and you do too.'

She leant over and hugged me tightly, with a look of not quite believing me yet. 'Thank you,' she replied softly.

'So, what are you planning to do about this book, Ava?' Rebeka asked as she returned to the table.

'Oh, I'm so sorry I haven't asked how it's coming on,' Grace said. 'How's it going?'

'She's bloody finished a draft, babe!'

'Well, a proposal!' I held the stack of paper up proudly. 'I brought you two a copy each – I printed it out this morning at the library, and it cost me seven quid so please, please don't lose them.'

Grace sat up in her chair, looking happy for the distraction from her love life.

'I figured I should send this on to a publisher or something. Then, in the meantime, I can actually write the book. I'll let you read it first in case it's shit, but I suppose that's the long-term plan.'

Rebeka let out a laugh.

'What?'

'Well, we all know a publisher, don't we?' She rolled her eyes towards me.

'A publisher that isn't Richard Tierney!' I insisted.

'Ava, I think you should talk to Richard. Reach out. I know he should have told you about Beatrice, but he was in an awful situation, too. He raised that child like his own and didn't have to!' Grace piped up.

'*And* he winched me, started this weird thing between us, introduced my daughter to her fucking sister without her knowledge, and never uttered a word about it!'

'But, hear him out. Maybe he could explain?'

I laughed. 'Grace, he hasn't contacted me. He got his bloody assistant to email me instead with new work, which is just plain awkward because Richard is cc'd in on every email but is like a ghost in the thread. Richard doesn't want to explain! He's a prick that has been caught out, end of.'

'Well, think of the book. Why don't you drop him an email? It wouldn't hurt. Get some advice on it.'

I snarled back.

Rebeka covered her face, listening to us disagree, and huffed. 'Look, fuck him, Ava, I agree. But don't fuck your chances of having a career you've dreamt about in the process, because of a grudge!'

'A grudge?' I questioned. 'Beks, it's been a fortnight, and in that time I discovered my husband got a girl pregnant, and the kid goes to the same school as my daughter. Oh, and the guy I kissed, who is also my new boss, knew all about it! And raised my husband's child like his own! This is serious *Jeremy Kyle* shit!'

They both agreed finally. 'It's up to you, babe, but I'm all about being selfish. You deserve a chance, and if Richard, the lying cunt, can give it to you, I'd be on my knees sucking his big old dick and playing along!'

I rolled my eyes. 'You've been there, remember?' I eventually smiled, and we all laughed around the table together.

The drinks arrived, and we began gabbing about Rebeka's shoot. I watched my sister try her best to engage in the discussion, but she slowly zoned in and out. I felt my heart break for her, watching her struggle, knowing how bad she must feel. How bad it always feels. That horrible gut wrench every moment it crosses your mind, similar to a death.

When Beks and I finished our lunch, I asked Grace to pop home with me for a girl's night, but she politely declined, craving her own space. So, together, we headed to the station, hugging one another tightly as we split up.

That evening, I began researching the best publishers in the UK – ones that didn't involve Richard. The entire publishing world seemed somehow attached to this cunt. Different divisions seemed to fall under the one umbrella of Richard Tierney's company. I sighed, then watched a YouTube tutorial on self-publishing vs traditional publishing. If I self-published, I'd be lucky to make fifty sales a year, never mind get my voice out there, and it wouldn't be on bookshelves. I started to doubt the chances of my book ever getting read. It seemed that writing the fucking thing was the easy part. I paced my living room and replayed what the girls had said at lunch. *Maybe this was my chance? Am I being stubborn by not asking Richard for help?* Would he even want to help after witnessing my daughter's teacher's cum slide down my living room wall? I mean, he didn't even ask me what that was about. He stood there watching the knickers glide down slowly, completely expressionless. *What must he think?* And the hurtful things I said. I racked my brain, remembering what I said to him. The entire Daphne/Johnny confession seemed like such a blur now. *Was I out of order*? I wondered. *What the fuck do I do?*

I opened the laptop cautiously and began typing an email to Richard. *Maybe if I act professionally, he will separate business from pleasure*. I'm sure a man with this much intellect can respond to a simple email regarding a business proposal. Maybe he would pass it on to another editor at his company?

Dear Mr Tierney,

I apologise for the delayed response on editing the new work. I have had a lot on

this week; I'm sure you can understand. I aim to have the edits completed by the end of the day.

However, I have emailed today as I have recently written a book proposal (see attached). Would you read over and pass on any notes, or perhaps pass on details of a contact who might? I understand how difficult it is to get published in this climate, so any advice would be welcomed.

Regards,

Ava Little.

Send.

Almost immediately, an email response popped up. My breath quickened, wondering what he'd reply. *Would he mention nearly knocking Johnny out?* Or were we pretending it didn't happen at all?

★This is an automated email★

Mr Tierney is currently on leave. If you have any queries, please email Dave Michael. Details below.

Shit! He'd never mentioned going anywhere. *Maybe he's done some damage to his hand from that punch? What if Johnny's charged him, and he's in prison?* I gasped and clutched my face in a panic. *Wait, calm down, Ava. The police would want statements if that happened*, I thought. I copied the email I'd composed to Richard and re-sent

it to Dave, hoping for a quick response. I gazed at the
laptop for ten minutes. I was hitting the refresh key
every few seconds. Nothing.

Beka: *What you girls up to? Xx*

Me: *Looking up book stuff for publishing, you? xx*

Beka: *One image attached.*

I clicked on the photo of her lying on the couch,
holding my proposal and smiling.

Me: *I need honest opinions!! If it's shite, TELL ME!!!*

Grace: *I'm doing the same! This is an amazing idea,
Ava. I'm so proud of you xx*

Beka: *Me too! Could we promote this on Rogue?? Xxx*

My face burst into a wide grin as my friends designed
all the ways to help make me a success.
Ping.

One new email from Dave Michael.

Hi Ava,
**Great to hear from you! And well done on
the writing!**
   **Unfortunately, I am inundated with
typescripts at the minute, and we only accept
work solicited from an established agency.
My advice is to submit your work to an
agent, and they will provide you with the**

relevant support!
Good luck!
Regards Dave

Ps. Look forward to receiving the edits.

I screenshotted the email and sent it to the group chat.

Me: *Great. I need an agent. This seems impossible.*

Beka: *No, he seems like an unhelpful cunt!*

Grace: *BEX! Hahaha xx*

I laughed loudly, glancing at the chat between us all.

Grace: *He's only doing his job! xx*

Beka: *Yeah, well, he needs to read your idea! It's fan-fucking-tastic! X*

Me: *Love you guys xxx*

Chapter Thirty-One

Ava

It was the morning of Georgie's return, and I woke with butterflies in anticipation of her happy ball of energy bulldozing through my door. I'd checked the flight scanner website throughout the night to ensure she arrived safe and sound at Heathrow. I wondered what Johnny would be like when he saw me again – well, if he saw me. He might let Georgie walk up the stairs alone. I hadn't spoken to him since he left my home after Richard's punch. I felt anxiety pound my arsehole at the thought of seeing him. I'd completely occupied myself with writing over the past fortnight, and I hadn't analysed the situation. Well, except for in bed, alone. I'd wake up and review everything in my head again. *Why didn't he tell me? What will happen now? Should I tell Georgie she has a sister?* So much wasn't spoken about, but I knew it would be discussed at some point. I glanced at my hand, trembling with nerves at the thought of facing him. I stretched it out and tried to settle myself, tidying up for Georgie's arrival. I opened the windows wide in an attempt

to let some sunshine brighten my mood, and blasted
Taylor Swift while washing the dishes and hoovering
my thin floral carpet.

Ping.

> **Beka:** *How did it go? Are they back yet, Ava?*

> **Grace:** *Let us know xxx*

> **Me:** *Should be here in ten. I'll keep you posted! I'm
> dreading seeing Johnny tbh. What are you guys up to?
> Xxx*

> **Beka:** *No wonder! Don't even acknowledge him!!!
> I'm just editing my latest shoot for some Insta posts!
> Xx*

> **Grace:** *Oh God, Ava! Don't blame you! I'm having
> a day in bed. I don't feel up to much. Give Georgie a
> big hug from me xxx*

I sighed for my sister, knowing how isolated she must
feel. I didn't want her to go through the torture I did
when my marriage blew up.

> **Me:** *Guys, I was thinking we should throw a wee
> party tonight. Just in mine? For Georgie coming home.
> I'll get some party food, and we can wear onesies and
> play board games! xxx*

> **Beka***: YES! But I hope you don't mean the adults
> wear onesies. Xx*

Grace: *I'm not sure. I feel a bit down recently, sorry, Ava xxx*

Me: *ERM . . . YES! Onesies are non-negotiable. You can pick up one in Primark! Oh, Grace, please say yes. She's missed her aunty, and I know a Georgie hug will make you feel a lot better xxx*

Grace: *What time? xxx*

Me: *Seven?? See you guys then xxx*

A sigh of relief washed over me. Operation 'Get Grace out of the House' was complete. I would have needed a fucking SWAT team this early on in the break-up, but I knew she was strong.

The door knocked, and I stood up straight. I walked slowly towards it. *Please don't be there. Please don't be a cunt in front of Georgie,* I panicked, feeling my pulse quicken. I turned the door handle and felt a small dive towards me.

'MUMMY!' Georgie's small arms swaddled my legs, and I laughed loudly. Completely surprised, I bent down and picked her up as she wrapped her little arms around my neck. She had on a beautiful princess dress and tiara.

'I have missed you so much!' I felt a bubble at the back of my throat, seeing her again. 'And look at your suntan!'

She giggled loudly, comparing her brown arms to my peely-wally colouring.

I peeked behind her to see Johnny with a soft smile on his face, his strawberry-blonde hair now icy-looking after a fortnight in the sunshine.

'Hi,' he said.

I half-smiled back politely and then returned my full attention to Georgie.

'Mummy, we saw the real-life castle where the princesses actually live!' she boasted.

I threw my head back. 'You did not!'

'We did! Didn't we, Daddy?'

He laughed at her excitement. 'We sure did. And did you tell Mummy what we got her?'

I glanced between the pair.

'Come get it, Georgie,' he said.

She wriggled out of my arms and walked back to Johnny. He passed her a little gift bag, and she handed it to me.

'WOW! For me!' I said, feeling myself blush. Why would he buy me a present? Was it an 'I'm sorry I pumped my best friend's teenage sister and got her pregnant just before our wedding day' gift? My mind was blown. Johnny had never been sentimental. I remember constantly dropping hints about birthday or Christmas gifts, and I'd end up with clothes chosen by his mother every year instead. 'Thank you, baby.' I bent down and kissed Georgie's forehead, taking a hold of the bag.

'She would have brought the whole of Disney World home to you if she could,' Johnny said.

I smiled towards my daughter, avoiding any eye contact with him, and stroked my fingers through her hair.

Georgie strolled past me towards the living room, and I stood for a few seconds.

'Well, I better go see to her. I hope you had a nice time, and thanks for this.' I flapped the bag around slightly.

'Ava. Wait. Can we talk?' he asked. I looked up from the ground. Why did he always look so good with a tan? He wore a plain white T-shirt and combat-style trousers, looking casual and handsome. I scanned his face for any signs of bruising from the punch, but it all seemed to have healed.

'Look, Johnny, I don't want to argue. Let me enjoy my day with Georgie, please. Can we talk about everything later?'

His brows raised slightly. 'I don't want to argue.'

'Well, what then, Johnny?' I said more sternly. 'What the fuck have I done now? Or what should I be doing?'

He shook his head, then lowered it. 'I miss you, Ava. I miss us. Our family, our life. I know I've done wrong, and I should have told you about Daphne fucking Tierney, I know that, OK? But we were just married. I didn't want to ruin my chances of happiness because of a stupid fling.'

When he said her name, I felt goosebumps travel down my spine.

I stood there speechless, motionless. This was all I'd wanted since we split up, all I had ever wanted him to say.

'When we were in Disney, every second Georgie mentioned you, '*Daddy, do you think Mummy would like that? Daddy, what do you think Mummy is doing? Daddy, can you tuck me in like Mummy does?'* And I realised how much she idolises you. How much we both do. I miss you two not being around the house, Ava. I've been putting up barriers and not getting close to you. I know how cold I was, but I was trying to protect myself. I put so much blame onto you for our marriage ending and I've realised it was all my doing. I can't do it anymore!' Johnny rubbed his face, looking unusually vulnerable, 'I want my family back. I need my family back.' His voice wobbled, sincere and faint.

'After everything?' I laughed at his timing. 'This has been the hardest year of my life. I tried so many times. I'm pretty sure I also begged at one point, on my fucking knees.' My face twisted with embarrassment at the memory.

He gulped. 'I know. I'm sorry.'

'You cheated on me, Johnny.'

'I know,' he whispered. 'But I've changed. I'm older, wiser, Ava.'

'You put me out. You made me start again. You made me feel crazy, and I was right.' I laughed slightly.

He sighed heavily. 'I think the more you accused me of things the more I pushed you away because I knew deep down you were right. I was terrified you'd find out. But you know now, and I need you back. No more secrets, Ava.'

I shut my eyes and stood quietly for a second. I wanted to let my brain have a moment to process all of this.

I felt his soft, warm hand slide down my face, and I had chills from the touch. I opened my eyes, and he

343

was close. I glanced up into his eyes as he stood tall above me. I could feel his chest against mine.

'I'm sorry,' he whispered, then reached down and kissed my lips.

It felt familiar yet strange. My heart pounded. I was static.

What the fuck was happening?

I felt his hand run through my hair as he kissed me again. I tilted my head and let him. I could feel his tongue wrap around mine; my heart pounded as he pushed his body against me. My nipples were turning hard, even though it was thirty degrees outside.

It felt strange . . . it felt wrong.

'Stop.' I whispered. 'Johnny, stop!' I stepped back, composing myself and wiping my mouth. 'I need to think, Johnny.' I walked into my hallway, pacing the floor, questioning everything. *What was I doing? He cheated on you, Ava. But it was a million years ago. You have a daughter now. This is what I wanted, what I prayed for. But why does it feel so wrong?*

'Ava?' he said, interrupting my thoughts.

'I need to wrap my head around everything.'

He nodded, wiping my lip gloss from his stubble.

'Daddy!' Georgie pounded out the door, noticing Johnny still there.

'Mummy, what's wrong?' Georgie asked, detecting my confusion.

I snapped out of it quickly. 'With me? Absolutely nothing, baby. I am just so bloody happy you are home!'

She giggled. 'Me too!' she cooed into my legs.

'I think Mummy needs some air, though. What about a walk, Georgie? Do you fancy it? To the park? We can show off that pretty dress of yours?'

'Yeah!' she replied, jumping happily.

I peeked at Johnny. He rubbed his hands over his face.

'Well, let's all go for a walk then. You don't mind if I join, Mummy?' he asked.

Jesus, the cunt was crossing the street to avoid me a few weeks ago, and now he won't leave me alone!

''Course not,' I said with gritted teeth, trying not to make Georgie uncomfortable.

We steered down the stairwell and passed Lina and Adam across the street hand in hand. I gasped, not expecting to see them, and Adam did the same, noticing Johnny. Lina waved over happily, and I pointed her out to Georgie, who waved back. *Things must be going well with them*, I thought, feeling a warm happiness for Adam.

The bustling streets were lined with pop-up food stalls from across the world. I smiled as I passed some of my local vendors. I could see Johnny's body stiffen at the culture and the crowded streets.

'Where will we go? This seems a bit rowdy,' he eventually said, as a stranger bumped into him.

I smiled. 'There's a play park around the corner.'

As we turned, Georgie sprinted into the park, and I sat on a bench with Johnny beside me.

'You look well, Ava.' He flicked my hair back from my face. 'This is the best I've seen you in a long time,' he admitted.

345

'Thanks.'

'How has your fortnight been?' He stopped himself. 'I'm sorry, it has been awful because of everything, hasn't it?'

I shook my head, 'No. I've been busy, really busy. I have been working, and I wrote a book proposal.'

He turned around, giving me his full attention. 'Wow! Back to the writing! Great! What type of book?'

'A self-help book. To help anyone who lost everything get back on their feet,' I said confidently, but it hurt confessing it to him when he was the one who made me hurt the most.

'Well, you're certainly back on your feet now we're on track,' he said.

I felt an awkwardness fall between us.

'Johnny, we have so much to discuss before we're close to being on track. What you did, the lies you told? How you've treated me. I don't even know if . . .'

He covered his face with his hands. 'I know, but I'm going to make it right. I've been a bastard, but I'm not a child anymore. I have to grow up. You're all I want. You and Georgie.'

I felt like a rod had suddenly been shoved up my arse.

'What about Beatrice?'

He looked uncomfortable. 'C'mon, she's never been part of my life, too much time has passed now.'

I shook my head at him making excuses.

'Ava, I promise things will be different.' He pulled my body into his and rested his arm behind my back.

'How, though, Johnny? Where do we even start?'

346

'The first step is moving you and Georgina back to Kensington. This place is unsafe and chaotic.'

I glanced around and screwed my face up, disagreeing in an instant.

'And the university students aren't back till September, so I have at least a month off before I need to prep and return to work. Let's spend the summer in the Lake District together at my mum's. We could go for walks; Georgie loves it down there, too. We would have time together, Mum could watch Georgina and allow us time to heal and get back on track.'

I felt my jaw drop. He had really thought about it.

'A month in the Lake District?' I sat up and turned to him.

'You love it there.'

I smiled. 'Yes, but I've just started working again. I'm writing, editing, spending time with my friends again. I don't want to turn my life upside down when I've just got it back.'

He gave me a sympathetic look. 'Ava, you don't have to work anymore. I got this. I got you. Just like before.' Johnny shrugged. 'We can return to how things were in Kensington.'

I paused, recalling my previous life.

Waiting in all day for my husband, who I'd be lucky to have a ten-minute chat with before he ate and then went to sleep. I spent my days staring at the same four walls of the house, overthinking scenarios in my head. I went to the hairdresser, hoping he'd give me a second glance or a compliment as he walked through the door, but he was more interested in his phone. *Yes,* the house was lovely, but I was empty. I was lonely and worthless there.

I couldn't do it.

'Johnny. No. Fuck me, I can't believe I'm saying this, but this . . . this life, this marriage, is never going to work.' I stood up with a wide grin of realisation.

I laughed and covered my mouth instantly. I was trying to mask it as a wave rushed over me.

'*Pardon?* What are you talking about, Ava?'

'I'm sorry, but *no.* I like, no, I fucking love living here. I love the people, my neighbours.'

Johnny looked disgusted.

'Look, I wanted this to work. I mean, honestly, *fuck me*, I fantasised about the day when you would finally change your mind more than anything else in the world. But that's all this is, isn't it? A fantasy. It's your fantasy where you have a perfect wife and child to come home to in the fancy home.' I shook my head, finally feeling relieved. 'But that's not me. We've tried it and failed miserably.' I was utterly empowered. A colossal weight swiped off my shoulders and was thrown away to space, and an overwhelming appreciation for myself radiated off me for the life I'd created *by myself.* 'But personally, if I was you, I'd get to know your other daughter. She seems great. And you, despite all of your issues, you are a wonderful father. At least pay her tuition, reach out to Richard, get to know her!'

'Reach out to Richard!' He scoffed at the idea.

'It's the right thing to do! But hey, it's your life,

Johnny.' I stood up from the bench.

'Ava, stop this. What the hell are you doing?' He stood up beside me, looking furious.

'I'm doing what I should have done years ago, Johnny.' I turned and spotted Georgie climbing the spider web. 'Georgie, come here, baby!' I called out. 'We're over, Johnny. Look at us. We're incompatible.' I held my hands in the air. 'I had tunnel vision that you were what I wanted, even when you treated me like an absolute cunt for no reason. You looked down on me, on the situation you put me in. I lost my home, because I thought I was wrong in our marriage. I thought it was my depression that drove us apart, but I can see clearly now that it was you. It was all you. Your lies and manipulation. Your snide comments about my parenting. I *hated* my life with you Johnny, cooped up in a house with no real friends or job. I drove myself mad. *You* drove me mad, and quite honestly, after the amount of shit you've put me through, can you blame me for never wanting to go back there?'

His jaw dropped.

Georgie ran towards me. 'Come on, then!' I held out my hand, and she grabbed a hold of it, and we started walking towards the gate.

'Ava, wait? Fucking talk to me!'

I continued walking.

'What about Daddy?' Georgie asked, looking back towards Johnny.

'Daddy's heading to his home,' I said cheerily. 'It's a Mummy day! And we've got a pyjama party to organise!'

Chapter Thirty-Two

Rebeka

Beks had finished editing her daily photography between emails and calls with brands, all hoping to collaborate with her. She packed her handbag and lifted her purse to head to the shops for the party. As she walked down the stairwell, she noticed a tall man's back leaning against the door. As she pulled it open, he moved slightly.

'Excuse me,' she muttered, glancing at her phone.

'Rebeka?' The strong New Zealand accent cut through her, and she glanced up at Mitchell's handsome face, staring down at her.

'What the fuck?' she hummed. 'What are you doing here, Mitchell?'

He smiled, his flawless teeth brightening up the street. 'I'm looking for you, I guess.'

Beks shook her head wildly and began walking away from him.

'Wait, Rebeka, please.' He grabbed her arm, and she turned again, pulling back her wrist from his grip. 'You didn't keep the cheque?'

Rebeka gulped down. '*What?* No.'

'Why?' he asked, frustrated. 'I've been wracking my brains and I don't understand why.'

'I don't need your money, Mitchell.'

'It was a generous offer, much more than you would get at a tribunal.'

'But this was never about money. Are you joking?' She laughed under her breath, shaking her head. 'But don't worry, I signed the non-disclosure, if that's what you're worried about.'

'I know you did,' he said, and glanced down to the ground.

'You know, you never asked me what happened that night, Mitchell. You just assumed the fucking worst. I tried phoning, messaging, emailing you, and you didn't reply once.'

He stood still.

'Yeah, well. Looks like it all worked out in the end,' she replied.

'Did it?'

'Well, you got rid of me and kept your money, babe,' she retorted, her voice getting louder as the anger ripped out of her body. 'My lips are sealed because *you* were scared I would air your dirty laundry? Well, congratulations, Mitch, you still have your reputation intact. Meanwhile, I'm the photographer from *Inner Me!* who got fired for shagging a prostitute!'

He groaned. 'It wasn't fair how I treated you,' he replied. 'I'm sorry. I was *so* angry. I thought you were the one, and on the day we were about to announce it, I heard . . .'

Beks laughed, 'You heard a bullshit story, babe! Ava shagged the prozzy, not me! I hired them to make her feel better so she didn't have to attend a stupid high school reunion alone. I didn't know she'd sleep with one of them. I didn't know he'd charge the fucking company. *Do you really think I'm that stupid?* The funny thing is, I went home early that night because I missed you!' She laughed under her breath. 'How pathetic, eh?'

Mitchell ran his hand through his hair.

'See you, Mitch. I have a party tonight. But I hope I cleared everything up for you.' She turned and walked away.

'Beks! Rebeka!' He continued yelling down the busy street, but she kept walking, feeling her entire body shake.

'REBEKA HAMPSON, I LOVE YOU!' As the words echoed down to her, Rebeka came to a standstill.

She turned slowly, trying hard not to cry.

'I'm sorry, and I love you.' He held his hands by his side. 'It's true,' he said, stepping towards her. She glanced around as people reacted to the public display, pointing as they recognised him. Some had their phones out, videoing the entire escapade.

He finally caught up to her, and Rebeka nudged her head towards the crowd. 'What are you doing?' she said quietly, looking around.

'It's true, and I don't care who knows it,' he replied, raising his shoulders in defeat.

Rebeka gulped. 'Stop this,' she said softly. 'It's too late!'

'Look, I told my family about you. They had their doubts but I wouldn't hear a word against you because you're the love of my life. And I knew it was killing you to hide it. It's why I fought to get that policy change through HR. It was meant to be the day we finally got everything we wanted. But then I heard the news. And I should have listened to you but I wasn't thinking at all. I just felt like an idiot for believing that anyone could really love me – me, and not the money or the fame - the way I thought you did. The way I realised later you do. But by then it was too late.'

He touched her lip and smiled as her gloss touched him.

'No buts this time,' he said, 'I need you, Rebeka.'

It was everything she'd wanted to hear; she wanted to jump into his strong arms and dry-hump him on the spot, but she couldn't. She was so hurt by him, she couldn't risk giving up everything she'd built.

'No buts?' she repeated.

Mitchell pressed his forehead against hers and gently shook his head, looking into her eyes. She could feel her heart pound inside. She had never loved anyone the way she loved him.

Rebeka paused, then stood back. 'I can't. I'm sorry. I'm not jumping in again. I have my Instagram page, and I have dreams to turn it into a real printed magazine. I know I can, Mitch. I've really built something here,' she said.

'Rebeka, I'd never ask you to stop. Your photographs are wonderful. The concept behind your work is inspiring! I've never felt prouder of anyone. I have never felt love for anyone like this!'

She giggled, having wondered for weeks if he'd stalked her page. *He saw them!*

Mitchell brushed back her hair from her face. 'Please, can we start over properly?'

A smile took over her face and she wrapped her arms around him. 'Of course, we fucking can!' He pulled her tightly against him, his strong arms around her body, as they kissed passionately in the street. She groaned as he moved his hand on her arse and squeezed her into him.

There was a small cheer from the spectators watching, and both of them burst out laughing and smiled towards them.

'Should we . . .' he tilted his head to her flat, and Rebeka hovered.

'Mmmm . . . Babe, you know make-up sex is like my favourite, but I have a party tonight. One of my friends needs me.'

'Well, perhaps I can come?' he asked.

She smiled, completely taken aback. '*Erm* . . . Yeah. Yeah, why not? But first, we need to hit the shops.'

He held out his hand, and she grasped it tightly. Beks could feel a basketball of excitement bounce around her stomach as she *finally* walked around the city with Mitchell Travers.

'Babe?'

'Yes?' he smiled.

'How do you feel about onesies?'

Mitchell raised a brow. 'What the hell is a onesie?'

She laughed wickedly. 'You're about to find out!'

Chapter Thirty-Three

Ava

Georgie and I returned to my flat laden with bags of her favourite Iceland party food bargain buckets. She was still chatting about Florida and how much fun she had had as we wandered up the stairwell. I giggled as she described the scary rollercoasters she had encountered and how many characters she'd met along the way. I was relieved to have her back home and grateful for her joyful energy again. As we continued up the steps, Adam and Lina met us on their way down.

'Oh, hello again, you two!' I smiled at the pair.

Adam seemed slightly flustered getting spotted with his new girlfriend after months of our shagathons. 'Hey, Ava. Good afternoon, Princess Georgina!'

'Hi, Adam!' she said back, still marching up.

'How are you, Lina? I hope he's taking good care of you?'

She beamed. 'He is!'

'What's all this? Feeding the street?' Adam pointed to my bags.

'Not quite, but we are having a little onesie PJ party tonight. You guys are welcome to come along. Just us and a few friends playing board games, celebrating the return of Georgie!'

Adam smiled cheekily to Lina, who enthusiastically laughed, 'Hell, YES!'

'We're in!' he replied.

'Great, pop in whenever. The girls are arriving about seven?'

'See you then,' he smiled back, and I continued trekking upstairs to make the food.

Just like clockwork, Grace arrived first with her perfectly ironed white linen onesie, harbouring a bottle of Prosecco under her arm. Georgie ran to greet her, and I could see my sister overwhelmed with love as she clutched her tightly.

'I've missed you!' she said. 'Come tell me all about Florida!' The pair wandered into the living room as someone knocked on the door again.

'Hey guys!' Lina and Adam stood in the hallway with their fleecy onesies on. I hugged them both, and we moved through to the living room.

'So, what board games have you picked for us, Georgie?' Adam asked.

'I think we should play Monopoly, and then Twister!'

He laughed, glancing at Lina.

'That is a great choice, Georgie!' Lina smiled, taking a seat.

'Can I get you two a drink? Wine? Prosecco? Juice?'

'Just an orange juice for me!' Adam replied.

'Ohh, a Prosecco would be lovely, thanks, Ava!'

My eyes darted to Grace, who had already started swigging her bubbles from the bottle.

'Ola, bitches!' Rebeka's voice called out from the hallway as she entered the flat. I tilted my head from the kitchen and laughed, noticing her abnormally tight Teletubby onesie.

'Look, Georgie, it's LaLa!' Grace said as Beks strolled in. 'Oh, and Tinky Winky!'

'Hi everyone,' said a male voice I didn't recognise.

I paused. *Who the fuck is that?* I dashed to them and spotted Mitchell Travers in my flat, squeezed into a Teletubby onesie.

'Everyone, this is Mitchell. Mitchell, this is everyone!'

He shook hands with Adam, then briefly waved to us all. 'I eh . . . didn't think I'd be meeting Rebeka's friends dressed like this, I must say.' He glanced down at his bulge, which looked like he was smuggling a half ounce of haggis, and shrugged.

My eyes flew towards Beks, who had failed to mention that she was bringing the multi-millionaire to my tiny flat.

'Lovely to meet you *properly*, Mitchell. Would you like some wine? Or Prosecco?'

'Likewise. I actually brought some beers, if that's OK?' He rummaged in a bag and took a can out.

Jesus Christ he is the only grown man who could pull off a Teletubby onesie.

'I'll pop the rest in the fridge then,' I swiped the bag from the floor. 'Rebeka, could you help me with the drinks?' I jerked my neck towards the kitchen.

'I think I will help, too,' Grace followed the two of us into the small kitchen.

'Beks, what the fuck?' I hissed.

'I know, babe, my fanny is eating me alive here. They only had onesies in the children's section left!' She squirmed. I glanced down at the yellow fleece engulfing her vagina and shook my head.

'Not your bloody camel toe, Beks! Mitchell!'

She puffed. 'I know, right? What the fuck? Completely unexpected. So, that little sort shows up outside my house in broad daylight, shouting that he loves me and wants to give it a go.' She squeezed her fists excitedly, then poured a large glass of wine.

Grace blew her nose loudly.

'What's up, Grace?' I asked.

She patted down her eyes. 'That's just such a beautiful story, Beka,' she cried.

'Oh my God,' I laughed. 'She began the sentence with *'that little sort shows up'*, Grace!'

We all began chuckling in the kitchen.

'Rebeka, he is just . . .' I threw my head back in desire at how drop-dead-perfect her man was.

'It's that voice, isn't it?' Grace added.

'Well, you should imagine it whispering in your ear during sex, babe! I'm wetter than an otter's pocket within seconds!'

We all squirmed with jealousy in my kitchen.

'Mummy! We want to start!' Georgie's voice called out.

'Coming, I'm coming!' I laughed.

'And I will be too by the end of the night, hun!' Beka smirked as I laughed at her and shook my head. I quickly poured the drinks, and we handed them to our guests.

'Ok, can I pick the dog, Georgie?' Adam asked.

Georgie shook her head. 'Mummy likes the dog,' she said.

I nodded. 'I do, but I can let Adam take a turn. I don't mind.' I winked towards her to play fairly.

The door knocked loudly again.

'Who else are we expecting?' Grace asked.

I shrugged. 'Beks will probably know!' I squinted at her, and she laughed as I stood up and headed towards the hallway.

'What one do you want, Mummy?' Georgie called out.

I opened the door, calling back, 'I'll have whatever is left, darling. Let our guests pick first.'

'Hello, Ava,' Richard said in his deep voice, and I immediately felt my brows rise as I turned to him.

'Richard, what are you doing here?'

'I can see I'm interrupting, and I don't want any trouble. I just wanted to give you this.' He passed me a large envelope.

I suddenly felt nervous. 'What? Why? What is it?'

Was he showing me proof about Johnny and Daphne that would most certainly ruin my night? Maybe he was going to court to demand money from him to pay for his daughter? Or maybe Johnny had been paying and I hadn't realised all this time?

My mind raced as quickly as my heart.

'It's nothing bad. I read over your proposal, Ava. And I think it's wonderful. Everyone at the office does, too,' he began. 'It's beautifully written, smart, deep, funny and painfully honest, but most of all it's incredibly inspiring.'

I looked at him dumbly, processing his compliment, before I pulled out a sheet of paper. My eyes fell on the words 'offer letter', unable to read any more.

'But . . . what . . . what is all of this?' I asked.

'Congratulations. We want to offer you a publishing contract,' he said softly, smiling gently at me. 'I know things between us aren't ideal, but I wanted to let you know personally.'

'What? Why?' I looked up into his dark eyes, my chest tight. 'Why are you doing this, Richard?'

He seemed confused. 'Because you're incredibly talented, Ava. You deserve a shot.'

My mind was racing, overlapping all the possible reasons he would want to help me.

'I know you and Johnny are perhaps patching things up, and he might disagree, but the offer is there regard-less. I have made sure you got—'

'We're not,' I interrupted.

'I thought . . .' he trailed off.

I shook my head quickly, still glancing at the paperwork.

'No. He wanted to. But I said no.'

He smiled slightly. 'I'm glad to hear it.' A brief pause fell between us. 'I'll let you get back to it then. I just wanted to pass on the offer in person. Take your time and if you want to discuss anything, please call me. I have B in the car downstairs so I'll let you think on this.' He turned and walked down a few steps.

'Why didn't you tell me, Richard?' I called out, stepping out to the landing.

He turned, his eyes heavy. 'I tried. I'm sorry. I just . . . I saw you standing at the church and you looked so happy. So perfect, in your white dress, and I couldn't allow myself to hurt you.'

I shrugged. 'But you did. By not saying anything, you did.'

'I know,' he said softly.

'Is this why you're helping me?' I waved the contract in the air. 'Because you feel bad?'

He screwed his face up and walked back upstairs. 'You'd be the one helping me. This book idea will get snatched up, Ava. There is no doubt about it. It's wonderful.' He lifted his head and looked at me directly. 'You're wonderful.'

I felt my heart pound, gazing at him. His tall frame, his sophisticated manner. His handsome face.

'But why did you not give your marriage another shot? Because of B?'

I shook my head.

'No, but I suppose that made me realise I didn't want to go back there again. Back to his lies, and overthinking, and back to his emptiness.' I paused, taking a moment to understand my own actions. 'I chose *this* life, Richard. I chose my friends, writing, my shitty apartment with cum on the wall!' I giggled slightly at the embarrassing memory, and he smiled back. 'I chose a flat full of laughter, clutter and love. I chose happiness.'

He stepped a little closer.

'And when you chose this life . . . Did you ever consider if there was room for me?'

My mind was blank. Richard Tierney stood before me, and all I wanted to do was kiss him.

I placed my hands on his shoulders, slightly on my tippy toes to reach him. 'I would like to say *yes*, but wouldn't that be a severe conflict of interest if we're working together?'

He grabbed hold of my waist and pulled me in towards him. 'I could always rip the offer up?' he teased.

'Hmmm . . . I mean, I do know an excellent lawyer! I'm sure she could find us a loophole.'

He pulled me in suddenly and kissed me deeply in the hallway, running his hands over my body like a starving man. I was panting heavily as the blood rushed to my fanny. I could feel his dick press into me as I finally gave in to him, skimming my hands over his chest and through his dark thick hair. It was electric. He tugged on my hair, biting my lip a little. *Jesus Christ,* I wanted to pull down my knickers and tell him to fuck me there and then.

'Richard, Richard,' I managed to mumble between kisses.

'Mmmm . . .'

'This is insane and I'm so into it, but I'm kind of in the middle of hosting a party. Do you want to join in?'

He stopped kissing for a second and grinned.

'I have Beatrice in the car, remember.'

I felt a chill as he said her name. *She's the innocent one, Ava.* I suddenly felt a pang of guilt for the years of neglect from Johnny. He had been such a good father to Georgie, but he'd never given this poor girl a chance.

'I mean, you could bring her in? Only if you want. Georgie's making us all play board games.'

He tilted his head, seeming surprised at the offer. 'If you're comfortable with that, then, it sounds great.'

'I am. I mean, we don't have to deal with the shit-storm just yet. Let's just have a nice night maybe?'

Richard leant forward and kissed my forehead. 'A nice night is exactly what we need.'

The evening of board games continued as we all giggled and told stories of our school days throughout the night. Beka spent most of her evening flicking back her hair and ogling Mitchell and his ginormous fleecy bulge, while Grace downed another Prosecco bottle, warning that anyone who even contemplated cheating during the games would be disqualified. Beatrice and Georgie played for a little while, then made up a dance routine and performed it for all the guests. I couldn't help but compare them both as they stood innocently together. They were similar, there was no denying it. They both seemed to have Johnny's eyes and smile. But luckily, they both had completely different natures from him. Beatrice was quiet, shy and very sweet, while Georgie was funny, bubbly and kind. They seemed to have a lovely bond, and I knew we'd have to figure out a way of telling them they were sisters eventually, but it was nice to just let them have fun together in the meantime.

I sat on the sofa as the boys and Lina battled it out for the Twister Champion and smiled as I watched Richard spin the wheel while Adam and Lina were trapped in some form of crab. Mitchell was creased at the side of the mat, spectating the game. *What a summer,* I thought. From tampons to prostitutes, make-ups to break-ups, our hot girl summer really seemed to cover it all.

Beks and Grace joined me at either side and cuddled in.

'I can't believe how much I've done this summer, girls, and it's genuinely all thanks to you two,' I said with a lump in my throat. 'You picked me up from the gutter when I thought I had lost everything.'

Beks nodded. 'And you two pushed me to create Rogue, or I'd be out on my arse, hun!'

Grace sighed. 'I can't believe what's happened to me this summer!' I reached over and held her hand. 'But I am glad we've found each other again. I couldn't have coped with the whole Steve thing alone.'

I nodded. 'We're not going anywhere, Grace.'

Beks smiled. 'Why are you two acting like this summer is over? We still have a good month *at least,* before it's autumn! And personally, I don't think we've even got started yet, do you?' She raised her brows suspiciously. 'I'm thinking our next task is setting up a Tinder profile for our Grace?' Beka and I burst out laughing as we watched the horror plunge onto Grace's face.

'No way! I am not going on Tinder, girls!' she insisted.

'Not right now, but you know, soon, babe.' Beka winked towards her.

Grace eventually broke into a smile, giggling at the thought. 'Well, here's to the future then!' She smiled, raising her half-empty bottle in the air. 'Back to life as a lawyer! And wait, wait,' she delved into her bag and brought out my book I had given her to read and slammed it onto the coffee table. 'My talented sister Ava is soon to be a *published* author, and our crazy Rebeka is the owner and director of the most body positive brand!'

We clinked our glasses together, and my mind suddenly flashed back to our first night as eighteen-year-olds, fresh out of high school, living in the city for the very first time. I remembered the ambition I'd felt, the drive and determination to do better and make something of myself and I felt the same energy surge around my body now. I was finally excited for the future. I had created this life myself – a life no man could take away. I could feel my buzz radiate to my friends, who rested their heads on my shoulders.

'Here's to our hot girl fucking summer, biatches!' I screamed loudly, pulling my manuscript from the table and throwing the pages up into the air.

The Best Friend's Guide to Feeling Like a Queen
Written by Ava Little.

Introduction.

This book isn't designed to be your guru. It's not based on scientific evidence or data. It's based on real love and experience. In the past few years, I've lost everything: my life as I knew it, my marriage, friends, home, money and confidence. I was rock bottom in a dark pit with no way out. I sought out professional help on many occasions and have since concluded that a lonely life packed full of antidepressants and dread was how mine would look. And I grew to accept that life. Well, that's until my best friends stepped in. After months of ignoring my friends, they let themselves in and demanded change, and since that day, I've never looked back. They have pushed me to look at things differently. They have made me acknowledge the shitty experiences I've been dealt and build on those experiences to accomplish my ultimate goals, which, quite honestly, I thought I'd lost forever. My friends and I rewound to our younger years, acknowledging and channelling the teenage confidence I forgot I had in me. Within a month of seeking out female friendships, I've found work, I've laughed and had more fun than I've had since my teens.

Most importantly, throughout all of this, in such a short time, I've seen a significant difference in my

mood, mental health, energy levels, and overall
outlook on life. I am not rich. I don't have some
secret formula to get rich, either. But for the first time
in my adult life, I am happy with my growth, and I
now know that I'm in total control of my destiny.

This brings me onto to why I'm writing this book.

After facing another mind-blowing trauma (which
would normally set me back to suicide watch), I
finally know I'll be OK no matter what happens in
the future. My best friends will step in. Like I'd step
in to help them with anything. There is no greater
love than what you have with your girlfriends. A
spiritual, deep, meaningful connection and admiration
for a group of other women. How beautiful! Eh?

This got me thinking: what do people who don't
have friends like mine do? Because quite honestly, I
don't know if I'd have made it out of my bed
without them.

I have written this guide for every woman who
needs a best friend. Let me help you. I will unlock
secret formulas to change your mindset and share the
blunt, hilarious words of wisdom that pulled me from
the gutter.

This book will help you navigate your way through
life and the problems it faces. It will guide you,
encourage you to have fun, and give you the self-belief
you need to become the best version of yourself. Any
problem you encounter, we can fix it. Let's get our
lives back on track together. Because honestly,
everyone deserves a best friend.

Acknowledgements

I would like to first thank my fantastic publishing company, Orion, for your support when writing my fourth novel. Significantly, the lovely Rhea Kurien who has filled me with confidence and continual comfort throughout the process. You have helped reassure me that I have more stories to tell, and you are always there when I need you. I honestly don't think I could do this without you, Rhea, and I'm so grateful you found me. Thank you from the bottom of my heart, and I can't wait to see what's next for us. Also, a special thank you to Sanah Ahmed for all your assistance over the past few years, Yadira Da Trindade and Frankie Banks for your excellent work and ideas behind promoting my books and the rest of the team at Orion. You are the best team, and I'm privileged to be a part of it.

I'd also like to thank Elliott Fillingham for his support and guidance throughout the past couple of years. You go out of your way to help in every aspect of this journey and my life! You have great ideas and suggestions and are always there when I need a boost. I'll always be eternally grateful for your help, and I can't wait to continue working together—special thanks to

John Kerr for introducing us. You crack me up every time I see you, John, and I appreciate how much you listen to and advise me on life, contracts, and men!

To the fabulous Rosie McCafferty for proofreading my book yet again! You are such a massive part of my journey, Rosie, and you sometimes understand the characters better than me. I am so grateful to have found you, and I don't think I could do this without your great ideas and suggestions (and, of course, your hahaha's in the margin!). Your talent doesn't go unnoticed, and I owe so much to you for your input while writing this novel.

A special thanks to all the Waterstone staff, in particular the Glasgow branches, who promote the hell out of these books! I am so fortunate to have you fighting my corner. Special thanks to the fantastic staff at the Glasgow Fort branch, who have smashed the sales for my previous books! I still get goosebumps walking past and seeing my work on the window display. It is genuinely a dream come true, and I'm not naive to how much this has contributed to the success of my writing.

To my Mum and Dad for your continued support. Thank you for promoting and boasting about your bestselling author daughter (even when you're not allowed to read my books)! I appreciate all your endless love and help with everything I do. Thank you for raising me to be independently fearless with my dreams. I owe it to both of you. Also, I thank Andy, Aidan, Arlene, Les, and Joyce. Thank you for helping me and my girls (including Wrinkles) while writing this book. I would never have had the time to be a Mum, complete the dance runs, work in the wards, and write full-time if it wasn't for you all stepping in. I never take how much you guys do for me for granted, so please know how privileged I am to have you all.

To all my fantastic work colleagues and friends in ward one, thank you for keeping the team going with your witty, crazy nurse banter throughout the past eight years. You guys keep me unbelievably grounded while still simultaneously supporting the hell out of this journey. I am so fortunate to be part of such a fantastic team, from nurses to porters to clinical support workers to domestics and medics; you inspire me daily to become a better person. I know how shit we have at times, but you still manage to keep the smiles and laughs coming every day on shift which keeps every one of us going. A special thanks to Maggie Donnelly, my work bestie, who is always there when I need advice on nursing, life or shitty men. You are one of life's special people and brighten up any room you walk into, and I'm so lucky to have you in my corner, Maggie.

To my very best friends, Michelle Patterson, Emma Mcauley, Lisa Scott, Sarah Scott, Lisa Murphy and Bianca Rinaldi, no man has ever come close to the love I have for each of you. Thank you for providing me with decades of entertainment, crazy stories and top-class banter. You girls keep me sane, keep me laughing and make me feel like the most loved person on the planet. There is no one like any of you, and without you guys, I wouldn't have the drive to keep on writing. I know you will support me endlessly with your painfully honest opinions on any dilemma I find myself in (and yeah, I know it's a lot at times), but hey, it's good book material, right? But, honestly, I don't know what I'd do without any of you. Thank you for being my people, my light in the darkness, and my true soul mates in this lifetime.

And finally, to my two favourite humans in the whole wide world. The most enormous, heartfelt thanks to my intelligent, patient, kind daughters, Olivia and Grace. I know it's not the coolest thing in the world to have an erotic writer as a Mum, but you guys encourage and remind me every day to keep on writing. Thank you for setting aside the time in your lives to let me finish another book! And yay, we've done it! I also appreciate all the sacrifices you have made while I've been working endless hours in the hospital and writing around the clock. I realise how much we've had to put to the side because Mummy works, but you get on with it and encourage me to keep going.

I hope one day you girls read this novel- (when you are A LOT older, of course) and feel proud of what it stands for. Women really can do anything they want in this world, and I can't wait to watch the amazing things you will both achieve.

I honestly couldn't ask for two more perfectly kind daughters,

I love you to infinity and beyond,

my gorgeous girls,

With love and eternal gratitude,

Sophie xx

Credits

Sophie Gravia and Orion Fiction would like to thank everyone at Orion who worked on the publication of *Hot Girl Summer* in the UK.

Editorial
Rhea Kurien
Sanah Ahmed

Copyeditor
Celia Killen

Proofreader
Francine Brody

Audio
Paul Stark

Contracts
Dan Herron
Ellie Bowker
Alyx Hurst

Design
Rachael Lancaster
Loveday May

Editorial Management
Charlie Panayiotou
Jane Hughes
Bartley Shaw
Lucy Bilton

Finance
Jasdip Nandra
Nick Gibson
Sue Baker

Marketing
Yadira da Trindade

Don't miss Sophie Gravia's filthy, hilarious and painfully relatable debut, *A Glasgow Kiss* . . .

A Glasgow Kiss [n.]
A headbutt or a strike with the head to someone's sensitive area

Meet Zara Smith: 29, single and muddling her way through life as a trainee nurse in Glasgow. With 30 fast approaching, she's determined to do whatever it takes to find love – or at least someone to sext! Cheered on by best friends Ashley and Raj, Zara embarks on a string of dating escapades that are as hilarious as they are disastrous. From online dating to blind dates, hometown hook-ups to flirty bartenders, nothing is off limits.

But when Dr Tom Adams, aka Sugar Daddy, shows interest, it's a game-changing moment. Zara has had a crush on Tom since her very first day at the aesthetics clinic she works at part time. As things heat up between them, Zara can't help but wonder: is this it? Or is it another disaster waiting to happen?

Then follow up with the laugh-out-loud
What Happens in Dubai . . .

Everyone's favourite Glaswegian girl is back!

After having her heart well and truly broken, Zara Smith is more interested in fun than forever. But she's starting to wonder if she's slept with every (somewhat) eligible bachelor in Glasgow... and if there's such a thing as too much fun?!

With competition ramping up in Glasgow, Zara and her friends at Individualise can't pass up an opportunity to promote their aesthetics clinic – especially not when it involves an all-expenses-paid quick getaway to Dubai! It's THE summer destination for the sexy, rich and famous. Cue sun, sand and disastrous flirtations for everyone. But it's okay because once they get back to Glasgow, what happens in Dubai stays in Dubai, right?

Warning: this is NOT a romcom. It's dating in the 21st century and Sophie Gravia is about to give you all the toe-curling, cringe-worthy, laugh-out-loud details.

And don't miss the laugh-out-loud summer read *Meet Me in Milan*!

Zara Smith is FINALLY in a healthy relationship . . . so why can't she stop thinking about her ex?

The shocking news of the summer is that Tom – the ex Zara always thought would never settle down – is ENGAGED to beloved actress and all-natural beauty Quinn Foxx. They're throwing a star-studded engagement party in Italy, and Zara is invited.

She isn't planning to go until she finds an old note from Tom that shows their feelings for each other were once mutual. And she needs to know – does he still feel the same way? And, just like that, Zara's on a plane to Milan to crash the most talked-about engagement of the year!

After all this time, could this be the moment Zara's been waiting for . . . or the biggest mistake of her life?